BOOK ONE
2008-9

Victoria Fox

TEMPTATION
ISLAND

HARLEQUIN®
entertain, enrich, inspire™

Harlequin MIRA is a registered trademark of Harlequin Enterprises Limited, used under licence.

Published in Great Britain 2012
Harlequin MIRA, an imprint of Harlequin (UK) Limited,
Eton House, 18-24 Paradise Road, Richmond, Surrey, TW9 1SR

© Victoria Fox 2012

ISBN 978 1 848 45067 7

59-0612

Harlequin's policy is to use papers that are natural, renewable and recyclable products and made from wood grown in sustainable forests. The logging and manufacturing processes conform to the legal environmental regulations of the country of origin.

Printed and bound by
CPI Group (UK) Ltd, Croydon, CR0 4YY

For Mark

ACKNOWLEDGEMENTS

Thank you to my editors Kim Young and Jenny Hutton, whose wisdom, guidance and commitment has meant the world to this book. To the whole team at MIRA, especially Mandy Ferguson, Tim Cooper, Nick Bates, Oliver Rhodes, Claudia Symons, Elise Windmill, Jason Mackenzie, Clare Somerville, and Donna Esiri and Debbie Clements for the beautiful covers. To Madeleine Buston for being a phenomenal agent, and to Clare Wallace, Mary Darby and Rosanna Bellingham for their stellar work. I'm also grateful to Tory Lyne-Pirkis at Midas PR who is the best publicist I could wish for.

Special thanks to Victoria Stonex and the Consultancy for her ideas at the beginning and her insight at the end. Also to Kieran Lynch for an afternoon of plotting in a Lake District pub; to Jo and Jeff Croot for bringing tea in the morning and wine at night; to Seth Dawes for talking to me about New York; to Ross and Angie Freese for their friendship (and to Louis for when he's older); to Kate Furnivall for her advice and encouragement; to Emily Plosker, Joe Martin, Matt Everitt and Ben Sanders. To Chloe, Sarah, Laura, Jimmy, Tay, Finny and everyone from school who remembers the LBM. To Mum and Dad. And to Mark Oakley for his patience, his imagination, and for believing that anything is possible.

Prologue
I

Present Day
Island of Cacatra, Indian Ocean

Had it not been such a clear night, the moon so bright and the air so still, her body might not have been visible where it moved uncertainly, facedown, at the surface of the water. As it was, the pale skin of her shoulder glowed sickeningly in the silver light, one strap of her gown fallen and bound to her like seaweed, its jewels glinting bright as the stars that pierced the sky above.

In the distance, the low thump of music and faraway cries of merriment. The megayacht twinkled on the horizon, its outline lit gold against the black ocean, a winking diamond guillotining the depths. The grand vessel was scene to the birthday party of the year: a lavish, abundant celebration for which no expense had been spared. On board, a host of VIPs, from Hollywood stars to Olympic idols, from dazzling supermodels to the government's elite, from singers, actresses and dancers—beautiful people the globe over—to the cream of the entrepreneurial world, partied as midnight came and went. All were oblivious to the quiet outside, around, below: unaware that, beneath their feet, a secret was drowned, soundless and stifled in the endless deep.

She had not been dead long, half an hour at most. The tide was strong, had rocked her body towards the shore, gently so as not to wake her, the water kissing her cold skin. Her arms were spread wide, her hair tangled like the ropes of a shipwreck, once bound to great beauty but now cut loose on the strange unknown. Her dress had been torn in the struggle, a red slit bleeding uselessly where the dagger had entered.

If she had been asleep, the coarse shingle would have woken her now. A scratch to the belly before, with a final, sad push, the water deposited her. Quiet as silk, it noiselessly retreated.

A little way down the beach, a small boy was hunting for sea turtles. His father had told him they came in to lay their eggs at night, leathery things whose shells shone white in troughs of sand. He wasn't supposed to be here— Miss Jensen, the housekeeper, would murder him—but it was boring waiting inside the mansion. He squinted at the yacht, hundreds of miles away, it seemed, and wished he could be there instead of here. They told him that one day it would all be his: his great inheritance. Crouching at the water's edge, the palm of one hand cradling his chin and the other blindly raking the beach, it was hard to believe. His knees were damp from where he'd been on them, combing the smooth, still-warm sand for that final, important discovery.

His fingers curled round it instinctively at first, like a baby's around its mother's thumb. It felt like net, the ones he caught crabs in, but it clung to him too unhappily for that, as if by holding on it could force him, maybe, to look.

When he did, he knew it was bad. His fist was buried in a knot of wet stuff, too sticky, too like cobweb, too... human. Strands of it across his skin, darkened by its journey over the water, a thickness so much like hair, and the solid bump of skull beneath; the yielding scalp.

The boy's scream ruptured the quiet. It came from somewhere in him that until then he hadn't known existed, somewhere basic and raw. The island gasped with the force of it, trembling in the vastness of its ocean pillow, and seemed to open one eye in recognition, as if it knew all along it was about to be discovered.

II

One day earlier
Twenty-four hours to departure

Reuben van der Meyde disembarked his yacht with the air and importance of a king. And he *was* a king, damn it—at least in this part of the world, where it was easy to forget that land and civilisation existed beyond the clean blue line of the horizon. The end of the earth, the van der Meyde sightline: as far as Reuben was concerned, Cacatra was it.

Despite the lightweight linen shirt he'd had his housekeeper leave out, Reuben was sweating buckets. He could feel it down his back, pooling in a horseshoe under his arms and sticking in the doughy folds he was trying half-heartedly to shift. Christ! When did he start perspiring out of his *ears*? Removing his baseball cap with an irritable swipe, he patted his head with a handkerchief and dug about a bit in his ear-holes. At last, satisfied, he strode purposefully off down the beach, thoughtfully scratching the ginger fuzz on his chin.

Preparations were in order: he had checked the boat, talked to the organisers, sorted the charity raffle...what next? In twenty-four hours everybody who was anybody would join him to celebrate his sixtieth birthday, a party in honour of, arguably (though Reuben saw no point in arguing an indisputable fact), the richest and most powerful man on the planet. Each guest had received their invite months previously, but it was hardly as if they could forget the only social event worth bothering about this year. All that time his people had been fielding calls from neglected stars—singers and models and actresses, politicians, art dealers, writers; names and faces who'd thought they were good acquaintances but clearly hadn't made the cut. He'd had to slash a few loose. You didn't get to where Reuben was without making a few sacrifices.

Initially he had purchased Cacatra as a business enterprise: an exclusive island getaway for the rich and famous, a destination for relaxation and rehabilitation, shelter from the glare of the spotlight. But these days he was living here more and more. The island's lush vegetation, its azure water and golden sands, offered a man exiting middle age the kind of respite he needed. Cacatra was a safe place, a beautiful place. There weren't enough of those left in the world.

Set back from the beach, up a series of winding stone steps, was the van der Meyde mansion. A white colossus overlooking the ocean, circled by glittering fountains and emerald palms, it had been built to a template of exacting standards and now, as voted for several years ago in a major US lifestyle publication, boasted the title of Most Desirable Residence in the World. It wasn't sufficient. Reuben had plans to improve the place further, beginning with extending the already gargantuan swimming pool to a multi-tiered affair that fed directly into the ocean. It was his entrepreneurial spirit, exactly how he had made his fortune: he would think of the most outrageous idea he could and then test himself—*dare* himself—to go ahead and do it.

Not today. He had a party to get on with first.

Margaret Jensen, his housekeeper, was waiting at the main entrance. She was a small, birdlike Englishwoman in her forties with poker-straight mouse-brown hair that hung limply to her shoulders and quick, darting eyes. She moved swiftly, purposefully and with a touch of fuss, in the way efficient people sometimes do.

'Is everything all right, Mr V?' she enquired as he swept past, flip-flops slapping the polished floor. It was what he liked to be called. 'The boat looks impressive.'

'Fine.' Reuben's brutal Johannesburg accent pinched the word thin. He threw his cap on to a dark-wood chest, a grossly expensive African piece he'd had sourced at an auction in the spring. The slogan across the front of the cap read: DO IT BEFORE YOU CHANGE YOUR MIND.

Reuben opened the door to his office, wishing that Miss Jensen could keep to the point and not feel it necessary to stick her beak in. He supposed she imagined she had the right.

Ill at the thought, he closed the door and strode over to his desk. Of *course* the yacht was impressive: that was the whole bloody point. Everything Reuben van der Meyde did was in pursuit of admiration. He was a god, and he expected his people to treat him as such.

He flicked on his Mac, wondering if he'd heard back about the Asian possibility. There was one unread message in his inbox, from a coded address he didn't recognise, and he clicked on it lazily, easing himself back in his chair with a greasy squeak of leather. Behind him the panoramic ocean view stretched out.

I'm one of them.
Tomorrow the truth comes out.

Reuben watched the message for a moment. He leaned in. He frowned at it. Then he got up from his desk and pulled open the door.

'Margaret.'

Instantly Miss Jensen appeared in the hall. 'Yes, Mr V?'

'Where is Jean-Baptiste?'

Margaret swallowed her nerve. JB was the man every woman wanted. It was wrong, because the things he did were terrible. She knew he was as cool and ruthless as her boss, and yet the Frenchman wore his secrets well. His were uncharted waters; she had always thought so. She would catch him, sometimes, deep in thought, and the way he was with the boy…

But Reuben only ever used the man's full name when something was the matter.

'I haven't seen him,' she said carefully. 'Is there anything I can help you with?'

Reuben forgot his manners. 'Do you really think an issue for which I require Jean-Baptiste could possibly be one you would be capable of handling?'

'I'm sorry—'

Reuben slammed the door.

It was a hoax. But how had this person got into his private

account? Only a small clique was permitted: Jean-Baptiste being one of them, and a handful of selected clients.

Pinching the material of his shirt between two fat fingers, Reuben fanned air on to his sweaty chest. Despite his self-assurances, his heart was throbbing against his rib cage.

Thump, thump, thump.

Fuck it. *No one* was more powerful than him. This party was going to go off without a hitch and then he'd trace whatever joker had dared stray into his personal business. For that was what it was: *business.* He was a businessman. The things he'd done...well, they were to make money. And make money they most certainly had. He wasn't about to start unravelling a moral fibre he wasn't even sure was there. Conscience was for pussies—not for him.

This time he buzzed for Margaret, couldn't tolerate facing her scarcely concealed rapture at whatever drama had now been thrown his way.

'Get me a girl,' he instructed as soon as she came on the line. 'And make it quick.'

There was only one thing he needed right now: a fucking blow job.

1
Lori

Loriana Garcia Torres was reading a novel. It was a good one. The hero was about to enter, a brooding, misunderstood lover with vengeance in his heart.

Dark hair fell over her face and she pulled the wild curls back with one hand, gathering them at the base of her neck. The *Tres Hermanas* beauty salon, a dusty-walled, graffiti-plastered enterprise in LA's Eastside was, as usual, empty.

Anita approached the counter. 'Trash needs takin' out,' she sneered, her features contorted with their usual combination of spite and boredom. 'Get to it.'

Lori tore herself away. At seventeen, with skin the colour of the desert at sunrise and wide, thick-lashed gold-black eyes, she was sexy, even though—perhaps because—she had never had sex. Hers was an irresistible age. On the cusp of womanhood, she still possessed a childlike innocence that rendered her very Spanish beauty incomparable. Her stepsisters, themselves a few years older and with none of Lori's charm or kindness, hated her for it.

'I've been here since six,' she replied. 'This is my first break.'

'This is my first break,' Anita mimicked as she chewed gum with an open mouth. It was obscene, the way she did it, because she was wearing so much lipgloss. The hand on her hip was crowned with curled fingernails, each one several inches in length, and heavy hoops pulled fatly at her earlobes. 'Been busy readin' that garbage?' She snatched the book, regarding its pages with disdain. 'There's jobs gotta be done round here, quit makin' excuses.'

'I'm not. I haven't stopped all day...' Lori trailed off under the scorch of Anita's glare.

'And you won't now.' Anita smiled sweetly and turned up the Jay-Z track on the radio. 'Or I'll tell Mama and Tony about Rico. And you wouldn't want *that*, would you?' Rico was Lori's boyfriend. The Garcias could never find out she was seeing him—they'd go crazy.

Lori's gaze raked over *Tres Hermanas*: the cracked mirrors bolted to the walls; the sickly pink of the salon seats, damp and rubbery in the sticky summer heat, their mock leather peeling like sunburned skin; the stained porcelain bowls where she washed through all that tough hair; the acrid smell of ammonia. She hated it. Every second she was here she hated it.

Life hadn't been easy since her mother had died, ten years ago now. Tony, her father, had swiftly remarried, acquiring a new family: Anita and Rosa, jealous of her beauty and dead-set on making her life a misery, and a stepmother, Angélica, whose mean stare and sideways looks gave Lori the impression she could well do without the nuisance of a ready-made daughter. Unable to abandon the hopes and dreams of her parents, Lori had left school and joined the business, working till her bones ached and her feet blistered. It wasn't enough. Her sisters' attitude had driven clients away and now the salon was spiralling rapidly into debt and disrepair.

Lori had no money and no prospects. The days were long and the pay virtually non-existent, and while Anita and Rosa wasted no time spending their share, on cheap clothes, cigarettes and men, Lori put hers straight back into the enterprise. She did it because she loved her father and she didn't want him to suffer—not more than he already had.

It wasn't a life. It was endurance.

Rosa emerged from the back, where she'd been smoking out in the yard. Rosa was the eldest and overweight. She sported a cap of slick dark hair, which she tweezed into little hook-like curls at the sides of her face.

'Loriana thinks she's done enough for one day,' chirruped Anita. 'Got better stuff to do.'

'Oh, yeah?' Rosa shot Lori a scornful look. 'Like what?'

Defeated, Lori rose from the counter. It was easier than arguing. Once upon a time she'd have stood up for herself, given as good as she got, but the reality was she was outnumbered. The only person on her side was Tony—or, he had been. These days he seemed to have given up, the endless loans and threats from the bank and demands for payment finally wearing him down. He'd become weak, let Angélica take over with her punishing schedules and harsh government, at least where Lori was concerned. No, she was by herself. That was all there was to it.

The salon door opened and Rosa's only appointment of

the afternoon wandered in, a mean-faced black girl with a tired weave. She slumped into one of the salmon-coloured chairs and threw a glance Lori's way. 'I want hair like hers,' she declared. It wasn't the first time a client had requested curls like Lori's, something that was impossible to pull off. Rosa glowered.

Anita released a satisfied puff as Lori began mopping the floor. 'You're lucky to have a job here, y'know,' she mused, leaning over the counter and lazily examining her nails. She'd always been a bully, was born with it in her character, intrinsic as genetics.

'My family started this place,' Lori fired back. 'So don't tell me I'm lucky to be here.'

It was a petty observation, but nevertheless the truth. Lori's parents had been proud, God-fearing, hard-working people: they'd been dirt poor but they'd been happy, arriving in America with barely two cents to their name and taking out a loan to build their own business. Purchasing one of a chain of beat-up shopfronts in a down-and-out part of LA, over the years they had watched it grow into something about which they could be proud.

Then her mother had died. Too quick, too sudden, too horrible. Through a shroud of grief, Tony had allowed himself to be comforted by the first person who claimed they wanted to listen. Angélica had pounced on a vulnerable man and an exploitable business. In the weeks that followed, *Pelobello* had become *Tres Hermanas*, and from there it had begun its descent. Lori tried desperately to keep its head above water but she worked thankless, endless hours. After a while, it got to a person. It made them feel useless and hopeless. It made them feel broken.

Lori refused to accept this was her future. A light glimmered inside her. Some days she thought it was her mother, still with her; others, the glowing, insistent ember that kept her alive. Change would come. She'd know when it did.

'I'm done,' she said now, shoving the mop back in its corner. Anita's horrified expression appeared in one of the salon mirrors.

'Don't you dare think about it!' she crowed.

'I'm not thinking about it.' Lori grabbed her bag. She changed from the uncomfortable plastic heels made obligatory by Angélica into her favourite worn Converse. 'I'm doing it.'

'You can't leave,' Rosa bitched, jabbing a pair of styling scissors in Lori's face. 'You've got another hour and you're workin' every second of it!'

'Or what?' She scooped up a stack of battered paperbacks from under the counter.

'You'd better not be meetin' Rico!' one of them screeched, but she couldn't tell which. 'You won't get away with it!'

Lori pulled open the door, hearing the familiar, hated metallic buzz that announced her departure. She held the books tightly to her, remembering the worlds they kept inside: other worlds she dreamed of when she lay in bed staring into darkness, imagining what opportunity, what possibility, tasted like. Sweet, she decided, like honey.

Things would be different. It was only a matter of time.

I will get out of here, Lori Garcia vowed. *One day. One day I'm going to be free.*

2
Aurora

'So, do you want to fuck?'

Mink Ray, sixty-something rock star fresh from a come-back tour with The Bad Brothers, put down his brush and gazed, stoned, at the canvas he'd been working on.

'Looks like shit,' he complained.

Aurora Nash ground out her half-smoked joint and sat up. She was naked. 'I'm offended.'

'I doubt it.'

'Let's see.' She peeled herself off the couch, one of several sunken offerings in Mink's Hollywood apartment. Aurora was tall, about five-nine, with short ice-blonde hair and glacial blue-grey eyes. Her tits were small and high on her chest, the nipples dark and stiff. She hooked an arm round Mink's waist. He was wearing his customary leather jacket and it felt weird, quite horny, against her skin. 'It's not that bad,' she pouted, secretly thinking it was dire. She couldn't work out if it was meant to be abstract or if Mink was just a crap artist.

'What's that?' She pointed at a jagged torpedo thing in the middle of the picture.

'Your tit,' he commented lazily, sparking up a cigarette and ambling to the bar, where he poured them both drinks.

'You promised me it would be tasteful,' Aurora teased, not minding at all. How tasteful was it ever going to be? She was posing nude for her friend's dad, rock star legend and now, apparently, frustrated artist.

'It is,' Mink said, chucking back the dark liquid and immediately filling another. '*You* couldn't tell what it was, could you?'

Aurora faced him, unabashed. She put a hand on her hip and felt Mink's gaze rake over her young body. Her skin was smooth, flawless, smelled fine…and she knew it. 'My turn.' She arched an eyebrow at his leather-clad crotch. 'Let me draw you.'

Mink snorted by way of reply. He fingered the blinds on the window, allowing a sliver of mid-afternoon light to stream in. It illuminated the crags on his face, features addled by years of alcohol and drug abuse and who knew what else. Aurora found it sexy. When he let go, the apartment returned to its den-like state. Aurora joined him at the bar and slipped on to a stool, crossing her long legs and in doing so folding away the light triangle of butter-coloured hair between them. She caught Mink watching.

'Wanna get bombed?' he asked, squinting as she took a slug of her drink.

'What are you offering?' She trailed her pinkie around the rim of the glass.

Mink knew he should suggest she wear a robe. He didn't.

'How old are you anyway?' he growled.

'Old enough to fuck.'

'Yeah, right, missy.'

'I'll be nineteen next year.' Aurora was guessing this was an acceptable number to him. Mink must've done all sorts in his day.

He narrowed his eyes. 'More like eighteen.'

'Whatever.' Finishing the drink, she pushed her glass out for a refill. Mink obliged. As she padded back to the couch she could feel Mink's gaze fixed on her ass.

Actually, Aurora was fifteen, but she was old for her age. She knew *loads* of girls who said that, but in her case it was actually true. It wouldn't be the first time she'd slept with someone older than her dad. Mink wanted her; she could tell it a mile off.

Settling on the couch, she tucked her knees up under her chin. Mink was getting an eyeful. Around her neck was a silver locket, from which she produced a vial of white powder. She tipped a small mound on to her little finger and expertly sniffed it up each nostril.

'Hey, let me in on summa that.' Mink swaggered over, glass in hand. He wore a lot of chunky rings with skulls and panthers on them and things like that, and his nails looked grubby. There was paint on his knuckles.

Aurora obliged and they both sat back. Whoa, that was good. She felt Mink's hand on her leg, creeping higher.

'I don't fuck kids your age,' he pronounced.

'I don't fuck men your age,' she countered.

He regarded her out of the corner of his eye, the way her chest was rising and falling as she breathed, the peaks of her tits coming closer and then receding, tempting him, teasing the growing bulge in his pants. When was the last time *that* had happened? These days it took more than a nice rack to get him hard. This girl was hot, real hot.

'Guess that makes us as bad as each other.' Desire curdled his voice.

Aurora smiled. The light in the room was purplish, and she could see tiny dust motes floating close to the floor. 'My parents wouldn't approve,' she said innocently, gazing up at him through pale lashes. She could see Mink struggle with the turn-on of her virgin-daddy's-girl protest and the undeniable truth of it.

Aurora Nash was the daughter of Tom Nash and Sherilyn Rose, mega-selling country rock legends and all-round respectable American couple. Initially they'd had separate careers—Sherilyn the sweetheart of the country and western scene; Tom regarded far more seriously than Billy Ray Cyrus but still attracting the comparison, one that pissed him off no end—but when album sales tailed off in the nineties they had joined forces and become a formidable duo, singing songs about the great and good of America, the land of opportunity, all that stuff Aurora privately thought was horse shit. It sold, though—boy, did it sell. They'd made millions.

As her parents' only daughter, Aurora had never wanted for anything. Every whim was indulged, every desire satisfied. The word 'no' didn't feature in her vocabulary. She liked her life, it was fun—and it *was* fulfilling, even if recently she'd been jumping from project to project without feeling much about any of them. Everything got handed to her on a plate, and it wasn't like she was *complaining* about it, it was just that she never, ever had to try. Then again, who wanted to try? Trying was boring. Succeeding was what it was about. In the last year alone Aurora had released her own teen-queen album, collaborated on a fashion range with a music icon, and launched a perfume called, fittingly, 'All Mine'. And she wasn't even sixteen yet.

'Who says your old man has to know?' Mink took her hand, guiding her towards the protuberance jutting tent-like from his pelvis.

He unzipped his fly and whipped his dick out. It was gigantic.

Aurora felt like laughing. But Mink was dead serious. 'You gonna suck my cock like a good little girl?' he breathed, the words catching at the back of his throat. One hand was absent-mindedly caressing the shaft, the other applying pressure to the back of Aurora's head. She resisted against it and Mink pushed harder.

'Wait your turn,' she told him, manoeuvring her body round. She lay flat on her back and parted her legs. Mink's mouth fell open, which was a good start. 'Girls go first.'

3
Stevie

There was a certain romance to exiting a New York yellow cab. As Stephanie Speller slammed the door and hauled her bag out of the trunk, watching as the vehicle rejoined a blaring stream of downtown traffic, she gazed up at the surrounding skyscrapers and believed, for the first time in a while, she had arrived.

It was like stepping on to a movie set. Drivers hollered from car windows. Commuters rushed past brandishing steaming coffee, bursts of animated conversation reaching her from every angle in layers of astounding clarity and detail. The aroma of something sweet from busily toiling street vendors, pretzels or doughnuts, masked the sourer odour of trash sweating it out in the summer heat. Stevie had to put her head right back, looking up and up and up till her neck hurt, trying to see the tops of the buildings, and even then—

Someone slammed into her, the force of impact nearly sending her flying.

'Hey, lady, get outta the street!'

'Sorry,' she mumbled, blinking behind her glasses. She'd developed the habit a lot of English people have where they say sorry for something when it's not really their fault.

She took refuge in a café with an Italian name, all red leather booths and an overhead ceiling fan, tickets being shouted for lattes and Americanos, and bustling, harassed baristas. After putting in her order and grabbing a folded copy of the *New York Times*, Stevie slid into one of the booths and took her phone out of her bag. She pushed the bridge of her glasses up on her nose, a nervous tendency she indulged in even when she wasn't wearing them.

As often they were, her phone proved to be a useful distraction. A guy sitting in the adjacent booth was eyeing her keenly. She was surprised at his unabashed scrutiny: she'd never before considered that looking someone up and down *actually* meant looking someone up and down. He was wearing a suit—it being a little past seven a.m.—and, judging by the laptop and stack of paperwork in front of him, ought to be focusing on something other than her. He was short, at least his top half was, and bald, with a muscular neck and shoulders. Parts of his body appeared inflated, as if someone had put a bicycle pump up a vital orifice and filled him with air.

Stevie glanced away. Even if she had found the man attractive, and even if she had become accustomed to picking up strangers in cafés within hours of arriving in a new city, the attention made her uncomfortable. What gave him the right? Was it the suit, the expensive shoes, the bulging wallet? It was the last thing she needed or wanted. It was the reason she'd come here in the first place, why she'd boarded a plane back in London and vowed never to look back.

Her drink arrived and she thanked the waitress, her English accent piquing the guy's interest. She focused on her phone, scrolling down the accommodation sites she'd had a brief trawl through before arriving. Any of her friends would have laughed at the idea that sensible Stevie would just turn up somewhere without a place to stay, but the decision had been so immediate that there'd been little opportunity for preparation. And anyway, they didn't know the context. She'd spent her whole life planning and arranging and playing by the rules, and look where that had got her: to a reflection in the mirror she barely recognised.

At twenty-seven, towards the elder end of six siblings, Stevie had always been described as the quiet, studious one. With that big a family it was easy to blend into the background and be tagged with a character, as much a means of identification as anything else. But it wasn't always possible to be how everyone else expected you to be, and, in any case, nobody was that clear-cut: nobody was immune to stepping out of themselves if the circumstances were right. Her behaviour over the past few months would stun them all.

She was tired after the flight and put more sugar than usual in her coffee. As she did so she made the mistake of briefly meeting her admirer's eye. She imagined how he saw her. Shy, probably. Nervous. Maybe a bit geeky, certainly she had been at school, when she'd worn braces and been timid with boys and hadn't grown into her face yet.

Stevie was petite, with dark, serious features and a precise, angular, pale-skinned beauty that had been described in the past as both 'classical' and 'timeless'. She was never sure how to take this: it made her think of the marble busts at the British Museum with their Roman noses and blank, staring eyes like peeled boiled eggs. Her hair was very dark red like the skin on a cherry, and she wore it back, in a neat ponytail. She used mascara but no other make-up—one of the preferences she'd recently reclaimed, because he'd liked a woman to look a certain way, and that had meant shadows and powders and waxy lipsticks. Stevie didn't need any of this. She was beautiful, in the way only someone without a scrap of vanity can be.

'Excuse me?'

Would it be rude to ignore him? Yes.

Reluctantly, she looked up. The man had packed his stuff away and appeared to be heading out.

'I couldn't help overhearing you,' he said. 'Are you from London?' Up close he had crescents of sweat under each eye. She didn't think she'd ever seen someone sweat there before.

'Yes,' she replied, with a smile that was neither encouraging nor dismissive.

'*Great* city,' he enthused. 'Is it your first time in New York?'

She nodded.

'Need someone to show you around?'

Stevie thought how to articulate her response: he seemed friendly enough, but she had no intention of getting attached to someone this quickly. Besides, while she hadn't been to New York before, she felt as if she knew it, however wrongly or remotely, from films she'd seen and friends who'd visited, and was confident she'd find her feet soon enough.

'Thanks.' She lifted her mobile to indicate she already had a network, and with it came the inspiration of a lie. 'I've got family here.'

'Sure, sure.' He grinned. 'But if you change your mind…?' From his pocket he removed a business card and slid it on to the table. His hands were soft, the nails clean. She sensed he had a lot of money.

When the man had gone, she returned to the flat-sharing site. Nothing new had come up since she'd last checked, and tapping in revised criteria didn't help.

The necessities of a flat and a job were about as far ahead as she could consider. When she'd made that snap decision only a few days ago, waking up one morning too many with the familiar hollow sickness, America had been the obvious place to go. Her father had originally been from Boston—he'd left when Stevie was a teenager, into the arms of another woman, and she had neither seen nor heard from him since: a while ago news came he'd died of a heart attack while skiing in Austria—and her American passport gave her a window to find work here and ascertain where she was heading…whether this really was a bolt hole or something more permanent. The way she felt right now, she never wanted to see London again.

She'd check into a hotel, at least for tonight. Tomorrow, she'd start her search in earnest.

Gathering up her things, save for the business card, Stevie downed the last of her coffee and rooted for some coins for a tip. She wasn't sure it was the done thing, but following a gruesome waitressing stint in her teens she'd been a strict twelve-per-center.

It was only as she was leaving that she noticed the bit of paper stuck to the café window. There were other notes, too, pasted over each other, photos and contact details and petitions—for lost dogs, nanny work, Pilates classes—but it was this one that jumped out at her. She crossed to look at it. The advertisement was scrawled erratically in red pen, an address and a number and a lot of exclamation marks, concluding with: AND I PROMISE WE'LL HAVE AN ADVENTURE!!!!

Stevie tapped the digits into her phone. Without thinking too much about it, she stepped out on to the street and pressed the green call button. She held it to her ear and waited.

And that was how she found Bibi Reiner.

4
Lori

Enrique Marquez worked the boats at the harbour at San Pedro. Lori spotted him straight away, bent over the rigs on one of the bigger pleasure cruisers, his jet tattoo creeping like oil from where it began at his collarbone and travelled down one arm. He was bare-chested, his black hair tied in a short high ponytail, strands escaping. His jeans were low-slung on his waist and a white rag, covered in some kind of grease, was thrown over one shoulder.

'Hello, stranger.'

He turned at the sound of her voice, a smile breaking out across his boyish face.

'I nearly forgot how gorgeous you are,' he said.

Lori waved away his compliment, but the fact of their time apart rang true. They hadn't been able to see each other for days—it was hard to escape her responsibilities at *Tres Hermanas* and, once she got home, forget it. Her father would explode if he suspected she was seeing a Mexican boy. Worse, one from the notorious Marquez family.

'Come here.' Rico held out his hand.

Lori stepped off the pier and on to the yacht. The LA sun bounced off the sleek white surfaces and crisp flat sails. Rico's strong grip encircled her waist and he drew her into a kiss. When the kiss became more fevered, Lori pulled away.

'This one's beautiful,' she commented, scoping the length of the boat. 'Whose is it?'

Rico shrugged broad shoulders. 'Beats me,' he said, 'I'm just paid to make sure it goes.' He grinned, showing his dimples. 'Someday *I'll* be the guy some kid's sweating his balls off for. *I'll* be the owner of a piece like this, you'll see.'

'And would you sail me a long way away?'

'Wherever you wanted to go.' He kissed her again, his hands running down her short dress and over her luscious hips. She felt him harden, his tongue slip into her mouth.

'Not getting distracted, I hope?' a voice admonished from behind. Lori turned her head to see a rotund man removing his shades and rubbing them on his shirt.

'Almost done here, boss,' said Rico, holding Lori firmly to him.

Rico's supervisor frowned. He scanned Lori's body, from her mane of wild hair to her bronzed calves and scuffed sneakers. 'You know I don't let girlfriends on the boats, Marquez.'

'It won't happen again.' But still he didn't release her.

The man watched them uncertainly before moving off down the boardwalk.

'Can you let me go now?' Lori teased.

'Can we wait till I'm in a position to move?' Rico laughed.

'Oh.'

'Yeah, oh. You know what you do to me.'

Lori glanced away. It was unfair of her to hold out on Rico—she liked him; he was good, he was kind and he treated her right. Yet instinct kept telling her she wasn't ready. She wasn't sure what she was waiting for: marriage, soul mates, a new life…? People talked about meeting The One, that single person you wait and hold out for because you love them more than anything else in the world and you'll always be together, always always no matter what… but that was fantasy, a plot from one of her books. Stories, only stories. Real life didn't work out that way.

Then why did it scare her that she didn't feel those things with Rico? If they didn't exist, why should it count?

But, it did. Somehow, it did.

They rode the freeway on Rico's bike. Lori loved the feel of the wind in her hair, the way it whipped round her legs and filled her lungs with air. For those moments she could forget. She could be a new woman, whoever she wanted.

Rico lived in a beat-up apartment with his mother but she was out of it on drugs and didn't hear them come in. His father wasn't around, and his brother Diego, chief of El Peligro, the most feared gang in Santa Ana, hadn't been home in a week. No one asked why.

'We should leave,' said Lori when they were in his room. 'Just go.'

Rico put music on. 'Where?' He lit a cigarette.

Lori sat cross-legged on his bed. It was a mess, strewn with unwashed clothes, and Rico hauled his T-shirt over his head with one hand and tossed it on to the crumpled mound. She knew he had it worse than she did. Her family was poor, the women were unkind, but at least she knew when she got in at night that she wouldn't find her father overdosed in a chair, vomit down his front and his tongue bit in half. The first time Rico had found his mom, he'd been only ten.

'Anywhere,' she said. 'Anywhere's better than here. I'm tired of LA.'

Rico inhaled smoke. 'You're tired of your end of it.' He opened the window and leaned out. A group of boys were fighting in the dusty street and the sound of it washed in, a dry shower of curses and the exploratory flare of violence. 'We just got the bad deal, didn't we? Everything you dream about is right here, Lori, just around the corner. You're on top of it. It's that close.'

'Hollywood?'

Rico lifted his shoulders. 'Something like it. You're pretty enough. Damn it, you're beautiful.' He set his jaw. 'You can do anything you want.'

'That's not what they say.'

'What do you care what your family thinks?' Rico's voice tightened. He knew the Garcias looked down on him. They and their stupid Spanish friends treated him like shit because he was poor, from a bad lot, and his parents had been first-generations. Hadn't they all started out in the same place? Hadn't they all crossed a border at some point? Just because the Garcias had been in this city longer they felt able to spit on him, judge him, dismiss him.

'Move in with me,' he said bitterly. 'Forget them.'

'You know it's not that easy.'

Rico tossed his smoke out of the window and joined her

on the bed. 'I wish you knew how special you are,' he said, gathering her into his arms. Perhaps Lori was right—they should pack up and leave, go somewhere no one could find them. But his mother needed him. He wasn't going to quit on her as his father had.

Lori breathed in her boyfriend's scent: salt and sweetness, heat and hard work. Was this love? It must be. She didn't want to lose Rico; he was all she had. And yet, as she felt his hands begin to roam, she was already preparing how to turn him away. Was there something wrong with her? None of the girls she knew had a problem with sex.

'You drive me crazy,' murmured Rico. He trailed his fingers down the front of her dress and over her curves. Man, she was hot. He didn't know how much longer he could wait. It would be her first time and she wanted it to be right, he got that, but this was sending him wild. He was far from inexperienced himself, but recently he'd forgotten what sex felt like.

Lori let herself be kissed and reclined uncomfortably, putting her head back when Rico buried his face in her neck. Every so often she experienced a brief, sharp dart of desire, but it fizzed and died like a match in water. Maybe she was incapable of it—some people were. Other girls talked about getting so turned on by their boyfriends they were prepared to do anything, anywhere, but, as always, the moment Rico's attentions became too fervent, a sense of claustrophobia overcame her and she had to get away.

'Rico, don't...'

He was moving down her body now, his hands on her breasts, attempting to free them as he kissed and bit her skin.

She didn't want to offend him, knew she kept leading

him on only to let him down. What was he doing with her? 'No, Rico…'

'Relax,' he responded, just a muffle, 'I promise I won't hurt you.' She felt his touch trail the inside of her thigh and hook the elastic of her knickers.

Roughly she pushed at him. 'I told you, I'm not ready.' She sat up, pulling down the hem of her dress, her face flushed.

Rico bit back his frustration. Instead he put his arms around her. 'I'm sorry,' he said. 'I shouldn't have…' The early evening sun spilled in and drowned his golden chest with light, the pool of ink there blacker, more absolute, because of it. 'You know I'll wait however long it takes. I'd never force you. I promise.'

Lori felt guilty. She was being unfair. What was she holding out for? She had to do it eventually—and it might as well be with a man she knew adored her.

'Do you trust me?' Rico asked.

'Of course.'

He nodded. 'I love you.'

She met his eyes. 'I love you, too,' she said, but she didn't know what the words meant.

5
Aurora

Aurora gunned the engine of her cherry-red Ferrari Spider. It purred beneath her as she waited at the lights. The sky was apricot and the air smelled sugary, the sun a melting orb that dipped hot below the horizon.

She and her girlfriends were on their way to Basement, their favourite Hollywood hangout. It was Friday night, which meant all the names that meant anything would be out and ready to party. Kids of famous parents, heiresses and socialites, child stars, models, they'd all be there: wholesome favourites with secret coke addictions, virgin starlets who'd spend the night promising a blow job to their managers, alpha-male young actors with an eye for the boys as well as the girls... Inside the car, a bottle of vodka was being passed round. Joints were being rolled. Lines being cut. They were totally baked and the night hadn't even begun.

At a red light, Aurora caught sight of a super-hot Latino

guy on a bike next to her. He had more than a passing resemblance to Rafael Nadal, who she had a major thing for.
A pretty girl was clinging to his waist—she looked like
a gypsy, with masses of black hair and long, tanned legs.
For a fleeting moment Aurora imagined being in bed with
both of them at the same time. Maybe she was a fucking
nympho—the thought had occurred to her before.

The lights changed and the boy sped off. In his place,
an open-top Jeep packed with surfers on their way back
from the beach. They were shirtless, still wet, whooping
at the girls to get their attention, their piercings glinting in
the fading light. One of them made an obscene gesture at
Aurora.

'You strapped in?' she asked the others. Farrah Michaels,
her best friend and daughter of the head of a mega Hollywood production studio, sniffed and coughed. Her eyes
were glassy.

'Your dad's gonna freak if you waste the car.'

Aurora revved the engine. Someone beeped. The driver
of the Jeep winked. One of the guys stood up, pulled down
his shorts and slapped his bare ass. The girls squealed.
Jenna Reynolds, in the back, lifted her top and jiggled two
enormous breasts in response.

'Jerk-offs.' Aurora floored it and the Ferrari roared to
life, nought to sixty in a matter of seconds. The other car
didn't stand a chance. In the rear-view mirror Aurora saw
the Jeep recede to a pinpoint before vanishing completely.

Jenna was thrown back against the seat. She struggled
to get her top down. 'Ow!' she complained. 'Fucking hell.'
Farrah was laughing.

Aurora took another swig from the bottle. She turned on
to Sunset at speed. The Ferrari's tyres squealed.

'Uh, hello?' complained Farrah, grappling to retrieve her smoking paraphernalia. 'Some of us are *trying* to get high?'

Moments later they pulled up outside Basement. Aurora was striking in a clinging white minidress, killer heels and statement arm jewellery. Her pale blonde crop looked incredible against her bronzed skin. Her blue eyes were lined with kohl. The other girls, though each attractive in her own right, paled in comparison.

The paparazzi were out in force. They clamoured for Aurora the instant she exited the vehicle. 'Aurora! This way! Look this way, Aurora! Aurora, over here!'

She chucked her keys at a waiting valet. He fumbled the catch and dived to the floor to retrieve them. Aurora led the way inside.

The club was pounding. She headed for the VIP area and proceeded to order them all shots. Farrah, a pretty redhead, scoped the place for the member of a teen boy-band sensation she'd heard would be making an appearance. To the public the band were all good innocent Christians, but rumour said different of at least one. Apparently he was into dildos.

Aurora was used to the looks she got. Everyone in this town knew who she was and who her parents were. A British DJ had remixed one of Sherilyn Rose's songs and it was currently storming the download charts. No doubt they'd play it tonight in her honour. Secretly she found it embarrassing. She was tight with her dad but her mom was another matter. Maybe it was the same with all moms: they were a reminder of what you could look like in fifty years or whatever. OK, not fifty, but close. She shuddered.

Last week had been her parents' anniversary. For some reason, every year, they celebrated it by buying her a gift, like she was the reason they were still together, or something. It was messed up. But she wasn't about to say no to a two-hundred-thousand-dollar ride, was she? Hence the Ferrari. Farrah had been right: Tom would throw a shit fit if he knew she was using it to party, but, still, what he didn't know couldn't hurt him. Aurora was his little girl and nothing she did could be anything short of wonderful. Did he even know where she was tonight? She couldn't work out if he and Sherilyn genuinely had no idea about her lifestyle or if it suited them to be ignorant. She guessed they had enough else to think about without a tearaway daughter who was bedding everything in sight.

Aurora ended up on the lap of Olympic idol Jax Jackson, who had a cock that was allegedly so huge it had acquired a myth-like status. From where she was perched it didn't feel like much. He had masses of bling around his neck and a solid-gold watch that probably cost more than the car. Across the bar she spotted Farrah pressed up against Boy-Band-Christian. Jenna, who'd starred in several kids' adventures when she was seven but had never lost the puppy fat, was dancing in a circle of admiring males. Aurora felt bored.

'Why'n't we skip the bullshit,' proposed Jax, 'an' you come home with me?' He shifted on the banquette, pressing his growing erection into her backside. 'Throw our own little party, whaddaya say?'

Aurora had never done it with a black guy; it'd make a change. But she was wasted, properly wasted. She felt kind of sick. Abruptly, she stood up. 'I'm leaving.'

'Jeez.' He slid his attentions to an adjacent blonde. 'Suit yourself.' It was an effort to get across the club. She managed to peel Farrah away from her boyfriend—'boy' being the operative word—and shout in her ear that she was going.

'Already?' Farrah was shocked. 'How'm *I* gonna get home?'

Aurora couldn't be bothered to answer. That was Farrah's problem. Either she was coming or she wasn't.

'I'm not coming,' said Farrah. Boy-Band-Christian grabbed her chin and stuck his tongue in her mouth. Aurora saw it slide in like a horrible slug and she experienced an intense rush of disliking her best friend. This whole scene was tired out. She'd had enough of it. Every day the same: endless partying, endless guys, endless everything.

If Farrah was staying, she could sort Jenna out, too.

Outside, the cameras lunged at her. In seconds her car was brought round and she jumped in, switching the ignition. Fuck. She was out of her head, shouldn't be driving, probably. But no one told her so. No one *ever* told her so.

She'd been on Sunset for a minute, maybe two, when she started feeling properly like shit. She'd done too much: her eyelids were heavy, her limbs shutting down.

I'm going to pass out, she thought. Car horns blared.

The last thing she remembered was her head hitting the wheel, hard, painfully. Then everything went black.

6
Stevie

Bibi Reiner was a firework. She was tiny, everything about her compact, with this amazing scrawl of frizzy auburn hair and huge, wide green eyes. Since welcoming Stevie at the door of her apartment over a month ago, she had barely stopped talking.

'You and me are gonna have *such* a blast!' she'd gabbled as she led Stevie through her place on West 54th, at once assuming their living together was a done deal, something Stevie found incredibly friendly. They were at the top of an impressive redbrick with views over Central Park, and inside were bright white walls, spotlights and parquet flooring. Stevie's room was spacious, light and airy, with tons of storage and a luxurious king-size bed. Over the summer it had been occupied by Bibi's brother, like her an aspiring actor, but he'd since relocated to LA, leaving the room free. Stevie had called at the right time. She couldn't believe her luck.

'How was your flight?' Bibi had chattered. 'What's going on in London? I *love* London. What do you do? What do you eat? I'm a vegan, which means I don't eat meat or dairy, but I *will* have a hot dog once a year because I love them. Also, I'm a Buddhist. I don't drink alcohol but I do drink champagne. I have to get nine hours' sleep every night otherwise I don't function and my skin turns to crap. Your skin's amazing, what do you use? You're so pretty, far prettier than me. I'd *love* to have hair like yours; it's so straight. Mine's a total mess. Don't you think? I've tried everything. Go on, be honest, it's too much, isn't it? I should dye it. Red? Or pink. I was thinking pink. And I want to get a tattoo on my back, here, of a butterfly.' She'd reached awkwardly around, failing to get to the exact spot and laughing at herself. 'Just a little one because they're cute. But my agent says I'm limiting roles. I just wanna stand out, ya know?'

Bibi didn't stop. But she was lovely, she was funny; she was sweet and she was kind. And for Stevie, who only talked when there was something to say, she was in many ways the ideal person to share with. The girls were different but they clicked instantly. Bibi thought Stevie was the most gorgeous creature she had ever seen because she had this air of calm and wisdom, something Bibi had always coveted in others because she herself was a ditz: things popped into her head and she just blurted them out, *pouf!*

Despite the fact that Stevie had moved in five weeks ago, she was still struggling to find work. Her rent was fair, in fact it was better than fair, but she was already scraping the barrel of her savings. It wasn't for lack of trying—she'd walked the city till her feet gave in, leaving her CV anywhere that looked as if it might need staff—but in honesty her lack of progress was more down to the fact that Bibi was constantly suggesting lunches out, parties, shopping and coffee with her friends so Stevie could be introduced. She was infinitely generous, with everything.

It was a Thursday. Stevie was lying on her front on the bed, intermittently yawning, her chin resting in the cup of one hand while the other tapped aimlessly through job sites. She didn't even know any longer what she was looking for. Every time she landed on one that seemed suitable, she'd spot that the closing date had already expired, or she had to be based in a different city, or it required a proven qualification she didn't have.

Always academic at school, she'd opted out of university to the disappointment of her teachers. Her dad had walked when she was fifteen and there followed an awkward few years: she'd wanted to get out into the real world and earn a living, because he'd left them with next to nothing and she'd decided that never again would she be in a position of dependency. Well, that was the reason she gave herself. More likely was that her mum was trying to raise and provide for an army of kids and a slug of university fees was the last thing they could sustain.

Working life hadn't been as glamorous or as productive as Stevie had imagined, however she'd found a niche that paid well and played to her skills. She'd been a PA now, in varying degrees of responsibility, for nearly ten years. She was efficient, organised and unflustered. Or, she had been, up until a year ago. But that depended on who you were working for.

There was a knock at the door. A beaming Bibi stuck her head round.

'Can I come in?'

'Sure.' Stevie smiled back. Her smile was one of the best things about her, the sort of smile she gave her whole face to. In repose she could appear quite solemn: it was more concentration than anything else, but all the same it made the contrast a dazzling surprise.

Bibi, dressed in faded dungarees and an eighties-style bandana, bustled in with two mugs of coffee. She laid them down and flopped backwards on to the bed.

'I need a boyfriend!' she announced dramatically.

Stevie snapped shut her laptop. 'You don't *need* a boy-friend; you *want* a boyfriend. There's a difference.'

'Are you a feminist?'

'Aren't you?'

Bibi shrugged and looked at the ceiling. She covered one eye, then the other, and did this a few times. 'I can see better out my left.'

'Maybe you need glasses.'

'Maybe. Wanna go out?'

Stevie sat up. 'I can't afford it, B.' She rubbed her fore-head. 'I need to find a job.'

'You *need* to?'

'Yes. Otherwise what am I going to pay you with at the end of the month?'

'Come *on*,' said Bibi, not listening. She yawned in her usual theatrical way, stretching her arms wide. She'd as-sured Stevie that the apartment belonged to some distant aunt and she was getting a 'ridiculously sweet' deal, but Stevie saw no reason why she should take advantage of this, and anyway she disliked not having work, it made her feel like a waster.

'Oh my God!'

Stevie was alarmed. 'What?'

'My friend's having a party tonight!' She sprang up. 'I just remembered! We should go!'

Stevie stared balefully at her laptop.

'Let's go now!' And she bounced off the bed.

'It's three o'clock.'

'So? We'll go shopping on the way.' At Stevie's expression, she added slyly, 'There'll be *guys* there. And you know what guys mean? Flirting. And you know what flirting means?'

'Waking up in someone's bed the next day without a clue what their name is?'

Bibi looked innocent. 'I was going to say a bit of banter, but if you—'

Stevie threw a cushion at her.

'Come on—' Bibi checked her reflection in the mirror and adjusted the bandana above her ears '—they're actors, it'll be fun!'

This was a further disincentive. Stevie loved Bibi and had no doubt that one day she'd be a famous and very talented actress—it was all she had ever wanted to do, Bibi vowed, her whole entire life—but she had, apart from where Bibi was concerned, a slight phobia of that world. Take the Aurora Nash scandal, for instance. Stevie felt sorry for the girl, she was only fifteen or something, and her mug shot had been all over the papers. Last month she'd crashed the car Daddy had bought her and ended up getting arrested. She'd had enough drugs in her system to tranquillise a horse. In fact one of the drugs *was* for tranquillising horses. It was a spoiled, desperate scene. All that mindless excess, it wasn't her thing.

Stevie's last job had been working as PA to the director of a firm dealing in high-profile celebrity court cases: divorces, injunctions, political scandals, they'd handled it all. As part of that she'd been obliged to attend the occasional industry bash and had found each one unbearable. Cash made these people invincible, or so they thought. Stevie recalled him working flat out on a case shortly after she joined involving a married news anchor who'd been filmed dressing up four twenty-something Russian prostitutes as characters from *The Wizard of Oz*—it was their job to keep the press off the scent. She resisted the memory. That had been the case that started it. The late nights...the way he'd stand at the window loosening his tie, the spires of London behind, silhouetted in gold...the invitation of a drink, and then...

'You do *like* men, don't you?' Bibi interrupted her train of thought. 'Because this one time I kissed my best friend, who's a girl, at holiday camp when I was, like, sixteen.'

Stevie shook her head. 'So...?'

'So are you gay?'

'No.'

'Just checking. Cos there are plenty of girls I could set you up with.'

'Who says I want to get set up?' Stevie removed her glasses and went to clean one of the lenses on her T-shirt. 'Believe it or not, I *like* being by myself.'

Bibi bit her thumbnail. 'Can you see without those on?'

'Pretty much. I just can't see things far away.'

'You should get contacts.'

'Hmm.' She slipped them back on, returning to her computer.

'You're really not coming, then?' Bibi folded her arms.

'I'm really not coming.'

'OK.' One of the nice things about Bibi was that she'd

try for her own way, but was quick to identify defeat and get over it without a struggle. 'I guess you need to save yourself for Linus Posen's party, anyway.'

'Who?'

Bibi had made to leave, and turned now, feigning surprise. 'Oh! Didn't I mention it?'

Stevie raised an eyebrow. 'No.'

'You must have heard of Linus Posen.'

She hazarded a guess based on Bibi's usual array of friends—and the more the name settled, the more she thought she recognised it. 'Director? Producer?'

'The first. My rep's going, she'll get us in. Honest, it's the party of the season. And Linus is a *very* big deal.' She clapped her hands together excitedly. 'If I play this right, he could really make things happen! So you will come, won't you? For moral support?'

Stevie cringed.

'For me?'

'That's not fair.'

'You're in New York City, now, sugar, you've got to live a little.' Bibi winked as she closed the door behind her. 'Stick with me and you'll be just fine.'

7
Lori

Tony Garcia folded his copy of *La Opinión* and slid it quietly on to the table. Lori noticed the stack of unopened envelopes gathered there, the red-stamped final warnings just visible in the windows. Dark circles shadowed her father's eyes.

'The shame!' Angélica, at her husband's wilted shoulder, had her thin arms folded and her black hair secured in a tight bun. Her lips were a bloody shade.

'I've done nothing wrong,' Lori replied coldly. She still had her bag slung over one shoulder, had scarcely returned from *Tres Hermanas* before Angélica embarked on her tirade. Anita and Rosa—those bitches, those *putas*—had grassed her up.

The tiny kitchen was the scene of their dispute. The house had barely been big enough for three when her mother was alive, but they had loved each other so it hadn't mattered. Now, Lori felt the walls closing in on her, unbearably close. Dirty plates piled up in the sink, awaiting her attention; laundry heaped in a corner, a pair of Anita's knickers thrown carelessly over the top; grime and squalor on every surface, tasks the women deemed beneath them.

'Rico loves me,' she attested, lifting her chin. 'He takes care of me.'

'Enrique Marquez is *not* one of us,' spat Angélica, as if this closed the matter. 'You are a disgrace to this family, Loriana.'

'What family? You're not my family. You'll never be.'

Angélica's eyes blazed. 'Tony, tell your daughter to show me some respect!'

Tony was an echo. 'You heard her, Lori. Show some respect.'

She wanted to hit him. *Come on*, she willed her father, *stand up for yourself!* Grief changed a man—but how much longer till she got him back?

'His people are dangerous,' blasted Angélica.

'You know nothing about Rico and his family.'

'I know about the dead baby!' she rasped triumphantly. 'Don't think for a second we don't know about *her*.' Rico's mother had given birth to a stillborn daughter the previous year: everyone knew it was the drugs.

'His brother will go the same way, you can be sure of that,' Angélica raged on. 'They are dirty, Loriana. They are *immigrants*.'

'And what does that make us?'

'*Tony!*' Angélica put a hand out to steady herself, appalled by the mere suggestion that she and her daughters should be classed in the same way.

Lori knew Anita and Rosa were behind her in the hallway, listening in. She pictured their rapt expressions and experienced a fresh surge of injustice. Nothing they did was ever wrong; everything she did was. She was an outcast in this house.

'You want to complain about people who don't work to support themselves? Fine. Ask your daughters. They're lazy; they do nothing. *Nada*. The work falls to me—just as it does here.' Her voice cracked. 'Mama would be so disappointed.'

There was a flicker in Tony's expression, but as soon as it appeared it was gone. Fury reignited Angélica, who was unable to tolerate reference to her predecessor.

'You ungrateful *puta*!' she spat. 'Do you think you would fare better on your own? Go ahead, then—try! You're living under our roof, remember—'

'I don't recall this house being yours,' interrupted Lori. 'And anyway, if you'd had your way I wouldn't even be here, I'd never have been born. So why don't you *let* me go out with a *dangerous* boy? See if *I* might wind up dead sometime. You never know, you might get lucky!'

'*Stop!*' At last, Tony snapped. The kitchen plunged into silence. Lori knew she had gone too far, but she had wanted a reaction, any reaction. Now she had got one.

But it wasn't the one she expected.

'If that is the way you feel,' said Tony evenly, 'then we will not stop you leaving. In fact, we will encourage it.' He rubbed his eyes, and when they met hers, red-rimmed with fatigue, she saw they were empty as a well.

'If you insist on seeing this boy, we will have no choice but to send you to Corazón.'

She was appalled. 'In *Spain*?' Corazón was Lori's elderly grandmother on Tony's side. The woman lived in the middle of nowhere in a remote mountainous part of the country.

Tony nodded. 'Angélica and I believe it is for the best.'

It made sense. 'That's exactly the way you want it,' she told her stepmother, almost admiring her nerve. 'Get me out of the way, maybe I'll never come back.'

'We are giving you a choice,' said Angélica, dripping mock-fairness. 'If you continue to see Enrique Marquez, you will leave us with none.'

Lori pushed her way through to the hall. Anita and Rosa scurried out of sight; Rosa's large behind waddling noisily up the stairs to the bedroom she shared with her sister.

She was blind with anger. It was unthinkable to split from Rico—he was her only refuge, the only thing in life that made her feel there was some escape, however, whenever. But equally she could not risk being sent to Spain. Her grandmother was about to die, she must be a hundred at least, and it would be like being sent to the graveyard herself.

'Loriana, you come back here!' screamed Angélica from inside the house, furious that she should be walked out on. 'I haven't finished with you!'

The beach drew her, the only place she could think of to go. She was desperate to call Rico but couldn't bring herself to tell him what had been said. Angélica's cruel words echoed, chaotic, in her memory, like a bird she had seen once, trapped in a room.

A truck horn sounded as she crossed Ocean Boulevard. A guy stuck his head out of the window and shouted something appreciative. In frayed denim shorts and a plain string vest, two thin hoops glinting in her wild black hair,

Lori was a siren without a clue how to use her beauty—and that was the best use of all.

The ocean was still. It wasn't yet dark. Lori removed her shoes and padded across the golden sand. At the water's edge, she stopped.

So this was the choice: quit seeing Rico or go to Spain. The irony was that if it were anywhere else she would have jumped at the chance—wasn't it the breakout she'd been wishing for?—but if she felt now like her life was moving nowhere, it would be nothing compared with the situation at Corazón's. Lori recalled the house in Spain only distantly, in the mists of her childhood, but the fragments she assembled created an image of quiet and loneliness and loss. What could there possibly be for her there? More waiting...waiting for her life to pass her by.

Mierda! Frustration gave way to unhappiness. She refused to weep; she was stronger than that. Tears achieved nothing. She needed a plan.

In the distance, a boat edged slowly across the horizon. Lori closed her eyes. In the months following her mother's death, she had pictured an island, somewhere remote and far away, the place she always went to when she needed to remember there was a wider world waiting to be found. She could picture it so clearly: its sweeping white shores and sparkling green waters, the chalky heat and the blazing sun. Now, at the ocean's lip, sensing the great expanse at her feet, she could almost believe such a place existed. An island that was all hers, her fantasy alone, which nobody else could touch.

One day...

Hers was a different fate. Maybe she knew it because of her mother: she had to live a life that was big enough for two. Maybe it was because she spent too much time poring over romance novels, gateways to those other glittering treasure-filled worlds. Or maybe, just maybe, it was because she was right. Her heart believed it and she trusted her heart.

Lori breathed the salty air deep into her lungs. One day she would visit her island, see it made real. See the destiny that awaited her there.

It was obvious what had to happen.

She and Rico had talked about it. Now they just had to do it.

They were going to run away.

8
Aurora

Tom Nash examined his reflection in the glass terrace doors. The record label was taking him out. Clad in tight leather slacks and an open white shirt, he teased the final element of his highlighted hairstyle into place. Aurora watched him.

'Don't you get hot in those pants?' she asked, sparking up a thin joint and reclining on the poolside lounger. Even through her Ray-Bans the sun was blazing, filling her vision with dots when she opened her eyes. 'They look like they're melting on your legs.'

Her father didn't appear to hear; he was way too concerned with his appearance. Aurora thought he was looking quite orange these days, understandable since they'd just had a sunbed installed in the mansion's basement, along with a gigantic spa, sauna and steam room. Tom was the only one who seemed to make use of it. Her mother, by comparison, was a pale-skinned beauty with a chronic fear of melanoma. She only appeared outdoors wearing wide-brimmed hats and covered in material head to toe. Physically, Aurora was unlike either of them.

She was used to being ignored when her father was preening. Her parents' latest hit 'Steady Rock', a gently lilting country ballad, emanated from inside the mansion, but was mercifully drowned out when Aurora screwed in her iPod and blasted some vintage Pearl Jam. Stretching out, she lost herself in the music. Oh yeah, she majorly dug rockers. A few weeks ago she'd attended a gig at the White Rooms, an indie group from Wisconsin on the cusp of a breakthrough, and ended up having sex with the lead guitarist right here in her mom and dad's pool. She turned to the blue water and remembered it with a tug of yearning: the way she had gripped on to the marble rim, each rough thrust sending an exquisite pain rushing through her, a spill of water over the side… Hmm. She was definitely hooking up with him again. These days she was certainly mixing with far cooler, and more mature, people than Farrah was. In fact she hadn't seen much of her best friend since the night she'd totalled the car. Personally she couldn't see the attraction in Boy-Band-Christian. She doubted he even had pubic hair.

A shadow loomed over her. Aurora opened her eyes a crack and reluctantly removed an earphone. She stank of weed but Tom pretended, as ever, not to notice.

'I gotta go, baby,' said her father, in a rich Texan drawl which years in LA hadn't completely washed out. He ruffled her hair affectionately. 'Be good, OK?'

'Always am,' she replied.

Tom raised an eyebrow. Once upon a time that line might

have worked, but given her recent disgrace it didn't say a great deal.

'Where's Mom?'

'Out.'

'Isn't she going with you?'

Tom made a non-committal gesture. 'She's got a session with Lindy.'

Lindy was her mother's therapist. Sherilyn had been seeing her since the couple discovered—shortly after Aurora was born—that they were unable to have any more children. Aurora found her continued reliance on Lindy and whatever psychobabble she regurgitated a touch offensive. Wasn't Aurora enough? She was enough for Tom.

'When's she back?' Aurora was pleased at the thought of an afternoon alone in the mansion. Maybe she could invite Farrah round, see if she had goodies to share. And maybe Boy-Band-Christian had an older brother.

Tom didn't know. It amazed her how career-wise her parents did everything together, but when it came to personal stuff they seemed to live practically apart.

'I mean it,' Tom said, trying his best to be stern. 'Behave.'

Aurora gave him her most winning smile. 'I'll be good, Daddy,' she said innocently.

Tom wasn't convinced, and who could blame him? Two months back Aurora had passed out at the wheel of her vehicle with a cocktail of drugs in her system. She could have died. The cops had arrived at the scene, realised the state she was in and taken her immediately to hospital, where she'd had her stomach pumped and been sick into a tray until her insides ached. Then came the inevitable arrest— and *that* photo. It had been splashed across the world's media: little Aurora Nash, once the bouncing blonde baby of two of America's most famous, most conservative and most clean-living country and western stars, was, now, at fifteen, a bleary-eyed mess, doped up on who knew what and, so it was widely reported, moments from death. But it was the attitude that seemed to shock people: the hard-edged glare in her eyes, the been-there-done-it-all weariness so at odds with her youth.

The Ferrari had been trashed, its hood concertinaed like an accordion. At first Tom and Sherilyn had been angry—well, as angry as they'd ever be. She'd been grounded for a week, but with Jenna's help had sneaked out on the second night. They never noticed. Tom had bought her a replacement car, though she'd had to wait a month—and she still wasn't permitted by the authorities to drive. Who knew how long she'd be without a ride! She was going out of her head.

'This has got to change,' Sherilyn had told her, but more with sympathy than rage. Sometimes she wished her mom had more balls. 'Perhaps you should come see Lindy.'

God! Seeing Lindy was a fate worse than death. She'd probably make them have mother/daughter sessions or something equally horrific. No, she'd handle this herself in the same way she always had: sweet smile, big eyes, promises to be good. Bingo.

'See you later, kiddo,' said Tom now, bending to kiss her cheek.

'See ya, Dad.'

After he'd gone, Aurora unclasped her bikini top and lay back down, slipping her earphones back in and letting her mind wander back to the sexy guitarist and the pool.

The next thing she knew, it was cold. Shit—she must

have fallen asleep. The sun was fading and the temperature had dropped. How long had she been out?

She checked the time: almost seven.

Gathering her things, she padded through the vast sliding doors and into the Nash/Rose mansion. It was a huge ranch-style place, with a mix of LA grandeur and Tom's more earthy Texan roots. She grabbed herself a glass of lemonade from the refrigerator. Tom's avocado facemasks littered the vegetable compartment.

The second the door shut, she jumped.

'Who the *fuck* are you?'

A man—at a guess he was only a year or two older than her—was standing in the doorway, arms laden with brown grocery bags. He was dark-skinned and dark-haired, short, with green eyes and a young, smooth-skinned face. He looked as startled as she did.

Aurora became aware that she was topless. She folded her arms across her breasts, but could see the effect her nakedness had already had on him. The boy's cheeks were aflame.

'Er… I am… My mother is…' His English was bad. Distantly Aurora remembered the Mexican housekeeper her parents had hired recently.

'You're Julieta's son?'

'Yes,' he said, relieved, but still not knowing where to look. 'She not well today… I come to help… The lady boss says is fine…'

'You've spoken to my mother?' Aurora demanded. She let her hands drop as she sipped the lemonade. It was cool inside, the air con made it so, and she felt her nipples stiffen.

The boy nodded swiftly. He dumped the bags on the central island.

'I will leave… You are busy…'

'You're not going to help me tidy these things away?' Aurora asked, gesturing at the groceries. 'I thought you'd come to help.'

He nodded. She'd never seen a blush under such dark skin before. He was five-six at a push, not the calibre of man she would normally go for, but something about him was attractive and she felt a stirring ripple through her. She wondered if he was a virgin.

'What's your name?' she asked.

'Sebastian.'

'Well, Sebastian,' Aurora said, setting her glass down and slinking round the counter. Her bikini briefs were tiny and she leaned over the bags, pushing her ass out for him to admire. 'Shall I show you exactly where I want you to… put things?'

He rustled pointlessly with the bags.

Aurora smiled, lifted herself up on to the counter and crossed her legs. His eyes were level with her breasts. 'Do you play pool?' she asked.

The boy gulped, gaze darting to the water outside.

'Not that sort of pool,' Aurora clarified, though she imagined they could have several entertaining games out there as well. Instead, she took his hand. He didn't object. She drew it to her right breast and felt his fingers cup tentatively round the soft flesh. His eyes were transfixed on her body, his mouth slightly open, in fear, desire or disbelief it was impossible to say. When she drew her own hand away, his remained. They stayed like that for several moments, the groceries between them. Sebastian's touch became firmer, beginning to knead, before his other hand seized the second breast and then he was pushing them together, squeezing and releasing. Abruptly he leaned in, took one of their peaks between his lips and sucked.

'Come,' she told him, slipping off the counter and leading Sebastian through to an adjacent games room. Centre stage was a magnificent green-felt pool table, the triangle of gleaming balls laid out in perfect arrangement and two slim wooden cues down each side.

Aurora settled on the edge of the table, enjoying the smooth, glossy veneer beneath her bare thighs. 'Strip,' she told him. When he looked confused, she added more softly, 'Take your clothes off.'

Fumbling, Sebastian removed his T-shirt, unbuckled his belt and stepped out of his jeans. He had a broad chest, muscular, and stocky, virtually hairless legs. The hard-on visible through his underwear was modest, but sufficient. Aurora raised an eyebrow. He peeled them down and over his ankles, kicking them to one side.

She appraised his dick. It was rock-hard and reasonable in length, his balls ripe and buoyant in a nest of dense black hair. Slowly she took off her own briefs, and the minute she parted her legs, he dived for her like an animal, plunging in with force.

'Fucking hell, hang on!' She pulled back, easing him out. 'Aren't you forgetting something?'

Sebastian's face had taken on a slack, robotic expression. He sank to the floor and started rummaging about in his jeans, at last removing a coloured wrapper. So much for being a virgin. The second time he entered her Aurora was thrown back on to the table, scattering the pool balls wide. She raised her arms and grabbed each of the top pockets with her fingers, the boy pummelling into her, deeper and deeper, all the way in then driving back out, his hands under her ass. He was half up on the table now, one knee bent on the felt, the other foot steadying him on the floor. Aurora didn't think she had ever in her life been nailed with such conviction.

He mounted the table, crouching, and flipped her round. She saw two of the yellow balls rush into the top pockets, heard the velvety *plunk* of one vanishing in another. Gripping under her belly with one hand, the boy pushed into her from behind, snatching her tits with the other, tugging them hard. She felt the slap of him against her and she grabbed one of the pool cues, sliding its length underneath till she could move the cold, flawless line of it back and forth, bringing her off. The boy took the lead, clasping its end and driving it between them. As she was on the cusp of coming he whipped it out from under her, slid his cock out and replaced it with the butt of the cue. With a strangled groan he ejaculated. Rocked forward with the motion, Aurora screamed aloud on the crest of her orgasm. The boy collapsed forward and they stayed motionless on the table, wrapped in sweat, gasping for air.

'Fuck,' was all Aurora could say. 'You're an outrageous fuck, Sebastian.'

He began kissing the length of her spine, from behind her neck to the top of her ass. She was still riding the gentle spasms of her first climax when he bent to lick her. Lazily she smiled, parting her legs to receive his tongue, feeling it flick and plunge between her till she was coaxed to the edge of another rising swell. He used his fingers, wetting them before, on the point of making her come a second time, he dipped the tip of his thumb into her ass.

Aurora cried in ecstasy, so loud she didn't hear the door to the games room open.

Sherilyn Rose dropped whatever it was she was carrying. Sebastian clambered back off the table, tripping over on to the floor, struggling to get his jeans on, mumbling something incoherent in Spanish.

Shit.

Triple shit.

Aurora looked up, blew the hair out of her face. 'Hey, Mom.'

9
Stevie

Linus Posen's party, or 'gathering', as it was creepily called on Bibi's invitation, took place in his penthouse New York apartment on a Sunday night. As soon as she saw Linus, Stevie understood he was exactly the sort of person who threw parties on Sundays, changing the rules simply because he could. He was a massive presence, tall and fat, and possessed a booming baritone of a voice and mean, quick little eyes that looked like raisins squidged into raw dough.

Stevie decided on sight that she didn't like him. Typically she'd never be so quick to judge, but his air of bored arrogance sat uncomfortably with her.

'Are you sure I look OK?' trilled Bibi as they stood at the entrance to the sprawling warehouse, suffused with mood beats and the hum of conversation. It wasn't like Bibi to be insecure about anything, but she hadn't relaxed since they'd set off.

In the cab, Stevie had been surprised. 'Don't tell me you *fancy* him.'

'Of course I do,' Bibi had confessed, insofar as Bibi could ever make a confession, because Bibi never seemed to be embarrassed or apologetic about anything. 'Linus Posen is shit-hot, Steve. He's the director that could build my career! My agent says he's casting for his new movie. Matthew McConaughey's tipped to star.'

'It doesn't mean you have to find him attractive.'

'McConaughey? Gimme a break.'

'Linus Posen, silly. Isn't he old?'

'Fifties, is my bet.' Bibi had checked her face in her compact for the millionth time. 'Frankly, I don't care. He could be in a wheelchair and I'd still show him the Bibi Reiner magic!'

'That's sick.'

'That's sensible.'

'What about whether or not you *like* him?' She knew she was giving Bibi a hard time. Just because she'd succumbed to a man with power didn't mean the disaster that had befallen her was going to befall everyone. It was just that she didn't want Bibi getting hurt, and instinct told her that Bibi didn't always think things through properly. Then again, that was hypocritical.

'That comes afterwards,' Bibi had explained patiently. 'All I care about right now is getting him to notice me.'

The party was packed with famous faces, some of whom Stevie recognised and some she didn't. The girls wound their way through the chatting, exclaiming sea of bodies. It reminded Stevie of the handful of celebrity soirées she'd attended through Simms & Court in London, but even she had to admit this was of a higher order. Back at Bibi's apartment she'd teamed a pair of black skinny jeans with boots and a top: it was definitely her style, not that she'd admit to having one, of quiet, understated glamour. Bibi had tried to insist she borrow a dress but she'd turned it down, compromising by letting her hair loose and slipping on a pair of heels, to which Bibi had exclaimed, 'We're the same size, ohmygod, it's meant to be!'

She regretted her decision. All the other women were in gowns and skirts and Stevie felt criminally underdressed, especially next to Bibi, who was clad in an imitation (a good one) Versace minidress and fierce heels.

'Are you OK?' asked Bibi, taking her arm.

'Sure. Why?'

'You seem a bit…I dunno, quiet. Is everything all right?'

It wasn't the first time Bibi had attempted to get her to open up. Being a relentless gossip, she'd been on at Stevie about ex-boyfriends and past experiences pretty much as soon as she'd got here, and doubtless could tell something was the matter. It wasn't as though Stevie didn't feel able to confide in her—on first impressions Bibi was a live wire, but underneath all that was a deeply caring and unselfish friend—it was more that she didn't want to think of it herself. She'd done a stupid thing, a reckless thing, and she regretted it. That was all there was to say.

'Honest, B. I'm fine.'

Bibi accepted it: she knew when to push her luck. She plucked two flutes of gold champagne from a passing tray and nudged Stevie in the ribs. 'There he is,' she murmured, the champagne vanishing in one. 'Let's go.'

'Will he know who we are?' Stevie disliked feeling like a groupie. She had no desire to meet Linus and even less to witness his ego being fawned over.

Bibi grabbed her hand and pulled her towards the group surging around the director, nearly colliding with an on-coming array of canapés that was more artwork than food. 'If he doesn't now,' she promised, 'he will soon.'

They got held up by Bibi's agent for a few moments, a flinty-eyed woman named Carrie Pearce, who had bobbed hair the colour of rat. From the way she spoke to her client it was clear she deemed Bibi incredibly lucky to have her representation. Stevie couldn't work out why, since Bibi seemed to go for endless auditions and never secure any lasting work.

'Stevie's from England,' said Bibi, in a way that managed to make it sound exotic.

Carrie looked bored. 'It must be quite something for you to be at a party of Linus Posen's,' she said unpleasantly. 'Are you in the business?'

Stevie shook her head. 'I'm a sales assistant,' she told her, correctly anticipating the admission would pass like a bad smell under Carrie's nose and feeling satisfied when it did. Why should she be made to feel self-conscious? After much searching, she'd finally landed a part-time position at a clothes store on Broadway and was proud of every cent she earned.

Carrie smiled tightly as Bibi blathered on, her eyes skipping across the room for a more interesting and important person to talk to. Stevie became aware of someone watching her and was compelled to turn round. A man with longish brown hair that curled under his ears was standing several feet away, his gaze unwavering even at having been found out. He raised his glass in her direction. He had a cute smile. She smiled back, regretted her haste and looked away.

'Come on!' sang Bibi, linking her arm once Carrie Pearce had departed. Stevie followed her friend through the crowd where, excruciatingly, they had to join a sort of queue to speak to Linus. She saw his spongy white head gleaming under the considerable lighting.

When at last Bibi's turn came to speak to the famous director, she introduced herself as though they were old friends, chatting away happily while Linus impassively listened, every so often chucking a soft salty devil-on-horseback between his fleshy lips and chewing ferociously. He ate with his mouth open, sweet prune pulping on his tongue, and stared blankly and brazenly at Bibi's breasts for the duration. Stevie, hovering behind, felt disgusted.

Men like Linus made her skin crawl. They believed their position gave them entitlement to any woman they felt like pursuing, confident there'd be plenty in reserve if that one said no. It didn't mean anything. They could speak all they liked of love and the future, of leaving their wife, of making it real—and they didn't mean a damn word. And before the object of their attentions could snap out of it, the spell cast—of sleepless nights and pining and lusting, of dreaming pointlessly of a happy ever after—she woke one day and realised she'd abandoned who she was, the morals and standards that she'd stood by, all for the sake of...

'Bibi, are you going to introduce me to your...*ravishing* friend?'

Stevie blinked. Linus was gawking straight at her. Bibi was bouncing up and down in the background and pointing frenetically: because she rarely drank, the champagne had gone straight to her head and her cheeks were flushed pink. Her eye make-up had smudged. 'Of course!' she squealed, ecstatic. 'Stevie Speller, this is Linus Posen.' She gave

Stevie a little excited thumbs-up when Linus leaned in to take her hand.

'The pleasure's all mine,' he said huskily, and she shivered as his lips met her skin.

'Steve's rooming with me,' said Bibi proudly. There was a protracted silence during which Stevie could practically see a reel of corresponding images turning over in the director's mind. 'Isn't she a doll?'

Linus smirked, his eyes hooded. 'I'll say,' he leered, absorbing Stevie's classic beauty, her pale, oval face and the dark, almond-shaped eyes hidden behind her glasses. A good girl. Sensible. The kind of girl who'd tell you off for misbehaving. 'She's irresistible.'

Discreetly Linus folded a card into Bibi's hand, then into Stevie's. For politeness's sake, Stevie took it. It didn't look like a business card, more a private one: simply the director's initials and a phone number. 'Look me up if you ever need work,' he said meaningfully. 'I sincerely hope you will.' And she could tell he was in no doubt of receiving her call: the cards had been dispensed with the same tolerant indulgence as with sweets to children.

Bibi seized hers with enthusiasm. 'Did you hear that?' she chirruped when he'd gone. 'He just offered me a job! Steve, he offered *us* a job! Can you *believe* it? This is it for us! It starts right here!' She clutched Stevie. 'Oh. My. God. We'll be like a double act. We'll be famous, like a famous duo, like Cagney and Lacey! Or Thelma and Louise!'

'I'm not sure, B, this seems a bit—'

'What do you mean, you're not sure? This is the hugest break ever! He'll make us stars, both of us! Everything he touches turns to gold!'

Stevie turned the card over. 'It looks kind of dodgy to me.'

'Dodgy!' Gleefully Bibi deposited her empty champagne flute and picked up another. She spotted Carrie Pearce and peeled off to tell her the good news. Stevie should have been relieved that Bibi was seeking her agent's advice, but something told her Carrie did not have her client's best interests at heart. She was unable to help the anxious feeling that had taken root.

Oh, she needed to get a grip! Linus might not be to her taste but it didn't automatically mean he was evil. She had to get over feeling as if every man was a threat and she was on some crusade to save womankind from surrendering to his charms. She didn't want to end up bitter and alone, but if she didn't get over it then that was exactly the way she was going.

Pocketing the card, Stevie scanned the room and landed on the guy who had been—and clearly was still—watching her. He mouthed 'hello' and she found herself mouthing it back. He was attractive, even though she knew the continually replenished glasses of champagne were likely contributing to that, and making his way over, taking her reciprocation as an invite.

'Hi.' He held his hand out. 'I'm Will.' He was maybe a few years older than her, with a dent in his chin that deepened when he grinned.

She shook it. 'Stevie.'

'I like your accent,' he said.

'Thanks.' She smiled, slipping into the groove of flirting though she'd left it to rust so long. 'I like yours.'

There was a lapse in conversation while Will's eyes lingered on her. He smelled good, like cinnamon. Stevie found herself wondering if it might help: just to do it, to be with someone else, so the time with him wasn't the last time it had happened, like listening once more to a song that caused you heartache because you had to face that pain and let it be before it went.

'D'you want to get out of here?' he asked, lifting an eyebrow.

Stevie glanced over at Bibi, who was happily chatting on at her agent.

'Sure,' she said, before she could change her mind. 'Why not?'

Will offered his hand. She took it.

Maybe New York was looking up, after all.

10
Lori

The hair got everywhere. Lori felt the coarse scratch of it beneath her nails, kept finding webs caught between her fingers, on her clothes, appearing on her pillow when she got into bed, bone-tired after another relentless day. She'd never imagined something so anodyne could cause her such torment. She was strangled by it, caught in a trap; it seemed to follow her, a constant reminder of the closed doors of her life, each strand thick as a chain.

But not any more. Today was her last at *Tres Hermanas*. After these final few hours, she would be shot of this city for good.

City of Angels. It hadn't been for her. There had been no one watching out for her here.

'Loriana!' Anita's summons sounded from the counter, where she was busy painting her talons, now so long they formed a corkscrew. 'Go get us coffee, an' make it quick, wouldya?'

Lori was prepping foils. 'I'll be right there,' she called, swallowing a biting response. If her sisters caught on, they could blow the whole plan with Rico apart.

She headed to a local bar for the drinks, distracted as she put her order in. It was no matter: the Hispanic baristo knew it by heart.

'There's a mess out back needs cleanin',' commanded Anita when she returned, scarcely looking up to take the drinks as she pulverised a stick of gum. She was reading a magazine article about tearaway starlet Aurora Nash going into rehab—again. The way the young girl had so many opportunities and yet had flown in the face of all of them confused Lori. What did she have to be so angry about? Surely with a life like that there could be no room for un-happiness. Aurora had money, fame, success…and parents who loved her.

Uncomplaining, Lori moved to her next task. Anita seemed confused by her lack of retort and threw in for good measure: 'The john could do with a scrub while you're at it!'

A carton of juice had been spilled and left to congeal on the lino. It had attracted flies and Lori got to her hands and knees to lift the sticky, cloying mess, dousing it with hot water and towels, wiping the floor with one hand and the film of sweat from her brow with the other.

She had given up complaining since the fallout with Angélica. Instead she had kept quiet, pretended her re-lationship with Rico was over and held her tongue over her sisters' taunts. All that time, she and Rico had been saving what little money they had and planning their route across America. She didn't care how it turned out—she was thinking only of tomorrow and what it would feel like to wake up in a different place. She could almost taste independence, could touch it, like something physical. It was close.

The yard was dusty and Lori picked her way over the lot to the heap of stinking trash, adding her load to it with an upsurge of flies. A cockroach scuttled out and across her foot. She pushed thoughts of her father away, of what it meant to abandon him in this squalor and near-poverty. But she could not carry on like this. When she was settled elsewhere, working as many hours as she could, for nothing could be as backbreaking as the toil she had known here, she would send him the money he needed. It wasn't abandonment; it was necessity.

As she was turning to go back inside she heard the rumble of an engine.

Rico. He pulled into the yard on his bike.

'What are you doing?' Lori cried, gesturing frantically for him to cut the ignition. 'If someone sees you…!' She didn't dare finish.

Obligingly Rico jumped off the bike and wheeled it towards her. Lori kept the door to the salon open and pulled him into the shadow behind it. She was about to reiterate her anger before she saw how pale he looked. The white vest he was wearing was covered in mottled dirt.

'Are you OK?' she asked, putting a hand to his head. 'Are you sick?'

'I'm not sick.'

'What's the matter? You look bad.'

'Nothin'.' He seemed to be in a hurry.

'It's all right, they're inside,' said Lori, misreading his concern. 'Even so, we shouldn't risk it—you can't stay. Is everything ready for tonight?'

'That's why I'm here.'

Fear seeped through her. Rico wasn't bailing—not now, when they were so close.

'I'll be late,' he said. 'An hour, maybe. There's somethin' I gotta do first.'

'What?'

'It don't matter. It's just I can't make midnight. I didn't want you waitin' around, thinking I wasn't gonna show.'

Lori searched his eyes. 'Is everything cool?'

'Everything's fine.'

There was something he wasn't telling her.

'OK,' she said uncertainly. 'Same place?'

'Same place.' He grabbed her hands. 'I love you, Lori.'

'I love you, too.'

'Do you?' He met her gaze, and there was desperation there. 'Because we've never…you know, we haven't… I've never loved you properly. In the way you know I mean.'

Lori looked away. 'We've talked about this.'

'I know.'

'And I can't say sorry.'

'I'm not asking you to.' He lifted her hand and kissed it. 'I just have to make sure you're not holdin' out on someone else. Someone better? Like I'm not good enough.'

She shook her head. It wasn't a question of being good enough. But if it wasn't that…

Fairytales don't exist, remember?

'Take this.' He fed a hand into the pocket of his shorts and produced a modest silver band. She let him slip it on to her ring finger. It glinted in the afternoon light and reminded her of a ring her mama had once bought, years ago when Lori was a little girl, but they'd been forced to sell it when the business began to fail.

'Why?'

'It's a promise.' He kissed her fingers again and she saw he wore a matching one. 'Between you and me. OK?'

She was confused. 'OK.'

'Whatever happens.'

'Rico, what is this—?'

'Shh.' He touched his forehead to hers. 'I'll see you tonight, yeah?'

Lori kissed his cheek. 'Yeah.'

Noiselessly he moved across the yard and mounted his bike, seconds later vanishing in a cloud of bitter dust.

It was cold. The moon shone bright in the clear sky like a pearl, an occasional gossamer cloud drifting across its spotlight.

Lori pulled her cell from her bag and checked the time. He was supposed to have shown up half an hour ago. *Where was he?*

They had arranged to meet partway down the Santa Ana Freeway, where Rico had organised a car to take them out of the city. Lori had planned her exit from the Garcia house with precision. She'd gone to bed early, leaving the volume on the TV high while she grabbed her stuff and hauled up the narrow window, which always stuck halfway. From outside she'd clicked off the set, tossing the remote back through. They wouldn't be any the wiser till daybreak.

Lori wrapped her jacket more tightly around her. She looked up at the star-punctured sky, the dwarfed outline of an aeroplane silhouetted against the giant moon.

Several cars stopped. Each time she was aware of her vulnerability—either the driver thought she was looking for business or she was hitching to the Southside. She moved between states of fear and upset at Rico's no-show and anger at him letting her down. What was he doing? Why hadn't he called or messaged?

What if he's changed his mind?

I should never have pushed him into it. It was me who wanted this, not him.

She twisted the ring on her finger.

It's a promise...

The wind was picking up. She would wait another half-hour. What else was she going to do? She dumped her pack on the ground and settled on it, huddling her bare knees up under her chin. Every time the glare of headlights filled her vision, each time a vehicle seemed to slow, her heart soared in hope, only to be dashed when it quietly passed by.

She waited half an hour. She waited another, then another. Three a.m. came round. She knew he wasn't coming.

She put out her arm and waited for a ride to stop.

Rosa was making breakfast when Lori emerged next morning.

'I heard you come in last night,' she commented.

Lori fetched a glass of water and didn't reply.

'Cat got your tongue?' Rosa slathered her pancakes with syrup and bit into them, releasing a clear grease that ran down her chin.

It was six. Lori had barely slept, maybe for an hour when she eventually collapsed into bed. *Tres Hermanas* opened shortly. The thought of returning to the salon she thought yesterday she would never have to see again was unbearable.

'I know you were out meetin' Rico.' Rosa slurped her

coffee. 'Hope he was worth it. Because when Mama and Tony find out...' She raised a painted-on eyebrow.

Lori turned her back, stared blankly at the wall. 'Tell them what you like. I don't care. Tell them to send me to Corazón if that's what they want. It doesn't matter any more.'

Rosa pouted, mocking her. 'He break up with you or somethin'?'

Lori didn't know. It was possible. Maybe he hadn't found the guts to tell her and that was what the ring had been about. She found it with her thumb.

'Quit feelin' sorry for yourself.' Rosa flicked on the radio. 'You'll get over it.'

The news reporter's voice filled the kitchen.

'In the early hours of this morning a young man was shot dead outside a convenience store in Santa Ana, California. Police have arrested twenty-year-old suspect Enrique Marquez, believed to have connections with the El Peligro gang, who were linked last year with six acts of violence in the area, two of which were fatal. Reports suggest Mr Marquez is the younger brother of Diego Marquez, thought to hold high rank in the organisation. The victim's family have been informed and a spokeswoman for them is expected to talk to the press later today...'

The pancake Rosa was holding fell to the floor with a slap.

'Lori, what the *hell*—?'

The item had moved on but the reporter's words looped hideously through her mind.

It couldn't be. It *couldn't*.

Lori fell into a chair. Thought she was going to be sick.

'You were there,' babbled Rosa, backing away. 'You were there!'

'No,' she managed to mumble, 'I—I wasn't. He never showed up.'

'Oh, you wait till Mama finds out,' Rosa spluttered. 'Rico Marquez, a *murderer*! We always knew it would happen, that he'd go the exact same way as his brother and the rest of that useless family—'

'Shut up.'

'—and now he's proved us right. What did Mama tell you? We were right!'

Lori put her hands over her ears. *'Shut up!'*

Rosa gave a burst of hysterical laughter. 'You're in so much shit it's not even *fair*! Loriana Garcia, in love with a murderer—'

Lori stood and slapped her sister round the face. It made a clean, sharp sound and left Rosa's cheek burning pink. She wanted to do it again, and again, till Rosa was silenced and she could be left in peace to think straight. It was impossible to focus. Her vision was swimming.

She remembered Rico's words in the salon yard: *There's somethin' I gotta do...*

The floor seemed to bend and shake till Lori realised it was her legs that were giving way. She collapsed against the wall. Rosa went for her, pulling her hair, calling her a bitch, a killer, clawing with her nails, but Lori didn't feel a thing.

11
Aurora

Rehab was a total waste of time. Aurora had known it would be—after all, she had only gone to please her parents and to help her mother get over the trauma of walking in on her young daughter in a state of such disarray, and everyone said that rehab only worked if the person genuinely *wanted* to change. She'd had a blast that day with Sebastian, got horny even now just thinking about it, and while it was unfortunate—and just a tad embarrassing—to have Sherilyn walk in at such an inopportune moment, she didn't regret it.

What she did regret was that Julieta had got fired from her housekeeping duties. On top of that being a rough ride for a poor Mexican family, it was also the end of any rough rides she could expect to enjoy with Sebastian again.

She'd spent a month at the Tyrell Chase Center with her consultant, a gnarled old shrink called Dr Lux, but it was always 'Call me Ed'—it wasn't the first time she'd been.

Dr Lux went over the same tired ground: her reckless behaviour was down to overindulgence, hedonism, lack of
boundaries, blah blah fucking blah. Sherilyn took this diagnosis as a personal affront and always wept heartily after
a meeting with Dr Lux: she hated Aurora going into rehab
as much as Aurora did. *Had she been a bad mother? Where
had she gone wrong? Was Aurora suffering from being an
only child?* While Aurora sat and picked her nails, wondering when the hell they could get out of there.

By the time she did eventually get out, it seemed
Sherilyn had just about recovered from the shock. Her
father informed Aurora she'd been upping her sessions with
Lindy the Therapist—no doubt Lindy would have several
things to say about the pool-table episode—and had some
new pills to pop that came in a fancy pink packet and sat
serious as a Bible by her mother's bed.

Today was the eve of Aurora's sixteenth birthday party.
They'd had people attending the mansion all week: caterers
and planners, stylists and organisers, even a horse trainer
attempting to map a route from the drive to the pool, where
a white stallion would enter with the birthday girl on its
back. She even suspected Tom was sorting a guest appearance from the Black Eyed Peas, and MTV was coming
to film a special all-star *Super Sweet*—it was going to be
amazing!

'You're lucky we're going ahead with this,' Tom had
said when they'd talked about the celebrations. 'After the
trouble you've got yourself in.'

'I know, Daddy,' she'd said, eyes wide. 'You and Mom
are *so* kind and generous—I know I don't deserve it!'

'As long as you've learned your lesson,' Tom had gone
on, as stern as he'd ever be and always with a twinkle that

suggested he didn't think whatever she'd done was *that* bad, 'we're not going to deny you your sweet sixteen.'

He'd ruffled her hair, and that had been that.

Ramon, her hair stylist, arrived. He was doing a colour before her big appearance tomorrow. Sherilyn had insisted on sitting in on the session: Dr Lux had told her she wasn't to be left alone with men—the girl had a sex addiction that temptation did nothing to ease.

'Mom!' she yelled up the stairs. The word bounced hollowly off the high ceilings, precise as a tennis ball. 'Ramon's here!'

Upstairs, Sherilyn Rose applied a flush of rouge to her alarmingly pale complexion. She looked bad. The lighting in her dressing room was unflattering, but, even so, she was tired, overworked and under-slept. Opening a drawer in her vanity table, she extracted a bottle of little red pills. She chucked a handful into her mouth and took a slug of water.

'All right, sweetheart!' she sang, her soft Alabama tones melting down the stairway to her waiting daughter. Sweet-As-Pie-Mom was a hard act to maintain, she thought grimly. It used to come to her naturally—recently she felt like a gruesome monster wearing a little girl's skin. Ugh, that was horrific. But that was the sort of image residing in her head these days.

It was hardly any wonder her nerves were shredded. The pills Lindy had given her were the only things that allowed her to sleep at night. She had been enduring terrible dreams of late: memories that she'd thought were buried deep in the past. And yet every time Aurora misbehaved—this latest episode the worst yet—they returned to her in vivid, appalling detail.

The vast Indian Ocean. The island. *That man...*

If it ever came out, the reasons why they'd done it, her life would not be worth living.

Another couple of tablets, that was all. Shakily she chucked them down her white throat.

Was her life worth living now?

Sherilyn took a deep breath, in through her nose, out through her mouth, just as Lindy had taught her. She tried to smile, making her way slowly down the mansion stairs, one step at a time. As always, she shuddered when she passed the open games room, its equipment cleanly polished and disinfected on her instruction. Nothing could have prepared her for the sight of her daughter in that context. It disgusted her.

Not that her husband seemed to care. People said fathers were always closer to their girls: that the mothers got left out in the cold. Perhaps that was it. Perhaps she was jealous of their connection, a bond she had tried so hard to feel, to *engage*, and, failing that, to manufacture. It hadn't worked. How could it, when week after week she was subjected to yet another reminder of her daughter's monstrosity?

What on earth had she and Tom raised?

Whatever it was, she knew they deserved every bad thing they got.

Aurora's first impression was that her mother could do with a visit from her own stylist: a recent dye job had rendered her hair the same colour as Barbie's and she wore tight frayed jeans and precarious white shoe boots. Dated.

She hitched herself on to a stool by the patio doors,

making sure she could see the poolside arrangement and issue preferences if necessary, while Ramon, young with a Mohawk, plonked down his cosmetics bag and laid out his tools. He was so clearly gay that any notion of chaperoning was absurd. Still, Aurora adhered to the new rules—it was a novelty to actually be made to do something.

'OK, honey,' he said, running his fingers through Aurora's blonde hair. 'What are we doing today?'

Sherilyn lit a cigarette and surveyed her daughter. Aurora noticed how her hands trembled with each puff. 'How about some layering in the length…'

'I want it all off,' announced Aurora.

Ramon was appalled. *'Shaved?'*

Aurora rolled her eyes. 'Not *shaved*. But nearly. Really short, like a boy's.'

Sherilyn blew out smoke. 'Darling, no!'

'Do you *mind*?' Ramon gestured to Sherilyn's cigarette, then to his cosmetics case filled with mousse and sprays. 'I've got flammable substances here.'

'Yeah.' Aurora nodded decisively. 'Dramatic. You *can* do drama, can't you, Ramon?'

'Anything for you.'

'We should dye it as well,' said Aurora. 'Bleach it. So it's kinda white.'

Ramon grinned. 'I like it.'

Sherilyn ground out her Marlboro. 'Are you sure? It sounds extreme…'

'I *am* extreme, Mom. And this is my party.'

'All right, if that's what'll make you happy…' She drifted out to the pool.

'Is your mom doped?' asked Ramon.

'Probably,' said Aurora as he began mixing the colour.

'I don't blame her. I've been a bitch lately.' And she did honestly feel bad about the pool-table thing, but the fact was that in its aftermath her life hadn't changed *at all*. Some days she thought her mother could do with an electric shock, or a cattle prod, something that frazzled her; something that *brought her back to life*. But if that hadn't done it, what would?

Ramon applied the cold mixture to her roots and didn't comment.

Aurora was watching a shirtless guy string lights in the trees by the pool. So was her mom by the looks of it. Ew! Weren't you meant to switch those bits off when you got married? An image popped up of Sherilyn and Tom getting it on. Maybe they didn't any more, seeing as they were now, like, way old. But they must have—at least once. Yuck yuck YUCK.

She spied a gossip rag poking out of Ramon's bag. On the front was her so-called best friend Farrah Michaels wearing a solemn expression above the headline: BFFs AT WAR: 'AURORA NASH SHOULD BE IN JAIL!' It was hardly a war, thought Aurora, since it was entirely one-sided: *she* wasn't the one mouthing off to the press at every available opportunity, all for a bit of cheap publicity. Farrah was just bitter because she'd split with Boy-Band-Christian after he was found cheating on her with a dwarf while on tour in Vegas.

She tossed the magazine down, pissed.

'Hold still!' commanded Ramon, swiping at her head with his brush. The dye stank and she told him so. 'Your hair will stink too if you don't do as I say.'

Outside, Sherilyn was on the phone. She was frowning and nodding. When she came back in, Aurora demanded to know what was going on. Weirdly, her mother ignored her. Instead, she addressed Ramon.

'How long will this take?'

'Don't hurry him, Mom, it's important.'

'So is this.' Sherilyn closed her cell. 'That was your father. He's got some news to share with you.' She took a deep breath. 'He's taking us for lunch at Il Cielo.'

'Is it about the party?'

Sherilyn hesitated. 'Not exactly,' she said.

'What, then?'

A pause. 'Let's wait till lunchtime, shall we?'

She could feel Ramon's curiosity wafting off him like heat. 'What was *that* about?' he asked when Sherilyn had disappeared next door.

Aurora yawned. 'I expect Dad's bought me another car,' she mused. 'They'll want it to be a surprise, but I guess they *have* to tell me if they want to co-ordinate it with the arrival of the stallion. To be honest, I don't know where I'll keep another one—and anyway, I don't even have my permit!'

'Your mother and I have one last gift for you,' said Tom over lunch. The waiter refilled their water. Cubes of ice tinkled and cracked in the glass, melting slowly in the afternoon sun. Il Cielo boasted a gorgeous terrace and, as ever, Tom Nash and his family had secured the best table.

Aurora, admiring her new bleached-blonde hairstyle in an enormous window, grinned. 'Cool! What is it?'

A gaggle of fans approached. Tom swore under his breath at the fresh interruption but smiled pleasantly enough as he and Sherilyn signed scraps of paper and the backs of tabs. Women fancied Tom Nash like crazy: his alpha vibe rendered them babbling incoherent wrecks. They fell for his Southern charm with its twist of LA polish; they adored his vocal Republican stance. Tom was all about tradition, about core values, work ethic and the importance of family. They lapped it up like kittens.

On the other hand, everyone regarded Aurora, and her new hairstyle, with a pinch of trepidation, as though she were a sitting bomb that could blast off at any second. Fine, fuck the lot of them. Aurora sighed loudly, impatient for her dad to spill.

Sherilyn forked her barely touched crab linguine. 'Go on, Tom,' she said softly.

Aurora frowned. What could they have bought her? Maybe it wasn't a car, after all. Maybe it was something sicker that even *she* hadn't imagined—and she'd imagined most things.

At last, Tom spoke. 'We're sending you to England.'

Aurora was pleased. 'London? Can I stay at the Dorchester again?'

'Not exactly a shopping trip, honey,' said Sherilyn.

There was an uncomfortable pause.

'Boarding school,' said Tom, clearing his throat.

WHAT?

'What?' shrieked Aurora, horrified.

Her parents exchanged glances. 'That's right,' said Tom. 'And it's not in London. It's a prestigious, little-known school in the North. You'll receive the attention you need there.'

Aurora's mouth was hanging open. She couldn't believe it.

'You can't do this to me,' she squawked. 'I won't go.

I'm not going. *Boarding* school?' The very word conjured images of prison bars and child labour.

Sherilyn touched her arm. 'We didn't take this decision lightly,' she crooned. 'But we do think it's the best thing for you. After what happened with—' she cleared her throat '—Sebastian Ortega. And crashing the Ferrari. And Mink Ray.'

'What do you know about Mink Ray?' Aurora's face was burning. Had they been *spying* on her?

'You'll be home every few weeks for vacation,' said Tom. 'And we've organised a guardian for you in London so you can be there for exeats.'

Aurora didn't even know what the word meant. This was a fucking outrage!

'You can't make me go,' she said, lip wobbling.

But Tom remained uncharacteristically steadfast. 'It's for your own good,' he said, sawing his veal in a manner that suggested the end of the discussion. 'Therapy doesn't work, rehab doesn't work... This is our last option and we believe it will be the making of you.'

'And this is meant to be my *birthday* present? Are you kidding me?'

Tom's face softened. 'Well—' he put down his cutlery and smiled tentatively '—I was going to wait till tomorrow, but since you asked... We've got you that Porsche you wanted as well.'

'Fuck the fucking Porsche,' lashed Aurora, scraping her chair back and getting to her feet. She lifted her mother's glass of red wine and emptied it pointlessly over the ciabatta rolls.

She was going to England over her dead body. There was no fucking way.

12
Stevie

Stevie woke to the glare of sunlight. She had a slight headache brought on by too many cocktails the previous evening, and foggily remembered the bar that she and Will Gardner had ended up in. Weeks had passed since they'd met at Linus Posen's party and she supposed they'd begun a relationship of sorts, insofar as nights out and occasional sex went. Will knew little of her life and she saw no reason why he should: she'd been frank at the outset that she wasn't in it for a relationship and he'd claimed he was happy with that.

Will's arm was thrown across her. She watched his sleeping face, handsome in repose, the eyelashes long and the jaw peppered with stubble. Will was good-looking, funny, and nice company—he was a good bet, surely, for any girl. Sex with him was fine, it was pleasant, but she rarely came and when she did it was only on top. Before Stevie had started at Simms & Court she'd had a string of short-lived boyfriends with whom sex had been the same way. Was she destined always to judge others against the man who had changed that? Why should she, when he had treated her so badly? It made her hate him more and more, because nearly a year after their parting he still had her in his clutches, refusing to let her go.

What had it been about him? What made him so special? Was it the way he'd listened to her, after years at home of being one voice among many, as if she were the most captivating woman on earth? Was it the attention he'd lavished, the compliments he'd given? Was it his authority, his age, his influence? That made her sound like a floozy secretary, and of course she knew it was the mother of all stereotypes. Boss works after hours, assistant fixes the drinks, maybe she even calls his wife to let her know he'll be home late... To her disgrace, she'd done that once. The sound of the other woman's voice would never leave her, and it was only after they were over that she was able to analyse what she'd heard in it: resignation, disappointment, but most of all sadness. Infinite, profound sadness—for Stevie understood now that it had happened before, probably many, many times. And through her inability at the time to think outside how she admired him, and how his marriage, she'd been told, was all but over, she'd pushed the woman to the back of her mind and pretended she didn't exist. It was shameful.

It was also what her father had done to her mother. That was the worst part.

Will opened his eyes, a contented smile spreading across his face. He rolled on to his back, and in an effort to forget the past Stevie moved to kiss him, feeling him reach around her waist, pulling her close. A groan escaped as he grew between her hands. She manoeuvred herself on top, desperate for release, slipping on protection and gasping as he entered.

Will gripped her as she began to rock back and forth. 'You're gorgeous,' he breathed, sitting to embrace her, grazing her breasts, moving with her, kissing her chin and then her lips.

Stevie's rhythm became more frantic. She could feel the surge rising and pushed Will back on to the pillows, riding him harder now, wanting him to fill her up and force her to forget everything. She gripped his hands, threw her head back and felt him free his fingers so he could stroke her throat and her tits, kissing her over and over.

She came fiercely, releasing a cry and feeling the blood in every fibre of her body. Will continued to thrust into her warmth, drawing out her climax, threatening to take her all the way again. He lifted her hips and withdrew, moving her on to her back and raising her legs high so her feet were on either side of his neck. Violently he pounded back into her, forcing himself so deep that Stevie had to push back on the wall behind her head to keep herself from slamming into it. Seconds later he reached his pinnacle.

'Christ, Stevie,' he breathed, burying his head in her shoulder as he rode it. 'What are you doing to me?'

She pulled on a shirt and padded to the bathroom. The shower blasted scalding hot then freezing cold. Will's downtown loft apartment was crummier than the one she shared with Bibi, but most times they slept together here. She preferred the detachment of it—plus she could do without Bibi's cross-questioning the morning after.

Speak of the devil. The minute she got out, Bibi called.

'I need you to come to an audition with me today,' she announced.

Stevie put her glasses on and sat down on the bed. Will released the knot on her towel, letting it fall to her waist. Lazily he stroked her back.

'What do you mean?'

'I need a partner.'

Stevie hitched the towel up and stood. 'For what?' She could see from the bulge under the sheets that Will was ready to go again. She returned to the bathroom and ran a comb through her hair, which wasn't easy with a phone under one ear.

'It's gonna make *all* the difference,' Bibi explained, 'if I read with someone I know—and I'll be most comfortable with you. And if I'm comfortable then I'm relaxed and when I'm relaxed I know I can shine. That's the problem with every other gig they've sent me for, Steve! I've been so nervous I totally blew it! So, I figure, if you're there too then it'll be just like it is when you help me at home, and you're really *good*, you know? You always bring out my best. So I need you.'

'I don't know, B—'

'Please,' Bibi begged, 'it's a serious part—the first one that's come up for me in ages! I really want it. Please, will you come?'

Stevie was puzzled. If the work her friend was doing for Linus Posen wasn't 'serious' then what was it? Since his party, Bibi had been collaborating with the director on several projects—she'd tried to cajole Stevie into phoning him too but had given up after a series of repeated refusals—but was always cagey about exactly what it was she was doing. All Stevie knew was that her engagements

with Linus always took place at some undisclosed location
and Bibi, when she reappeared, was terse in her replies
about where she'd been. It was unlike her: Bibi waxed lyri-
cal about everything, especially when it came to her career.

'But—'

'All I'm asking is for you to say a handful of lines,'
Bibi barrelled on, 'that's all. I'm desperate for this, Steve,
please. I mean it. *Please* say yes. *Please?*'

It was the least she could do after Bibi's kindness. 'Yes.'

Will approached her from behind, lifting the towel and
pressing his erection against her.

'When do you need me?' she asked into the phone.

'Now,' he murmured, attempting to direct himself inside.

Bibi's relief was audible. 'Park Avenue. Two o'clock. I
appreciate it, I really do.'

'Are you all right?' Stevie asked. 'You sound funny.'

There was a brief silence, before: 'I'm fine!'

She tried to bat off Will's attentions. 'You're sure?'

'Sure. Just be there, OK?'

'I will.'

Stevie clicked her phone shut, concerned about her
friend. Something wasn't right. But then maybe she just
hadn't spent enough time with Bibi recently. She had to
rectify that.

'I've got to be somewhere,' she said.

Will took her hips in his hands and tilted her forward.
'Five minutes,' he growled. 'And then I'll let you go.'

The casting took place on the second floor of an old office
building on Park Avenue. There was a little waiting space
outside the room, packed with hopefuls. When Bibi and
Stevie arrived, they attracted a wave of catty looks that

Bibi assured her was par for the course. They went down the corridor to get a watered-down coffee.

'Here,' said Bibi, thrusting a wodge of paper into her hands at the same time as a boiling hot drink, 'this is it. You read Jerry.'

'Is it a man?' Stevie asked, fumbling before putting the coffee down. She flicked through the pages.

'No. Like Jerry Hall.' She grinned. 'Or like Steve!'

'Oh…' Stevie had never done anything like this before. 'And who're you?'

Bibi adopted a dreamy expression. 'I'm Lauren. Secretly I'm in love with your husband, but you can't *ever* know because we're best friends. But even *more* secretly, you're in love with me! And you're like a really prim housewife and you can't begin to contemplate leaving your marriage for another person, let alone a woman! Shock, horror and all that. Juicy, isn't it?'

'Jerry's part sounds more interesting than Lauren's.'

Bibi shrugged. 'But Lauren's part is bigger. The whole movie's about her, basically. Which means—' she struck a pose '—that if I get it, the whole movie's going to be about me! Oh, I *really* hope I get it!' She chewed her lip.

'I thought things were going well with Linus's projects,' Stevie said softly. She was determined to tread carefully. 'You seem awfully keen to try something new.'

Bibi linked arms with her. 'Come on, or we'll miss our call.'

The audition went adequately. Stevie managed to speak her lines clearly and not let Bibi down, which was a feat for her because she didn't like performing and spent the first few minutes fudging the phrasing until she hit her stride. Unhelpfully, the panel—two producers and a casting agent—asked her to remove her glasses halfway through, which made the task of reading a challenge in itself. Bibi herself delivered a melodramatic performance that was more reminiscent of Shakespeare than a Hollywood independent. Stevie thought she had great charisma, but couldn't help feeling she was running a little over the top: the script required a degree of subtlety, an invitation to viewers to draw their own conclusions about who was feeling what. But what did she know? She wasn't the actress.

Afterwards, the jury conferred among themselves for a while before dismissing them with a brisk, 'Thank you, that's all.'

'How great was that?' squealed Bibi when they were back outside.

Stevie smiled encouragingly. 'You did brilliantly. I don't know how you memorise all those lines. I don't think I could.'

'Ah, don't be dumb.' But she blushed at the compliment. 'You really think I did OK?'

'Definitely,' Stevie reassured her. Bibi had been word-perfect and her enthusiasm was second to none. 'When are you likely to hear?'

'Carrie will be in touch as soon as they are.' She hailed a cab. 'Keep your knickers crossed for me!'

'My knickers?'

'Sorry,' said Bibi, in a much better mood than this morning. 'On the contrary! I forgot you were with Will.'

'That's gross. And anyway, I'm not "with" Will. I'm not with anyone.'

Bibi narrowed her eyes. 'You're a commitment-phobe,' she said. 'That's what it is.'

Stevie laughed. 'I'm not,' she said. 'Fine, maybe I am, but just for the time being.'

'Ah, but love's the best thing in the world.' Bibi pressed her palms exaggeratedly to her chest as a cab pulled up. 'Love richly and love well. Isn't that a saying?'

'I don't think so.'

Bibi pulled open the door. 'You know what I'm getting at.'

She did. Only she'd been the one loving. He hadn't said he loved her at all. Not even when she got rid of the baby.

'Thanks for coming today, Steve.'

'Any time,' she replied, with a faint smile. 'It was kind of fun.'

As she was climbing in, a young woman with a scruffy blonde ponytail emerged from the building, glanced once up and down the avenue then waved in their direction. Stevie recognised her as the casting agent from their audition. She had to nudge Bibi to get her attention.

'B, that woman's waving at you—look!'

Bibi followed her gaze. She covered her mouth with her hands. 'My God, Steve! Do you think she wants to offer me the part? What if she offers me the part? What do I do?'

Stevie giggled. 'You say yes.'

The woman strode over. 'Are you able to come back inside?' she asked, eyebrow arched. 'We'd like to hear you read again.'

'Of course.' Bibi flushed with pleasure.

The woman's gaze flicked over Bibi, as if she'd only just noticed her. 'Not you,' she said dismissively, turning back to Stevie. 'We'd like to hear *you* read again, for Lauren this time. We've been looking for someone like you for a very, very long time. We think you're absolutely right for the part.' She grinned, exposing a row of small neat teeth. 'What do you say?'

13
Lori

When Tony and Angélica found out about Rico's involvement in the gang homicide, they resolved to send Lori to Spain without further delay.

'It's the only place we can be sure you'll stay out of trouble,' her father said.

The last Lori had heard from her boyfriend was a rushed phone call shortly after he was arrested. She had asked him if the reports were true. They were. It broke her heart. She didn't know him any more. Rico, the gentle Rico with the kind eyes and the tender promises, was gone. He was a killer, capable of taking another person's life.

Things moved fast. Her flight was tomorrow. When she arrived, she would take a taxi out of Murcia and travel south, to the outskirts of a remote town where her grandmother resided in the same rural house Tony had grown up in. It was falling apart, too sprawling and dilapidated for one person to look after. Ancient, tired out, like its sole occupant.

Tony was dropping her off at *Tres Hermanas* for the last time.

'Please don't send me away,' she begged. 'Can't you see I've been punished enough?'

Angrily, Tony changed lanes. 'I've done everything to make things right, Loriana—I've tried my best with that business, I've tried to secure you the future your mama wanted. I found us another family—'

'I never said I wanted another family. I had you.'

'And who did I have?'

Her voice was small. 'Me.'

'You were a child. I had to look after you.'

Lori tried to reach him. 'Mama always said it didn't matter how small you were, you could always make a difference.'

Tony pulled over amid an explosion of sounding horns. 'Will you *stop*?'

'Stop what?'

'Accept that she's dead.' His voice was bitter. 'I've been trying for ten years to find a different happiness, while you dream only of the past—'

'Moving on isn't the same as forgetting.'

'Do you think I can forget? Do you? How can I, when I look at you and all I see is her?'

'Is that why you want me gone?' Lori wept then, proper tears she had been keeping in check for too long. For a second she thought Tony might comfort her, but the embrace she had been hoping for didn't come. Instead he signalled and rejoined the stream of downtown traffic.

'You are going to Corazón because it is the right thing,'

Tony said evenly, 'and because I hope it will put an end to this pointless rebellion. That boy and his family are dangerous. I cannot lose you as well.'

The working day began like any other. There was no reason to suspect what was to come, the event that would change Lori's life irrevocably and for ever. Her sisters had spent all morning doing zero work, gloating about how miserable she would be bundled away in Europe with a rotting old crone, while Lori answered the phones, sorted the orders, prepped the treatments and cleaned up after them. Her head was numb and her heart was numb, going through the motions and that was all: a living doll, with a face and hair and arms and legs, but when you unscrew its neck and turn it upside down and shake it around, nothing inside, just empty.

It was a little after two o'clock and she was alone, unpacking a delivery on the salon floor. Anita and Rosa had slipped cash from the register, informing her they were 'heading out', which meant they were down on the beach sipping coladas, examining their nails, bitching about her, and would be till half an hour before close.

The boxes were heavy, filled with stuff they didn't need and could not afford, but the girls had to spend their time somehow and it would be Lori who made the returns. A guy in a van had dumped them by the door and told her to sign. Afterwards, she would remember scribbling her name in the space he indicated, and would that night, and in the nights to come, think back to how it was a different girl signing from the one she was now: that the Lori Garcia she'd been before had given her very last autograph and was finally checking out.

She was bent, her back to the door, when she heard someone come in.

Preparing to apologise for her sisters' absence, since this was no doubt a forgotten appointment, she turned—and came face to face with a man. He was dark, short and stockily built, with a hard, low brow and a nose beaten out of shape. He possessed deep-set, unblinking eyes, and wore a black vest that exposed meaty, painted flesh at the neck and shoulders. His arms were sketched with tattoos, a cobra winding up one arm, its head emerging beneath his thick jaw, cut from a bad shave, where the serpent's thin forked tongue escaped.

Diego Marquez. Rico's brother.

'What do you want?' Lori asked coldly.

Diego's mouth moved into a thin, satisfied smile. 'A word, *chica*. That is all.'

'I'm busy.'

'So am I.' He kicked the door shut with one foot. 'Which is why you're going to give me what I need and you're going to make it quick.'

She backed off. 'Don't come any closer.'

'What you gonna do about it?' His eyes flicked behind her, scoping the place. 'Looks like you might be getting a little lonely in here.' He reached out, attempted to touch her but she pulled away. 'You saying you don't want company?'

'I mean it. I'll call the police.'

He laughed. It was cold, dead, utterly without humour. Lori felt the push of wood against her back as she came into contact with the counter. Diego was close now, his breath in her face.

'An' how d'you think that's gonna look? One Marquez boy not enough for you?'

Panic was rising, a steady, obliterating tide. 'Please. I won't tell anyone you were here.'

Diego narrowed his eyes. She could see the hard sinews in his neck, a trapped muscle pulsing like there was something living beneath his skin, writhing, contorting, trying to get out.

'Oh no,' he snarled. 'Not until I get what I came for.' This time, he grabbed her chin, the impact of it so hard, so sudden, she bit the inside of her cheek. 'Are you gonna be a good girl and tell me what happened that night? Think carefully, now, 'cause I don't want no mistakes.'

'I don't know what you mean.'

'Sure you do. You were with Enrique. You were with him the whole time, the whole damn night. He never left your side, not once.'

'That's a lie. You know it is.'

Diego tightened his grip. 'D'you think Enrique gives a fuck about the truth where he is right about now?'

Hate burned in Lori's eyes. 'You've done nothing for Rico,' she countered. 'You never have. All you've done is hurt him and ruin him and take away any chance of a life he might—'

This time Diego pressed his iron-hard body against her, pinning her in place. She could feel every contour, heavy as a brick, inescapable, suffocating. He made a sound of teasing disapproval, shaking his head with grim amusement. Up close she could smell him—the scent was of rotten sweat and something sharper, more astringent, like vinegar.

'No, no, no,' he taunted, 'you're not *listening*. This is how it works. I ask you for something, Loriana. You give it to me. Easy. Shall we try again?'

'I'm giving you nothing.'

'Then I won't spare you nothing.' Diego lunged for her—to kiss her, to take her by the throat?—but she was too quick. Darting from his grip, she ran. She went for the door, forgetting she had cleaned that morning and the floor was still slick with wet. Her feet vanished from under her. Uselessly she reached out to break the fall, spraining her wrist, and when her chin hit she felt a warmth of blood escape, so quick, as always blood was, as if her skin were an eggshell, or a balloon filled with water, thin-membraned and fit to rupture. A heavy foot landed across her back, pushing down on her lungs so that it hurt to breathe.

She heard the click of a cigarette being lit. Seconds later, the door opened, tantalisingly close to Lori's desperate, up-turned face, but at the same time impossibly far away. For a brief moment she imagined help had come.

It hadn't.

Three other men walked in. Her ears felt cloudy so it was difficult to understand what they were saying. Her mouth tasted thick, the smell of antiseptic in her nostrils.

'She causin' you trouble?' One of the boots nudged her lightly with its toe, then, when she didn't protest, a bit harder, like a child prodding a frightened animal with a stick.

Diego hauled her up, holding Lori to him, her arms behind her back.

'Let me go,' she whimpered, making a futile attempt to break free.

One glance told her that wasn't going to happen. Circling her was Diego's gang. She looked from one to the next, with each pinched, expressionless face feeling hope dwindle—then, worse, a shoot of fear that blossomed and spread, climbing into her throat. The way they were eyeing her, sharply, greedily, and with a satisfied reticence that she had not the experience to consider but knew instinctively put her body at risk. One had a long, thin ponytail down his back. He licked dry lips.

'Try again,' said Diego, menacingly quiet in her ear. 'And get it right this time or we are gonna fuck you up so bad that when you look in the mirror you won't even know who's lookin' back. You got that, *chica*?'

'Rico didn't show,' she spluttered. 'It's the truth. I don't know what more you want.'

Diego tugged her backwards. Pain shot up her arm. 'Give it to us, Loriana.'

She knew what they wanted. An alibi. The words that would set Rico free.

He was her boyfriend. *The man I'm supposed to love.* But she couldn't.

'I can't lie for him,' she choked. 'I can't.'

'Aw.' Diego arranged his mean features into something like pity. 'There was me thinkin' you were his girl.' Roughly, he pushed her. She landed in the scrawny grip of the guy with the ponytail. 'Girls do right by their men, wouldn't you say, boys? But then if you *ain't* his girl, then we ain't gonna *treat* you like his girl. We're gonna treat you just like what you are—a dirty fuckin' whore.'

The scrawny grip was wrestling her. Violently she was thrust into another pair of arms, then another, and another, passed between them, playing with her like a kitten on a string, making her dizzy, her vision gather and dissolve like ink in water. The shoving got more and more forceful, she was conscious of hands seizing parts of her, wrenching at her with ferocity. She heard her dress tear. Someone kicked her, pulled her hair.

'Stop,' she begged. 'Please, please, stop!'

'Nah—not till we've had our fun.' She didn't know who spoke. Through the ringing in her ears she thought she heard a belt buckle being unclasped.

'You heard her.' A new voice. 'Stop.'

Lori was thrown to the floor. Through red panic a splinter of blue appeared, like water poured on flames. A hot current travelled down her spine, the hairs at the back of her neck prickling, thousands of needlepoints, each tip like fire. She became aware of her breathing, low and shallow, and her frantic heart.

Diego spoke. 'This ain't nothin' t'do with you, man. Back away.'

The stranger moved. She heard the clean smack of his step as he approached. Smart, controlled, precise. 'Wrong. Let her go.'

Lori raised her head, taking the newcomer in in pieces— the oil-black shoes, the expensively tailored suit pants, the way a strip of crisp white shirt emerged from each sleeve of his jacket. His suit was the sharp, thousand-dollar sort she had seen on models in magazines and on businessmen who dealt in money and gambling and sex with their secretaries. He was tall. One of his hands was visible. Strong knuckles. His hair, the colour of sand after the tide's been in; his precise profile and square-sharp jaw; his mouth. In his right earlobe he wore a flat black stud, which was ill-matched with the attire and spoke of something exotic.

The man regarded her directly and with a gaze that was bluer than the colour itself, light blue of a kind that seemed artificial. She saw his top lip was scarred, a jagged groove that ran like lightning, almost ugly, through his philtrum.

'You got no business comin' round here,' warned one of

Diego's gang. They were hesitant with the stranger—they outnumbered him and yet they did not make a move. 'Walk away now an' no one gets hurt.'

The man reached down to Lori and held out his hand. With the gesture, his sleeve lifted a fraction and she saw a thin band of leather encircling his wrist.

'Get up,' he told her.

Diego was quick but the stranger was quicker, bringing Lori to her feet as if she weighed nothing at all. Smoothly, swiftly, he positioned his body in front of hers, simultaneously catching Diego's punch in one of his fists.

'I wouldn't do that if I were you.'

Diego's eyes flashed a caution. One of his guys freed a gun. The weapon was raised.

'We ain't gonna tell you again,' growled Diego. *'Walk away.'*

One of the crew lunged but the man seized the strike, twisting the elbow back at such an angle that the body crumpled to the floor.

'My arm!' the guy howled. 'My fuckin' arm, you've broken it, you sonofabitch!'

A second swing; the audible rush of swiped air as he evaded the blow, landing his own fist squarely in the throat of his assailant, who performed a sickening pirouette and was slammed back against the wall with a force that made something crack.

The next she knew, they had the gun. The last of Diego's crew still standing was making a run for it. 'Fuckin' get outta here, man!' he urged his chief. 'Fuckin' let's *go!*'

Diego stared down his own weapon. 'You don't know who I am,' he said. 'Do you?'

The gun didn't waver.

Lori saw Diego hesitate, a ripple of fear behind his eyes.

'Take your men away from here,' the stranger said, in an accent she could not place. 'And don't ever come back. If you come back, you will disappear. Nobody will know what happened to you. Your wives will not know. Your friends will not know. Your brothers will not know. Your children will not know. Your lovers will wait for you in a cold room in a cold bed but you will never come. Do not doubt this will happen. If you come here again, it will happen to every last one of you.'

And in a rush that felt like flying, the stranger had taken her hand, she was with him, next to him, and they were moving, out of the door and into the blazing sun. She saw his car, a gleaming, purring Mercedes, black and silver, opened to an interior of plush, heavy-scented leather, a secret world. She hadn't time to question her actions. They were inside, the door slammed shut; he was pushing a button and giving instructions to someone up front, concealed behind a screen of dark glass, to drive. He turned to her, eyes so blue, so blue.

'I won't let you go until I know it is over. I'm not going to hurt you. You're safe with me.'

She found her voice, only it sounded like someone else's. 'Do I know you?'

'No.'

The car was moving at speed. 'Who are you?'

'I am no one.'

Lori wanted to touch him. She wanted to touch him in a way she had never before encountered—raw, necessary, primal. The stranger was facing away, his profile still, his mouth set in a line of grim determination, as though he were trying to resist unseen temptation.

And then, she didn't know how it happened, they were kissing each other, their bodies apart one second and together the next. His lips, his tongue, that scar she had noticed that felt, beneath her mouth, like danger. The smell of leather and the smell of him: his neck, his skin, the softness of his mouth and eyelashes. His hands held her face, one thumb on her chin where it was cut, the fingers behind her jaw, beneath her earlobes. She had never been kissed like that. She could kiss him for ever. She could kiss him till her mouth bled.

Not once did his hands move lower, though she ached for them to. She wanted him to touch her in all the places she had refused her boyfriend: all the emotions she was meant to feel with Rico but hadn't, imagining something must be the matter with her. His fingers reached round and pressed the very top of her spine, his touch so deft, electricity, the heat of his body and the soft insistency of his mouth, and she felt the blood rush like fever, trembling, to between her legs. For the first time in her life, Lori experienced desire. Prolonged, exquisite, concentrated desire that entered her like a knife and twisted her heart, sliding its smooth blade down her stomach, opening her up to that place whose existence she had always denied.

The car stopped. The man pulled away, his expression closed, but angry, like an argument happening behind a shut door.

The only sound was their breathing, painfully intimate in the silence.

Lori sensed the certainty of their parting and grasped for more, abandoning restraint because that was what he had done to her.

'I have to find a way to thank you—'

Sunlight flooded in, hurting her eyes. They were back outside *Tres Hermanas*. His driver stood on the sidewalk.

The man took her hand. 'You'll be all right,' he told her, in that soft, strange accent. 'I'll make sure of it. I always will.'

Lori was helped on to the street, the light blinding: a new world. She was shaking.

His arm reached to close the door.

'Wait! Will I see you again? What's your name? You have to tell me. I have to know.'

The man lifted his mouth slightly, the corners, not much, like a cat that wakes from a deep sleep and raises his head once to look around before settling again. It wasn't a smile. It didn't come close to the eyes, whose look of benevolence had hardened like a frozen lake.

'It does not matter who I am.'

And with a last, lingering stare, as quick as he'd come, he was gone.

14

Present Day
Island of Cacatra, Indian Ocean
Four hours to departure

Reuben van der Meyde was a self-made industrial entrepreneur with tens of billions in the bank. He had come
from nothing: orphaned as a baby, he had grown up with a
lukewarm, uninterested foster family in the South African
city of Johannesburg. At thirteen, after being expelled from
school for bad behaviour, he had started his own trade on
the streets, selling stolen cut-price jewellery to travelling
businessmen. One such businessman, an unhappily married tycoon who had recently lost a son Reuben's age, took
him under his wing, trained him and served up a job in one
of his fledgling telecommunications companies. With the
Soweto sprawl in the seventies came massive investment
in the suburbs—Reuben was in the thick of it and, as each
year passed, his flair for business grew. Aged twenty, he
launched VDM Communications. Soon he was rivalling

the man who had taught him everything and, as his business swelled, so did his fortune, his reputation, and his ambition. Today, VDM was the most lucrative company in the world.

Reuben van der Meyde was not a man prepared to be taken down.

He paced the terrace, pausing occasionally to put his hands on the balustrade and glare darkly at the water. He checked his chunky silver watch, grimaced when the links caught the reddish hairs on his arms. Four hours. It wasn't enough.

'I'm telling you, JB, the damn thing's got me in a sweat. I'm like a pig in shitting heat.' He removed his cap and swiped at a persistent fly.

Jean-Baptiste Moreau loosened the knot on his tie and didn't respond. He was facing the ocean, concentrated on calmer waters. Emerald palms rustled in the salty breeze.

'I hope to fuck you're coming up with a solution,' said Reuben. 'Because it's not just me being threatened, boy, it's you as well.'

JB remained where he was, on one of the high-backed wicker chairs that peppered the rugged veranda of his white-stone villa. Despite the sun, he did not perspire. His dark-blond hair was immaculate, neat at the neck, and his expression still. The only betrayal that he was deep in thought was the slight twitch to the scar across his top lip, a giveaway since he was a boy.

'Shit!' Reuben slammed down his fist. 'After all the work I've put into this—'

'It might not be what you think.'

'What else could it be, hey? A fucking strip-o-gram birthday cake?'

Finally JB turned. The strength of his gaze compelled an already struggling Reuben to sit down. His eyes really were extraordinary, an untarnished blue with flecks of silver, uncannily light.

'Nothing in that message suggests this person knows anything about what we're trying to protect,' JB told him. 'Keep it together.'

Reuben laughed bitterly. 'You don't think *I'm one of them* has a certain ring to it?' He ground his teeth. 'I spent all night trying to look at it a different way. Bottom line is I've got a bad feeling. This person got into my private mail. When was the last time that happened?' JB didn't answer. Reuben sprang to his feet. 'Let me tell you. *Never.*'

The Frenchman's gaze slid back to the ocean. 'You worry too much. We're in control.'

'It's OK for you, isn't it?' Reuben blasted. 'Swanning around Hollywood, scouting for pretty girls, while one of us is trying to run a business!' JB didn't react. 'Damn! It's my reputation on the line here, not yours.'

'Are you insinuating I don't have my own problems to deal with?'

Reuben caught the menace in his words. 'It's not my fault you're hard up for the Spanish broad,' he said. 'I knew that girl was trouble from the start. Ones like her always are. Too wild for what we had in mind. Young, dumb and desperate—remember?'

'You know nothing about her.'

Reuben grimaced. 'I know she was meant to be a job, for Crissakes. Try tying your dick in a knot next time—it helps.'

JB stood. Instantly the shorter man, despite his wealth and power, took a step back. He'd regretted the words as soon as he'd said them. Moreau was not a man he wanted to piss off.

'Keep your voice down,' he said quietly. 'Rebecca is inside. And stop cowering like a dog. Fear achieves nothing.'

Reuben matched the younger man's glare until eventually he was forced to look away. 'I'll assume you're right.'

'I'm always right.'

One of JB's assistants emerged from the villa. Reuben was about to explode at her for interrupting a private conversation but stopped when it became clear JB was expecting her.

'The caterers have arrived, Mr Moreau,' she said, smoothing her skirt down, chosen because she'd been told it made her ass look good. Ridiculous. One night was all it had been. She knew JB Moreau took women to bed like he ate hot meals, and didn't know whether to curse herself for having allowed it or to thank everything good in the world for those hours.

'Thank you, Sara.'

'What do you want to know about the caterers for?' Reuben frowned once she'd gone.

'I've requested updates on all arrivals.'

'Yeah, but I got people looking after that.'

JB ran a hand across his jaw. 'Let's stick to business, shall we?'

Reuben leaned in. 'Fine,' he said impatiently, 'but I've got enough else to think about without this...*inconvenience*. The organisers are climbing up my arse and the captain hasn't bloody showed up yet. It's all very well decking the place out like a pair of frilly knickers but if the thing doesn't sail I might as well have a floating turd out there, hey! What am I going to do, give them a swimming lesson?' He scowled. 'Believe me: soon as I find out who sent that message I swear I'll rip their fucking throat out.'

JB had neither the time nor inclination to watch Reuben fall spectacularly to pieces. He headed inside. 'I have to make a phone call.'

'Make it quick. We'll rendezvous in an hour. This party's going to be one hell of a stunt to pull, my friend.'

The Frenchman turned at the open door. 'As long as it's the only stunt getting pulled, I'll be happy.'

Margaret Jensen did not like other people being in her kitchen. She worked in this place three hundred and sixty-five days a year, and yet, on these occasions, it counted for nothing. It was like allowing strangers into her home and letting them touch things, move them, put them back in the wrong places. She found it easier to stand apart and let the caterers get on with it. The company hired for tonight's event ran with a military precision that rivalled even her own.

Hovering at the threshold, she observed the food being prepared. The fastidious detail of the champagne caviar, the pink lobster mousse, the gold-leaf mint and basil tarts, the seven-tiered miniature cakes, belied the chaos: white-aproned staff running back and forth, wanting to get every-thing perfect. It would never be enough. Mr V would find something to complain about, whatever the standard.

This afternoon, however, Margaret Jensen had more pressing things on her mind.

She wiped her hands on her skirt. She could feel her pulse, fluid behind her clavicle.

The plan she would execute in just a few hours' time was

years in the making. Eight, to be exact. Oh, she hadn't settled on Mr V's gruesome fate until more recently—not till she'd met the man who could make it happen—but a long time she had fantasised of a vengeance that fitted his cruelty exactly. His abhorrent scheme was one she had always been privy to. After all, she'd been one of the women who had allowed it to happen. She'd been stupid enough to believe his hollow pledge, his guarantees of money and security and a better future—in exchange for what? The most precious thing in the world. How could she even have considered it? But she'd been a different woman then, a wretched woman with no way out. As they all were.

Only she'd been more than he bargained for. She'd stood up to Mr V. She'd refused to give him what he wanted and he'd been forced to offer her a compromise, a position as his lowly housekeeper, guardian to his son, pushing her to the shadows and pretending she didn't exist.

He should have known she wouldn't stay there for ever.

Margaret exited the van der Meyde mansion and stood at the top of the stone steps that led down to the beach. She raised a hand against the glare of the sun and squinted down the pale sandy stretch. Mr V's yacht was moored a hundred yards away, dark spots milling round it like ants, everybody desperate to get involved in the big man's day. Adoring minions, nothing more, blinded by his riches and his power, with no idea what he was truly capable of.

It was ambitious. It was outrageous. It was wrong. But it was revenge, and revenge was usually all of those things.

As far as Margaret was concerned, there was only one person to protect.

'Ralph!' She called for the boy, knew he'd been playing on the beach all morning.

There was no reply, so she walked a little way down the steps and repeated his name. In moments she caught sight of the child's small frame weaving haphazardly down the beach. As always, he brought a smile to her face and happiness to her heart. The years hadn't all been in vain. He waved at her and she waved back.

'What have you been up to?' she asked as he ran, panting, up the steps, bursting with enthusiasm. He was carrying a red bucket and held it out for her to see. Inside was a hard, moving scrape of crabs' legs, their burned-orange shells lifting and dragging over each other.

'Shall we eat them?' she asked.

Ralph nodded happily. 'Where's JB?' he said excitedly. 'I want to show JB!'

'He's not here, darling.'

He held out the crabs, his fingers small and sticky where they gripped the rim of the plastic lest anyone try to steal his loot. 'Do you think Daddy will be pleased?'

Margaret swallowed. Ralph idolised Mr V, more so because he believed him to be his only living parent. It was what he had always been told.

If only.

'Very,' she said. 'Come inside, my love, we've got to get you ready. Look at your fingers!' He had grubby sandmarks under his nails.

'Can I go to the party?' he begged as he trailed her inside. 'JB said the whole world's coming! That means I have to come!'

Briskly she shook her head. 'Absolutely not. You heard what Mr V said.'

'He said I'm not old enough.'

'And he's right.'

Ralph was disappointed. 'Please?' he tried again, hoping Miss Jensen might be a softer touch. Usually she let him have his way.

'I've said no and that's the end of it.' Outside the boy's bedroom, she turned and crouched down to his level.

'Besides, we'll have fun here, won't we?' She smiled. 'Just you and me. Safe on the island. Because, my darling, who knows what could happen at sea?'

BOOK TWO
2009-10

15
Lori

The taxi Lori took from Murcia San Javier airport was driven by a slight, middle-aged Spaniard with a hook nose and thick eyebrows. A rosary swung from his rear-view mirror and the upholstery smelled sweet, like lemons, or vanilla. Dusk had fallen. The gloomy shapes of mountains reared up on both sides as the car wound its way between, tyres throwing up dust.

They drove through a sharp bend, then another, and she realised they were climbing. Each twist required the car to slow completely, almost to a stop, and she knew the ascent must be steep. She wound the window down and breathed the unfamiliar air. Crickets gave off their whistling night-time rhythm; the sea was close because she could smell its salt.

Lori had travelled an ocean. She had gone halfway across the world. And yet all she had thought about, incessantly and without reprieve, for the past forty-eight hours, was the man who had saved her. Every time she closed her eyes, she saw his face and his hands; the leather band around his wrist; the twist, almost cruel, of his top lip. That day felt like a dream, impossible—something out of a novel about which she'd half laugh, half swoon. The way he'd arrived from nowhere, strange as though he'd come from another world, far far away, and how he had kissed her, the urgency in his eyes as he'd tried to resist... Details became her addiction: a specific suddenly surfacing, shedding new light.

Who was he? Why had he come?

And then the soft comfort of her recollection would be punctured by shame. Guilt at having denied Rico the lie that would set him free; the way she had run from her commitment to him, into the arms of another man. She felt as if she had leapt from an aeroplane into wide blue sky, off the top of a mountain, over the rim of the earth, abandoning every principle that had guided her through seventeen years. Never had she endured a sensation so strong it eclipsed every other, stifling her conscience, making her selfish, reminding her that those same principles by which she'd lived so strictly had never made her happy or fulfilled, and in that way drawing her, tempting her, towards a new horizon.

For what? A stranger she knew nothing of?

Lori ran the bud of her thumb over the ring Rico had given her the day they had planned to escape. It felt like centuries ago, another life, another her.

They passed a red and white church buried in the hillside, momentarily bathed in the gold of the headlamps before retreating to its shroud of darkness. By the side of the road was a box, lit by a lone, uncertainly flickering candle: a shrine for a child, tipped from a crumbling precipice. The motion of the car, winding and turning, rising ever higher, began to lull Lori to sleep.

When she woke, the moon was high and bright in the sky. The car was rumbling along a bumpy track and Lori realised her head must have been resting against the window, for it was this motion that roused her. They were in the middle of nowhere. On either side what looked like orchards, clusters of trees whose fingers brushed questioningly as they passed. At the foot of the drive was the dark shape of her grandmother's house, bordered by the shadowy outline of an olive grove, and a single lamp glowing in the porch.

She thanked the driver in Spanish and heaved her bag from the trunk. She watched as his red taillights disappeared, listening to the silence of a depth and quality entirely new to her.

There was no sound coming from inside and when Lori knocked it seemed to disturb the sleeping hills. She began to wonder if anyone was in when, eventually, a light came on. The slow patter of footsteps approached, accompanied by a wet snuffling.

When the door opened, something quick and small rushed out and Lori felt a damp nose attacking her legs.

'Pepe!' the old woman chided. 'Come back here. *Tsk!*'

Lori petted the dog as it sniffed enthusiastically at her knees. Corazón watched her, the old woman's ancient, pale face cracked by the lines of time and the losses she had known: she had dressed in black since her husband, Lori's *abuelo*, passed fifteen years before. Even in the dim glow of the porch her eyes sparkled with happiness.

'Loriana. *Querida*, my darling.' She held her arms out, eyes brimming with emotion.

They embraced, Lori clinging lightly because holding Corazón was like grasping a bundle of sticks and she didn't want to break them. She told her hello and her grandmother touched her face, her mass of wild hair, and kissed her forehead.

'*Has crecido!*' she marvelled, taking her hands. 'You have grown. *Te heche de menos*, Loriana; I have missed you.'

Inside, Corazón boiled a pan of water and gave Lori a cup of sweet, hot liquid that smelled of herbs, and a bowl of vegetable stew that through her hunger and fatigue tasted incredible. Pepe the dog darted between her legs, begging for food and attention. They spoke about Lori's journey and her memories of Spain (what Corazón called her 'home country'), and why she had come back here. While Lori didn't go into detail about her strained relationship with her father, she suspected Corazón knew more than she was letting on.

Despite being over ninety, her grandmother was shrewd. Lori didn't know if it was the tea and the soup, or her exhaustion, or arriving in Spain after dark, but she soon found herself opening up, telling her about her stepsisters, the way she missed her mother, her hopes for the future—and finishing up with Rico, the killing and the arrest. She didn't tell her about Diego Marquez, or the stranger with the accent, or what had happened afterwards… This was a secret she kept close, a fragile form she couldn't yet be sure would survive definition.

The old woman listened patiently, nodding sagely once or twice.

'I am glad you have come,' Corazón said at last. 'Important things will happen to you here. I feel it in my bones.' She looked down at Pepe. 'Don't I, *chiquita*?'

Lori went to her room a little after midnight. It was humble, just a single bed made with floral linens, a small square closet and a wooden desk. On the desk was a lamp, the only source of light, which cast a pale yellow glow and was not enough to read by. At the head of the bed was a finely carved crucifix. The ceiling was sloped, with thick black beams running across it, and the floor was scratchy and cool beneath her feet. An old rug covered a portion of it.

She opened the window. The catch was stiff and she wondered how long it had been left unused. The air was balmy and still. Outside was what appeared to be a yard, though it was difficult to tell at this time of night. Mountains in the distance, darker than the air that held them, stared back, old as time. Lori drank the air in through her nose, fragrant and sweet.

Whenever she pictured the man in *Tres Hermanas*, she experienced a nagging throb deep inside, delicious and frightening. She had been feeling it on and off for hours, and it kept coming back, stopping her from sleeping and making it hard to eat. Was this what people called love? How could it be, if she didn't even know his name?

The moon was full, a white outline in the inky sky. Lori leaned out, imagining that somewhere, wherever he was, by some trick, a hole in the sky, it would mean they were looking at each other.

The dragging sensation in her belly returned. She closed her eyes. Her heart quickened. She tried to picture him, not too hard else the image fell away like shattered glass. She tried to hear him, but could not conjure his voice. What was happening to her? She felt possessed, under a spell, the back of her neck tingling in that spot where his fingertips had touched, the accuracy of it, the assurance, how he knew what she wanted and how he was going to give it to her.

A little while later, Lori shrugged on her white cotton nightdress and climbed into bed. The sheets were cold and slightly damp, but the heat from her skin soon warmed them up. She was tired past the point of being able to sleep, and lay with her eyes open, staring into the black. The pillows released an old, musty scent.

Ten minutes passed, then twenty. She could not sleep. Each time she came close, something woke her: that hot feeling, again and again, in her stomach. After another half-hour, she sat up and flicked the lamp on. The room was as it had been only now it seemed brighter, sharper, as if she was looking at it with renewed vision. She returned to darkness and lay back.

Faintly she became aware of the swell of her chest as she breathed. She realised her nipples were hard against the cotton of her nightdress. A jolt rushed through her and she raised a hand to touch herself. She ran her fingers across her skin, over the material at first and then underneath it, feeling the softness of her breast. The tingling sensation in her gut was stronger than ever, calling her down, telling her what she must do. Exploring the lines of her own body, she trailed her hand over her stomach and parted her legs, releasing a gasp as she met the surprise of her own wetness. She tilted her hips up, her breath lowering to something wilder as she ground against her own touch. Lifting her knees and spreading them, she stroked gently till she discovered a spot so sensitive it whipped the air from her chest. She pictured him lowering his head, in the way she had heard men did, and as her fingers slipped in and around she imagined it was him, exploring her with his tongue, tasting her, wanting her, what would have happened had the kiss gone on, in that car, across the leather, against the windows. The fire was raging now, flames licking down her legs to the tips of her toes and racing to the blinking lights behind her shut-tight eyes till a great blinding wave crashed over her and every fibre in her body surged. She arched her back, meeting the point of ecstasy. Unable to move, she let the current pass through her, shaking, trembling, shivering.

Recovered, Lori dressed and padded down the dark corridor to the bathroom, where she vigorously washed her hands. She saw her reflection in the mirror. Her eyes were darker than they'd ever been: total black, the most basic of colours.

Shame washed through her. What had she done? She had heard about people who touched themselves… It was wrong; it was dirty; it was sinful. She scrubbed at her fingers and splashed cold water on her face, before killing the light and returning to her bedroom.

The next time she closed her eyes, she fell instantly asleep.

16
Aurora

St Agnes School for Girls was a massive, austere building in the heart of England's Lake District. Grey, bleak and circled with turrets, it resided next to the slate quarry from which it had been built. Aurora thought it the ugliest, most miserable thing she had ever seen.

Her chauffeur-driven car wound up the imposing gravel drive, rounded a stone figurine with its roots submerged in a stagnant oval pond, and deposited her at the main entrance. Immediately she lit a cigarette, smoking moodily while she figured out what to do. She'd get expelled, that was it. There was no way she was staying here longer than a week. What had her parents been thinking? Clearly they had never laid eyes on this shitfest: all she had to do was send a picture to Tom and she felt sure her father would remove her at speed. He would never consent to her suffering. She'd turn the tears on for her first call home and then it would be over.

A woman with a grey bob was bustling across the drive. Grey, grey, grey—even the sky here was grey. How fucking depressing.

'Can I help you?' she demanded in a clipped English accent. She had a little moustache tickling her top lip and a mouth tight as a dog's ass.

Aurora blew smoke in the woman's face. 'I'm new,' she said, enjoying how her brash accent made the lady wince. She spoke louder to make the most of it. 'Name's Aurora Nash.'

'We weren't expecting you until tomorrow.'

'What do you want me to do, camp in a field? I'd like you to show me to my room and then I want a phone call.' This was just like getting arrested—only it looked as if this cow wasn't going to be won round with a sob story and a reapplication of Clive Christian No. 1.

'We do not permit our girls smoking,' said the woman. 'I'm sure you understand.'

Aurora pulled on her cigarette. 'Not really.'

Plucking the stick from Aurora's hand, the woman tossed it to the gravel and ground it out with a steel-toed boot.

'Hey!'

'*I* am Mrs Durdon,' she said briskly, 'your housemistress. From now on you will do exactly as I say—or you're going to wish you'd never set foot in this school.'

'No kidding,' Aurora muttered grimly.

'Come with me.'

Mrs Durdon led the way through the main doors, a scowling Aurora loping behind. She was all too accustomed to spoiled teenage girls needing taking down a peg or two. The international ones were the worst. Here they had them all: princesses, heiresses, daughters of sheiks and oil barons, and, her least personal favourite, the brats from America with famous parents. Glimpsing the girl out of the corner of her eye, she sensed this one would spell no insignificant amount of trouble.

Aurora wondered why no one was offering to take her bag. Where was the doorman? Instead she had to drag her impractical Louis Vuitton wheels behind her as they entered the hall. Grave portraits of headmistresses-past glared down at her from their frames on the wall; an enormous fireplace sat cold and unused beneath a great black hood; doors peeled off from the space, most of them closed. There was a disgusting smell like soup.

'You'll meet the Head this afternoon,' said Mrs Durdon as she mounted the staircase. 'I'll let her know you've arrived.'

'Great,' Aurora mumbled. She was tired of lugging her stuff. 'Where's the elevator?' She stopped and leaned against the wide mahogany banister, folding her arms.

Mrs Durdon was revolted by the word. 'We do not have a *lift*, I'm afraid. If you can't manage, leave your things down here and you'll have to come and collect them piecemeal.' She eyed the suitcase, bursting at its seams. If there were drink or drugs in there, the school would soon rinse them out. 'We'll need to organise you a trunk. That...*bag* is hardly suitable.'

Aurora didn't know what a trunk was but it sounded far from hot. 'Can't you get one of your staff to carry it?'

A frigid smile. 'This way.'

Upstairs, a door opened and a gaggle of girls came rushing past. Aurora had to back up to avoid being slammed into.

'Girls!' Mrs Durdon boomed. 'No running in the halls!'

Giggling among themselves, the girls slowed their pace, arms linked as they vanished into what appeared to be a dining room. Aurora caught a glimpse of long regimented tables: as the heavy door opened a massive waft of the soupy smell came rushing through to greet her.

'Don't they have their own clothes?' asked Aurora, grossed out by the grey skirts and shapeless jumpers. So unflattering!

'That's the school uniform,' Mrs Durdon confirmed. There was a carpeted corridor at the top of the stairs. Several doors down, she stopped. 'And *this* is your dormitory.'

Aurora raised a hand. 'Wait a second,' she said. 'First, I'm not wearing some dumb uniform. I've got a fashion line to protect. And second, I am *not* sleeping in a dormitory. I demand a private room. I'm sure my dad paid for one, so I'd appreciate you taking me to it, please.' She lifted her chin.

Mrs Durdon was amused. 'All girls share dormitories,' she said. 'You'll get used to it.'

When the door opened, Aurora knew categorically and absolutely that she would *never* get used to it. There were at least ten beds in here! It was like some ghastly hospital room. Where was she going to put all her clothes? A small closet parked by each mattress wasn't going to come close. What the *fuck*? What was this place?

'Uh-uh, no way,' said Aurora. But Mrs Durdon was charging down the central aisle between the beds until she stopped by the one closest to the window.

'This one is yours,' she said smugly. The revelation of the dormitories was always her favourite bit. Aurora Nash wore a look of sheer horror. 'I'll find your guide—we assign every new student here one—and she will help you unpack your suitcase. Once you've settled in you can meet Mrs Stoker-Leach.' She departed without another word.

Aurora felt like bursting into tears. She missed LA, she missed her dad; she missed the glittering ocean and the warm sunshine. She even missed Farrah and Jenna. How had this happened? How did she end up in this raging dump? She stormed to the window and gazed bleakly out. It had started to rain. Down below, girls in navy blue skirts ran pointlessly around a hockey pitch and a fat Games teacher with pasty legs blew a harsh whistle. Beyond the school gates, the severe, rugged line of the hills stood cold and immovable, trapping her, forcing her into this unimaginable situation. Did anyone seriously *live* here? Never mind the castle-slash-orphanage-slash-prison she was expected to reside in, but the whole freaking place was abysmal. All she had seen on the drive up was endless motorway going into hills, hills and more hills. She couldn't imagine how anyone could exist here in Dullsville and not want to shoot themselves between the eyes after about five minutes.

In the quiet deadness of that empty dormitory, Aurora felt acutely alone. Fine, it *was* kind of her fault for getting into trouble, but hadn't her parents gone a bit far? Wasn't this total abandonment? Didn't people get arrested for this kind of neglect?

She could see her reflection in the pane, distorted as the rain pooled and slithered and ran in rivulets down the glass. They looked like tear drops.

Fuck it—she *wasn't* a crier, and this place wasn't going to make her one.

All she needed to do was come up with a plan. Fast.

* * *

Her guide was a girl called Fran Harrington, Queen Dork of Dorkdom. She had mouse-coloured hair and the most boring face Aurora had ever seen—in fact it was so boring it didn't even merit description. Her personality was boring, too. Everything about her was boring. Everyone in the whole school was boring. The world was boring. Aurora was bored, bored, bored. She craved California and lamented the parties she was missing; the *guys* she was missing. She was desperate to fuck. The frustration! That was another matter entirely.

A week had passed since her arrival and she was learning a few things about St Agnes School for Girls. First, it didn't matter how boring everyone was because they'd never need worry about acquiring a personality: all the students were daughters of shipping magnates, government officials, royalty… In comparison, being Tom Nash and Sherilyn Rose's kid meant squat. Second, they were all suck-asses and never seemed to do anything even remotely rebellious. The girls she shared a dorm with were mostly English and called things like Camilla and Verity and Poo-Poo. Third, the teachers seemed to hate her. They were all ancient with bad breath. The only decent one was Mr Faulks, who taught Chemistry and was reasonably sexy if you looked at him through squinty eyes, but the one time she'd attempted to flirt with him had backfired when she'd got her substances confused and caused an explosion in one of the research chambers. Fourth, Mrs Stoker-Leach was a total witch. No surprises there. Was it possible for someone with that name to be anything but?

It was Tuesday afternoon. This meant only one thing: hockey with Eugenie Beaufort.

Eugenie Beaufort was a grade-A bitch. Her mother was a

screenwriter Aurora had never heard of but was apparently famous in the UK. She walked around as if she owned the place, while her devoted troop of followers—weak-chinned girls who nodded and yah-yahed to everything she said— trailed her like puppies. Her dislike for Aurora seemed to be instant. Whenever they shared a lesson, Eugenie would glare at her from across the room. Whenever she ate lunch by herself in the dining room, Eugenie was gossiping and looking over, laughing and sneering with her friends. One night Aurora had found a dead spider in her bed, and some of the girls she shared with had collapsed in tinkling laughter—the next day they were sitting with Eugenie. Aurora didn't care: they were morons. What was more, they were fakers. Eugenie was always rattling on about how she'd hung out with Prince William and Kate Middleton the previous summer on a snowboarding holiday, an acquaintance Aurora could tell was exaggerated because Eugenie went on about it in a way she wouldn't have to if they were, like, her real friends. The stories Aurora herself could tell about the rich and famous... Whatever, it didn't impress her, she was way over it. She doubted half the girls had even heard of some of the stuff she'd done to Hollywood's celebrity cocks. Let them suck on that if they wanted scandal.

Aurora had never cared much for sport and wore a lacklustre expression as she changed into her Goal Defence bib.

Within minutes Eugenie Beaufort was attacking her legs.

'Fuck off,' Aurora told her as they locked sticks.

'Fuck off yourself,' Eugenie hissed. Her dark hair was plastered unattractively over her forehead. She was one of those girls to whom team sports meant everything. Win-

ning was the be-all and end-all. Aurora was already thinking about when they could finish so she could sneak into
the bushes for a joint. Maybe if she broke Eugenie's shins
she might get suspended.

'OW!' Eugenie howled out in pain as Aurora's hockey
stick slammed into her. She lifted her leg and clutched it at
the knee, hopping up and down.

'Oops, sorry,' said Aurora sweetly. The fat Games
teacher came panting over and blew her whistle unneces-
sarily close to Aurora's ear.

'Off!' she blasted, red-faced and angry as she pointed
to the sides. Eugenie appeared satisfied, as if being sent
off mid-match was the worst fate she could imagine.
Aurora didn't know whether to laugh or cry. *That* was the
punishment? She'd have to come up with something far
worse if she was going to make it home within the month.
Her phone call to Tom last week had been rushed and
unsatisfactory—her father had a spa session he was loath to
miss—and despite her declaration that St Agnes was worse
than death row (mainly because there was no chance of a
lethal injection at the end of it), her tearful pleas and impassioned begging that eventually descended into a litany of
*I hate you!*s, he had remained firm: she was to see out her
first two terms and then they would rediscuss. Yeah. Like
that was going to happen.

On the bench was a girl she hadn't seen before. She had
long straight black hair, pale skin and a compact, petite
body.

'How come you're out?' asked Aurora moodily as she
slumped down.

'I don't like exercise,' said the girl, not bothering to look up. She was reading a book, and when Aurora peered over she saw it was written in another language.

'What's that?' she asked, sipping from a bottle of water and crossing her legs. She thought she spied Mr Faulks loping into the Science block and adjusted her bib to reveal a little more flesh.

'It's a book,' the girl said flatly. This time Aurora noticed the strong accent.

'You're French?'

'Bravo.'

Aurora kind of liked her blatant lack of interest—it piqued her own. 'I'm Aurora Nash,' she said, sticking out her hand.

Finally the girl looked up. She was startlingly pretty, with a perfect white complexion, blood-red lips and cat-like green eyes.

'I know who you are,' she said. 'The loud American.' She frowned. 'Is your tan real?'

Aurora was unoffended. 'West Coast sun, baby.' She withdrew her hand and sat back. 'You should get some.'

'I don't like how it looks.'

'Thanks very much.'

The girl returned to her book.

'Sport sucks for me, too,' Aurora said. 'How come you get off?'

'I refuse to do it.'

'Sounds like a great tactic.'

The girl flipped her book shut. 'I am exempt from these lessons. My parents have a doctor friend—he wrote me the diagnosis.'

'Which was?'

She shrugged. 'Simply, I am not a team player.'

Aurora laughed with genuine amusement. 'What are you, then?'

'I'm me.'

She raised her left brow. 'Does "me" get high?'

The girl narrowed her eyes. 'Do you imagine you can be my friend?'

Aurora pulled up her scratchy, fashion-bankrupt socks. 'I don't care either way.'

'Because I'm not here to make friends.'

'Suit yourself.'

They sat in silence for a bit, watching Eugenie Beaufort roar and pump the air with her fist whenever her team scored a goal.

Aurora noticed the girl didn't reopen her book. After a while she turned to Aurora. 'I'm Pascale Devereux,' she said, and held out a small, pale hand.

Aurora took it. 'Pleased to meet you.'

'You will be.'

'Why's that?'

'Because now you have,' said Pascale, 'things around here are about to get a lot more interesting.'

17
Stevie

Stevie took the part. How could she not? There it was, laid out before her, the role thousands of girls had dreamed of. Including Bibi Reiner.

'B, this was meant to be yours,' Stevie said when the role was formally offered. 'You wanted Lauren. I wasn't even supposed to be here.'

Bibi kept her smile in place. She was not the sort of girl to begrudge a friend's success, even if her pride stung. Stevie could never know why she'd wanted the role so much, why she'd had her heart set on a gig free from Linus Posen's grip—she probably thought it was just another failed audition. Bibi was used to rejection, wasn't she?

'Take it, Steve,' she said, giving her a hug, and despite her disappointment pleased for her. 'Your turning it down won't bring it my way, will it?'

'If it would…' She meant it.

'I know. Really, it's OK.'

Stevie felt bad. She had never harboured desires to be an actress, far from it, and yet the opportunity had landed straight in her lap. To her surprise the script in its entirety interested her, and people were telling her she had talent and that maybe she should give it a go. What did she have to lose? The studio had long been searching for an antidote to blonde-haired blue-eyed California, captured perfectly in Stevie's cool, detached beauty, which, once the spectacles were off (she'd finally succumbed to lenses), everyone agreed was astounding.

'You've changed my life, B,' she told her friend. 'I owe you so much.'

Bibi squeezed her hand and promised herself her time would one day come. It had to.

In the meantime, she asked Stevie to run her a small favour. *Lie to Me* would be filmed in Los Angeles, where the studio would put her up in a modest apartment complex. Bibi's younger brother was already in the city, struggling to get parts, heavily in debt and currently residing on randoms' sofas. Would she be able to accommodate him for a while?

Naturally, Stevie agreed.

Six weeks later, she was filming on location. Dirk Michaels, Hollywood powerhouse and legendary money-spinner, was producing. Stevie was living out of her suitcase in LA and getting four hours' sleep a night. Things were moving unbelievably quickly, her name public property virtually overnight, her image suddenly appearing on Google and friends she hadn't seen in years clamouring to make contact and claim they'd once been close. Everyone wanted a piece of her. She was being invited to an endless stream of parties and functions, awards ceremonies and photo shoots, scarcely having time to register that this was a world she'd been set against for years but now had welcomed her with open arms. Word was spreading about the hottest new actress in town: Stevie Speller was being billed as the next Great British Star, combining all the haughty London beauty of Keira Knightley with the shy intellect of Natalie Portman.

After the awkwardness of that first audition with Bibi—at least she'd felt it was awkward—she found herself taking to the game with surprising zeal. Her first time on set had been terrifying, she felt like a total sham, but before she knew it the director was calling 'Cut!' and the scene was nailed. All her life, as for so many, she'd been OK at a lot of things but never excelled in one. When she was immersed in a role, speaking words that had already been written, living a life in which the outcome was safe and known, she found refuge. She was able to forget where she'd been and what she'd done. When she watched her performance she was amazed to see so many versions of herself coming back. Ways of behaviour she'd never thought she had.

It was a sunny Hollywood Wednesday morning and Stevie was in her agent's downtown office. Marty King was top dog, a power agent with a host of superstars on his books. She couldn't believe it when he'd approached, and when she told Bibi over the phone the other girl squealed, *'I just peed in my pants!'* Bibi went on to inform her that Marty King was renowned for his knack of spotting a star on her way to the top. He also represented major Hollywood blockbuster names like Cole Steel. Cole's films had been staple viewing in Stevie's family while she'd been growing up and the idea of sharing representation with him was mind-blowing.

'Have you got a boyfriend?' Marty asked. For a second she thought it was a loaded question—she'd heard enough about fledgling actresses getting promised the stars and ending up on their hands and knees—but he regarded her seriously from across his desk. Marty had ruddy cheeks and a soft thatch of orange hair. Stevie could tell he'd been handsome in his younger years, and he had a genuine smile she was learning was rare to come by in this town.

She thought of Will, who'd been less than enamoured with news of her moving out to LA. 'I'm not sure,' she replied.

Marty made a face. 'That means no.'

'It does?'

He picked something out from between his teeth—a remnant from lunch, perhaps—and examined it before sucking it off his fingers. It told Stevie all she needed to know about how powerful Marty was. He didn't need to impress; his name spoke for itself.

'Sure it does.' He linked his hands across his belly. 'From here on in it's about who you're associated with. Stevie Speller spells class, she spells…sophistication. Some boyfriend you couldn't give two craps about ain't gonna cut it.'

'Who said I don't give a crap about him?'

'I said two craps. You might give one: you're still with the bozo. Do I know him?'

'No.'

'Good. The ones I know are the ones that cause me trouble. Take my advice and stay single. It'll make my life a hell of a lot easier, not to mention yours.'

'OK…'

'With your looks and talent,' he said matter-of-factly, 'there's no place to go but up. That accent right there's gonna have every major studio shitting money out their asses to sign you.'

She laughed. He didn't.

'You heard of Xander Jakobson?' Marty asked.

'Yes.' He was a thirtyish actor-turned-director, quite handsome. He'd been nominated last spring for an Award.

'I want him to see you.' Marty rolled up his shirtsleeves. 'His new project's got your name all over it.' There was a knock on the door. He looked up, distracted. 'Yes?'

A pretty blonde opened the door. 'Rita Clay called. I told her you were in a meeting but she made me promise to ask you personally to return it.'

Marty pinched the bridge of his nose. He stayed like that for several seconds before saying, 'Thank you, Jennifer.'

When his secretary had gone, he turned to Stevie. 'In the middle of a complicated negotiation,' he said by way of explanation. Stevie shrugged; it was none of her business.

'Xander Jakobson?' she prompted.

'See what you make of the script, I think you'll like it. Let me get on to him. I'm sure we can strike a deal.'

On impulse she asked, 'What do you know about Linus Posen?'

Marty sat back and narrowed his eyes. One whole wall of his office was glass and outside the green tops of palm trees quivered in the warm breeze. 'Why d'you ask?'

Stevie shrugged.

'I know you're not gonna be working with him any time soon,' said Marty.

'Oh?'

'You met him?'

'In New York, last year. He offered me work. I thought I should mention it.'

'What kind of work?'

'He didn't say. He gave me his card but I never called.'

'You know what line he's in?'

As far as she knew Linus directed mindless action blockbusters. She told Marty so.

'That's right,' he said, and she detected a note of caution in his voice. He let the silence hang before adding, abruptly back to business, 'So it's not what we're going for.'

'I didn't think so.'

'Good,' said Marty. 'Take my advice, it's what you pay me for, and steer well clear.'

When Stevie got back to her apartment, Will Gardner was waiting for her. Bibi's brother was due to arrive this afternoon and her first reaction was one of annoyance. Couldn't Will have called?

'Hello, beautiful,' he said when she exited the cab, drawing her into his arms and planting a kiss on her lips. She didn't know what to say.

'What are you doing here?' she asked eventually.

'Do I need a reason other than this?' He looped his arms around her waist and kissed her again. Stevie was hot and her top was clinging to the skin on her back: she wanted to get in the shower, change into a baggy T-shirt and sit by herself. It had been a hectic week and she realised now that Will was the last person she felt like seeing.

She didn't want to be a cow about it. 'Come in,' she said. 'Sorry it's a bit of a mess.'

The apartment was in a basic, unfussy compound, laid out like the motels she had seen in films: a one-storey cream building that formed an L-shape around a central shared swimming pool. She doubted if the novelty of a pool would ever wear off. Since arriving she'd adopted a routine of early-morning swim followed by a healthy breakfast and a review of the day's scenes.

Inside, Will helped himself to some apple juice out of the fridge, which he drank straight from the carton. He wiped his mouth on the back of his hand and pulled Stevie into an embrace. She felt yucky and wanted to change, but Will's touch was all over her, his tongue in her mouth, sticky from the juice. Maybe if she slept with him now she wouldn't have to later.

As they had sex he delivered a virtually non-stop stream of accolades, such as how gorgeous she was, how much he'd missed her, what a great body she had, how she was the hottest lay in the world. It felt wrong. Stevie had never been vocal during sex—and, besides, what was she meant to say back? *Thank you. Now would you please hurry up and come?* She realised then that Will had always been more into this than she was, despite what he'd said in the beginning. Breaking up would be horrible, but it was unfair to keep stringing him along.

Afterwards, he showered. Stevie took the opportunity to call Bibi. While Marty King hadn't expressly said anything negative about Linus Posen, his remarks had unnerved her. Bibi hadn't seemed herself recently: she wasn't the sparky, carefree girl Stevie had met in New York.

Her friend picked up on the fourth ring. 'Steve! How're you?'

Stevie pulled the bed sheet up and lay back. She could hear the steady thrum of the shower, the change in rhythm as Will's body moved beneath it. 'Did you know Will's here?'

'Wow. I thought you guys were taking it slowly.'

'So did I.' She sighed, rubbing her temple. 'What's new?'

'Well,' began Bibi, 'I was all set to call you, actually. I've got something I've been just *dying* to tell you!'

Stevie sat up, willing it to be a successful audition. 'Go on, then, spill!'

'I'm moving in with Linus!' Confused, Stevie waited for more. 'He's relocating to his house in Beverly Hills, and I'm coming with him! What do you think? Isn't it incredible?'

'Really?'

'Yes!'

'I didn't even know you were dating.'

'We kind of are, we kind of aren't.' Bibi cleared her throat, and for the first time in their acquaintance Stevie detected something forced in her enthusiasm. 'We're sleeping together. I mean, I don't know if I'm the only one. But truthfully I don't mind too much! And he must really like me, right? To ask me to come with him, I mean. Because the stuff I've been doing up till now hasn't been great, but Linus says that once we're in Hollywood he's putting me in touch with all the major casting agents and when he starts spreading the word then it's practically *definite* I'm going to make it! How can I go wrong? Steve, this is it for me. I know I said it before but this time it's for real. I'm going to be a star!'

Stevie didn't know what to say. 'I'm so happy you're moving here,' she said at last, the only honest comment she could think to make.

Bibi and Linus were dating? How had *that* happened?

'Tell me about it!' crowed Bibi. 'We're gonna have the *best* time. I've really missed us living together.'

Will opened the door to the en suite and padded naked across the bedroom.

'Me too,' she said. 'Listen, B, I've got to run. Call you later?'

'Sure.'

Stevie put down the phone. Despite the blast of warm steam that had accompanied Will's emergence, she shivered.

18
Lori

Lori changed while she was in Spain. As the weeks passed, the quiet seeped into her, the stillness and solitude bringing a peace long forgotten to her heart. For hours she would walk in olive groves, read books in her mother tongue, wander the narrow streets of the nearest village or play with the dog. She realised how beneficial loneliness could be.

Though she tried to resist, Rico Marquez was in her thoughts. One minute she worried for him and wondered if he was OK; the next she was consumed with anger at the risk he had brought, quite literally, to her door. Had Rico known about Diego's visit? Had he requested it? At night, in her dreams, she was terrorised by images of the gang, the hunger in their eyes and the rasp of their threats, of what might have happened if her stranger hadn't arrived...

Gratitude towards the man whose name she did not know flourished by the day. Time, rather than diminishing her obsession, only heightened it. The thought she would never see him again was unbearable. Once back in LA, she would seek him out. She had no idea how, where she would even begin, but if she did not try she would never forgive herself.

Corazón was old, but she was sharp as a pin. Often they would sit on the veranda, sipping lemonade and playing cards, speaking about the past, or when Tony was a boy, or not speaking at all, just listening to the crickets or the low chatter of her radio. They would prepare meals together. Lori learned recipes she recalled her mother making in happier times: she, too, had been taught them here. In so many ways she felt that she was treading the same stones. It was clear Corazón had cared for her mother like her own daughter.

'You know that Tony loves you very much, don't you?' she asked one night. They were preparing a feast: salted bread and chillis and peppers dark as cherries. Lori was chopping red onion and its sting caught her in the eye, but if Corazón thought it was tears she didn't say so.

'It has been difficult for him,' her grandmother went on.

'I know.'

'He remarried quickly because he believed it was best. He wanted you to feel secure.'

Lori couldn't help herself. 'He thought he'd better replace Mama, you mean?'

Corazón stopped what she was doing. 'Oh, Loriana, that is not true. Tony struggled. He did not know how to be both a mother and a father to you.'

'So he stopped being either?' Lori wished she could let go of her bitterness. It was ugly, it ate her up, but she couldn't help it.

'When Maria got sick, it tore his heart out, right from his chest. I saw it, *querida*, spooling to the floor like a ribbon and gathering at his feet, and I knew I could never fold it back in. You cannot judge a man's behaviour because of his grief.'

A long silence followed. Lori returned to the board but there was nothing else to do, she'd cut everything, so she drove the point of her knife into the wood and twisted.

'He had to keep you safe,' Corazón said.

'Safe from what? My own decisions?'

Corazón put her head to one side. 'Perhaps.'

'But I don't *want* to be safe!' Lori found her hands were shaking. She thought about how reckless she had felt that afternoon at *Tres Hermanas*. How until that moment she had lived her safe, miserable life and no one had been there to show her there was more; a different way of feeling. Until him. 'That's the point! I want to be more than just the poor kid whose mama died.'

Corazón shook her head with infinite sadness. 'No, *querida*. That is not how it is.'

'I hate Angélica.' She threw the vegetables into a waiting pan. Blue heat licked up the sides. 'And I hate her daughters. If it weren't for them—'

'The blame cannot rest with Angélica. Tony changed after your mother died, and he did that all by himself... Maria was the love of his life.'

Lori nodded, biting her lip to stop the tears.

'I cannot know what has been in his mind,' continued Corazón, 'the places he has gone to. But I *can* understand his decision to be with Angélica. She is strong, she takes control—'

'She is unkind, she is hurtful…she has spent all our money—'

'She is your father's wife.' Corazón watched her. 'Whether you like it or not.'

Eventually her grandmother put a brittle arm round her shoulders. 'Come,' she said. 'Didn't I promise good things would happen to you here? You don't get to my age without learning to trust your instincts.' She kissed Lori's head. 'Wait and see, Loriana. Wait and see.'

Lori took the bus into Murcia twice a week. She hadn't seen it after dark before, so, the following evening, Corazón encouraged her to venture into the city.

'Are you sure?' Lori had asked. She was nearing the end of her stay. 'What about you?'

Her grandmother had smiled. 'Go, have fun,' she said, settling into her favourite chair with the radio by her side. Her eyes closed. 'Watch the river for me.'

There was a fiesta happening in Murcia, a vibrant band of colour pouring through the streets. Locals in costume sang and blew fire into the night, the air was alive and the atmosphere infectious. Lori had worn her hair loose, an abundance of thick curls tumbling past her shoulders, and a simple yellow dress. The tan she had acquired in Spain was rich and deep, a burned amber—the sun was different here, more intense. Two small hoops glinted at her ears. She crossed the *Puente de los Peligros*, stopping to look out at the black and gold rush of the Segura. Beyond the rooftops and the spire of the gothic cathedral, mountain ranges soared into the sky. Lori imagined he was standing next to her. He would feel for her hand and hold it, his touch on her pulse, the engine of her blood.

She settled in a café in the *Glorieta*, the city square, and did not notice the woman staring at her from the bar, checking a small leatherbound book and then making her way over. Lori ordered a glass of red wine that was so sticky and viscous it clung to the sides like syrup.

'Excuse me?' a voice asked in Spanish.

Lori glanced up to see a striking woman, older than her, with a long sheet of glimmering dark hair. She had an unusual face with fine, high cheekbones and a large beauty spot in the middle of her cheek. 'Could I use your ashtray?'

Lori didn't smoke. She offered it to the woman. 'Sure.'

Uninvited, the woman pulled out a chair. 'I'm Desideria Gomez,' she said, extending her hand. 'I caught sight of you earlier, from the bar. I hope you don't mind me joining you.'

Tentatively, Lori shook it.

'Que linda.' She lit her cigarette with a flourish. 'You are very beautiful.' With a questioning expression, she slid the pack across the table.

Lori smiled uncertainly. 'No, thanks.'

'Do you live here?'

'I live in America. Los Angeles.'

The woman was surprised. 'Really? That's a coincidence. My company has a branch in LA.' Desideria started talking English and Lori thought she was less attractive when she did. She blew out smoke in a thin, efficient stream. 'I'm a talent scout, which means I get to do a lot of travelling—and hopefully, though rarely, come across girls like you.'

Lori wasn't sure what her companion was getting at. There was a silence during which Desideria didn't elaborate. Instead she continued to stare at Lori, so intently that after a while Lori began to feel uncomfortable. For something to say, she volunteered, 'I'm vacationing with my grandmother. She lives out of town.'

'But you'll be going back? To LA, I mean.'

'Yes.' Her face must have betrayed regret because Desideria leaned forward.

'What's your name?' she asked in Spanish.

'Loriana Garcia Torres.'

Desideria put her head to one side. 'Lori Garcia... I can see it.' She appraised her. 'I work for La Lumière.'

Lori waited.

'Modelling agency? Best in the world?' She flicked ash on to the ground, making Lori wonder why she'd wanted the ashtray in the first place. 'Though, I suppose I would say that.'

'That sounds fun.'

Desideria grinned, as if she couldn't quite work the younger woman out. 'Would you be interested?' she asked.

'In what?'

'Work.'

Hope soared. 'Yes, yes, I would,' Lori began. 'As it goes I have a job in a beauty salon already—nothing impressive, but I have a lot of skills, with hair, make-up and clothes as well as treatments. And I'm a very fast learner so anything you show me how to do, I'll be quick to pick it up...' She trailed off when Desideria started laughing.

'I meant on our *books*.' She sat back, her face moving in and out of shadow as lights from the carnival seeped over.

'What books?'

'As one of our models?'

Lori was baffled. 'Your models,' she repeated blankly.

'You're very sweet,' observed Desideria, nodding as though a previous notion had been confirmed. 'Innocent.'

'A model?'

'But with a sexy edge.'

Lori was embarrassed at the compliment.

'It was a lie,' said Desideria, 'when I said I'd spotted you from the bar. The truth is I've been following you all evening. If you're working behind a salon counter now, sweetheart, I can guarantee you won't be for much longer. You're gorgeous.' She eyed her keenly, licked her bottom lip. 'I mean,' she said huskily, 'I take it you're straight?'

'Yes.' Lori wasn't sure what that had to do with anything.

'Do me a favour,' said Desideria, reaching into her purse for a smart black card. On it, a stylish spotlight illuminated her name and number. 'Soon as you're back in LA, call me. We'll bring you in for a shoot, see if the camera likes you, and, if it does, we'll sign you up.'

Lori was dumbfounded. She took the card.

Again, Desideria laughed. 'Promise me you will?'

'I promise.'

'Good.' But Desideria insisted on scribbling Lori's details down all the same. 'I'm going to tell my boss about you.' She looked up. 'He's a very big deal. If I don't bring you back, Lori, he'll *never* forgive me.'

19
Aurora

Pascale Devereux was something else. Within days the two girls were inseparable. Never had Aurora met such an impressive, strong-minded person, so different from her so-called friends back in LA who thought only about cars and clothes. Pascale was cultured, she had travelled; she was intelligent and interesting; she told Aurora things about the world and taught her what she didn't know. She was clever and spirited and defiant in the face of the St Agnes teachers—she was also someone who, for whatever reason, the other girls, including Eugenie Beaufort, didn't want to mess with. Pascale's parents were Gisele and Arnaud Devereux, French politicians who held high positions in their country's government. She was from powerful stock.

At last, Aurora felt she had met her match.

The girls did everything together—they sat in a disgruntled pair in lessons, they bunked off when they felt like it, they crept into each other's dorms at night and lay in bed whispering secrets, they sneaked out of school after dark and smoked and drank miniatures that Pascale kept in a locked box under her bed. The nearest settlement was miles away, but somehow, with Pascale, it didn't matter where they were. Aurora could talk to her new best friend for hours.

'I suppose you'll be sharing a tent with your *girlfriend*!' crowed snotty Eugenie Beaufort ahead of a camping trip led by Mrs Durdon. 'Everyone knows you're lezzers.'

Aurora smiled sweetly as she shoved the last of the camping equipment into a bag. Screw Eugenie Beaufort and whatever she thought. She was just jealous because everyone wanted to be friends with Pascale and nobody was.

They were on the Games pitch and it had started to rain. Aurora caught her reflection in the glass of the main building and shuddered: her tan had faded entirely since being in England, and, without Ramon to see to her hair every few weeks, her blonde crop had grown out to her shoulders, still golden but without the shine the LA sun allowed. It majorly sucked.

'Chop-chop, girls!' bellowed Mrs Durdon, done up in a tragic flat cap and breeches. She was brandishing some sort of stick that she kept striking the ground with, as if she were rallying a herd of sheep. 'The weather's set to get worse and I want to make camp in three hours!'

Aurora groaned and caught Pascale's eye. The French girl glanced away, uninterested. Aurora wished she could perfect that look of indifference: it was far more effective than bitching.

They hiked out of the school grounds in a trudging line.

Fran Harrington hadn't caught the hint that Aurora was over needing a guide and glued herself to her at every opportunity. Today she was sneezing and complaining of a cold.

'Can I camp with you two?' she whinged, her waterproof trousers rustling maddeningly with every step.

'I don't know who I'm camping with yet,' Aurora lied. God, if she'd never met Pascale an expedition like this would be nothing short of deadly. Tramping off into the hills with a lead-weight attached to her back—and, courtesy of Fran Harrington, to her side. It was like those lousy boot camps she'd heard about. Worse.

'But I don't know how to put my tent up!' Fran cried pathetically.

'And I do?' snapped Aurora. 'Someone will do it for us.' The very idea of erecting a tent was laughable.

Hours later, shoulders aching and faces stinging from the driving rain, the dejected party arrived at a valley clearing. Mountains loomed all around; hostile clouds brooded overhead. It was barely four o'clock and yet dark as night. Didn't this country ever see sunlight? Aurora had forgotten that the sky was meant to be blue.

As it was, Pascale put their tent up in a matter of minutes. The other girls struggled fruitlessly with theirs, Eugenie Beaufort bossing her self-appointed team about the best way to do it and ending up tangled in canvas and tent pegs. To get her off their backs, Aurora helped Fran untangle hers and said she could pitch next to her and Pascale. They made a mess of it and Fran ended up with a sagging construction that whipped and billowed in the bad weather. Pascale sat in her perfectly erected tent and painted her fingernails.

'Who wants to orienteer tomorrow?' asked Mrs Durdon, charging round the camp, such as it was, like an army general. The girls were sheltering in the tents, front zips open. 'Aurora?'

Aurora resisted giving her the finger. 'Fran wants to, don't you, Fran?'

Fran poked her head out and looked around, never more like a twitchy-nosed mouse. 'OK,' she said, happy to have a job to do.

'Fine,' said Mrs Durdon. She scowled at Pascale, who met her gaze with a blank expression. 'Pascale, you will organise the fire, and then we'll make supper.'

Supper was a metal tin full of slimy orange pulses that Eugenie's crew was inexplicably loving. 'Ooh baked beans!' they cried. Was this what their lives had come to? *Baked beans?* Aurora couldn't think of anything less appetising. She had an acute craving for lobster—not likely, especially with Mrs Durdon off preparing some sloppy dessert. The redeeming feature was Pascale's fire, which burned bright and hot and warmed their aching bones. As nighttime fell a dozen faces gathered round in the flickering glow.

'Let's tell ghost stories!' Fran suggested, hugging her knees to her chest.

'As if you've ever seen a ghost,' snarled Eugenie. One of her cronies, a waify slip of a girl called Allegra, sniggered at her side.

'I don't have to see them to believe in them,' said Fran.

Eugenie yawned. 'Well, *I've* seen one,' she said.

'Ooh, tell us, tell us!' Allegra chimed, braces glinting in the shivering light.

'OK,' said Eugenie, basking in her audience's rapt attention. 'Well, there was this one time, at school, last term, where I woke up in the middle of the night and there was this...*thing* at the end of my bed. I can't describe what it was like, except it was this thing, like a black shape, like a misty black swirling cloud...' Next to Aurora, Pascale snorted. Eugenie went on, unperturbed. 'And it was short, like midget-sized, and it was wearing this cape that was flapping all over the place like wings. And it was *ugly*—I mean, what I could see of it was ugly. And then it started pulling back the covers, dragging the sheets off the end of my bed, and I tried to call out but my voice didn't work, I was paralysed! And all the while my sheet was getting lower and then I saw the midget's shoulders moving up and down, like it was laughing...'

'Are you sure it wasn't Durdon?' Some of the girls sniggered at Pascale's comment but knew enough not to identify themselves.

'Piss off, Devereux,' said Eugenie. 'You wouldn't understand.'

'What happened next?' Allegra murmured.

Eugenie bristled. 'I went back to sleep, didn't I? It was freezing, mind you.'

'Why didn't you pull the covers back up?' asked Aurora.

Eugenie shot her a withering look. 'Every time I did,' she explained slowly, 'this midget or whatever it was pulled them back down, didn't it?'

'So this thing just stood at the end of your bed, all night, holding your sheet?'

'Oh fuck you, it's not my fault you've got no imagination.'

'Or you've got too much,' snapped Aurora. 'Has anyone here *actually* seen a ghost?'

There was silence before Pascale spoke. 'I haven't seen a ghost,' she said. 'But I have seen something... extraordinary.'

Eight pairs of eyes turned to her.

'Perhaps I shouldn't tell you...'

'Go on, tell us! You have to now!'

Pascale inhaled deeply. 'Very well. We were in the Dordogne, many years ago.' She repositioned herself, waited for the last rumbling objections to die down. 'The house is old; it belonged to my father's parents and his grandparents and their parents before that. When I was young, my cousin would tell me a story: a village superstition about a split in the ground that led straight to the Underworld. The village was built on this fissure. They used it to frighten children into behaving, he told me, and it worked because I was afraid that if I did anything wrong then the Devil would come up and try to find me, and take me back down there with him.'

She paused. No one spoke. 'But one day I did do something wrong. My cousin saw me do it. We had a cat, you see, and she gave birth to a litter of kittens...'

Allegra shrieked. 'Oh no, I don't want to hear this!'

'*Shh!*' the others hissed. Even Eugenie looked faintly interested. Aurora wondered if Pascale was making it up.

'One of them was born sick, so my uncle killed it by hitting it on the head. He put it in a sack with heavy stones in and he said, "Take it to the well, Pascale, and drop it in the water." But on the way I felt its tiny body wriggling about in the bag, just a mess of fur and bones. He hadn't finished it off, it was still alive, in all that pain...'

'Oh nooo!' Allegra plugged her ears with her fingers.

'And I knew I should have killed it again. Properly, this

time. But I was afraid. So I dropped it straight into the well and let it drown. I let it drown—a slow, horrible, agonising death. And I knew what I was doing, but I just waited there. Waited for it to die.'

'You're sick,' Eugenie announced. But Pascale wasn't finished.

'My cousin knew what I'd done. He told me bad things would happen. I'd let something helpless suffer. I'd ignored my responsibility. He told me I would be punished.'

Silence.

'It snowed that night, very heavily,' Pascale went on, barely a whisper, 'so when we woke up the next morning there was this undisturbed blanket of white covering everything. It was deeper and thicker than any snow I have seen before or since. Beautiful and pure, so white it hurt to look at it for too long.' A beat. 'And only one thing disturbed the immaculate snow. A chain of footprints that seemed to come from nowhere, so abruptly did it begin and end, as if whatever had made it had landed here and flown away there. And I say footprints, but these were like...' She searched for the word. '*Horseshoes*. But the horseshoes had two toes at the front. An animal's print, or a bird's? Or a man's. We could not tell.' Pascale looked at each of her audience in turn. 'Odd that they did not appear in pairs, but in a single straight line, as if the person making them had only one foot, or a certain...*twist* to their walk...' Another pause, a longer one. 'But the strangest thing about these footprints?'

'What?' someone breathed.

'They did not run only across the ground. They ran up the side of the house, over the roof and down the wall to the river. They ran across the garden and up a tree and around its top, on branches, up, down, here, there, everywhere. I believe the Devil came for me that night. Only the Devil could not find me. Not that time, at least. But whenever I am out in the country—like now—I wonder if he might try again…'

Silence enveloped the group.

'Is that true?' Fran Harrington wailed, her mousy face panicking in the half-light. Eugenie Beaufort looked sick.

Pascale started laughing. 'What do you think?'

'I think you're full of bullshit,' said Eugenie.

Mrs Durdon came back and they ate their gelatinous dessert in pensive quiet. Afterwards, some of the girls still visibly unsettled, they went to bed.

Inside the tent, Pascale was undressing, wriggling out of her hiking clothes and slipping on a Raconteurs T-shirt. It wasn't the first time Aurora had seen the French girl's body: whenever they showered, or tried on each other's clothes, she had no qualms about getting naked. All the girls back in LA were painfully body-shy, all in competition with each other about who had the perkier ass or tits. Pascale didn't care.

'*Was* it true?' asked Aurora once they were in their sleeping bags.

'What?'

'That story.'

Pascale faced her in the dark. 'Does it matter?'

'I suppose not.'

They lay in silence for a bit. 'Tell me about when you were a child,' said Pascale, pushing herself up on one elbow. 'Tell me a story like that.'

Aurora thought about it. She was conscious that her youth had been one excess after another. Tom and Sherilyn had never taken her away, the three of them, somewhere where they just chilled out away from it all. Come to think of it, they had never done much as a family.

'I don't have any,' she admitted. The words hung between them in the darkness, hollow and sad, and Aurora thought about qualifying it but she didn't have anything else to say.

'Do you ever wonder what life would be like if they weren't your parents?'

The question was so unexpected, and Aurora so exhausted, that she felt tears prick her eyes. 'What do you mean?'

The rain had started up again. They could hear it pattering on the tent.

'Doesn't matter.'

'No—go on.'

'Just that yours is kind of a messed-up life.'

'Thanks.'

'Don't be sensitive. All I mean is that it's hard to be you—just you, for what you are—because you're Tom Nash's daughter. You'll always be Tom Nash's daughter, all your life.'

Aurora hadn't thought of it like that before. Now she did, she felt horribly claustrophobic.

'So?'

'So you have to be your own person.'

'I know that.'

'And make your own choices.'

'I do make my own choices,' snapped Aurora. 'No one tells me what to do.' But she knew that for all her proclamations of independence she lived the life she did solely because of her parents' status. Tom Nash was a world-famous A-list performer. Sherilyn Rose was the darling of the country scene. Aurora Nash was…well, she was their kid. Nothing more. She never would be. She'd never be exciting and original like Pascale.

Pascale's voice dropped. 'Have I upset you?'

'No.'

'Sorry.'

'Don't be.' Aurora bit her lip. She had always been content with her cars and cash and clothes, her status as Hollywood princess, but her friendship with Pascale was widening her horizons. Maybe there *was* more to life than album sales and wild parties and boys. She was lucky, right? So lucky, just like everyone said. Why, then, did she feel empty? A salty teardrop slid down her cheek.

'Are you OK?' asked Pascale.

'I'm cold.'

'Come to me.' Pascale reached out and put her arm round Aurora. She unzipped their sleeping bags so their bodies were touching, warmer in the embrace. The French girl smelled clean, like violets, her hair touching Aurora's cheek.

The wind was picking up, tugging at their canvas shelter. Pascale began stroking Aurora's skin, at first over her tank top and then, as though it were the most natural thing in the world, slipping her hand beneath it. Aurora didn't breathe. Pascale's touch was light, barely there, her fingers small, the nails long. She traced over Aurora's stomach, slowly, affectionately, and then, almost by accident, it became something different, her touch creeping up, finding the crescent swell of Aurora's left breast, following it till she met the bud of her nipple. It didn't occur to Aurora to object. She hardened under Pascale's touch, moved her position ever so slightly, without really meaning to, so she filled Pascale's palm.

'Can I kiss you?' Pascale whispered, her accent stronger in the dark and with the quiet.

Aurora was aware of every hair on her body, every pore. 'Yes.'

Pascale's lips were soft and yielding, her tongue inquisitive. She was wearing gloss and the girls' mouths locked, their tongues entwined in sweet curiosity. Gently Pascale bit Aurora's bottom lip. It sent a charge of desire through Aurora and she found herself reaching for the other girl's body. Pascale lifted her T-shirt and peeled it off, then her knickers, revealing a smooth-skinned body that shone whitish in the moonlight. Between her legs, a bush of dark hair, two pale nipples high on her chest. Aurora took one in her mouth and tentatively kissed it. It was a new sensation but at the same time oddly familiar, as if she were loving her own body and knew all its contours and pleasure points. Carefully she bit the tip. Hearing the French girl's sigh, she pulled harder, till Pascale was holding her and drawing her close.

Aurora had never made out with a girl before. Pascale had skin like silk, her touch tender but firm, fragile but strong. Overcome, she felt for the other girl's wetness, sliding once into it, then raising her fingers to Pascale's mouth and between her lips, feeling her tongue wrap around. Aurora kissed her again, more passionately this time. She felt like she was imitating the boys she'd been with, not sure why she assumed the role of the man. Not that there had to be a man. In fact, the way she felt right now, there had never been need of boys and never would be again.

'I am going to show you something,' Pascale whispered,

manoeuvring Aurora on to her back. Moving her head lower, she kissed Aurora's stomach and then the ridges of her hips, till she reached the band of her knickers. Peeling the material to one side and kneeling between her legs, she inserted one small finger, then two. A thin sound escaped Aurora's mouth. She shivered, hot and cold, raising her hips, pushing herself on to the other girl, marvelling at the exactitude of Pascale's touch. The French girl ran a thumb over that sensitive swell, then the very tip of her tongue. Without warning Aurora crashed over waves of pleasure. It was the quickest, and most intense, orgasm of her life.

Afterwards they lay together, their foreheads touching.

Pascale dressed and rolled over. 'Night,' she said, as if nothing momentous had occurred.

'Night,' said Aurora. She stared into the dark and listened to the rain outside.

20
Stevie

Ben Reiner, Bibi's nineteen-year-old brother, was a pain in the arse to live with. Stevie had been patient at first—he was broke, he'd split up with his girlfriend, his esteem had taken a knock: she knew from her own younger siblings it'd get better—but since arriving at the apartment all he seemed to do was sit around getting stoned, eating chicken drumsticks and watching internet porn. Ben had little if anything in common with his sister, especially where work ethic was concerned. After appearing in a couple of anti-zit adverts that he complained made him look like a 'chump droid', he seemed to have given up. Still, she abided him for Bibi, and if that meant picking up balls of discarded socks, turning the telly off late at night when Ben forgot to (invariably still set on the Adult Hardcore channel) and occasionally thinking he was dead because it was three o'clock on a Tuesday afternoon and he still hadn't surfaced from his room, then so be it.

One thing Ben had been useful for, however, was in the resolution of her situation with Will Gardner. Coupled with the fact they were living in different cities and scarcely saw each other, Will hadn't taken kindly to the fact that Stevie was about to let a bum teenager into her house, who, despite the Bibi connection, he stated she hardly knew. His attitude over the whole thing had been cheap and ungenerous. It had been the push she needed to make the break. Marty King was pleased. Now she was free and single, Stevie could throw herself into the publicity circuit unencumbered—and the timing couldn't be better. Things were taking off with the wrap of *Lie to Me*. Critics were calling it 'a shatteringly truthful portrayal of friendship and the many shades of love', while her performance was hailed 'a stunning debut'. It felt as if she'd walked straight into someone else's life—which, in a way, she had. It never left her mind that the role of Lauren was meant to belong to someone else, and she vowed that one day she would find a way to repay her good fortune.

Bibi herself arrived in LA towards the end of the month. Stevie dropped several hints about Ben taking one of the rooms in Linus Posen's sprawling Beverly Hills pad, but, according to Bibi, the timing was never quite right: *'Sorry, Steve, you know what it's like—new relationship and all! Could he crash with you just a little bit longer?'* Reading between the lines, Stevie decided that Linus had no intention of helping Bibi or her family and had likely vetoed the idea, serving only to confirm her bad instincts about the man. Try as she might, Stevie couldn't shake the impression that there was more to the director than met the eye. She didn't trust him.

Though she'd had plans with another friend tonight, she

had cancelled on hearing about Bibi's housewarming. Bibi and Linus were throwing an extravagant party to mark his relocation and Bibi had made her promise to be there.

'Cool,' Ben had grunted when she told him. He was permanently attached to his phone, reclining as he was now on the sofa, examining what he said were football scores but would just as likely be downloaded filth: he was obsessed. 'You can get me talking to some people.'

Stevie tried not to let it get to her. Ben was always demanding to trail her around and get introduced to as many influential faces as possible, but then did little to establish or nurture those relationships. She found it awkward: it wasn't that she didn't *want* Ben accompanying her to parties, exactly, more that she felt it a liberty to constantly be appearing to pioneer an out-of-work actor in need of a break. Nevertheless, she kept reminding herself, this was a favour to Bibi. Wasn't she riding on one humongous favour herself?

She and Ben shared a car to the Posen mansion. Ben had harped on about accompanying her in for the benefit of the paps but she had refused, saying speculation would be rife once it was revealed he was Linus's sort-of-brother-in-law (which she suspected was exactly what he wanted). Now, predictably, he was sulking. Stevie glanced at him on the back seat. The only physical similarity he had with Bibi was the hair, which was curly and gingerish. He was getting chubby around the chin and was struggling to cultivate a beard. She'd seen pictures of Ben when he was young and he'd been cute then, but cuteness often didn't translate into adulthood.

The paparazzi were out in force. Ben was first to enter

the fray and attracted a minor flurry when the association with Linus's new girlfriend was revealed. He hovered about a bit once the cameras had done their thing then loped off in search of a drink.

Stevie's reception was at the other end of the scale. Clad in a white Stella McCartney number (she was always advised to wear British) cut short at the thigh, she emerged to a cacophony of exclamations and demands for her attention. Bulbs glittered in an almost continuous stream of light. The glasses were long gone and the hair was let loose, tumbling in gentle deep-red waves to her shoulders. She possessed a Mona Lisa smile that sent the paps wild.

Inside, Bibi found her straight away. 'I'm so happy to see you, Steve, I've missed you *sooo* much! Can you believe the reception you got? I suppose you're used to it by now, but *wow*! You look amazing, by the way. Do I look OK? I wasn't sure about the dress but it *is* my party, you know, so I figured I should stand out.'

Stevie liked Bibi's dress but the rest of her looked bad. Her green eyes were glassy and there were dark rings beneath them that she had tried to conceal with foundation. Her hair, that reddish frizz once so charmingly shambolic, was bluntly cut and dyed a severe, waxy blonde. There were still shades of the old Bibi, but it was as if a light, a vital one, had gone out. 'It's gorgeous, B,' said Stevie, kissing her friend on the cheek. She fought the urge to wrap a blanket round her and bundle her home where she could take care of her. She looked like she hadn't eaten in a week. 'I haven't seen Linus. Where is he?'

'Oh—' Bibi flapped her hands '—he's about. Is Ben here? How's it going?'

Stevie turned round. Ben was making small talk with a

nonplussed Scottish-born actor and drinking too quickly. She was about to say something evasive like, *You know what teenagers are like*, then realised that made her sound about fifty.

'Fine,' she said. 'He's settling in.'

The Posen mansion was outlandishly decorated. Crystal chandeliers dazzled from lofty ceilings; plaid chaises longues studded the marble floor of the entrance hall accompanied by faux-Regency three-legged tables; huge gilt mirrors hung on the walls. Artwork from Linus's greatest movies was dotted around: action-shot stills of gorgeous actresses, all running from some point of menace. It was elegant, if you liked that sort of thing, but strangely void of character.

'There he is!' Bibi had spotted her aged, overweight boyfriend as he weaved through the crowd of assembled faces, flinty eyes scanning the guests. Stevie hadn't seen Linus since they'd been introduced in New York, and she was reminded of how physically off-putting she found him. He'd got fatter in the intervening months, and his white hair was now cut brutally short, military-style, which emphasised the pink fleshiness of his cheeks.

'Stevie Speller,' he greeted her with a damp kiss, 'I always knew you'd be going places. Didn't I say so when we first met?'

She couldn't remember exactly what he'd said but it hadn't been that. In a flash she recalled the card he'd handed her, a matching one to Bibi's.

'Make an old man happy,' he said, licking his lips as his eyes scoped her body, 'and promise you'll work with me some day...'

Ben joined them. Bibi's haunted expression was immediately replaced by a happier one.

'Little bro!' She had to reach up to hug him, she was so tiny. 'How's it living with my best friend?'

''S OK.' He shrugged.

Unfortunately Linus took the opportunity to step closer to Stevie.

'I mean it,' he said quietly. 'Dirk tells me you're the business. The offer's there whenever you want it.'

She hadn't a clue what he was doing speaking to Dirk Michaels about her. It stood to reason they'd compare notes, but the way Linus was going on was unsettling, as if they'd been discussing her behind her back.

'I'll bear it in mind,' she replied, though she had no intention of doing so. Linus returned by placing a heavy hand on the small of her back and instantly she moved away.

'Can you believe we're all here?' Bibi was exclaiming, though her wholehearted enthusiasm was matched only by Ben's lack of interest and Stevie's unease, as the print from Linus's touch seared into her.

Linus looked momentarily thrown, as though he'd forgotten all about his girlfriend. He glanced down at Bibi, as if she were a pet.

'Run along, darling, our guests need seeing to.'

An uncomfortable silence ensued. Stevie was shocked at the director's rudeness, and even more shocked by her friend's response. The old Bibi would never have cowed to such misplaced authority. This one nodded meekly and moved away.

Bibi Reiner went straight upstairs to one of the guest bedrooms—she had taken to sleeping there recently. She couldn't stand it. Her head was spinning and she had a dry, sick taste in her mouth. Shakily, she fished about in a drawer and found what she was looking for. She unscrewed the cap and poured the dark liquid down her throat.

Before she'd met Linus Posen she had never drunk. These days, forget it.

Damn Linus. *Damn him!* Bibi oscillated between needing him desperately—alone, panicking, *What am I without him?*—and loathing the man with every fibre of her being. He had promised her the world: the moon, the stars and everything in between. Instead he had fed her into a different, sordid game. One she felt powerless to get out of.

Linus Posen ran a lucrative sideline in the porn industry. By day he directed surefire Hollywood blockbusters; by night he directed movies called things like *The Girl Who Couldn't Say No* and *Six in a Bed*. He'd been doing it for years. Oh, it wasn't the money—he'd made his fortune long ago—but he liked it. It gave him a kick. His favourite hobby.

Bibi closed her eyes, surrendered to a shudder. The things he had made her do…with men, with women, with objects—ever since she had foolishly taken his card. Stevie had told her not to call, but had she listened? No. She'd met Linus the following week, dazzled by his guarantees of fame and celebrity, willing to do anything he asked. Initially he'd been pissed that she'd come alone, he'd wanted the girls as a package: Bibi with her wild hair and huge innocent eyes and Stevie with her cool, slender beauty. She'd been forced to give him head as 'compensation'. Even if she had wanted to confide in her friend, she couldn't: she hadn't been able to talk right for days afterwards.

That episode had set the tone for their working

relationship—and now it was degradation of the highest, or lowest, order. Before Bibi realised what was happening, Linus had drawn her in, dangling the carrot of stardom and having her follow it blindly into a long dark tunnel. By the time she wanted out, it was too late: she turned, looked back the way she had come, searching, searching, and could no longer see the light.

Some days, the good days, she believed she was on a necessary journey. Linus promised her she was a natural and that the camera loved her: she was born to do this. Bibi would beg—when could she star in just one of his other movies? And he kept making that vow, just this last gig, just this last time, and then he'd get her the breakthrough audition…

It never came. Meanwhile just about everything and everyone else did, in her mouth, in her hair, on her body, between her legs. She'd thought when she became Linus's official girlfriend, the way out would be clear: he wouldn't want to risk people seeing her in that context, would he? It had to stop. But Linus had a solution for everything. Instead he capitalised on it, engineering movies more sordid and perverse than ever, introducing her to the underground scene as 'The Faceless Vixen', forcing her body into every unthinkable position but always severing the headshot. It was a double strike for the Posen empire: a host of new devotees who got off on the anonymity; and for him, supreme protection.

Somehow the very worst thing was sleeping with Linus himself. He was away a lot of the time, Bibi could only guess at where or with whom, but each night he returned it always went the same way. He'd be drunk, and he always sweated when he drank. Bibi, anticipating his arrival, would get stoned out of her head. It was how she got through sex on-set—that and more coke than she knew what to do with. For Linus's pleasure she would be required to get changed into something school-girlish; they'd engage in the first part of a role play that involved her getting on all fours and having her ass spanked while he whacked off, then he'd be so drunk he dived straight in, rutting her from behind with a half-limp dick. She supposed it was some small mercy (and it was small) not to be forced to face him, but as she accommodated his heaving bulk, suit pants round his ankles, shoes still on, grunting and wheezing as he ploughed into her for ages and ages, making her dry, making her sore, she wondered when the hell it had gone so wrong.

She had wanted to be an actress—a proper, serious actress. Now she was little more than a high-paid whore. Because in return for the work she did for Linus, she got a roof over her head, her status as his girlfriend, everything she thought she had wanted. She just hadn't known at what price. Walking out now would mean the months had been in vain, and there was still a chance her time would come. Wasn't there? How much longer could she stand it?

A tear plopped down her cheek. It wouldn't do to cry. She had a party to get on with and guests to greet. The Bibi Reiner show must go on.

Before she went downstairs, she cut two fat lines and inhaled them in quick succession, so hard it made her teeth hurt. There, that was better.

Stevie was talking to Dirk Michaels, head of Searchbeam Studios and, she was learning, close friend of Linus. He was good-looking in a predatory, self-satisfied way, with black, deep-set eyes and a mop of dyed mahogany hair. He'd also been giving her serious come-on chat.

'How's your daughter?' she enquired, deciding to remind him of his family. His only child, Farrah, was constantly in the press with her crew of fellow teenage starlets.

'Keeping out of trouble,' he leered, 'for now.' Stevie, accurately sensing he was about to deliver an awful line about making trouble themselves, cut in.

'That must be a relief.'

Dirk sighed, replenished both their drinks when a waiter swept past. 'Her best friend was the troublemaker. Now Tom Nash has finally seen sense and deported her, we can all rest easy.'

Stevie puzzled over the connections. 'Aurora Nash has been *deported*?'

Ben joined them, no doubt wanting her to put a word in.

'Sent her to school in the UK,' elaborated Dirk, barely registering Ben's presence. 'You must have read it. She kicked off such a fuss mid-air that their jet had to be brought down.'

'Oh, right.' That would explain why she hadn't seen Aurora on the newsstands recently. The girl intrigued Stevie. She carried an air of greater intelligence than the party she hung with.

Ben's voice snapped her back to reality. 'Aren't you going to introduce me?' He was like a panting dog begging for scraps. Stevie obliged. As the men shook hands a tinkling of glasses hushed the crowd, accompanied by a ripple of urgent shushes.

Linus Posen had taken to the main staircase, where he jovially raised his drink.

'Listen up, everybody.' He was slurring his words. The

gathering dutifully turned. 'Tonight marks my permanent relocation to Los Angeles—a move I've been planning for some time. But I'm also taking this opportunity to ask a special question to a special woman in my life.' He scanned the assembly, veined face flaccid with drink. 'Where's my girl?'

Stevie watched as Bibi made her way forward, smile fixed in place, shaking a little on her heels. Linus helped her up next to him, his massive frame dwarfing her miniature one.

'Baby—' he directed it to the crowd, Stevie noticed, rather than to Bibi '—we've been together a little while now. I think we've got a good thing going —' a self-deprecating shrug '—an' this old dog's not getting any younger.' There was a polite murmur of disagreement from the crowd, which he lazily waved away. 'So, whaddaya say? How'd you like to be my wife, B? How'd you like to be Mrs Linus Posen?'

A cheer went up.

Bibi found Stevie's eyes. Stevie thought she detected a quiet panic there—and shock, definitely. Celebratory cheers and backslaps were being passed round. Linus held his wife-to-be's hand in the air as if they were champions in a great race.

Bibi blinked, before seeming to recover herself.

'But she hasn't said yes,' murmured Stevie.

Next to her, Ben yawned. 'Of course she's going to say yes,' he said. 'It's B.'

21
Lori

Corazón had loaned her enough money to get settled in a place of her own. Initially she hadn't wanted to take it, but, after it was agreed she would repay every cent, objection seemed mulish. And so it was that Lori returned to America with a heart full of promise.

Her sisters were apoplectic with jealousy when they heard about the mystery scout and the modelling agency.

'*You? A model?*' they screeched, as, on her first night back, Lori relayed her news. They trailed her up to her bedroom, shouted through her closed door. 'You'll never make it. They probably just felt sorry for you!' But it was when she explained she was moving out and quitting her position at *Tres Hermanas* that the shit properly hit. Horrified, they appealed to Angélica. 'Mama, *do* something!' The thought of Lori pursuing something they weren't involved in was abominable, something as glamorous as this, monstrous.

Over the phone, Corazón pleaded her case with Tony. It

didn't mean Lori was running away, nor did it mean she was set on misadventure—what it meant was that she had to grasp opportunities when they came along and explore a world separate to the one she had grown up in. To deny her that freedom would be to lose her. It wouldn't be Rico Marquez who took her away, or rebellion, or drugs or sex or any of that—it would be the slow suffocation of a life in which no decision had been hers to make.

Two weeks later, Tony helped her move her possessions into a modest, basic apartment in West Hollywood. As she explored the plain grey block, for once she didn't notice her father's quiet.

'Spain was good for you,' he observed. 'I was right about something. You're different, Lori, you've grown.'

It was true. The last time she'd been in LA was as a child. Now, she was a woman.

'I haven't been here for you,' he admitted. 'It's been easier not to be…a coward's excuse, but an honest one. I'm sorry.'

Corazón had helped her understand. Tony might not have been much of a father over recent years, but he had done his best. 'You don't need to explain,' she said.

He ran a hand through his thinning hair. She saw his regret was real. 'You will always be my daughter, the most important thing to me. You do understand that, don't you?'

They embraced. Tony held on so tight that Lori felt a tear spill from her eye, like he had squeezed it out of her.

The apartment was comprised of just two rooms that she planned to divide into independent living areas. Lori had few belongings and positioned them with care, relishing the novelty of her own space. She thought about the giant mansions in Beverly Hills and didn't know how people could live in them—it would be like a penny rattling around in a jar.

The walls were bare, awaiting her imprint. She hung two pictures: one, a photograph of Corazón when she was a girl, young and full of laughter, standing on the *Puente de los Peligros* where Lori herself had been just a few weeks before; the second, an image she had spotted in a glossy publication on her flight home. It showed a private island called Cacatra, an exclusive celebrity rehab spa in the middle of the Indian Ocean, owned by a South African business entrepreneur whose name was often in the press. The mansion featured in an article about the world's most desirable places to live: JEWEL OF THE OCEAN—A PRIVATE PARADISE. With its sprawling grounds, golden sands and lush foliage, it had easily stolen the top spot.

Lori had torn the picture because it mirrored so closely the island of her imagination, the one she visited in her dreams. Over the years she had fleshed the image out in such detail that, the moment she saw its counterpart, the resemblance was astonishing. Not the grand house or the pleasure cruisers or the luxury villas, but the landscape and the water, the fundamentals, like if the island had been a painting it would have been the canvas that drew her, not the oils.

As the golden sun set over Hollywood, Lori ordered takeout and settled on her bed. She withdrew a file of paper she'd put together at Corazón's and studied it with intent: everything she could remember about the man who had come to *Tres Hermanas*—what he looked like, what he wore, the car he drove. The latter was the only real lead she had, and, after tapping 'Mercedes' into a Google search and trawling through the catalogue of images it supplied, she'd at last landed on the model she recognised. How she cursed herself for not memorising the licence plate. In her mind it began with a J, but after that, nothing. What she did recall was the very specific colour: a silvery charcoal-grey, like wet slate, with black-tinted windows. It wasn't much to go on, but it was a start. Determination would carry her the rest of the way.

Tomorrow, her search would begin. What would she do when she found him? Would he take her in his arms once more, tell her he was glad she'd come? While in every other respect her musings on the stranger were ripe with colour and invention, here her imaginings hit a wall. He just didn't seem *real*; she couldn't picture him in any context other than the strange dreamscape of that mystifying afternoon. Routine, the mundane, didn't fit. Where did he live? She couldn't see him in a house. Where did he work? An office, a desk, wasn't right. Who were his friends? What did he talk to them about? What made him happy? What made him sad?

Always her thoughts returned to the same. What did she think she could offer him? A poor Spanish girl from the wrong part of town…she had nothing he could possibly need.

Cautiously, Lori withdrew Desideria Gomez's card and ran a thumb across its surface. All was dependent on securing work with La Lumière: it was the only way she could afford to see this through. She vowed to call them in the morning.

The La Lumière offices were on Sunset, a stuccoed building with an expansive parking lot out front filled with gleaming vehicles. Lori felt conscious of her plain string dress and the battered satchel she had slung over one shoulder—she ought to have bought a new outfit, but after paying her deposit and buying in basic groceries she'd had no money left. Approaching the main entrance, she gripped the card in her hot palm till its edges went soft.

A friendly redhead called Hayley greeted her in the lobby. Four aubergine-leather banquettes were positioned in facing pairs, a glass table between them, on which was centred a neat square stack of fashion publications. Headshots of beautiful women were arranged on the walls behind the main desk. All were black and white, but each incorporated just one splash of vibrant colour: the bleeding-crimson of a top lip, the vivid purple of a smear of eye shadow, the fiery orange of a lock of hair.

'Didn't they tell you not to wear make-up?' Hayley asked as she led the way to the bank of elevators. She walked on sharp heels and her hair bounced glossily around her shoulders.

Lori nodded. 'I'm not wearing make-up.' They had told her to come natural so she had worn her curls untamed and scrubbed her face clean.

Unconvinced, Hayley pushed the button to the eleventh floor. The girl's features were too dark, too intense: people just didn't look that…extreme. Even the models she was used to working with needed a little help to achieve their optimum glow.

Desideria was waiting for them, along with a short woman with bobbed black hair and glasses, who flashed a brief, professional smile. She introduced herself as Kirsty Belafonte, the agency's managing director, and shook Lori's hand with purpose.

'Didn't I tell you she was something else?' said Desideria, pleased. 'She's even lovelier than I remember.'

Kirsty put a hand on each side of Lori's face and peered in close. Lori didn't know what to do. She felt self-conscious. The other woman was so near she could have kissed her.

'She's beautiful,' said Kirsty in a matter-of-fact way.

Hayley was dismissed. Lori stayed standing as the women moved around her, nodding to each other, touching her hair and scanning her body, every detail absorbed. Gently Desideria drew her shoulders back and put a finger under Lori's chin to lift it.

'Quite short, isn't she?' Kirsty commented. 'What are you, five-seven, five-eight?'

'Five-seven.'

'Hmm.'

'She'll be magic with the camera,' put in Desideria. 'We needn't use her for runway.'

Kirsty nodded. 'OK,' she said briskly. 'Let's get some pictures.'

They travelled down to the building's basement. A rangy photographer was snapping at a pouting brunette with stringy pale legs.

'Be with you in a minute, darlin',' he called out in a British accent.

A frazzled stylist rushed over and took her arm. 'This way!' She checked a clipboard. 'Loriana, you'll be doing me a favour if you can move quickly. We've got a lot to get through.'

Behind a curtain she was shown several rails of clothes. Only they weren't clothes, exactly, more like scraps of material. It was about stripping the models down, encouraging their looks to shine through. Several girls were in today—like her, they had been talent-spotted. Today was about meeting Kirsty and getting a feel for the camera. The successful candidates would go on to meet the owner of La Lumière, the boss Desideria had mentioned back in Murcia. He would decide whom the prestigious agency took on.

She ended up in a torn pale pink top with a wide, loose-fitting neckline, and an ordinary pair of blue shorts. Despite the shapelessness of the outfit, against the deep shade of her skin the effect was dizzying. Her curves were enhanced, her hair a windswept mass. When she emerged into the studio, Desideria audibly gasped. Kirsty smiled and the women exchanged words, though Lori couldn't make out what they were saying.

Initially she was self-conscious in front of the camera, but as the photographer guided her through with instructions to look this way and that, smile and not smile, run a hand through her hair, sit down, stand up, cross her legs, turn around, bite her lip, tilt her head, she settled into the rhythm and began to fall into the poses without trying. It was the quickest ten minutes of her life. The photographer kept consulting with Kirsty. 'Gorgeous,' he said, over and over. 'Every single shot, she's absolutely gorgeous.'

Desideria helped her get changed. 'You did great,' she said, leaning against the dresser as Lori stepped out of her shorts. 'I knew you'd be a natural.'

Adrenalin was charging through Lori. She was still buzzing when Desideria took her back upstairs to the lobby.

'We'll call you once we've shown the boss your prints.' Lori must have looked unsure because she added, 'Try not to worry. Mr Moreau isn't as terrifying as people say. At least, not once you get to know him.'

'Moreau?'

The name was familiar. She had seen it in magazines, on expensive shopping sites, heard it on the lips of celebrities walking the red carpet—*'I'm wearing Moreau; no one dresses me like it'*. He was the son of the legendary Paul and Emilie Moreau; so the rumour went, their reluctant heir. Before the Moreaus' untimely deaths—they had been killed in a tragic boating accident while holidaying with their son—they had been designers on a par with Valentino and Lagerfeld. As two of the industry's greatest innovators, the celebrity circuit had clamoured to work with them: from movie stars to supermodels, politicians to royalty, they had dressed the world's most famous silhouettes. Their son and successor was notoriously private and rarely seen out in public. Word was he had little to do with his inheritance, masterminding the Moreau fashion house from behind the scenes but employing a dedicated team to execute affairs.

It couldn't be the same man...could it?

Lori felt giddy. She was way out of her depth.

'That's right.' Desideria looked amused. 'You seem surprised.'

'I didn't realise—'

'Welcome to the big league, honey. You just wait till he sees you.' They made their way into reception. 'If you don't already know,' she elaborated, 'JB prefers to keep a low profile. He's very—how should I put this?—*secluded*. The industry respects that. He won't make it easy for you, he hasn't for any of us, but once you've earned it, he'll do anything for you.'

'Earned what?'

Desideria smiled. 'Trust.'

The door behind Lori opened. She heard someone step inside, shoes on a polished floor. *Smart, controlled, precise...*

Something gave way in her chest, an underwater explosion, like footage she'd seen once of a submarine torpedo. Devastating and silent.

Desideria straightened. Lori thought she saw a shadow of conspiracy pass across the woman's features, a kind of confirmation, there and then gone, quick as a flashlight.

'Ah,' she said. 'How about that for timing?'

When Lori turned, it was his scar that caught her attention. Then the line of his jaw, square and straight, absolute, as if it had been drawn cleanly, in one stroke, with a sharp pencil.

He was sexy. Sexier than she had made him, even in her fantasies. He was sex.

'JB Moreau,' said Desideria, 'I'd like you to meet Lori Garcia.'

22
Aurora

Aurora passed the spring half term at Creekside, her father's Texan ranch retreat. Tom Nash had spent his childhood in the South and when fame hit had purchased the land as a hideaway. With its six hundred acres of rolling hills and prairie land, catfish lakes and cattle farms, it was an opportunity to get back in touch with nature: his own personal slice of Utopia.

Not what Aurora needed after months buried in a rural craphole in England. But Sherilyn had decided that Hollywood life might risk unpicking the work St Agnes had done, so she'd been directed to the lodge in Texas, where Tom was busy writing material for their new album.

It seemed to Aurora that her parents weren't spending much time together at all these days: whenever she'd Skyped or called from the UK, they'd scarcely known the whereabouts of the other. She hoped they weren't on the brink of a divorce. Despite the wealth of clichés attached to their names, this was one they had so far managed to avoid.

There were several cabins and lake houses on the ranch, of which Creekside was the biggest. It was a rambling wooden lodge with bearskins on the floor and antlered deer heads bolted to the walls. Aurora thought it was weird since her dad was the least macho guy she could imagine. In fact, with all his cosmetics and clothes and his gentle manner, he was quite, well, feminine. He hadn't hunted the beasts down himself, of course, but it was as if he enjoyed parading the alpha thing. Sometimes, when he was writing, he'd pace the floor, hands on hips, and stand wide-legged in front of one of them, Stetson on tousled head, for minutes on end. A man with highlighted hair gazing into the eyes of a stuffed dead deer. One mousse looking at another moose. She supposed it was his creative prerogative.

'Dad, I'm going out!' Aurora yelled up the stairs. She counted the seconds to his reply, always ten when he was working, as though it took this long for her words to reach him.

'Sure thing, baby,' it wafted down eventually. 'Be careful.'

Be careful? What could she possibly get up to here? She wandered out on to the wide porch, a summer seat swinging gently in the breeze. The prairie grasses whispered and sang; a wild duck flew low over the horizon.

She missed Pascale badly. Life seemed so mediocre without her. Despite the rigours of boarding school and how much Aurora disliked it, Pascale always found a way of making things exciting. She could be anywhere with Pascale and enjoy herself.

As Aurora wandered down to the creek, the sun sweltering overhead in its hot blue sky, she wished her best friend were with her. They had slept together numerous times now, but it hadn't affected their relationship. Pascale always acted as if nothing had happened, and after the first few occasions Aurora caught on that this was the way things were: sex was just another thing they did together. At first it had crossed Aurora's mind that she was gay. Despite the number of guys she'd been with, it was possible—look at Lindsay Lohan! But with Pascale it was like she could be a guy or a girl, old or young or thin or fat (maybe not fat) or whatever, it didn't matter. She was just…Pascale. She was fascinating and alluring and you wanted to be with her all the time and that was it. Pascale talked about her boyfriends in Paris and no doubt was screwing one right this minute. Aurora chose not to care. The bond they shared was unbreakable. It was a different thing, separate to the baggage of a conventional partnership.

At the water's edge, she knelt down and trailed her hand through the glittering silver. Her reflection stared up at her. Though the weather in England had done zilch for her skin, Aurora appeared younger than she had before she went away. Her eyes had lost their steeliness, her mouth its cynical line. She saw she was more of a girl again.

'What're you doin' down here?' The strong, lilting Southern accent made Aurora jump. 'It gets dangerous by the water, y'know.'

The man was about forty, broad and well built, and wearing a red and brown lumberjack shirt and work pants. She recognised him as one of the farmhands, Billy-Bob. A real hick: thick as you like, would probably shag anything that moved, but with a hot labourer's body. Perhaps this break didn't have to be so uninspiring, after all. Aurora stood, dusted off her bare knees and fixed him with an ice-blue stare.

'Does Tom know where you've got to?' Billy-Bob asked. He had fair stubble round his chin, on the cusp of growing into a beard.

'How dangerous?' Aurora asked.

Billy-Bob frowned. 'Huh?'

'You said it got dangerous by the water.' She took a step forward. It had been too long since she'd had a man. 'I asked how dangerous.'

He stayed where he was. 'Let's get you back up to the house, little girl.'

Aurora reached out and put a hand on his chest. It was warm and solid. She could feel his steady workman's heart beneath her palm. He didn't flinch.

'I'm good at handling danger, you know,' she murmured. 'I'm good at handling a lot of things.' Her eyes flicked down to his crotch—even through his jeans she could see the size of him. She came closer, pressing herself up against his body. He smelled of sweat and grease, and the invigorating cool of someone who spends their time out-doors. Sure enough, he stiffened.

Billy-Bob glanced over his shoulder once or twice, seemed to think for a moment, before fumbling with the buckle on his belt. Aurora smirked. Men were so easy.

Up at Creekside, Tom Nash gazed out of his studio window at the expanse of grassland that ran down to the river. He watched as Billy-Bob Hocker came into view, check shirt sweating from his morning's work, his strong, wide back and the swagger of his gait as he made his way up from the water. As the farmhand rounded the stables, stopping to pat their prize stallion on the nose and scratch the animal's muzzle, Tom backed away from the glass. He felt like the yearning pariah hidden up in the attic, craving a reality that could never be his.

Tom ran a hand across his forehead, imagining it was a slate he could wipe clean. He picked up his favourite Gibson acoustic and started to strum absent-mindedly, reluctantly turning his thoughts to Aurora and wherever she might have got to. He knew he ought to spend more time with his only daughter while she was here, but this darned album wasn't going to write itself.

Ordinarily Tom didn't find the creative process quite so difficult. Perhaps it was because, this time, his wife didn't care about being involved. Sherilyn was too out of it: it was enough for him to get the material down, stick her in front of a recording mic and encourage her to deliver the notes. Or maybe she was still reeling from Aurora's behaviour last year. Even now her legs shook whenever she was forced to venture into the games room back in LA, and he himself thought twice before using any of the pool cues.

On darker days he worried Sherilyn was at risk of blowing the whole thing open, jeopardising all that they had worked for; the reasons why they had made that choice in the first place. And there *were* reasons, of course there were. How could America's number one duo, advocators of good, clean-living Christian ideology, possibly confess to…?

What his wife needed was to get away, drink in some air and stop listening to that shrink Lindy Martin once and for all. He swore Lindy made up all kinds of horse shit to keep Sherilyn coughing up the cash, and the more shit she got fed, the hungrier she became for it. Was he the only sane one left in this family? *Women!* No wonder he was the way he was.

Maybe he'd organise her coming down here by herself for a few days—that might help her get things back on track. They were both concerned for Aurora, but at least school seemed to have calmed her a bit. Even so, what Aurora needed right now, above all else, was her mother.

That reminded him.

Putting down his guitar, Tom opened his desk drawer, pulled out his chequebook and flipped it open. As he did every time, he paused a moment before, teeth gritted, he filled in the amount of money. Writing it in figures was preferable to penning it in full: it was enough to feed a small country for a week. Tom felt nauseous after he'd done it, but this was coupled with a pinch of respite. Another three months before he had to do it again. He could rest easy till then.

He flicked on the radio, hoping for inspiration. Instead, Billy Ray Cyrus blasted into the space. *Sonofabitch!* He slumped back down in front of the equipment. Was it a sign this record was jinxed?

No way. Tom Nash was in a different league. He was a megastar, the heart of the country and western music scene and the core of conservative Uncle Sam. Keep paying the bills, four times a year to make sure they kept quiet, and long may it stay that way.

He checked himself in the mirror.

Billy Ray, eat your heart out. For starters, he had better hair.

Aurora had been back at school a month when she found out she was pregnant.

'You look rough!' diagnosed Eugenie Beaufort in the dining room one morning. Aurora was spooning sugar on to her cereal in an attempt to garner energy. Her body felt wracked and tired, and she was having difficulty keeping food down.

They sent her to the san. Nurse Cranley put her in a horrible room with bars on the windows and a creepy picture of a Pierrot clown on the wall, a drooping yellow flower hanging from its downturned mouth.

'Is there any possibility you're pregnant?' she asked straight away.

'Um, I don't think so,' said Aurora, concentrating solely on not being sick.

'No, or you don't think so?'

'I don't think so.' She got into bed and pulled the starched white linen up to her chin. Nurse Cranley brought her a bucket and told her to stay put.

Pascale visited at lunch with a test. 'I can tell you are without you even doing it.'

'Don't say that,' Aurora groaned.

'Well, I can.'

'How?'

'The colour of your skin.' She helped Aurora sit up and peered down the corridor for approaching staff. 'Better you find out with me than with that old hag. Come on.'

In the bathroom Aurora peed on the little white stick and waited, anxiously twisting her thumbs. Pascale sat with her the whole time, on the edge of the bathtub, and told her when her two minutes were up. Sure enough, two blue lines appeared in the tiny window.

Aurora whimpered. This was the very worst thing that could have happened. She had slept with her dad's farmhand on three occasions while at Creekside, but it was only that first time they'd neglected to use protection. She had to admit she'd been careless with guys before and nothing had happened—trust Billy-Bob Hocker to have some super-sperm potency. Come to think of it, there was every chance he was inbred. Which meant she probably had some six-legged freak scuttling about inside of her.

'What the fuck am I going to do?' she despaired.

Pascale was unfazed. 'You'll have to have an abortion,' she said bluntly.

Aurora's head was spinning. She was too young to have an abortion. The word itself was cold and ugly, reserved for other women, not her. What if it hurt? What if it left her barren?

But she knew she was also too young to have a child. She was still a child herself, for God's sake! And she couldn't deal with a normal baby, let alone one whose dad was also its brother or whatever. There was no other way. Pascale was right. It was the only option.

'My mom and dad can't know,' she said, still sitting on the loo with her knickers down by her ankles. 'They'll murder me.'

'Don't worry, my parents will organise it.' Pascale stood. 'They'll organise everything. They've done it for me before.'

Aurora looked up. '*You've* had one?'

'Two, actually.' She paused. 'The only way you can keep this to yourself is if we take it out of school. Come to Paris for the weekend. All we have to say then is that you got sick again and needed to stay in the apartment. When you're better, you can come back.'

Aurora chewed her lip. 'You'd do that for me?' She

thought of Gisele and Arnaud Devereux, those fierce, powerful politicians of whom everyone seemed afraid. '*They'd* do that for me?'

'Of course.' Pascale shrugged, plucking the stick out of her hand. 'You're my friend. But for now we need to get rid of this. Quickly.'

Girls weren't typically permitted to get out of school for the weekend unless it was exeat, but clearly the Devereux family commanded exception. One phone call from Arnaud Devereux, combined with an expertly forged note by Pascale on Sherilyn Rose's behalf, and the trip was organised for Friday. The girls would travel down to London's Kings Cross, where they'd take a first-class Eurostar shuttle to the heart of the French capital. Aurora would have been excited were she not so horrified. At night she tried to sleep, that ugly word 'abortion' looping over and over in her mind, keeping her awake, staring into the dark and listening to her dorm-mates' gentle, untroubled breathing.

Aurora decided not to think of the germ of life inside her—because it wasn't alive, not really, not yet. Unexpectedly Sherilyn and Tom's inability to have any more kids popped into her head and she endured an irrational twist of guilt. It was stupid. What did she fancy herself to be, some surrogate for her own mother? The thought was fucking ludicrous. Going to Paris, getting the abortion, it was the right thing to do.

The night before they left, one of Tom Nash's old music videos came on in the common room. Everyone jeered as his leather-clad body ground to the screaming crowd of overweight Middle America. A pair of knickers got thrown at him. Aurora bolted, unable to take either the embarrassment or the guilt trip, as Tom gazed into the camera, beseeching, seeming to ask her, *Why?* Sure, she'd misbehaved before, she'd done bad things, but nothing that came close to this. This wasn't a stupid lie like the ones she told her dad from time to time—this was serious. Would she ever again be able to look him in the eye?

In Pascale's room, they packed. Aurora had brought along her designer cases but Pascale advised her to keep it compact: they were supposedly only going for two nights and didn't want to give themselves away before they'd even left.

'You can wear whatever of mine is in the Paris apartment,' said Pascale. 'Or my mother has plenty of clothes.'

From her friend's bedside table, Aurora picked up a framed photograph of two men and a woman. One of the men—Arnaud Devereux, she guessed—had his arm round the woman. They possessed serious, angular features, and judicious, though not unfriendly, faces.

'Is this them?' she asked.

Pascale nodded.

'Who's he?' She pointed to the man standing with them, a small distance away though she imagined the photographer had told them to pose together. He was younger, maybe thirty, and shared some of their physiognomy—you could tell they were related. But where Arnaud and Gisele had softer edges to their expressions, this man did not. He was arresting to look at, almost unkind. A deep scar ran between his nose and top lip.

'That's my cousin,' said Pascale, folding a dress into her Mulberry valise. 'JB.'

'Is he close to your parents?'

'His own parents are dead.'

Aurora put the photo back down. 'He's the one who told you that story.'

'What story?'

'The one about the Devil in the Dordogne.'

Pascale smiled in a way Aurora disliked: as though Aurora was missing some obvious point. '*I* told you that story.'

'But he told it to you first. He told you the Devil had come to get you…and that's what made you afraid.'

Pascale zipped up her bag, and, with it, the conversation. 'I was never afraid.'

A throng of chattering girls bustled into the dorm, squealing and laughing over a minor rebellion. Aurora and Pascale scooped up their bags and took them downstairs to the hall, ready for tomorrow's pick-up.

They went to the bushes for a cigarette and smoked in silence, each girl lost in her own thoughts and not quite ready to share them.

23
Stevie

Marty introduced her to Xander Jakobson over lunch at The Ivy. At thirty-two, Xander was a young writer/director who had made his name in a popular US sitcom about doctors. He was very dark, Jewish, and had a serious, searching stare that made him look as if he was about to ask some examining question of the person at the end of it.

Xander's new movie was a sharp, satirical spin on life on the Vegas Strip. Stevie was in talks for the lead role: a showgirl with a troubled past who receives an irresistible offer from a mysterious stranger. The script attracted her straight away: it was clever, daring and empowering. Xander had managed to get inside the female head seamlessly, every word, every feeling, rang true. The showgirl's character combined everything that Stevie recognised from her own experiences of falling in love with the wrong man. She knew it would echo through the hearts of women everywhere. According to Marty, it signalled a break-through project for both of them.

The following Friday, her agent called with news that she had the part.

'You're going to *Vegas*?' Ben Reiner whined. These days he barely left the apartment, slumping into evidence mid-afternoon following a heavy night in which he'd drunk what little money he had, or having spent a morning in a marathon session with a box of tissues and his repulsive downloads—sometimes both. Stevie could no longer stand him.

'Yes,' she answered tersely. 'And it's probably for the best.'

'Who's gonna get the food in?' he muttered, yanking open the fridge and surveying its scant contents.

'You could buy stuff,' she said. 'It's not that difficult.'

'We're not all rolling in it,' he retorted snappily.

Stevie knew her own career was highlighting a bitter contrast with Ben's, but it seemed she couldn't win. If she were sitting in the LA apartment all day, out of work, sure, it might make him feel better. But who, then, would pay all the bills and provide him with endless pizza takeaway and Oreo cookies? All he seemed to do was hole up with the blinds drawn, watching DVDs and eating Ben & Jerry's. It was like he had a permanent bout of PMT.

Vegas was a welcome alternative.

The cast and their entourage were being put up in the Desert Jewel Hotel, a monster enterprise on the North Strip. Stevie was met by Wanda Gerund, her PR, a glossy brunette with all the chat and charm of an exemplary pub-licist, but with Rottweiler tenacity.

'We've promised the press a photo op this afternoon,' Wanda said once they were up in Stevie's suite. 'Save us all the pleasure of them trailing you about on-set.'

Stevie was too busy absorbing her surroundings. It was her first time in Sin City and the awesomeness of it surpassed her expectations. She'd never seen anything like it. People claimed the old glamour had faded, and that nowadays it was less the mob and more Mickey Mouse, but no one could deny the sheer *ambition* of it. With its kitsch cabarets, novelty hotels and the relentless drum of the casinos, it was the sort of place she ought to have felt uncomfortable. Certainly where the shy girl who'd arrived in New York last year would have felt uncomfortable. Now here she was, amid the opulence, *part* of it, an actress with her own publicist. It was mad.

'This is unbelievable,' she murmured as she checked out the enormous silky-gold bed, fully stocked bar and lavish bathroom complete with Jacuzzi and steam.

'Yeah.' Wanda was punching digits into her BlackBerry. She'd seen it all before, found it rather hideous, actually. 'Welcome to Vegas.'

Under Xander's direction, filming turned out to be the best experience of Stevie's life. They were shooting in a purpose-built auditorium that in reality felt a little like a project put together with scissors and sticky-back plastic, but on camera got elevated to the calibre of Vegas's finest theatres. Stevie's was a varied part: she'd be singing one minute and crying the next. She'd go from dancing in sequins to spilling vitriol in a conversation with her estranged mother; from pulling off a jubilant performance to going backstage and finding her best friend with a needle in her arm; from falling in love to falling into dark despair. She was mesmerising, able to embody the role without reservation. Cast and crew were impressed by her humility, her beauty, and an aptitude, despite her early misgivings, that was God-given.

Xander demanded total focus from his actors. Stevie caught on quick that he was a perfectionist, but he was also fair. He was uncompromising in his vision, particularly in regard to her character's love affair, and every last detail was considered and approved. She decided this script had been a long time in the making, and it revealed something of Xander himself, though she didn't know him well enough to tell what that was.

In any case, his methods commanded respect. People worked hard for him. There was a sense of pulling together for a shared cause, something she hadn't experienced in her debut.

A week into shooting, Xander pulled Stevie to one side. They were in the middle of getting her pivotal love scene in the can.

'How do you feel about top-half nudity?' he asked, straight to the point.

It wasn't the fact that nudity hadn't been addressed in Stevie's contract, nor was it the fact she might have a problem with it. All she could think about was how it might feel getting naked in front of someone on whom, she realised now—with a curious mix of surprise and relief—she had a monolithic crush.

'Well, I…' She wasn't sure what to say.

'The scene isn't working as it's written,' explained Xander, brows gathered in concentration, tapping his bundle of notes with a pen. 'It's unnatural. I'm concerned we're forcing the modesty.' He glanced up at her. 'That said, you've no obligation. The last thing I want is for you to feel uncomfortable. It's your role and your call—I only want your view.'

She nodded. 'I don't have an issue with it.' And she didn't: nothing about Xander's script or style of working was gratuitous, and this was no different. The scene hadn't been working for her either—it was a passionate, obsessive moment between two soul mates, and, while in theory it worked without exposing skin, in practice it felt contrived.

'If I speak to Tyler, would you be happy to try it out, see how it fits?' Tyler was her male lead. In real life he was gay as Christmas. 'If you feel unhappy at any point, shout out.'

Xander was right. The scene was shot in one and Stevie was pleased with the wrap. Privately she blushed when she saw it. Tyler's fervent kissing, his hand unclasping the neck of her dress, the material falling to reveal her breast… and then cut. She wasn't embarrassed because of the eroticism—in fact she found love scenes straightforward. She was embarrassed because to her it was plain that the ecstasy on her face was from imagining Xander Jakobson was caught in the moment with her; what he might have felt or thought when she was exposed like that. It was the first time since leaving London that she had wanted to get to know a man—really get to know him, because he interested her. It was different from before. Xander was considerate and smart and sincere. He was down the line.

'You're brilliant,' Xander told her afterwards. 'It's rare I see talent like yours. Honestly,' he added when she brushed the compliment off. 'It's easy to see why Marty snapped you up.'

'That's kind.'

'Only stating a fact.' He was wearing a baseball cap, which he now took off, ruffling his hair, which was messy and sticking up at a strange angle at the back.

'Weird to think how it happened,' she said. 'I never imagined any of this when I moved.'

'So I read. Desk job in London, right?'

Stevie flinched at the reference. 'Yeah. Long time ago.' She tried a smile. Xander was regarding her fixedly, so she added, 'Well, I guess not. Just seems that way.'

'Life changes quickly, huh?'

'You could say that.'

Did Xander have a girlfriend? She wasn't sure. He hadn't mentioned one, but then that didn't mean anything. Someone like him must have a girlfriend.

'Are you going to the Fashion Awards tomorrow?' she asked, grappling for something to say. Frontline Fashion was a charity gala in aid of American troops based abroad. This year Vegas was host city and all the big names in town would be there.

Xander's demeanour instantly changed. He stiffened and looked away. 'No.'

Stevie felt like a teenager who didn't see the point of attending a party unless her crush was going to be there. She tried to hide her disappointment. 'Oh. OK.'

Xander must have sensed that he'd come across rude, because he elaborated, 'I don't go in for that kind of thing.'

'Celebrity parties?' It figured.

'Some.' His body language was utterly new. Gone was the easy confidence. He appeared nervous, jumpy. 'It depends who's going.'

Stevie made a dick of herself by misunderstanding. 'I'm going.' It sounded horribly, pointlessly, flirtatious.

Luckily, he smiled, but there was little humour in it. 'You're not who I'm worried about.'

'Oh?'

Xander thought twice before speaking. 'Old adversaries,' he said, and the words seemed weighty, laced in shadow, as though they'd been left a long time in the dark. 'It's boring.'

Stevie frowned. 'I'm sure it's not.'

'The guy running it—we, er, don't see eye to eye. Long story.'

She recalled seeing a picture of him once. Cool eyes, a sharp suit. She had read about him in a magazine, his surname as synonymous with the fashion world as Versace, Armani, Lacroix. *Moreau.* Since his parents were killed, he had become the reluctant face.

What history could Xander possibly share with JB Moreau? It was too soon to pry.

'I'll have to be careful, then, won't I?' she teased.

He didn't return her smile. 'You will.'

24
Lori

'*I'd like you to meet Lori Garcia...*'

Shocked and flustered, caught off-guard, Lori had been unable to form the words she'd envisaged herself saying a thousand times. Even if she had, what would have been the point?

JB Moreau had pretended not to know her. He had met her gaze and extended his hand, those still blue eyes regarding her without a hint of recognition. Blankly, she had accepted it, thrown off course by the unexpectedness of a coincidence she could not understand.

'*Lori's the girl I found in Spain. We've taken her picture, she's a natural.*'

If he was surprised, he hadn't shown it. If he remembered, he'd given nothing away.

Lori's mouth had gone dry. Her throat had closed up.

'*It's a pleasure,*' he'd said. '*I hope we've been looking after you.*'

Dazed, she'd nodded. Later, she would wish she hadn't, for the moment she consented to their introduction it became impossible to claim what had passed before.

JB's skin had been dry and cool. Her own hot. As their hands had connected, she'd recalled his touch that day in the car, how unbridled they had been, all over each other, the temptation they had been powerless to resist. She knew he'd felt it too: if she knew anything, it was that.

How she had wanted to blurt, *'It's me, don't you remember?'* Instead, just a burning humiliation, like a child in trouble though they didn't understand why.

Lori could not make sense of it. She got that he was an important man, more so than she could have anticipated, and that with Desideria standing right there it was never going to be an impassioned reunion—after all, the nature of their first meeting was hardly something he'd be prepared to advertise. Yet, even now, weeks down the line, he had made no attempt to see her. Seeking him out through La Lumière was impossible. His army of personnel— mostly, to her agony, long-limbed women with possessive, mistrustful eyes—made sure of that. Besides, it would make her feel like some kind of stalker, a kid with a crush, a desperate admirer. It wasn't as if she were the only girl at the agency fixated with Moreau. Everyone was.

Didn't she deserve an explanation? He had entered her life—the circumstances of which, now she knew his identity, were more perplexing than ever—and left it in pieces. She had tried everything she could to explain his dismissal, clinging on to the vain hope that he would eventually make contact and extinguish the misery of her pining. He didn't.

Lori's appetite vanished. She wasn't sleeping. At night, in her apartment, she would stay awake for hours trying to picture his face, trying so hard that the details imploded and JB Moreau morphed in her uncertain half-dreams into Rico, her sisters, Desideria, sometimes even herself. When sleep finally claimed her, it would be just for a short while. Woken by desire, she would battle the gnawing ache in her gut—all types of hunger, physical and emotional and sexual—until she gave in, and, thinking of him, would pleasure herself, vowing it to be the last time, ashamed at her craving, addicted to the fleeting relief but frustrated by its impermanence. The only cure for her sickness, for that was what it was, was the man himself.

In darker hours, she became convinced this was her reckoning. It was what she deserved for wronging the man she ought to have stood by. Rico Marquez was languishing in a prison cell because she had refused him help. She, who was supposed to love and uphold him, had run that day and not once looked back. Selfishness, her desire for another man, had overtaken what a small, scared part of her still labelled her duty. She found she was unable to remove the ring her boyfriend had given her, as though it would make her jinxed: a final rejection of her responsibilities. *It's a promise...*

It could not go on. She had to find answers—and, if JB Moreau was not prepared to give them, she would have to uncover them herself.

Desideria wanted her in Vegas for a party the agency had organised. It would be a chance for Lori to meet the industry's notables as well as get a feel for the lifestyle she was set to embrace.

'Learn to adore your celebrity,' said Desideria. 'Because

it might not be tonight, it might not be tomorrow, but sometime soon it'll happen.'

They arrived in Vegas on Friday afternoon. It was the first time Lori had been and the scale and sparkle of the Strip dazzled her. This time a year ago, she'd never have seen herself as part of a world so glamorous. It didn't seem real, just another of the improbable storylines that had kept her going back home, and in a heartbeat she'd wake, bleary-eyed from a midday sleep, resting on the counter at *Tres Hermanas* with the sound of Anita's scolding ringing in her ears.

At the Mirage, they settled into their rooms. Several girls represented by La Lumière were performing in tonight's show and had suites adjacent to Lori's. She had seen them arrive: tall, steel-faced beauties, alarmingly thin; black, white, Asian, all ravishing.

'They seem nervous,' she commented as she and Desideria headed to one of the hotel's magnificent bars. The show was taking place at the Parthenon, a little way down the Strip, but, while a handful of celebrities had already started to arrive, Desideria wanted Lori to hit the carpet a fraction after everyone else.

'That's because they are,' said Desideria. Her hair hung sheer and straight, fluid as oil.

'Of what?'

'Tonight's a big night.' She ordered drinks, vodka martinis with a twist. 'It's the biggest showcase of the Moreau house there is.'

'I thought it was a fundraiser?'

'It is. But it's also a publicity gambit—not just for the fashion line, for the models, too. They've got to make a good impression. It's not every day they get to exhibit their abilities in front of the man himself. It's rare he attends events like this.'

Carefully, Lori sipped her drink. It was strong. 'They want to impress JB.'

'Our girls know what they want. They're ambitious, they've got their heads screwed on—they're not puppets in lipgloss. But, even so, the minute they clap eyes on Moreau it all goes out the window.' Desideria watched her sideways. 'I hope that's not going to happen to you.'

Lori laughed. It hit an odd pitch, like an instrument being tuned.

'All he has to do is snap his fingers and they come running. It's the French thing: that accent ought to carry a health warning. And they think he's what they want, you know? Rich, handsome, driven, successful...' She shrugged. 'The next day, they're history.'

Lori felt sick. 'He's known a lot of women?' she asked.

But not in the way he knows me. He didn't do for them what he did for me.

Desideria nearly spluttered out her martini. 'What are we in, the nineteenth century? Honey, he's known them and *then* some. Are you getting the picture?' Her expression was grave, her voice soft. 'Look, you're a sweet girl. I like you. I don't want you getting hurt. Do you hear what I'm saying?'

She nodded.

Desideria reached for her hand. She opened her mouth to speak, lowered her gaze then closed it again. In her eyes was a glimmer of conflict, as though she wanted to say something but couldn't.

'Just be careful. OK?'

* * *

The women took a cab to the Parthenon. Desideria had a brief word with the La Lumière officials manning the carpet and ushered Lori in between a Czech supermodel and a movie star couple who were friends of Stefano Gabbana.

She had dressed in vintage Moreau: a dusky pink off-the-shoulder figure-skimming dress, her hair harnessed in a loose bun below one ear, its darkness offset by a blooming lilac flower. It was a simple look, one that showed off her coppery skin and exotic black eyes, in one glance a virginal Spanish girl-next-door, in another an icon.

Cameras danced and throbbed, the wall of paparazzi a moving shadow giving way to bursts of light. Desideria had told them her name and they shouted it again and again.

'You starting to believe it now?' she asked, placing a hand on Lori's arm once they were inside the lobby. Trays of champagne circulated; jewels glittered and gowns shimmered like light on water; TV crews interviewed the biggest names in the industy. Everywhere she turned, Lori saw faces she recognised. All except his.

'Believe what?'

'That you're going to be as famous as them all,' said Desideria, collecting two flutes from a passing tray. 'More, I should think. You're incredible-looking, Lori.' Her eyes flashed. 'You know that's what I think.'

Not for the first time, Lori had to drag her gaze from the other woman's. She didn't know much about Desideria's private life and didn't want to make assumptions.

There was a reason he avoided nights like this.

The spotlight—that solitary, staring eye—was a lonely place to be. Everyone here, despite their wealth and riches and glamorous connections, craved its heat and at the same time despised its scrutiny. It was a trap he had become adept at eluding. JB Moreau was in the business of not getting caught.

Nevertheless, his evasion fuelled their gossip. WHO IS JB MOREAU? headlines demanded. MOREAU HEIR AN ENIGMA. Speculation raged on his whereabouts and how he spent his time. MOREAU IN SECRET CULT was a popular line the previous year. FRENCH TYCOON HOLIDAYS IN SPACE. Or, less imaginative: ORPHAN MOREAU RETURNS TO FRANCE TO SCENE OF PARENTS' DEATHS. Then, last month, his favourite: JB MOREAU ACQUIRES REMOTE TERRITORY TO INITIATE CLANDESTINE BUSINESS.

That was the closest they had got. Even the prowling eye of the media could never guess at the truth. Hacks were hacks: they wanted a quick, easy story. If the curtain were ever pulled up on Cacatra, its ruse exposed, he doubted they could even find the vocabulary to write it up.

For a man ill at ease on a public stage, JB didn't let it show. Making his way through the teeming lobby, graciously greeting acquaintances, he played a perfect game. Absence and reappearance: the oldest trick there was. A white rabbit out of a hat. JB's charm, his intelligence and his brutal beauty were quick to secure the devotion of women and the admiration of men.

Poise and proficiency ran through his veins. From the earliest point, JB had been treated like a man and expected to behave like one. Infancy had been nothing of the sort, an inconvenient prelude to the time when he would eventually become useful. His parents, the notorious Paul and Emilie, would be absent for months on end, working, travelling, honeymooning. There'd been no brothers or sisters—he, the accident child, was enough of an exasperation—and for long stretches he'd been left alone, until, at the age of five, he'd been sent away to a series of international academies. There had never been time to be young. Life was a challenging issue and the sooner that was realised and confronted, the better.

Another reason why JB resisted attending parties: the industry's unrelenting interest in the Moreaus and their legacy. His upbringing was not a territory he wished to revisit.

Do you remember them fondly? *They were my parents.*

What does such a tragedy do to a teenage boy? *It was a difficult time. Painful.*

How have they inspired you? *I choose my own inspiration.*

He was steered into an interview with a rampant TV crew. Tonight's gala was in aid of troops fighting abroad, a fund-and-awareness-raiser.

'What is Frontline Fashion hoping to achieve, Mr Moreau?'

The reporter was new on the job. JB had a way of separating the green from the ripe like sorting buttons. Inexperience was something he could sense.

'This evening is about demonstrating our support,' he replied, 'to the men and women risking everything, miles away from home. Fashion might seem an unorthodox approach, but it's what we do and we do it well. Every industry should be looking to offer assistance to the forces.'

'Are you planning a stay in Vegas?'

'No.' He smiled on one side of his scar. 'Vegas and I don't get along.'

'Are you a gambling man, Mr Moreau?'

'Only when I know I can win.'

The reporter couldn't help himself. 'Reuben van der Meyde was a close friend of your father's. Is that why he's with you tonight?'

One of JB's assistants moved him along. 'That's all,' she sharply told the crew.

As they slipped into another interview, JB glimpsed Lori Garcia across the room. Careful not to look too long, he focused on the dialogue at hand. For the moment, at least, she was safe in conversation with Desideria Gomez. Right now she was too scared and confused to dare confront him—and he was counting on it. He knew he could not guarantee her silence for ever.

JB had not wanted her here. Yet what choice did he have? He should never have become involved. He should have walked away, turned his back and left her alone to her fate. It was beyond unprofessional to target a possibility so brazenly, and if JB could hold one thing aloft and claim it was entire, it was his professionalism. But to see her so helpless, so desperate—and he could not imagine what might have happened had he not intervened—for only the second time in JB Moreau's life, impulse had reigned over logic. Against every principle on which Cacatra thrived, Lori Garcia had seen his face, he had spoken to her, and the path he had taken to reach her had become one he could never retrace.

Perhaps then, afterwards, he could have let it lie. *He should have let it lie.*

Only it wasn't that easy. He had to make sure she was safe, just as he'd promised. It was a question of protection…

An acclaimed designer had pinioned him in conversation. Among JB's abilities was sustaining a conversation while considering another matter entirely, and he managed to conduct himself with characteristic ease. In any case, he found that people were most content when they were talking about themselves.

Soon as the man drifted off, his wife wasted no time in making her move.

'You and me,' Arabella Kline murmured huskily, leaning in so he could detect the cloying fragrance behind her ears, 'after the show.'

They had shared nights together before. She was a brittle lover, but capable.

Taking her hand, JB slipped a fold of paper into her palm.

'You know where I'll be.'

Lori was seated five rows back from, but directly behind, JB Moreau.

With his entrance, the theatre had fallen quiet. Despite the hundreds of guests, the excited babble of conversation and the anticipation of the night ahead, a reverential hush had descended. JB was that breed of man that demands veneration without even trying. It was a grace, an impression: an abstract thing. Lori understood for the first time what it meant to have *it*.

JB had it. He had it in spades.

Centre-front by the catwalk, he was flanked on one side by a middle-aged woman with a deep red chignon, gazing straight ahead with an expression still and sad. On his other was an unshaven, slightly scruffy but gamely suited Reuben van der Meyde, the world-famous entrepreneur.

Lori recognised him from the magazine piece on Cacatra Island.

'I didn't know Reuben van der Meyde had an interest in fashion,' she whispered.

'Van der Meyde has an interest in anything that makes money,' Desideria replied. 'He's in with all the major Hollywood players.'

'Really? Who?'

'Dirk Michaels, Linus Posen... They were a four-man gang back in the eighties. All the powerhouses, drinking, partying...no doubt womanising.'

'And the fourth?'

'Paul Moreau. JB's father. Van der Meyde and the Moreau family go way back.'

'How did they meet?'

'Who?'

'JB and Reuben.'

'I'm not sure,' said Desideria, bemused by her questioning. 'I know he was around when JB was growing up. The Moreaus would vacation on his island.'

'Cacatra seems like a beautiful place.'

'Hopefully you'll never need to go.' At Lori's expression, she went on, 'Cacatra is the finest rehab facility money can buy. Celebrities use it for recovery—pure isolation, no vice, no distraction, *nada*. Van der Meyde's got his own stake of nirvana. Who says you can't buy paradise? Clever guy.'

Up front, Reuben was fidgeting, digging about in his ears and shifting in his seat. He made a marked contrast to the woman on JB's other side, who sat so immovable and solemn it was as if she were made of wax.

'He doesn't look that clever,' she suggested. 'He looks like a boy.'

Desideria rested a hand on Lori's knee. 'That's what makes it clever, I suppose.'

Lori watched the back of JB's head: the dirty-blond hair cut precisely above the collar of his shirt, the angle where the skin below his ear caught the hollow of his jaw.

Who are you? What are you hiding?

Before the lights dimmed, JB took the podium. Lori was aware of Desideria's hand still on her dress and withdrew under the pretence of crossing her legs. As she did so she exchanged glances with Stevie Speller in the bank opposite. The women smiled at each other.

Silence enveloped the space without needing to be summoned.

JB glowed beneath a single spotbulb. When he dipped his head it emphasised the carve of his features. Lori felt herself opening up to him, a flower to sunlight.

'When I was a boy,' he began, his accent hypnotic, 'my uncle asked me what courage was.' A beat. 'I told him what I believed. That it was being brave.' The quiet was absolute. 'Yes, he said, but what is being brave? I told him it was when the helpless need our help.'

His words came back to her. *I'm not going to hurt you.*

'Like an animal, my uncle prompted, when it's sick? Yes, I agreed, like that. Even when you are afraid? Even when you don't know if your help will be enough? Yes, I said. Even then.'

You're safe with me.

The hush was profound. JB allowed it to stand before continuing.

'As I grew up, so did the analogy. Animals evolved into people. Sickness became more than disease. It became corruption and sorrow. It became poverty...'

Lori was unable to tear herself from the way his mouth moved as he talked, the scar and the starlit eyes, which in dim surroundings seemed to glow brighter, like something nocturnal. If she could memorise every line, every contour, she could fold it away till later, when she could unravel the image and lay it flat, examine it, savour it, in the only way she knew.

You'll be all right...

'And so, too, did courage take on new meaning. Bravery was not as easy as it had been once upon a time, no longer a simple question of rescue or relief. For how can we be sure of the right time to move? How can we be certain our help will be welcomed? Help is only what it means to the person receiving it—in all other ways, a martyr's illusion.'

I'll make sure of it...

'Tonight, while we celebrate, far away in a distant country, ordinary people are forfeiting their lives.' He paused. 'I didn't know it when I was a boy, but that is what courage means truly. It means sacrifice.'

I always will...

'Help is not an easy thing to give. Courage is not an easy thing to have. But that does not detract from my certainty that they are the two most important assets we as humans possess. Through the works you are about to see, the feats in invention and creativity, the House of Moreau and its affiliates pledge their allegiance to both. I hope you will join me.'

The audience erupted in applause. JB stepped away. Aside from a short nod of acknowledgement, he remained impassive. He reminded Lori of a stone in a river, water rushing between and around, smooth and solid against the flux.

The show began. Lights drenched the runway. Music thumped, heralding the arrival of the models. Clad in the latest trends, six-foot-tall beauties, men, women and something in between swaggered down the walk. A pose at the end, photographers snapping, those sharp angles of elbows and shoulders and swan-like necks. All the while Lori sought JB's response—what he was looking at, what interested him; the outfits and models that made him react. She wanted to be up there, having him see her. She wanted him to remember what they had shared, to say to van der Meyde, *That's the girl I met. The one I told you about.*

She had to find a way.

Lori didn't stay long at the after party. She was tired and any hopes she had of talking to JB evaporated when Desideria told her he was dining with sponsors and wouldn't be around till later. She decided to go back to the hotel—it had been a long day.

Desideria insisted on coming with her. They took a car to the Mirage. Desideria tried to persuade her to indulge in a nightcap, a game of blackjack, but Lori was dead on her feet.

At the door to her suite, the older woman leaned in for an embrace. She smelled of cigarettes and aniseed. Several uncomfortable moments passed before Lori tried to ease her off, but Desideria renewed her hold, pulling their bodies closer till Lori could feel the squash of her breasts against a pair of much flatter, harder ones. Desideria must have felt it too, because she released an involuntary, guttural sound and buried her face in Lori's neck, swaying slightly.

'Do you want me to stay?' she whispered, her breath hot and ragged.

Lori pushed gently. 'That's not a good idea.'

'I know you're a virgin.' Without warning Desideria's hands flew to Lori's ass and clasped. 'I know a lot about you, sweetheart. More than I should.'

Lori attempted to wriggle free. 'I don't want to offend you. Please...'

'Then don't. I can show you things, Loriana. Things a man never could. The moment I met you, I wanted you. Couldn't you sense it? Forgive me. I can't help the way I feel. Whenever I see you I want to touch your lips, your beautiful breasts... I want to love you with my mouth and taste you and teach you the things I long for you to know...'

'No.' Lori shoved her this time. 'I don't have those feelings for you... I'm sorry, I don't.' It didn't matter if it was Rico or Desideria or whoever it was, why couldn't people take no for an answer? She wasn't ready. She was a virgin. At least, she hoped she still was. The things she did to herself...they didn't count, did they? No. She was saving herself.

For who?

For him.

Desideria was hurt. 'I see.'

'I like you,' explained Lori, wondering why she was the one making amends. 'But not in that way.'

'I'm not sure what I was thinking,' responded Desideria tightly.

'Let's forget it.' Lori hoped they could. 'See you tomorrow?'

'Sure. Tomorrow.'

Lori closed the door and rested against it. She was aware of the other woman waiting outside, for a minute at least, before her footsteps padded quietly away.

* * *

Three a.m. The dead hour.

JB Moreau stood from the bed, looking down at the sleek contours of Arabella Kline's naked back. Her golden hair was swept across one bronzed shoulder, a white sheet gathered round her waist. Soundly, she dreamed.

They'd had sex for hours, hard and urgent, the release that both of them craved. Only, JB had never been one for sleeping after he fucked. Fucking left him empty, the pointlessness of it once the fact was done. Little existed between him and Arabella, just a concise encounter every now and again that, for all the heat and skin and fervour of the moment, meant, in the lonely hours, nothing at all.

His suite at the Orient Hotel overlooked the Strip. Pulling on a pair of jogging pants and silently sliding the balcony doors, JB stepped outside. He inhaled. At the apex of Vegas's grandest enterprise, it was possible to see the entire sprawl of Sin City, her vast array of sparkling lights and golden spires and summits. And yet not a soul could see him.

It was the way of his life. Always the observer, never the observed.

The blinking red light of an aeroplane passed across the night sky. JB rested his elbows on the terrace rail and gazed up at a star-pricked dome.

They'd said it about him since he was a child. He was a closed book, a distant ship. Something missing. At first, shy. Later, disconnected. A conversation he'd overheard one summer, when he was back in France on school vacation, hovering unseen by the drawing-room door, his mother and father discussing him in hushed tones while they drank gin cocktails and planned their next party and hadn't a clue who their only son was.

The boy has no heart.

And people said it again, and again, after the accident. *What's wrong with him? Any other child would be in pieces...*

Some time ago, he had started to believe it himself. It was easier to be fixed against the memories of the past. Easier to freeze over. He was missing something, of course, had always missed it, because it had never been given to him.

And there were times, like now, when he was looking over the city and feeling as if this ought to be right, a destination of some kind, that the hollow in JB threatened to consume him entirely. He thought of Lori, so different from the women in his life, those tough, grasping women against whom her innocence shone like dawn. She drew him, had drawn him ever since the first time he'd laid eyes on her at the San Pedro harbour with her boyfriend. It was her goodness, her kindness, for he had watched her for weeks and come to know the hardships she faced, and in a lifetime of building walls he had begun, piece by piece, to dismantle.

Little wonder he had given in to temptation. It was impossible to forget the way she had kissed him that day, her eyes like the ocean, a blink and he was beneath the surface, treading water, leagues of silence underfoot. Peace.

Despite the inconceivability of their situation, how he could never have her, not in this lifetime or the next, JB knew he could not have abandoned her that day. Vulnerable, a girl.

Look what had happened the last time he had done that.

25
Aurora

Aurora and Pascale arrived at Gare du Nord in Paris early Friday evening. Aurora was tipsy after the champagne Pascale had insisted on getting on the Eurostar (a little inappropriately, she thought), nevertheless it was probably better that way. Whenever she remembered the reason she was here, the A-word, she felt even sicker than normal. She was unable to address her fears with Pascale: Pascale had undergone two of these things in the past—what was the big deal?

Arnaud and Gisele Devereux had sent their chauffeur, a hot young Parisian called Alex, to pick them up. Pascale clearly knew Alex well and nattered away in French as they sped to the couple's apartment in Montmartre.

Aurora was accustomed to luxury, but only of a certain type. She had grown up around money, lots of it, and all the shiny wonderful things it could buy. But she hadn't grown up around sophistication, or taste, or, dare she say it, class, and when those things were combined with cash, the results were potent. Pascale's parents lived in a converted penthouse at the very top of one of Montmartre's oldest buildings. The apartment was enormous. It was filled with art. You could see the whole of Paris from an oval window: the glittering spike of the Eiffel Tower, the twin columns of Notre Dame and the silky twist of the Seine.

Alex noticed Aurora's expression. *'C'est jolie, n'est-ce-pas?'*

Aurora didn't know what he was on about, though she did know that Angelina Jolie's surname meant 'pretty'.

'Yeah...*très.*'

'A bientôt!' Pascale called to Alex when he left. She turned to Aurora and snorted unkindly. '"*Très*"? You're going to have to do better than that. There's nothing worse than an American who can't be bothered to speak the language.' She padded into the kitchen and pulled open the fridge. It was less of a fridge and more of a chilled room, wall-to-wall filled with supplies, from bottles upon bottles of Veuve Clicquot to little jars of *cornichons* and caviar. 'My parents will fully expect you to know the basics.'

Aurora was horrified. She tried to play it cool, though secretly she was shitting it about meeting the fearsome Devereux couple. No doubt they were out right now with the president or something. (Did France have a president? Or was that a prime minister? She wasn't sure.)

'What, like *oui* and *non*?' Her accent was dreadful. 'And *sieve-oo-play*?'

'I wasn't going to turn up in England not speaking a word, was I?' Pascale grabbed a couple of glasses and popped open yet another bottle of champagne. 'It's a courtesy.'

'I suppose.'

'Anyway.' Pascale lit a cigarette. 'You'll get the hang of it. Want one?'

Aurora was shown to one of the guest bedrooms, a pearly-pink princess of a room complete with golden candelabra and a four-poster bed. She had visited Paris with her parents before, ages ago when they'd been on tour in Europe, but she'd been holed up in a hotel for most of it eating novelty French chips out of a bucket and watching MTV. Tom and Sherilyn had spent the whole trip sniping, as if actually having to spend that much time in each other's company was too much for either of them, and the only mitigation had been Tom taking her to EuroDisney on their last weekend. Needless to say, her mom hadn't come.

Now, as Aurora explored the costly antique furnishings and claw-footed tub in the bathroom, she wondered how people knew where to *get* this stuff. It was, like, easy enough to spend money on cars and shoes and what everyone *said* you ought to have, but these things came from someone's personality. And that personality was elegant, refined…all the things she, and her own family, weren't.

She was unpacking when she heard the door go, followed by a flutter of greetings in French. Aurora heard her own name occasionally puncturing the surface, the Rs making it sound like someone clearing their throat—*'Or-hor-ha'*. She stepped out to meet them.

Pascale and her mother were smoking, Gisele still in her coat, slim cigarette held between the long fingers of a chocolate-leather glove. They were chatting more like sisters than mother and daughter, so similar in appearance, both raven-haired, both petite, and with a fast, matter-of-fact way of speaking. Arnaud was pouring brandies. He was extremely French in appearance, and didn't smile when he saw Aurora. Grey-haired, lean, rangy. Long nose. Liquid eyes. A white linen shirt that was open at the neck, a thin gold chain resting on the crinkled skin.

Pascale jumped up. 'Maman, Papa, meet Aurora Nash, *ma meilleure amie.*'

Gisele embraced her. 'A best friend of Pascale's is a best friend of ours,' she said. Her voice was sweet and girlish, but you knew she could drop it in a second and eat you for breakfast. 'Did you have a good trip?'

'Uh…*oui, merci. Très bien. Merci.*'

Pascale rolled her eyes but Aurora didn't know what she'd done wrong. Arnaud extended his hand and she shook it. *'Bonsoir.'*

They had dinner—or, three of them did; Gisele just smoked—and Pascale talked about school, sometimes in French, sometimes in English, and Aurora contributed where she could. She wasn't used to feeling self-conscious or like a sitting idiot: normally she was the one in control. In fact she'd never felt inadequate before in her whole entire life, and that was really the only word. Because despite her wealth and privilege, what did she herself, not her parents, not her PR people, not her rep—what did *she* have to bring to the table?

When Gisele politely enquired after her parents, *'les chanteurs'*, Aurora felt embarrassed. It was horrible to say, but Tom and Sherilyn seemed so cheap and cheesy in comparison with the Devereux lifestyle. Gisele and Arnaud discussed history, politics, art…no wonder their daughter was so well informed and sure of her mind. The only things *her* mom and dad discussed were their record-breaking album sales or the ratio of honey to cinnamon in Tom's hair. And she couldn't remember the last time they had eaten a meal at home together.

She tried to remember as much of Madame Taylor's French lessons as she could. She'd never paid attention, had lost interest during an enforced debate with Eugenie Beaufort over the respective merits of a *croque monsieur* and a *croque madame*. Having to pretend she gave a *croque*.

'*Ils sont...bon...*' she began, before giving up and speaking English slowly.

Pascale interrupted. 'They're fluent in seven languages,' she said witheringly.

Seven? She had barely known there *were* that many. Gisele laughed, not unkindly, and Aurora suddenly longed to clarify that just because Tom Nash and Sherilyn Rose were her parents, she didn't always feel like their child, in fact she hardly felt similar to them at all, and anyway, it didn't mean she had to end up like them, singing corny all-American rock ballads to hordes of hollering housewives. She herself might well end up a member of some high-flying intelligentsia or political cabinet or a writer or artist or something like that. It could happen.

The reason for her visit, the A-word, wasn't mentioned. She felt as if she should, to thank them, but it wasn't the sort of thing you dropped into conversation over *tarte tatin*. Besides, Pascale had assured her it was no big wow, and the only one who thought twice about it was her. Part of her wished her friend could be more sympathetic. But Pascale wasn't a terribly sympathetic person, and why should she get sympathy anyway? It was her own dumb fault.

Once, Arnaud talked about *demain*, and mentioned a *docteur*, but that was it. Aurora went to bed feeling strange in her head and her stomach, and tried very hard not to overthink what she was about to do.

It happened the following morning, the Saturday. Pascale came with her to the private clinic, armed with a stack of French gossip magazines and not appearing fazed by any aspect of it. The doctor performing the procedure, an esteemed private physician with silver hair and capped teeth, was a close friend of Gisele and Arnaud. He was careful to conceal his disapproval.

They used a sucky vacuum-cleaner-type thing. Aurora wasn't sure what she had been expecting—probably something akin to a Caesarean, if she were honest—but in the event it was a rubber sort of tube that they stuck inside her and flushed the growth out with. She didn't want to use the word 'baby', even though the doctor kept saying it. *Bébé*. Why did he have to keep saying that? She wondered how many of these he had done. Had he done Pascale's?

Aurora concentrated on the ceiling. She kept waiting to hear the doctor's horrified gasp as he saw the six-legged freaky inbred whatever-it-was shoot down the tube. But he didn't. It was just a baby. *Bébé*. Or might have been.

A tear slid out the side of her eye and coursed a hot track past her ear. Stupid! Why was she crying? This was a necessary thing. But all the same it made her think about what it might mean to one day become a mother herself. When she'd heard of girls back in LA getting rid of unwanted pregnancies, Aurora had always felt she belonged on some theoretical higher ground: she'd *never* get herself in that sort of situation—what kind of a woman did? And now here she was lying on her back in the middle of France having an abortion.

At that moment Aurora vowed things would change. She was a woman now, not a kid. She'd been foolish in the past, chasing the next thrill without a thought for anyone else, because that was how it worked being Aurora Nash. But this…this *bébé* was a wake-up call. It had to be, otherwise what was the point? What was the point of anything if you could make a life and then get rid of it, the most miraculous thing in the world, just like that, all in a morning while your best friend sat outside reading *Paris Match* and eating pain au chocolat and next week would have forgotten all about it?

Afterwards they gave her some pills and warned her of cramps. Pascale took her back to the apartment and propped her up in bed. Aurora drifted in and out of sleep. At points she was aware of Gisele and Arnaud returning: hours passed, light turned to dark. Her door opened, a silhouetted figure checking on her, the back of Gisele's hand pressed against her forehead, whispering kind words in French. Pascale slept next to her in bed and stroked her hair. Aurora had strange dreams, dreams about rivers travelling into the sea, and woke at four a.m. and sat on the loo and felt all the red stuff fall out. She thought about where the *bébé* had got to. Was it in a bin somewhere? Wrapped in a plastic bag? She knew it was just a blob, it wasn't really a person, but she had it in her head that way so it was difficult to get rid of.

Sunday morning, she felt a bit better. Pascale had to go back to St Agnes and Gisele telephoned Mrs Stoker-Leach to tell her Aurora had been beset by a further bout of flu and would be remaining in Paris for a few days.

'Don't be long or I'll kill myself,' Pascale informed her when she departed.

'See you in a few days,' Aurora promised. Her experience had left her feeling fragile and emotional, like clinging to her friend and saying thank you over and over again. But Pascale hugged her briefly and said goodbye to her mother and was gone. In that moment Aurora knew that when the day came where the girls no longer spent every minute in each other's company, and that day would come, holding on to Pascale would be like holding on to water. Pascale didn't need anyone.

Gisele stayed with her. Around lunchtime Aurora surfaced in a towelling dressing gown and sat on one of the sofas, her legs curled up under her. Her body felt contained that way, more held in. She still felt like her guts were about to fall out all over the carpet whenever she got to her feet.

They drank bitter, grainy coffee and ate sweet biscuits and Gisele told her about when she and Arnaud had met. They'd been eighteen, at university, involved in student politics. It sounded so romantic, so...*intellectual*.

'Was it love at first sight?' Aurora asked, pleased to have another thing to think about.

Gisele was so elegant. She leaned on one elbow and gazed out of the window. 'It was his brother I loved first,' she said, with a little expression of apology. 'Paul.'

'Did they fight over you?'

Gisele laughed. 'No. Paul loved Emilie. We all knew each other—Arnaud and Paul did everything together, same school, same college...but, really, they were very different. Paul and Emilie thought we were very boring, I am sure.' Another laugh, a softer one. 'We loved our sociology, our history, our revolution, the things our country was capable of. They loved fashion and music, money and parties.

But Paul was very handsome. And they say that opposites attract.' She smiled, remembering. 'Well, they did for me.'

'What happened?'

Gisele sipped her coffee. 'He introduced me to his brother, Arnaud. Perhaps he felt sorry for me.' Aurora couldn't imagine anyone feeling sorry for Gisele. 'So Arnaud and I became friends, then lovers. And then we married.' A lift of the shoulders, a half-shrug, as if sometimes that was how life turned out.

'Do you still see his brother?'

Gisele frowned. 'Paul and Emilie died.' Aurora kicked herself—she remembered Pascale telling her that. The cousin's parents dying. That cousin with the scar on his top lip.

'Oh.'

'Paul and Emilie Moreau?' Gisele prompted.

Aurora's mouth fell open. '*The* Paul and Emilie Moreau?' The Moreau fashion house was major league. Aurora had several pieces in her closet at home, each with a price tag that made your eyes water (not that she'd know: her dad had bought them).

'Of course. He and Arnaud had different fathers, hence the name.'

'Shit. I had no idea!' She was shocked. The boating disaster had happened years ago, before she was even born, but it was the stuff of industry legend. So Pascale wasn't just the daughter of famous French politicians, she was also the niece of fashion legend Paul Moreau! And she hadn't mentioned it once!

'The guy in the picture...' She struggled to untangle it. 'There's a photo by Pascale's bed at school. Of you and Arnaud, with a man. He's their son?'

Gisele's manner changed. 'Yes,' she said brusquely. 'Though we hardly see much of him these days.'

Aurora recalled the image. 'Aren't you close?'

'We were.' Gisele stood and took the cups. 'I should say, he and Arnaud were. Arnaud always wanted a son. More coffee?'

'No, thank you.'

'When JB was young,' she said as she made her way into the kitchen, her voice becoming fainter as she disappeared behind the partition, 'we thought he was a troubled child. Some children are. He didn't say much, just used to sit by himself, always by himself. You could tell he was a thinker and he had a good brain, but when people have good brains and they don't share them, you wonder what they are doing with what's inside.' She came back in. 'He liked Pascale, as far as he liked anyone. I wasn't fond of him, but then Arnaud would say, "You cannot think that, he is an eight-year-old boy."'

'And then his parents died?'

'That was later,' she said, resuming her seat. 'JB was fourteen when that happened. Poor thing was on the boat with them. Arnaud stood up for him unconditionally, of course. A tragic accident...' She trailed off.

'But you never liked him?'

'It's not that I never liked him. I just didn't know him. JB Moreau has been in my life for thirty years and I didn't—I don't—feel I know him at all.'

Aurora wanted to find out more. 'He and Arnaud, do they still see each other?'

'Until recently. Several years ago JB became involved in...well, let's just say we didn't approve of what he became involved in. Arnaud has seen less of him since then.'

'What did he get involved in?'

But Gisele wasn't saying. 'Come now, you ought to get dressed.'

'Surely he's in charge of his parents' legacy?'

'Among other things.'

'Like what?'

'Never mind.'

'I want to know.'

'No.' Gisele's vehemence shocked her. 'You don't.' There was a pause wherein it became clear the conversation had ended. The French woman shook her head once, her expression grave, and Aurora knew that she could not be pressed on the subject.

26
Stevie

Back in LA, Stevie's apartment was shrouded in gloom. The blinds were drawn and there was a bad smell of bins and washing up. Clearly nothing had changed since she'd been away. Depositing her keys in the hall, she steeled herself for the familiar sight of Bibi's brother languishing on the sofa under a duvet, his hand buried in a tub of popcorn, avidly watching TV.

But the sounds emanating now from the living room were altogether different: moans and groans, and a woman's voice chanting, 'Fuck me, baby!' over and over again, punctuated by frequent references to the man's 'bigfathardthickcock'. Any notion that Ben himself was having it off in there was quickly dispelled—she'd seen him emerging naked from the shower once or twice: he was moderate, and that was being generous.

God! Putting up with it was bringing out the worst in

her. She had to ask him to leave before she turned into a total bitch.

Outraged, Stevie stalked in to join him.

She stopped in her tracks, mouth open, incredulous.

Instantly, she knew. The ambiguities of the last twelve months, the secrets and the dodged questions…it all came together now, pieces slotting into place with terrible clarity.

The woman's face wasn't visible—that was the point—but the voice, however forced, was one she recognised. She recognised the tiny frame. She recognised…

I want to get a tattoo on my back…of a butterfly…

Stevie remembered the day they'd met. Bibi's ramblings about her appearance.

Just a little one because they're cute…

The air got knocked out of her. She couldn't speak.

Sweet, funny, happy-go-lucky Bibi. Starring in this gratuitous filth.

Rigid with horror, she turned to Ben, who was sitting in profile, eyes wide on the screen, his fist delving into his jeans, oblivious to her presence.

When at last she found her voice, it came out little more than a croak.

'*What the—?*'

Ben shot up from his position on the couch, zipping his fly. She spied a box of man-sized tissues on the floor and practically gagged.

'What the *fuck* is going on?' she managed. The bags she was carrying fell to the floor. Horribly transfixed by events on-screen, she stormed over and furiously killed it.

'S-sorry,' he mumbled, 'I, er, didn't think you were coming back till tomorrow…'

'Ben—' she was trembling all over '—do you have any idea—?'

'It won't happen again,' he muttered moodily, as though she were the one imposing. 'Thought I had the place to myself, didn't I?'

With dismay Stevie realised he had no clue what he'd been witnessing...*who* he'd been witnessing. It was bad enough watching any woman pushed into such a vile, exploited position—for fun, for kicks, for what? She didn't get it: it was despicable—but this...

'Where did you get that?' she demanded quietly.

He shrugged like a kid. 'Downloaded it,' he grumbled, and she saw his laptop was plugged in under the cabinet. Next to it was a stack of DVDs, all boasting a close-up of the ubiquitous star's naked back, complete with the butterfly tattoo that told Stevie all she needed to know. Each was crowned with hot-pink lettering: THE FACELESS VIXEN. And it seemed the Vixen had been busy. She'd faced cyborgs from the future in *The Ejaculator*. She'd been paid a flying visit by *Harry Rutter and the Philosopher's Bone*. She'd even taken the reins in the Christmas *Big Dong Merrily on Thigh*.

'Get out,' she said coldly.

'What?' he puffed. 'Because of some lame porno?'

Stevie was struggling to process how things had got this far. How could she have failed to notice? How long had B been embroiled in this sick game? How many films had she done, five, ten, a dozen? More? And if she knew, if she ever found out, who'd been indulging...

'Ben,' she said slowly, unable to stop the words coming. 'That woman—' she gulped '—that woman you've been... The Faceless Vixen. *That woman is your sister.*'

He blinked. Then he laughed.

'Fuck that,' he said. 'She's just some tart.'

'"Some tart" is Bibi.'

He'd gone pale. Greenish, like pea soup. 'How would you know?' he spluttered.

'Because *I know B*.' She was close to tears. 'And so should you. Here!' She snatched up one of the DVDs, brandishing the cover, forcing him to look. 'See this? *I know* she wanted that tattoo, she told me! Look at her shoulders, her hands! *I know* she won't be frank with me what she's doing for a living. *I know* she's about to be married to a depraved human being…a *movie producer*. It doesn't take a genius to see what's staring us in the face, Ben.'

He stood for a moment, swaying gently like an axed tree about to be felled, and she saw what remaining colour there was in his face drain out like dirt through a plughole.

'I'm gonna barf.' He clamped a hand over his mouth and darted from the room, staggering and tripping in his haste, holding out a hand to break his fall and heaving with a ferocity so basic and wrong that the upsurge belonged more to some grisly underworld, an inferno of the damned, a burbling River Styx. Seconds later she heard him retching over the loo.

Stevie remained in the gloom for she didn't know how long, the DVD in one hand, eyes closed to the facts, letting silent tears run.

She watched it. Or, she watched as much of it as she could manage before she felt so appalled she had to turn it off. Nothing could have prepared her for seeing her friend in that revolting context. So this was what Linus Posen had been working with her on all this time. This explained the vanishing light in Bibi Reiner, the spark being put out.

Within moments, her headless body naked and violated. It was hardcore. Brutal. Twisted. Old and young, skinny and fat, men and women, front and back.

Of course, Posen's name wasn't attached to it. Even if it had been, the thing would stay underground. She wondered who else was in on it—Hollywood's prominent hustlers dipping their fat hands in the honey pot for some extra cash. She remembered the way Dirk Michaels had ogled her at Bibi's party. Men so powerful they were above the law. Never mind the law of the state of California—the laws being contravened here were ones of human decency and respect.

Once she'd gathered herself, she stormed into Ben's room. He was lying facedown on the bed with a pillow over his head.

'I hope you're ashamed of yourself,' she said grimly.

Ben tossed the pillow aside. She saw his eyes were red-rimmed, his complexion ashen, but she dug around for sympathy and found none. Yes, his discovery was heinous, but any man who got a hard-on for that kind of brutality deserved every inch of it.

'How was I s'posed to know?' he whinged. 'It's not like I was getting off on the fact she's my… It's not like I could tell she was…' He baulked, flirting once more with nausea. 'This is fucked up. I can't be dealing with this.'

'*You* can't be dealing with it? Try asking B how she feels!'

Ben stood. He retrieved his smoking miscellany from the chest of drawers. 'I need to be alone,' he said. 'I need to think this shit through.'

'What, so you can wank off on it again?'

'Fuck off, Stevie.'

'It's people like you who let it continue,' she raged. 'You let it happen in the first place!'

'What? You're blaming me now for the entire porn industry?'

'Supply and demand.'

'Get a life. At least she got a cheque at the end of it. 'S more than some of us have.'

Stevie wanted to slap him. The arrogant, ignorant little—

'Face it,' he snapped, whipping round, 'you've been handed all this on a fucking *plate*, haven't you? What about Bibi, huh? All this was meant to be hers and you stole it, right from under her. So don't you stand there and tell me I'm to blame when you know full well she'd be in a different position right now if it weren't for you.'

Stevie's heart froze over. 'Don't you dare talk to me about B. Not after what I've just seen. Not after you've been salivating over that dirty little skin flick, you prick.'

'Oh yeah?' He barked a laugh. 'And where were you, then, Saint Stevie? Well? Off living your glamorous movie star life in Vegas while she was back here getting boned up the ass? If I hadn't downloaded that scene you'd never have known!'

'I'm not having this conversation.'

'Get out of my fucking room, then.'

She was glacial. 'It's not your room any more. I want you out.'

'Tough shit. I'm staying.'

'You're not.'

'What're you gonna tell B, hey? The truth? That you

caught me whacking off to her latest release and now I'm being thrown out on to the street?'

'If I have to.'

But she wouldn't. She couldn't tell Bibi—it would break her. And Ben knew it.

She tried a different tack. 'We've got to find a way out of this,' she said hollowly. 'We have to help her.'

He sparked up the joint. 'I'm keeping out of it.'

'That's helpful of you.'

'What else am I meant to do?' he snarled, returning to the bed. 'If I don't forget like it happened I'll drive myself insane. I'll end up in a fucking asylum.'

'Do you ever think about anyone but your *goddamn self*?'

'Leave me alone.' He switched on the TV and turned the volume up till Stevie could no longer hear her own voice shouting over the noise.

She left the room and closed the door, wondering what the hell she was going to do.

Stevie was desperate to speak to Bibi but knew she had to handle it carefully. Eventually she resolved to call the one person whose integrity she felt she could trust: Xander Jakobson. They'd agreed to stay in touch, having become close during filming, and, in spite of how Stevie felt about him, she figured she'd sooner have him in her life in a platonic capacity than not at all.

They arranged to meet for a drink at a low-key bar downtown. Xander listened while she spilled everything—about Bibi's situation, about Linus and finally about Ben.

'Her own *brother*?'

'Yes.' Saying it out loud was so bizarre that she fought the urge to burst out laughing.

'Jeez.' Xander shook his head and ran a hand over his unshaven jaw. About Bibi's situation, he didn't appear shocked.

'I feel for her,' he said. 'You'd think in this day and age this sort of thing might have gone out of fashion, but it's more rampant than ever.'

'Can we do anything?'

He raised his glass to his lips. She liked that he drank draught lager.

'You could expose it,' Xander reasoned. 'But you'd be opening up a shitstorm of controversy if you did. These people run the town, they're big fish.'

'And in comparison I'm a tadpole?'

'Something like it. Look, the industry's old as time and now it's more accessible than ever. It doesn't make it right, it's as abusive and wrong as it ever was, but it thrives. Sex always does. Over time these movies are likely to gross more for Posen than his above-board projects.'

'You don't seem surprised.'

'I'm not. I've heard talk of Posen and his cronies before. Dirk Michaels is another one. Nobody cares that much, Stevie. People let him get on with it.'

'He's conned Bibi,' she said tightly. 'He promised her a different life.'

Xander raised an eyebrow. 'And he might yet get it for her. It's in his interests, after all.'

'How?'

'If your friend's career does one day take off, in a legitimate field, then her appearances in these sidelines are going to spell gold dust.'

'I didn't think of that.'

'Hmm.'

Stevie put her head in her hands. 'I should have noticed. I feel awful.'

'It's not your fault,' commented Xander. 'And it's not too late to try and help. My advice would be to speak to her.'

'And say what?'

'That you want to get her as far away from this guy as possible. Once you do that, you can decide objectively whether or not you want to take this battle on. Not all fights are worth it.'

'You sound like you speak from experience.'

He nicked his jaw with his thumb. 'Experience I'd sooner forget.'

'She's marrying him.'

'Then stop her.'

Stevie sat back. 'You're wise,' she observed.

'It's easy to be wise when you're not involved.' Xander signalled for the check. 'But you know what you're doing— you'll find a way.'

They sat in comfortable quiet for a moment, before Xander said, 'I never asked you about the Frontline Fashion gig. How was it?'

'It was fine. A bit boring, actually. It's fun to see the models for the first five minutes then they all sort of blend into one. The clothes go over my head, if I'm honest.'

'Some clothes do that.'

'Ha.'

A pause. 'You saw the man himself?'

'JB Moreau? Yeah.' She was so bound up in thoughts of Bibi that she forgot Xander's strange reaction when the name had come up back in Vegas, and didn't pick up on his tone now.

'How did he look?'

She remembered only too well. Moreau's appearance was unusual because it flirted on that line between impossibly good-looking and an edge she could only describe as cruel. It brought to mind the pleasure/pain theory, the notion that something could be so exquisite that the endurance of that exquisiteness required a degree of suffering, and only in that suffering could the exquisite truly exist. Moreau was beauty and he was pain; she knew it from looking at him.

She didn't bother saying any of this to Xander, of course. 'Handsome,' she said instead.

'Who was with him?'

Stevie recalled a dark-haired woman with a chignon. 'I'm not sure,' she said, making a mental note to ask Wanda Gerund about it. 'Reuben van der Meyde was.'

Xander was visibly uncomfortable. Just as she was about to enquire after the significance of the men, he seemed to recover his demeanour. 'A friend of mine works for the agency. She's been telling me about a new protégée of hers, a Spanish girl. Lori Garcia.'

'I saw her.' Stevie remembered the gorgeous—and that was the only word for her, really—girl sitting on the opposite bank, a few rows back from Moreau. She'd been like Eva Mendes, with a pinch of Natalie Wood in *West Side Story*.

'I think she's quite taken with her.'

'It's not hard to imagine.' A beat. 'You should have come.'

'I wasn't in the mood.'

The bill came and they split it.

Stevie asked the question that had been bugging her. 'Do you know JB Moreau?'

Xander grabbed his jacket, electing not to answer. 'It was good seeing you.'

She wasn't sure if he'd heard the question. Maybe he hadn't. Anyway, what business was it of hers? He'd been good enough to her already.

'Of course. I've kept you.'

'Not at all. Let me know how your friend gets on?'

'Sure.' She stung at his imminent departure. She thought of Ben, rotting in his mortification back at her apartment, and poor dear Bibi and what on earth they should do. 'Look me up next time you're in town.'

He pulled on his jacket. 'As it goes, I'm in town tomorrow—and I know a great place for dinner. Want to join me?'

27
Lori

Mac Valerie—*the* Mac Valerie of Valerie Cosmetics—
wanted to meet her. Desideria called Lori early on
Wednesday morning with the news.

'Get ready,' she breathed. 'Your star's about to shine.'

Lori couldn't believe it. Mac Valerie was the big league,
the biggest there was. If she secured this, the world would
be there for the taking.

And so, surely, would the man she desired.

She caught a cab to the beauty mogul's Bel Air mansion. Desideria was waiting outside, dressed entirely in
black and drawing on a thin menthol cigarette. The night
in Vegas was never mentioned, for which Lori was grateful: she'd woken in the morning feeling foolish, could only
imagine how Desideria felt. But since then she'd been the
epitome of businesslike.

Another woman was with her. She was in her twenties,
blonde, with shrewd green eyes and a dimple in her chin.

Desideria introduced her as Jacqueline Spark, a PR princess on her way to the top at One Touch, the publicity firm used by La Lumière. Jacqueline shook Lori's hand with purpose and gave her a warm, friendly smile.

'You look great,' she said, taking in Lori's plain camisole and hip-tight jeans, a fresh white jacket thrown over the top. 'Ready for this?'

'Always. What do I need to do?'

'Be yourself,' advised Desideria, extinguishing her cigarette. 'Mac's seeing four girls today, so we need to impress. Don't talk unless he asks you a question. You're just the face, remember. The rest is for me and Jacqueline to look after.'

Jacqueline added more tactfully, 'We want to make sure he hears the right noises. Personally I think the other girls will be out soon as he claps eyes on you.'

Mac Valerie's place was a sprawling one-storey villa with a glinting crescent-shaped swimming pool, bordered by palms that rustled in the balmy LA breeze. Lori told herself to be cool even though she'd endured a twist of anxiety in her stomach since breakfast. This was the big boys' playground. The gatehouse alone was the size of her childhood home.

As they approached the main entrance a scrabble of white tight-curled poodles shot out on to the drive, their claws scratching the melting ground. Some had pink bows nestled in their hair, their wet, shiny noses searching the new scent.

'Trixie! Tiara! Tillie! Come back here, you naughty dogs!'

A woman in a coral-coloured jumpsuit with candyfloss hair hurried out after them, precarious on a pair of tiny-heeled slippers with feathery baubles on the front. She scooped the dogs up, her painted fingernails buried incongruously in their fur. Two of the dogs licked her face with quick, sandpapery tongues. Lori guessed the woman was in her fifties, or even sixties, though she'd had a lot of surgery. Chalky foundation gathered beneath her eyes and set in the crinkly skin like clay.

'Val Valerie!' she cried. 'Mac's wife. Come with me, you must be Loriana.' Formal introductions were made and she led the way inside.

'Val Valerie?' Jacqueline mouthed as the three of them followed. Lori tried not to laugh.

They were taken through the main atrium and out the other side, where Lori was surprised to see a lush green golf course stretching away as far as the eye could see. A squat man wearing Hawaiian-print trunks and sporting a very dark hairy chest was in conversation with two more formally dressed players. When he saw the party, he came puffing over.

'Mac Valerie.' He thrust out his hand with all the grace and ceremony of a wooden stick. He didn't seem interested in chitchat and gestured for them to settle beneath a wide cream parasol, from where he'd presumably been watching the round. Judging by the shambolic array of photographs and paperwork laid out on the table, Lori had the impression that Mac's business meetings were normally quite relaxed.

'You wanna be my Valerie girl, then, do ya?' He slipped on a pair of shades and sat back, plump fingers locked over a generous stomach.

Desideria answered. 'Lori has an irresistibly fresh look. She's a healthy contrast to what's out there right now.'

Mac spotted someone inside the house and yelled, 'LEMONADE!' Then he turned to the women. 'You like lemonade?'

'Sure.' Desideria smiled tightly. 'Who doesn't like lemonade?'

Mac removed his sunglasses and squinted at Lori. 'What makes you think you've got what it takes? I got broads queuing for this contract, big names, too.'

'Lori may be new to the industry,' put in Jacqueline, 'but we've had a fantastic reaction to her across the board. People are ready to embrace something different. She's a *real woman*, not just skin and bone. That's who the Valerie brand speaks to. Real women. We see it as the perfect partnership.'

'No offence, lady, but can you do me a favour and zip it?'

As Jacqueline had suspected, Mac Valerie was a jerk-off. A huge-breasted blonde wandered out brandishing a tray. She was clad in a lime bikini, the bottom part of which did little to cover her ass. As she deposited the drinks and turned to go back inside, Mac slapped her on it.

At last his gaze fixed on Lori. 'Well?'

Lori wanted this contract. She needed it. It was another step away from the life she'd left behind, and another step towards the only thing she truly wanted.

'What Jacqueline said is true,' she began. 'A superskinny image of women isn't helpful to anyone. As I understand it, the Valerie range is about creating a natural, glowing look, something that makes women feel well and that makes us happy in our own skin, working with what we already have instead of fighting against it. And when we feel well, we look well, whatever our shape and size. I believe I can be the person who says this for you.'

Mac slurped his lemonade. Without preamble he snapped at her with a Polaroid camera, flapping the prints in the sun. Lori noticed how hairy his hands were, loads of hair all down the knuckles and wrists, like a wolf. On his fingers he wore fat gold rings. The hair on his head was receding and the diamonds left by its retreat sweated in the sun.

'Pretty nice.' He scrutinised the photos. 'She's got what my wife calls "best friend eyes". But that kinda depends who's lookin' at it, don't it?'

'"Best friend eyes" sums it up,' confirmed Jacqueline, pleased.

'She's…cute. Like if I were a girl I'd wanna talk to her, confide in her, whatever women do.' He raised a bushy eyebrow. 'But if I were a guy…well, to be frank, I'd wanna f—'

'You'd have Lori exclusively as the Valerie Girl for a twelve-month contract,' Desideria interjected. 'She'll be all yours—and, guaranteed, Mac, this is going to be an electric year for her. Valerie needs a fresh style, it needs reinvigoration, and none of the old names can do it for you. It's time to innovate, push things forward.'

Lori held her hands together in her lap, tightly, as though she didn't trust herself not to reach out for a golden opportunity that was close enough now to touch. She thought of the sticky salon walls at *Tres Hermanas*, the flies that buzzed round the counter and her stepsisters' bitching and whining. It was miles away. She thought of her father, of Corazón on her veranda back in Spain, listening to her radio. And Rico, the boy she'd adored but never loved—if love was what she felt for JB Moreau—alone, in jail. The totems of her old life.

'I like her,' announced Mac. 'And it's about time I did business with Moreau.' The name, in whoever's mouth, was like a poem. 'I'll be in touch.'

They didn't have to wait. Mac called on the drive back to La Lumière.

'No point seein' the others,' he told Desideria. 'It's her I want.'

A week later, JB invited them to celebrate. The Mac Valerie contract was a coup.

'Moreau doesn't meet with everyone,' Desideria told her. 'Consider yourself lucky.'

Lori did. This was it, at last, her big chance. She hadn't seen him since the Frontline Vegas event, a night that had made clear the gulf between them. Perhaps now she had tied the deal with Mac they would finally have a legitimate reason to speak. His behaviour had puzzled her at first, but now she understood. When JB Moreau, mogul of the fashion world and a man with both reputation and responsibilities, had walked into her life that day, he'd never expected to be confronted months later with the same girl. No wonder he had closed up. He had probably felt as embarrassed as she had. And what real occasion had they had to speak candidly about what happened? None whatsoever. She felt certain that this lunch invitation was a sign of his intentions. She had secured this contract for them both: for the sake of what might be.

She spent ages deciding what to wear. It was strange having this much choice—her wardrobe now consisted of gorgeous clothes she would never have dreamed of owning but had been told to keep after shoots—and while every one was beautiful in its own way, none was quite right. It looked as if she was trying too hard. *That's because I am.*

In the end she plumped for a cream vest top, silk high-waisted trousers and shoe boots, her hair tied back in a ponytail.

They were lunching at exclusive LA eaterie La Côte. In the car, Lori spritzed fragrance in the hollows behind her ears and attempted to slow her breathing. She was so accustomed to JB in pieces, fragments she would take away with her and turn over in her hands and her memory— glimpses of him at the agency, at parties, facts people told her—that the realisation of him in his entirety was difficult to fathom. What would he say to her? What would she say back? Would there be a chance to talk alone?

La Côte boasted an ocean view of Venice Beach, the glittering green of the Pacific carving a line through the hot sands of her anxiety. She asked the car to drop her a block away. Her heart was thrumming wildly. Several times she started towards the restaurant then turned back, walked the avenue and gathered herself.

This is so dumb! He's just a guy! Only, he wasn't. He was something else.

Passers-by regarded her strangely. They seemed so care-free, enjoying the LA sun, the beach and the shimmering blue as they bladed waterside, caught a tan and licked ice cream.

Remember the way he kissed you. He meant it, he meant it...

She took a deep breath. *Do it before you change your mind.*

As Lori had imagined, he was seated on the terrace with

Desideria, Jacqueline and Mac. She spotted them straight away, made as if she hadn't, so Desideria had to wave and gesture for her to come on over. The walk to that table was the longest of her life.

JB stood to meet her. In seconds she had absorbed every detail, attraction honing her powers of observation to something animalistic. Loose white shirt rolled up at the sleeves, open at the neck; hair darker than she remembered, but those on his arms were lighter, bleached by the sun; a smile that lifted, just a fraction, the groove of his scar. She recalled kissing it, the strange pleat that had felt against her lips that much more pronounced, like a tongue probing a missing tooth.

'Lori.'

He made her name sound like a marble he was rolling around inside his mouth. He kissed her on both cheeks—properly, not one of the air kisses to which she was getting accustomed—and the smell of him was achingly clean and new, like something just born, but at the same time steeped in the experience of vast ages, as if a part of him had been living for ever.

'Sit down, please, we were waiting to order.'

'Thanks.' She was amazed it came out as steady as it did. 'Sorry I'm late.'

JB leaned back in his chair, reaching behind to a chilled wine bucket. A waiter dashed over to assist but was dismissed with a subtle gesture.

'You're in time for champagne.' She loved the way he said 'champagne'.

'A Valerie Girl should always be a bit late.' Jacqueline smiled, lifting her glass for JB to fill. 'Isn't that right, Mac?'

Mac Valerie winked, his squat dark head protruding

out of a garish shirt. 'Nothin' like makin' an entrance.' He tossed an olive into his open mouth. 'An' I should know.'

'To the new Valerie Girl,' proposed JB, raising his own glass. As he drank he watched Lori over the top of it. 'And to all she will become.'

Lori peeled her eyes away. She couldn't look at him. He made her feel naked. How could the others fail to notice the effect he was having? She felt like a quivering schoolgirl, all the confidence and courage she'd willed back at the apartment evaporated like steam.

The women fell into conversation with Mac. JB signalled their waiter and ordered oysters as an appetiser. At last, he turned to Lori.

'Was it a surprise?' he asked.

His question threw her. 'Excuse me?'

'I said: Was it a surprise?'

From his tone Lori didn't think he was asking about the Valerie contract. Then again, maybe he was. 'Yes,' she answered.

'It was for me, too.'

The blue eyes shone and she remembered what Desideria had told her: *All he has to do is snap his fingers and they come running... The next day, they're history...*

Groping for something to say, Lori noticed the extra place set at the table.

'Is Val joining us?' she enquired.

At this, Mac flipped open his menu, greedily eyeing its wares. 'No, thank Christ. Which means I'm orderin' a feast guaranteed to shoot my cholesterol to shit.'

Desideria made a face, which she concealed in her champagne glass.

'Rebecca's running late,' she explained to Lori, with an expression of apology.

Lori was confused. Who was Rebecca?

But Desideria's eyes switched to JB's and in that moment she felt the light slip out of her, discreet as a door closing on a sleeping child.

'Rebecca?' she asked, in a voice too small.

The oysters arrived, pearlescent innards on a shell like rock. The smell of the sea.

JB gestured for them to begin. 'I'm sure she won't mind.' He glanced at Lori, and before he even said it she knew.

'Rebecca is my wife.'

28

Present Day
Island of Cacatra, Indian Ocean
Three hours to departure

'**S**onofa*bitch*!'

Reuben van der Meyde exited the shower, cursing under his breath. Couldn't a man get ten minutes' peace ahead of a major event? It seemed not. No sooner had he digested his crisis meeting with JB than he got buzzed with news that one of his A-list guests had arrived early. The guy clearly deemed himself so important that he thought nothing of rocking up hours before he was due. Fucking stars!

Reuben charged down the stairs, stark naked and dripping with water. He favoured stalking about nude. Towels were a constraint.

'Miss Jensen,' he bellowed when he reached the hall. In moments, his housekeeper appeared, unsurprised by his nakedness but conscious that his young son was about.

'Mr V!' she chided, presenting him with the first thing

that came to hand, one of Ralph's comics. In truth she was disgusted by Reuben's body—how dare he parade around in such a state? Was he playing with her, teasing her? Did he imagine she found him desirable? The sight of his shrivelled penis, hanging miserably in its greying fuzz of coppery pubic hair, revolted her. His pale, muscular thighs and short, bulbous calves...the picture was horrifying. She heaved at the memory of her own nakedness entwined with his all those years ago, the way, for he had been a skilled lover, she had enjoyed it and begged for more. Small comfort was the thought that his body had been different then, though whether it really had, or if it was just her view that had changed, she wasn't sure.

'I'm not available till seven, understood?' he snapped, snatching the comic and tossing it to one side. 'No matter who shows up.'

Margaret nodded. 'Are you expecting an early arrival?' She hoped her contact hadn't fouled up before they were even out of the starting gates: after all, he was only young. The slightest whiff that Reuben suspected anything amiss sent her heart plummeting.

'Already here,' Reuben said bitterly, hands on hips. 'And take a wild guess who?'

Margaret had no time to respond before they heard a commotion on the patio steps that sounded dangerously like a star with his entourage.

'Goddamnit!' Reuben turned and shot up the main steps, two or three at a time, like a bare-bottomed monkey mounting a tree. 'Stall 'em, you got it? I'll be there in a minute.'

It was five minutes, in fact, till Reuben appeared out front, pristine in white shorts and a loose cotton shirt, reddish chest visible where the top buttons were undone. He spotted his guest straight away, a marvel of a man with his broad back to the house, clad in a vanilla linen suit as he faced the wide ocean. A crew of ten or fifteen hangers-on fussed around him.

'Jax Jackson,' Reuben boomed, extending his hand to greet the Olympic megastar, 'this is an unexpected pleasure.'

Jax Jackson turned, his manner and bearing that of someone who knew there was a part of every man that wanted to be him—not be *like* him, but *be* him. It was a nice philosophy.

'What's up, Roob?' He shook Reuben's hand, who tried not to baulk at the crass abbreviation. 'Not a bad place you've got.' He leaned against the marble balustrade, tilting his face to the sun so it gleamed off his black skin. If Jax had been a painting, or a sculpture, he would have been hailed a masterpiece. At over six feet tall, he was a pillar of pure dark muscle, as strong and graceful as a stallion. His was the body of a god, a warrior, a titan: physically, he was nothing short of exquisite. He was also the fastest man on the planet, the World Record Holder for the 100-metre sprint. Jax's Olympic training meant he was often booked into the rejuvenation spa for rest and recuperation, hence the over-familiar greeting, no doubt.

'Trust you've been happy with your stay?'

'Hell, yeah.' Jax whipped a pair of shades from the pocket of his shirt and slipped them on. 'I'm windin' it down, man, takin' it easy.'

Reuben wondered if he could palm Jax off on JB, or even Rebecca, while he had the chance to gather himself, maybe get a shot of brandy, try to stop thinking about the disaster of a morning he'd had. He just couldn't shake the fear. Those words, they were too close to home.

I'm one of them...

There was no way. Not now. It couldn't all come crashing down tonight.

'Jeez! It's hot.' Jax raised his arms and sniffed both armpits in succession. It brought to mind a dog spraying a tree. 'Fresh,' he informed his entourage, all of whom nodded enthusiastically. 'Hey, Roob, we was hopin' for a grand tour before things kick off.'

Inwardly, Reuben groaned. This was the last thing he needed. He knew he wouldn't be able to get rid of Jax. Honest to Christ, the number of celebrity asses he'd had to wipe over the last thirty years! Wasn't he a celebrity himself? Who was wiping his goddamn ass?

He smiled. 'Of course, I'd be delighted.'

Discreet as a shadow, Margaret Jensen slipped back inside the mansion. That was the beauty of being a nobody. You never got noticed.

Mr V wouldn't be pleased at the Jax interruption. She had surmised he was upset, though about what she couldn't fathom. There was only one person who knew about the plan and he wasn't due for another hour. No, it had to be a different concern: one that had her boss disappearing into meetings with JB and prowling the place like a hunted man...

Her sole priority was getting him on to that boat, him and all the rich, arrogant devils that had set the island's great misfortune in motion. For her vengeance wasn't just about Mr V. She was taking revenge for all of womankind, for mothers everywhere. On top of her private injustice was a wider one: the vile enterprise she had watched unfold from the start. She'd experienced it first-hand, what it meant to be one of the mothers, lied to and exploited and cheated out of the most important thing there was, because Mr V told them one thing, he made out as if it were *humanitarian*, a kind of gruesome *charity*, when in fact he pocketed every dime himself. No wonder he was the rich bastard he was today. Stealing off the blind and stupid, couples who'd cough up any amount to protect their precious reputations, sleeping soundly at night as they imagined the women they were...*helping*. Margaret shuddered at the word. Those women had received no help. She'd been lucky, permitted to stay in the boy's life because Mr V had decided he wanted an heir to his empire, and this one was as good as any.

Lucky. She didn't feel it.

Would Hollywood's elite have time to figure out what was happening? Would they have seconds to regret, to repent? Or would death come in a bright hot flash?

Margaret busied herself, laying out a Moreau couture suit for Mr V to change into when he returned from the tour with Jax. Minutes with the Olympic idol had been plenty enough for her. She'd met many famous faces in her time, but he had to be one of the most delusional. Who did he imagine he was, some sort of deity? He'd barely deigned to glance her way; his radar didn't pick her up: she wasn't rich or celebrated, and she wasn't young or especially attractive. It was a universally known fact that Jax liked women. One of her colleagues at the island's Reef Spa had told her he was, in fact, being treated here for sex addiction. Never mind this rest and relaxation foil, the donkey simply couldn't keep it buckled. Oh, Cacatra saw it all. Only last month the spa had treated a global R&B star for his obsession with lifting heavy weights—at the height of his preoccupation he'd been attempting to lift anything he could get his hands on: tables displayed on a shop floor; strangers' cars in the street... Never mind the weights at the gym, this guy wanted to lift the *machinery*. She'd heard how his therapist had been forced to nail office furniture to the floor in exasperation of them repeatedly being moved.

When all this was over, perhaps she'd write a book.

An edited one, naturally.

Margaret consulted the time. Once Enrique Marquez showed up, a little under an hour from now, she knew there would be no turning back. Not that she'd considered it, but of course there was a small, scared part of her that clamoured to call the whole thing off. All those people perishing, suffering in the water... And what next? Sharks? They were rife in this ocean, she knew. She had seen their black fins slicing through the water, quiet and deadly, too close to the shore for comfort. She imagined beautiful bodies torn limb from limb, designer gowns shredded and pampered skin bloated, the screams that would pierce the sky...

This was no time for conscience. The word didn't exist out here, in any case. It belonged to a vocabulary that had been swallowed up long ago, drowned on the seabed, rusted as a wreck. Mr V had created a game without rules, without mercy, without pity—and forgotten he wasn't the only one with a piece in play.

She had to go through with it. For Ralph, for her, for their future. For all the women in her position. For the ones who weren't so lucky.

She'd waited a long time, too frightened, too weak, to

take action, believing Mr V to be the one with the power when, in fact, it was her. It had always been her.

At long last, Margaret Jensen was taking back what was hers.

On the opposite side of the island, in the villa where she spent most of her days, Rebecca Stuttgart watched her husband. She realised, with startling clarity, that she no longer hated him.

A long time she had hated JB Moreau, but not in the conventional sense. She had hated him because she adored him, had adored him from the moment they'd met, and yet through the course of their ten-year marriage she had been unable to make him feel the same way.

She observed his body in the pool below. Strong arms carving through the water, before a length, silent and still, beneath the surface, his shape fractured and fluid as a ribbon in air. He was a purposeful swimmer, fast and committed. Once, in a rare confidence, JB had told her that for months following the accident he had swum every morning. Miles and miles he would swim until his muscles gave in, then the same the next day, and the next, and the next after that. The sea became his obsession. It could not beat him.

Their courtship had been swift. JB had been twenty-three, she, a decade older. Her father had steered them into a union through a series of lunch invitations and industry parties. At the time Rebecca had turned a blind eye to the orchestrated romance. She had believed that despite her father's machinations there was something real to pursue. There had been for her.

Moreau was the sexiest man she had ever known. He

exuded sex like musk. Good looks were one thing; charm was another. But sex... It was in his eyes, those shades of blue that changed like an ocean storm. It was his mouth. His skin. His scent, as cool and clean as snow.

But more than that, and the cement to her infatuation, was her husband's wounded soul. Rebecca had trusted she could reach him: whatever he needed, she could give. She wanted to access a new part of the man she loved, a place left cold and quiet from years untouched. She felt she understood him in a way nobody else did: his indifferent parents, distant at best and neglectful at worst. How he had never been cared for as a child or received affection in its purest, selfless sense, how he had never been made to feel wanted or valued or cherished, how he'd been pushed to the background, a mistake, an oversight. Despite the nature of their meeting, she believed in time he would grow to feel for her what she did, and always would, for him.

At the start, he had made love to her as if it were their last living hour.

Make love...

She thought of the words differently these days. For that was what JB had been trying to do. The urgency she had mistaken for ardour was an attempt to break through, to feel, to *acquire* the thing that should have been given freely. To make love that had been missing from the start.

Rebecca backed away from the window. She could look no more.

Time had taught her one thing. JB Moreau was like winter, and no sun she could conjure would ever be warm enough.

Tomorrow, after Reuben's party, Rebecca would leave this island for good. She had never wanted to follow him here, but through the heady mists of her passion had tossed her scruples aside. Their marriage was over. JB treated her well, had shown her kindness in the past that even now it stung her heart to recall: when her father had died, the way he had held her tight and kissed her over and over till her body stopped shaking. But she knew he didn't love her. She knew he had only entered the marriage because he didn't believe there was anything more.

Was it any wonder they both sought refuge elsewhere? Rebecca, searching endlessly for fervour in another that could come close to matching her own, and JB for the thing in whose existence he doubted but nonetheless whose possibility he would chase to the ends of the earth.

She hadn't been so reconciled when she'd first found out about the others. Maybe that was from where the lie had sprung. In any case, it did little to ease her conscience.

For years they had tried for a child of their own. In her mind it would be the switch in JB, the event that would change him. But Cacatra Island was poisoned in more ways than one. The child she had longed for had never arrived.

Terrified of losing him, grasping at ways to make him stay, Rebecca had blurted the fallacy: that it was he who was unable to conceive. She'd wanted to hurt him, make him see the result of his inability to love. And once the lie had been told, there was no way to unpick it. It was a vicious, evil mistruth—and tonight, finally, it would be revealed.

Hate that sprang from love was the very worst kind.

I'm one of them... The truth comes out...

Rebecca met her reflection in the closet mirror. She nodded, an assurance.

How could she have stayed silent, knowing what she did? And to whom, exactly, did she owe her allegiance?

The Spanish girl had been a shock, and like all shocks it had shifted the landscape. JB had sourced so many over the years but none had affected him as she did. At first, Rebecca had felt only disbelief at their working together—*after what he had meant her for*—but now she understood that Lori, and the secret she carried, was the only way out for any of them.

Once, Rebecca Stuttgart had been a powerful woman. Perhaps she still was. If knowledge was power, then she was mightier than them all.

BOOK THREE
2010-11

29
Lori

Over the summer, with the launch of the new Valerie Girl and Mac's latest sought-after cosmetics range, Lori Garcia became the most in-demand model on the fashion circuit. She graced billboards across the country, into Europe, out to Japan. Sexy, sultry, shy in her beauty—the market went crazy for her look. Each day was packed with photo shoots, magazine interviews, radio and TV appearances, red carpet events and lunches with the movers, shakers and heartbreakers of LA. Lori was growing into America's sweetheart. In the eyes of the press, she could do no wrong. She'd been a poor, struggling Spanish girl from the wrong side of the tracks, rescued into a world of wealth and stardom by the guiding light that was La Lumière.

In many ways fame was how she'd imagined, in many ways it wasn't. It was hard work. There were barely minutes to eat or sleep and her time was no longer hers. Little was permanent: gigs came and went, countless hotel rooms a place to crash; friends were made and drifted away.

Her virginity became an enduring fascination. It was the combination of wide-eyed virtue and a glint that promised something more, and it was one of the first things Jacqueline Spark had raised when discussing publicity angles. She promised it would secure the fans' devotion. It did. Lori became an example for young girls, not in a square, this-is-a-role-model-my-parents-think-I-should-have way, but in a way like an idolised older sister, a sharer of dreams and secrets. To guys she was irresistible, the suggestion that she was saving herself—just for them—in a celebrity world where innocence was a rare commodity.

But Lori wasn't the innocent. She felt further from innocence than ever she had.

It wasn't that she'd kissed a married man. That was part of it, of course—but it was more. It was that she had been forced to harden, to develop an exterior that was toughening by the day like the rind on a piece of soft fruit. To Lori's nascent heart, the deceit she had suffered at the hands of JB Moreau was the most profound betrayal imaginable.

She thought back to that terrible lunch at La Côte with a cringing sort of ache. How his wife had approached the table, so elegant, so poised: secure in the knowledge that he was hers. Rebecca Stuttgart, daughter of the late Crawford Stuttgart, billionaire financier and owner of an American banking corporation, was, at forty-two, a decade older than her husband. She was ravishing in a classic, screen-siren way, with sleek, plum-coloured hair and pale, flawless skin, everything about her expensively immaculate, from her delicately drawn make-up to the gems that glinted on her wrists and fingers. Lori recognised her from the

Frontline event in Vegas, the solemn woman at JB's right-hand side. How could she have been so blind?

It had taken every ounce of will to respond to his admission, like talking through mud.

'I—I didn't realise you were married.'

It became horribly clear why he'd blanked her. The married man found out.

Stupid stupid stupid!

Every taunt, every insult her sisters had ever thrown her way she now pitched at herself—for once, apposite. *Whore! Tramp! Slut!*

She was furious with herself. JB had taken her for a ride and she had fallen for it. He was a cocksman, everyone said so: she understood now that he probably dropped in on legions of teenagers in the poorer parts of town, delivering his smooth come-ons, whatever he needed to, playing the hero, all for the sake of a kiss, maybe more. It was probably a turn-on for a man like him, knowing he could have anyone but choosing to slum it once in a while—bored with his wife's attentions, looking for something a little rougher round the edges.

He must have had the surprise of his life when Desideria brought her back from Spain, a girl he'd written off as too insignificant, too poor and wretched, to ever darken his door. But any small comfort she felt at that was quickly overshadowed by the realisation she was now working for him, entirely under his power, and to walk away from this opportunity, because of the impossible position he'd put her in, was not a sacrifice she was prepared to make.

Whatever had passed between them that day at *Tres Hermanas*, it clearly meant nothing.

She hated JB Moreau. Where once she had nurtured

adoration, she now tended loathing, growing it from the soil, a tangled vine she was eventually able to bind herself in, and in that containment instruct herself to set him free.

Hours turned into days, days turned into weeks, and gradually she learned to forget. Each time he emerged in her memory, she concentrated on holding him down, like someone pushing an adversary underwater and waiting for them to drown. She trained herself to let go and found she had a greater capacity for it than she knew. She stopped replaying every second of the altercation with Diego Marquez and his crew. She stopped thinking about how it felt in the interior of JB's car. She stopped trying to conjure his voice in the lonely hours of the night. The kiss shivered in her memory until finally it became still.

The mansion was enormous, more space than Lori would ever need. With tennis courts, a basement gym and a huge infinity pool, it was excessive: she would never use half the stuff, and when she crawled, exhausted, between the sheets at the end of another long day, she felt the vastness of her new home around her. Everyone assured her this was fitting for a model in her position—she couldn't live in that crummy downtown apartment for ever.

In August, she called her father. She'd been putting it off. It wasn't for lack of wanting to see him, it was because she no longer felt like the girl he'd known and was afraid that would make them strangers.

The sight of him pained her. Tony had dressed for the occasion in a jacket and trousers and smelled of astringent cologne. Lori hugged him at the mansion door, where he presented her with a limp bunch of flowers. In the kitchen she ran a basin of water and positioned the bouquet so the stems were submerged.

'Let's sit outside,' she said, sensing his discomfort at her new surroundings. She gave him a look between pride and apology, didn't want him to think she was showing off but aware that was how it might look. 'Want to try the pool?'

Tony smiled. 'Aren't you going to give me a tour?'

She led him upstairs, through the guest suites with their adjacent bathrooms and walk-in closets, then her own bedroom, its stripped floors and mammoth white-silk bed and the views of downtown Hollywood that stretched to the skyline.

He stood at the window, hands in pockets. 'You took a chance, Loriana.'

'Some days I feel like it was chance that took me.'

His face relaxed and she caught a glimpse of the father she used to know. 'Your mama would be proud.'

Lori thought of her mother's treasured salon, the place in which she'd endured the greatest misery of her years—and, just once, the greatest joy. But she turned her back on that.

'Did you receive the money?' she asked.

Tony nodded. 'You shouldn't have sent it.'

'Why not?'

'It's yours. You earned it. I don't want you bailing me out, Lori. It's not your responsibility.'

'It's both our responsibilities.'

He appraised her, searching for something. When he found it, he said, 'Thank you.'

Back downstairs, they settled by the water. Tony appeared awkward, too heavily clothed for the heat, and removed his jacket and loosened his shirt.

'How are the girls?' Lori enquired. She couldn't care

less for Rosa and Anita, but was prepared to acknowledge this was the only common ground she could tread with her father. What she wanted to ask was how they felt about her new-found fame—Angélica, too. But Tony wasn't saying, and her pride didn't allow her to ask.

'The same.'

'And you? How are you?'

'Apart from missing my daughter, I'm getting by.'

'Oh, Papa.' She touched his arm but he waved away her concern. 'Now I'm settled we can see more of each other. I'll make sure of it.' But the promise was faint.

'Are you happy?'

She considered the question. 'I think so.'

'This is a big place for you to live all by yourself…'

'It feels it.'

Tony licked his lips, clasped his hands together. 'And our place is small…for the four of us. What I mean to say is, Angélica feels we might…'

She could tell where this was going. The thought appalled her. She stood up. 'I'm sorry, the answer is no.'

Tony reached out, caught only the tips of her fingers as she moved away. 'Angélica wanted me to ask you. She said there was no way you could need all this to yourself—'

'And what has it got to do with her?' Lori bit her lip to stop her anger escaping. She'd spent the past few months convinced she'd moved on from that downtrodden girl at *Tres Hermanas*, the unhappiness of her life with her step-family, and couldn't tolerate the notion that all those sensitivities were still there, waiting beneath the surface.

He shook his head. 'I'm sorry. I shouldn't have mentioned it. I told her it was unreasonable.'

'Couldn't she have mentioned it herself?' Lori folded her arms.

'She didn't feel she was welcome.'

'But she feels welcome enough to invite herself to live in my house, is that it?'

Tony glanced to the ground. Here was the father she had become so exasperated by. What was he now, merely Angélica's puppet? This was the reason she had got out in the first place. If he thought for one second she could return to that scenario, he was dead wrong.

'Papa.' She came to him, her voice softening. 'You know there is always a place for you.' Her omission was clear.

'I understand,' he said. 'It was wrong of me.'

'No, it wasn't.' She wanted to add, *It was wrong of Angélica*, but didn't. Her conscience buckled. If Tony was her responsibility and they, in turn, were his, where did that leave them? She had this whole mansion to herself, while he was cramped in his old age in a tiny house barely big enough for one. Guilt pawed at her. What would her mother tell her to do?

'I'll think about it,' she told him, sick in her soul at the glimmer of hope in his eyes.

'I have a proposition,' said Jacqueline, stirring mint tea. 'His name's Peter Selznick.'

'Who?'

'From *No Husbands Needed*.' Her publicist cited a mega-hit year-old sitcom. 'Getting into movies. Tipped to be big.' She winked. 'And *very* good-looking.'

The women were at a café on Melrose Avenue. Barely twenty-four hours had passed since the Valerie deal without the women talking, and while Jacqueline had started in a junior, apprentice-type role at One Touch, with her first client's stratospheric rise to fame she had swiftly been promoted. Though Lori knew little of the ins and outs of the PR machine, she could tell that Jacqueline was extremely good at her job.

Lori frowned. 'OK…'

'It'd do wonders for your profiles to be seen out together. Even better, to take it to the next level.'

'Sorry.' She was confused. 'You'll have to slow down. The next level?'

Jacqueline smiled triumphantly. 'Weren't you saying Bay Heights was too big for you?'

Lori never used the mansion's formal title—it made it sound like a hotel. 'Yeah, so…?'

'So, Peter's ready to move in!' She shrugged, as though it were obvious. 'Everything's been finalised and we're all on board. Now we just need your OK.'

Lori was shocked. 'Hang on: you want a *complete stranger* to move into my house?'

'He's not a *complete stranger*; he's well-known—just not to you.' Lori tried to make sense of this logic while Jacqueline took the opportunity to plough on. 'And the house is plenty large enough to accommodate you both leading independent lives. Think of it like advertising for someone to share your apartment! People do that all the time.'

'Hang on.' She was struggling to keep up. 'Why?'

Jacqueline made a so-so face. 'Think of it like you scratch his back, he scratches yours.'

'I don't want to scratch his back.'

'Come on, you know what I mean. This is a fantastic

publicity opportunity for you *both*, and like I said you'll only really be roomies. There's nothing to lose.'

'Yes, but—'

'But what? Who knows,' she teased, 'maybe after a while you won't want to keep things so separate.'

Lori blushed. She was conscious of a gaggle of girls on the sidewalk opposite taking her photograph. 'I hope he wouldn't be expecting—'

'Of course not.' Briskly Jacqueline shook her head. 'Peter's fully aware of your situation and the importance of, well…'

'Keeping me intact?'

Jacqueline smiled. 'What do you say?'

Lori thought about it. Reporters had been unremitting in asking about boyfriends and fiancés—a handsome guy on her arm could be just what she needed. Even better one who, at last, accepted her virginity.

And it would show JB Moreau I'm over him.

She ignored the voice that added: *I hope it hurts.*

'I'd want to meet Peter first,' she said.

'Naturally.'

'And make sure I like him.'

'Obviously.'

'And then…' She recalled the conversation she'd had with her father. Angélica wouldn't want to move in if she had a man living there, would she? 'It could work. I guess.'

'Excellent.' Jacqueline glanced at her hand. 'You'll need to take that ring off for starters.'

Lori followed her gaze. She had gotten so used to wearing Rico's ring that she could almost forget it was there. Initially there had been speculation, before One Touch had assured the world it was a family heirloom.

'Oh. Right.'

Jacqueline sensed her hesitation. 'If you'd rather not...'

'No, it's fine.' Lori twisted it. It caught on the knuckle then slid off with ease. The ring had been on her hand for over a year, and its absence left behind a thin whitish band of skin.

Rico.

It's a promise...

'Will La Lumière know about Peter?' she asked.

Jacqueline took a sip of her tea and set the cup down. 'The fewer people are aware of the arrangement, the better—that's how it works in this town. Though I'd imagine Moreau would back it. He's tyrannical about his own press, or lack thereof.'

Lori bit the inside of her lip. Of course JB would back it. He'd seen her in the first place as some kind of prostitute— why shouldn't he pimp her out, invite others to have a go?

The words were out before she could stop herself, a slight but satisfying stab at revenge.

'Did I mention JB and I met before I was signed to the agency?'

Jacqueline looked up, surprised. 'No.'

'He came into the salon where I worked. Some guys were giving me trouble and he stepped in to help.'

'That's odd. Are you sure it was him?'

The idea of mistaking JB for anyone else was laughable. 'Positive. But when we met again at La Lumière, he made like he didn't know me.'

Jacqueline raised an eyebrow. 'I wouldn't think you're the first.'

'That's the conclusion I've reached.'

'Then you're catching on fast. He probably didn't remember.'

'Probably.'

'Between you and me, he's an asshole.'

'Hmm.'

Jacqueline sat back. 'Oh no.'

'What?'

'Not you as well.' She rolled her eyes. 'Look around, this city's *packed* with hot guys; he isn't the only damn one! The way you lot carry on, you'd think he was the last man alive. You're best off out of it, Lori. I'm sick of seeing women being pathetic over him, he's not all that.'

'What about you?'

'What about me?'

'Weren't you ever...?'

'Tempted? No.' But Lori saw how her gaze flickered.

'It's irrelevant now,' Lori concluded. 'I'm over it.'

'You'd better be,' warned Jacqueline, pushing back her chair. 'Because there's more going on with that guy than you even want to know about.'

'There is?'

'Come on.' Jacqueline grabbed her purse. 'We don't want to keep Peter waiting. I've got phone calls to make.'

30
Aurora

Aurora was back in LA for summer vacation. It had been ages since she'd returned to the Nash/Rose mansion and she was surprised to discover that she missed England. She missed Europe, she guessed, another continent, because that was where the most momentous events of her life so far had taken place. Here, she was just another starlet with an empty head and pockets full of money. She didn't want to be that person any more.

Her first night back, Farrah Michaels called.

'Hey, you wanna party?' It seemed that, after months apart, Farrah was prepared to bury the hatchet. Aurora couldn't remember what they'd fallen out so publicly about, but she'd never been one to hold a grudge.

'Sure.' Though, her heart wasn't in it.

They went to Basement—for old times' sake?—and drank shots of dark, intoxicating liquid and got high in the back of Farrah's BMW. Aurora couldn't begin to explain everything that had happened since she'd started at St Agnes—Pascale, the abortion, Paris—and anyway, Farrah didn't ask. Instead she yabbed on about how her dad was pulling strings for her to take the lead in one of Searchbeam's upcoming movies. It went over Aurora's head; she wasn't interested. The conversations she had with Pascale were enlightening, intelligent; about real, important things... She drank through the mind-freeze of Farrah's dialogue and thought about the difference between women and girls.

Farrah could never understand the stuff she'd done. She'd be grossed out at the idea of Pascale and wouldn't be able to grasp the concept of a connection, a soul mate, regardless of sex. And as for the abortion... For endless nights Aurora had cried into her pillow, hollow inside, worried she was a murderer. Pascale had been hard about it—'Get used to it: nobody cares except you'—telling her she had to forget what happened; even, once, saying how bored she was of being Aurora's sole confidante. In retrospect it had been her salvation. Pascale's coolness meant everything was still normal and she wasn't some victim or leper people had to tiptoe around for fear of contamination. From Farrah's perspective she'd be both of those and more.

The following week, Tom Nash flounced out on to the patio where Aurora and her mother were sitting by the pool. Aurora was in a scant bikini, making the most of the California rays, while Sherilyn was wrapped head-to-toe in pashmina, settled under a parasol and gazing vacantly into the middle-distance from behind a pair of dark super-UV-protection sunglasses.

'Kiddo, I've got news for you!' Tom took a seat at the

end of Aurora's lounger and she lazily withdrew one of her earphones.

She hoped it wasn't anything to do with returning to the ranch in Texas. Every time she met her father's affectionate gaze she experienced a ripe mixture of sadness, disgust and regret when she thought about Billy-Bob Hocker and the ensuing crisis she had endured. She doubted she'd ever fully get over it. She never wanted to set foot there again.

'What?'

'That was Rita Clay on the phone.' Excitedly Tom pushed a recently dyed honey strand from his face. 'We've been in touch for a little while now and, well…she's agreed to represent you! Isn't that brilliant?'

A couple of years back this would have been quite cool. Rita was one of Hollywood's top female agents and responsible for hauling many a sagging career back on track. But Aurora couldn't summon her father's enthusiasm. As Tom went on about promotion and recording and image reconstruction she felt the exact same way she had with Farrah the other night: as if there was a great barren distance between her and it.

'So?' he pressed. 'What do you think?'

Aurora sat up. 'Great.'

'We've been talking about you doing a new album. I even suggested we collaborate, the three of us!' He threw an eager glance at Sherilyn, who failed to react. 'If we can get Strike to commit…' Strike Records was her parents' label, and the one on which she had released her own, poorly received, album.

The collaboration idea chilled her blood. Nevertheless she said, 'Thanks, Dad.'

'No worries, baby.' He stood and kissed her forehead.

'We're just happy to see you getting well again.' He made it sound like she was in remission. 'Aren't we, Sherilyn?'

It was difficult to tell if her mother was asleep behind the glasses. 'Hmm?' She raised her head, not listening.

'Exactly.' Tom squinted into the sun. A couple of seconds passed before he returned his gaze to Aurora. 'Rita's coming to the house this afternoon. You can meet her then.'

Rita Clay was a striking black woman, tall, with cropped blonde hair. No sooner had she arrived at the mansion than she suggested to Aurora that they head back out: 'If we're going to talk about your future then we can't do it sitting in your past.' Rita was forthright and plainspeaking, said what she meant and meant what she said, and listened as well as talked. Aurora knew she handled a lot of the big names and it was easy to see why.

They went to The Blvd at the Beverly Wilshire. Several paparazzi had caught wind of the arrival and snapped ferociously as they exited Rita's car. 'Aurora, over here!' 'Aurora, how was the UK? Are you going back?' 'Aurora, are you signing to a new agency?'

When she had first started getting papped, Aurora had loved it. Recently it had lost its sheen. Today, however, with Rita Clay at her side and aware of the positive speculation that would cause, it felt a little more like it had at the beginning.

They ordered drinks. Rita asked, 'Where do you see yourself a year from now?'

Aurora hadn't thought that far ahead. It occurred to her that she only had one more year of school before she was back in the States for good.

'I'm not sure…' she began.

Rita had been told to expect a Hollywood brat—certainly everything she'd seen and read about Aurora Nash supported this verdict—but, to her surprise, the girl seemed rather hesitant, rather uncertain…even rather shy. Perhaps the boarding school boot camp had worked after all.

'Go on,' she encouraged.

Aurora felt compelled to tell Rita the truth about how she felt—at least, some of it. 'It's my mom and dad…' She shook her head. 'This is going to sound totally nuts.'

Rita waited.

She took a deep breath. 'OK, so, it's like I was kind of born into this life, you know, Hollywood and everything, and now I'm not sure I want it. But I can't get out. I'm Aurora Nash—and it's normal to me, I guess, because it's all I've ever known, but some days it just feels really… *empty*…and I think there could be so much more to life that I haven't found yet. That makes out like I'm really ungrateful, but there it is, that's how I feel. And it's like my dad's got this grand plan for me, and I love him and everything, but he's never ever asked even what you just asked—about where I see myself. So maybe that's why I don't know the answer.

'I don't feel as though I know them—my mom, especially—and they don't know me. And none of us really cares. It's like we're strangers, living in the same house.' Her brow creased. 'I can't explain it. My mom's stoned off her head 24-7 and that can't be me in however many years' time, with my husband or whatever—it *can't*—because they never seem to talk, they don't even seem to *like* each other. It's not like a normal marriage, and we're not like a normal family. If normal families exist. But I never thought about this stuff before, and now I am it seems so *wrong*, somehow. So I guess what I'm trying to say is, I appreciate your being here and the fact you've met me and all, but I can't honestly say my heart is a hundred per cent in this, and I don't want to waste your time, so I figured I might as well be straight about it.'

Rita raised an eyebrow. This was certainly a breath of fresh air. When she was positive Aurora had said all she wanted to, she prompted, 'How long have you felt like this?'

'A while.'

Their drinks arrived. Rita added sugar to strong coffee. 'OK,' she said, 'I hear you. And there are too many girls in this town who mess up their lives because of it.'

'You think?'

Rita nodded. 'I know. Too much, too young. Nothing left to aim for.'

'Am I spoiled?'

'By most people's standards, incredibly.'

'So why aren't I happy?'

'You're clever enough to answer that.'

Aurora chewed her lip. Rita continued, 'My advice? Don't make any rash decisions. If you don't know yet what you want out of life, there's plenty of time to find out.' Her voice softened. 'And the only way you're going to do that is through exploring your options. Don't close doors on yourself, Aurora—not yet.'

'I should sign with you, then?'

'Your experience of a career like your parents',' commented Rita, 'a career here in LA, hasn't got off to the best start.' She touched her lips to her drink. 'Your album bombed, your fashion collaboration got slated and, I'm sorry to say it, your perfume stinks. I don't know a single person who'd wear it.'

'Is this meant to make me feel better?'

'It's meant to make you see things as they are. The point is that, with me, it'll be different. Success changes everything. I've seen it happen. Honey, I've *made* it happen. See how you feel a year from now. Things might change.'

Aurora sat back. She felt better having confided in someone, though she wasn't sure she'd communicated accurately what she meant.

Maybe Rita was right. She was seventeen: it stood to reason she didn't know where she was headed...who did? Apart from Pascale, who said she wanted to be an astronomer and talked about those distant moons with their strange, wonderful names—Ganymede, Io, Europa—and, knowing Pascale, was destined to one day reach them.

She wanted her own personality, just like Pascale: a personality that was nothing to do with Tom Nash or Sherilyn Rose. Working with Rita was a good opportunity, one Aurora wouldn't get again, and unless she grabbed it now she might never know whether she could make a go of it, achieve something in her own right.

'OK,' she told Rita, raising her Coke for a toast. 'I'll give it a shot.'

Sherilyn Rose's therapy session took place twice a week at Hollywood's Tyrell Chase Center. It was a popular choice with celebrities and, in the past, to her dismay, she'd run into many a face she recognised. Of course acknowledgement was never made on either part. It was accepted that people in their line of work should need an outlet, and

Tyrell Chase offered the best there was. Specifically, Lindy Martin did.

'Talk to me about the past few days,' said Lindy now, in her calm, soothing voice, once they had gone through the customary relaxation techniques. Sherilyn was reclining on Lindy's black leather couch, her eyes closed.

'Sleeping hasn't been easy,' she confessed. That was the understatement of the century: she wasn't getting off until four each morning.

'I'll sign you a repeat prescription,' said Lindy. Sherilyn omitted the fact she'd been taking so many of Lindy's magic pills that she'd developed immunity to them, at least as far as sleeping went. Instead they made her feel spacey and numb, her mind alert and her body weak. It was how she was operating.

'You have things on your mind?' pressed Lindy. She crossed thin, tanned legs, compact in a navy pencil skirt.

'Always.' Wearily Sherilyn raised a hand to her forehead, every inch the damsel in distress. And that was the word: *distress*. The past twenty years had been distressing, right from the moment she'd married Tom. 'I can't stop thinking about what we did. If it was a mistake…'

'We've been through this before, Sherilyn. It was seventeen years ago. You have to let the past be.'

'It's been a lie.' Her lips were cracked, her eyes filled with warm, stinging tears. 'All of it. I can't even look myself in the mirror any more. Do you know what it's like to live a lie?'

There was a pause. 'Let's keep this about you,' said Lindy evenly.

'It eats away at you.' Vacantly she gazed up at the whirling ceiling fan, as measured in its motion as Lindy was in her words. Round and round, round and round, its effects rendered nothing to her the moment she left this room.

'Can you be more specific about what's troubling you?'

More specific. Yes, she could be. If she revisited that place.

'The island,' she choked, the previous night's insomnia catching up with her, lulling her into drowsiness and transporting her back across that wide green Indian Ocean, Tom Nash's hand in hers. *'Cacatra.'* The syllables sharp as daggers, slicing her jugular.

'And what was the man's name?' Lindy knew, of course. Her client needed to say it, to put a name to her fear.

Sherilyn struggled. *'Reuben van der Meyde,'* she uttered at last, the words laced in shame.

Lindy nodded. The first time she had treated a client who had experienced the same thing on Cacatra—for Sherilyn Rose and Tom Nash were not the only ones— she had been appalled, disgusted, speechless. Most of all, staggered that someone in van der Meyde's position would facilitate a scheme like that. Now she saw it *was* exactly why: having all that wealth and power was the very reason he could. When someone had that much money, where did they go next?

Lindy had never discussed the enterprise with any of her colleagues at the Center—not even her husband. What got said in therapy stayed in therapy.

'And what is your daughter's name?' she asked.

'Aurora.'

'That's right. Aurora *is* your daughter, Sherilyn. And you *are* her mother. Remember?'

Sherilyn wrestled the feelings her child's name evoked.

'Tom thinks it's all sweetness and light now she's been in England,' she croaked. 'But nothing's changed.'

'What do you mean by that?'

She was snapped from her reverie, frustrated by Lindy's stupid line of questioning. 'I mean you try walking in on your kid with a snooker cue up her ass and then try telling me she's changed into an angel overnight!'

Lindy was accustomed to clients' outbursts. She waited while Sherilyn composed herself. 'It hasn't been overnight, has it, Sherilyn? It's been twelve months. People *can* and *do* change.'

'Not her.' Sherilyn had convinced herself. 'She's evil. And it's karma, retribution, whatever you want to call it. Punishing me.'

'Can you explain to me why you feel that way?' Sherilyn Rose's sessions always went the same: despair, anger, paranoia. Regular as clockwork.

'What we did was wrong,' barked Sherilyn. 'The *way* we got her was wrong. Our *reasons* for getting her were wrong.'

'Tom and you were never going to have children of your own.'

'Of course we weren't. But still we married. I thought it would be easy. After all, it was right for us: the money, the music, the publicity. How hard could it be? We were friends; there was no expectation. At the time it was bearable, but now...now *it's slowly killing me.*'

'Have you told your husband how you feel?'

'My husband?' she spluttered. 'You make it sound like we're holding hands in bed each night and whispering sweet nothings.' Her mouth twisted. *'Hardly.'*

In fact, even if she had wanted to talk to Tom about

any of this, it would scarcely have been possible. In recent months he had been consumed by their new album, barely giving her a chance to get involved—and he knew the creative sessions were her favourite part—and bolting to his ranch in Texas whenever the mood struck. She shuddered when she thought about what he might be getting up to with that farmhand of his. Oh, she'd seen the way Tom ogled Billy-Bob Hocker's labourer's body when she'd been out there to visit.

'Despite your arrangement,' suggested Lindy, whose preference wasn't normally to dispense her own opinion, 'you can still be friends.'

'It's too late for that,' said Sherilyn. 'It's too late for any of it. The moment Aurora turns eighteen I'm taking Tom through the divorce courts. I don't care who finds out why. We've kept this to ourselves way too long. It's high time the world found out our dirty little secret.'

31
Stevie

At night he'd wake her to make love to her silently, the bright moon swimming in through the window and bathing them in ghostly light. In the middle of the day she'd meet him on-set and they'd snatch ten minutes inside his trailer, in the nearest washroom, hidden behind a screen, against a wall. This morning they had done it twice already, tangled between Stevie's bed sheets, unable to get enough of each other after two months of dating. She'd believed Xander to be sexy but not like this, not in a way that made it impossible for them to be apart, for her to crave him every second he wasn't there. Just as she'd reconciled herself to letting passion go, accepting in exchange something more constant and sustainable, she realised she could have it all.

Xander moved down Stevie's body, parting her legs and disappearing between them. She opened wider, pulling at his hair as he brought her to rapture, making her wetter and wetter, his tongue sliding into her, suffocated with the task.

It was past eight, a rare day off for both of them but they ought to be getting up, there were things she had to do...

'Fuck me,' she breathed, not wanting to come till he was in her. As his face came close and she kissed him, tasting herself on his lips, she reached down and grasped his cock, guiding it, feeling it vanish inside. Raising one knee to her chest, she sharpened the angle of his entry, allowing him to sink unbridled into her heat, wrapping her other leg round his waist and tying him to her. Rock-hard, he thrust so deep it hurt. This wasn't like sex she'd ever had and she knew the reason for it: they were two people who felt the exact same way about each other. No power struggles, no game playing. She was coming alive again.

'I love you,' she whispered.

And then they both gathered pace at the same time, catching sight of a bright light, climbing towards it like explorers staking new territory, their breath coming quickly, battling to the top, not resting till they reached it.

Stevie came first, Xander moments later, and then she again. He collapsed on top of her, his head in her neck, and she held his strong shoulders till they were both spent.

'Fuck,' said Xander, rolling off.

They lay side by side. His fingers found hers and held them. Stevie turned to face him, adoring the way that when he had his eyes closed she could see how long and soft his lashes were as they rested on his cheek. This was how it was meant to be. When she'd come to America she'd never have imagined this would happen: her career was one thing but finding Xander was another. How was it that a heart could be broken, beaten beyond recognition, but still resurface and risk doing it again? Because the risk was worth taking. The prize was too good.

Xander opened his eyes and fixed on a spot beyond her shoulder. It was a look she had become used to, his dark gaze private and pensive, frowning slightly in the manner of someone trying to remember. Remember what? She had decided not to press him. She trusted Xander, and that meant having faith that if there was something she needed to hear, he'd tell her.

Abruptly, he sat. 'Come live with me,' he said. 'Let's make it official.'

Surprised, Stevie pushed herself up on one elbow. 'What?'

'I mean it. Why not?'

She shook her head, sitting straighter. 'Where's this come from?'

Taking her hands, he kissed each of them in turn. 'I know this is right. And you know this is right. Because it's right.'

She laughed.

'Marry me.'

'Xander—!'

He smiled the smile she loved. 'Come live with me and marry me and let's live happily ever after.'

'But we haven't…' Giddy, she laughed again. 'I mean, it's only been a few months. Are you serious?'

'Deadly. I know it's not the most romantic setting, but, hey, this bed means a lot to me.'

She put a hand on his cheek and spoke gently. 'Ask me again.'

'I want to be with you always, Stevie,' he said solemnly. 'I want us to be together. I want us to be married. Say yes?'

Bibi Reiner had been married to Linus Posen for less than six months, and every moment of it had been hell. Linus wasn't bothering to conceal his infidelities any longer: he brought girls back to the house like they were going out of fashion. Once upon a time he'd tried to get her involved but he knew not to ask any longer. It wouldn't matter so much—be a *good* thing, even—if it put him off sex with her. It didn't. Soon as her day's work was done—whatever debased, agonising work he had in store for The Faceless Vixen that week—he wanted to get his own kicks. He loved playing her DVDs while he fucked her, and she would lie there, smothered beneath his damp, revolting bulk, gritting her teeth and praying for it to be over.

Tomorrow, she was attending a very different wedding. Stevie and Xander had wasted no time in organising their big day, an intimate ceremony in the Bahamas, only a matter of weeks after their engagement had been announced.

Stevie knew, of course. The day she'd called, with none of the usual niceties, and asked to meet, Bibi had known instantly why. Her friend didn't say how she'd come across *Goldicocks and the Three Bares* and Bibi didn't ask. She'd told Bibi she was getting her out, away from Linus, flipped open a case on the bed and started bundling belongings into it.

Only it wasn't that easy. Yes, she was desperate and unhappy; yes, she was damaged and addicted and taken advantage of; yes, she wanted out, but Bibi wasn't yet ready to accept that the things she'd been subjected to had all been in vain. Where would that leave her? Despite the humiliation of Linus's movies, he still promised that her big break would come. He was loathsome to her, and at the same time he was essential. Without him, she'd be an ex-porn-star with no chance of switching to the mainstream. With him, she was miserable as sin.

'Please, B,' Stevie had begged that day, cradling Bibi's head as she sobbed her heart out. 'All that matters is your happiness. You can't carry on like this.'

But the way Bibi saw it she had no other option. She was close to snapping. There was no way out. How come Stevie's life had turned out so different? It wasn't fair.

'I'll get you a place,' Stevie had pleaded. 'We'll set you up on your own, OK? Pay me back when you can, money's not an issue. I'll put you in touch with Marty—'

Bibi had laughed sourly. 'Like Marty King's gonna look twice at me,' she'd mumbled, wiping her nose. 'The minute they sniff out my past, it's over.'

By the time Bibi had persuaded her friend to leave, Stevie was almost more upset than she was. Stevie made her promise they would speak every day, and that if Bibi changed her mind, she'd be there in a heartbeat... What else could she do?

Now, Linus was sprawled in a chair on their hotel terrace, the Caribbean sun pouring on to his globular white body. He was sleeping, tired after their flight, lips parted, snoring. Xander and Stevie had paid for their guests to stay in a resort close to Nassau. The ceremony would take place the following afternoon on the shores of nearby Paradise Island.

The sight of her husband filled her with disgust: his flaccid nipples, the greying hairs on his chest, and his big ugly feet with their claw-like, yellowing toenails.

Bibi unpacked her bag quietly, not wanting to wake him. After sleep he was always horny, would grope for her and pin her down, never mind about foreplay, or if she was sore—Linus thought only of his own satisfaction. She'd lie there and let him tear into her, rip her apart in body and mind, silent, salty teardrops coursing into the pillow. Every time the same. He knew she cried but he didn't care. If anything, he liked it.

Carefully Bibi extracted her cosmetics bag and slipped into the bathroom, closing the door noiselessly behind her. She chalked up and inhaled the white powder. The day ahead became bearable. She was ready to face the world.

Stevie had wanted a quiet affair, no cameras, no media, no spotlight—just friends and family. The setting, the golden shores of Paradise Island, lent itself perfectly to the occasion. She was resplendent in a dress conceived by an edgy British designer, a classic, demure style with a scoop neck and full-length, Spanish-lace sleeves. With the sighing blue ocean behind them, the warm Pacific air quiet and still, she and Xander were married beneath a petal-strewn pagoda.

Afterwards, they drank champagne on the beach.

'Congratulations, Mrs Jakobson,' said Marty King, enjoying the canapés. 'Have to say, I didn't see this one comin'.'

'You didn't?' Stevie hadn't eaten much and the bubbles were making her hot-faced and woozy. 'And by the way it's not Jakobson. I'm keeping my name.'

Next to him, Wanda Gerund nodded in approval. 'Good,' her publicist said. 'I always thought Stevie Speller had a ring to it.'

'She does now!' Stevie brandished her hand.

'What I *meant*,' elaborated Marty, 'was that you kids seemed so tight on your careers.'

'We are,' said Stevie. 'It doesn't mean we can't be married.' Their joint project, the Vegas showgirl movie, had been released to critical acclaim. Wanda had warned her that cynics would surmise their marriage was a scam, engineered to hit the headlines in the same week as the film's release, but it didn't bother her. Too many conspiracy theorists in the world.

'You never know, Marty,' Wanda teased, 'it could be you next.'

'I doubt that.' Marty made a face. He'd been a bachelor all his life, was too busy for a relationship. He was yet to find a woman who could match him ball for ball. In the meantime, career was paramount, always had been.

Stevie spotted Bibi and Linus by the water. Bibi had taken her shoes off and was clutching them under one arm so her feet could get wet…a shade of the untroubled girl she remembered from New York. If only her friend would accept her help.

Excusing herself to Marty and Wanda, who were now locked in a fiery conversation about married couples in Hollywood, Stevie made her way over.

'Here comes the beautiful bride,' leered Linus, sweat patches gathered beneath the armpits of his grey suit.

Stevie hugged her friend but couldn't bring herself to greet the director. If it hadn't been obligatory to invite him she wouldn't have wanted him within a hundred miles of the event.

'I was just telling Linus about when we lived together in New York!' Bibi's eyes shone. Stevie could tell she was drugged up again. Couldn't Linus see it, too? Didn't he care?

'It was a blast,' she agreed.

'Sure was.' Bibi scanned the guests. 'How come my little bro didn't make it?'

Because I didn't invite him.

'Something came up,' she said instead. The truth was she'd only managed to get rid of Ben a matter of weeks ago, when he'd finally acquired a new girlfriend and decided he'd move out and leech off someone else for a while. He'd been useless about the Bibi situation, his own shame and repulsion overriding his sister's far greater need. By the time he'd left, Stevie found herself loathing him. His selfishness, his indolence, his predilection for cheesy puffs that got orange powder all over the kitchen counters, and how by the time Xander came on the scene he'd lope around the apartment late at night, like a child listening ardently at a bedroom door. The image of him beating off to The Faceless Vixen was scorched for ever into her memory.

'A job?' Bibi asked brightly.

'Not sure.'

Xander joined them, slipping an arm round Stevie's waist. 'Hello, lovely wife.'

'I can't get used to being called that.'

'You'd better.'

'"Wife" is a feeble word,' Stevie mused. 'Not like "husband".' She said it again: '*Husband.* Hardly fair.'

Bibi giggled, but didn't express an opinion, just clutched tight to her drink.

Linus screwed up his face. 'You better keep that one in check,' he lewdly counselled Xander. 'Can't tell what she's on about.'

In response, Xander regarded him blankly. 'I always know what she's on about,' he replied, with a controlled smile. There was another silence and Stevie felt glad she was drunk.

She saw Bibi turn to the water, lost in thought. The pink sun was kissing the horizon, melting as it got there, the ocean like rippling silk.

'Are you honeymooning here?' asked Linus. He winked unpleasantly. 'I could've done with a bit more honeymoon, if you catch my drift. Non-stop, we were.'

'Actually we've decided to hit Europe,' said Xander, in an attempt to dispel the image. 'A friend of mine owns a boat off the Italian coast.'

'Xander's a competent sailor,' Stevie proudly confirmed.

'Europe's a great place,' huffed Linus self-importantly. He flashed a look at Stevie. 'European women, they're a breed of their own.'

Bibi was still gazing at the ocean. Stevie was conscious of bleating on about her and Xander's plans, their newborn marriage, their happiness. Touching Xander's elbow to indicate her departure, she linked arms with her friend.

'Come on,' she said, 'let's go for a walk.'

The women made their way down the beach, cool clear water washing up between their toes. Stevie held up her dress so the bottom of it didn't get wet.

When the others were out of earshot, Bibi stopped.

'Steve,' she said, facing her. 'Can I tell you something?'

Stevie frowned. 'Of course.' She let the dress go and took Bibi's hands. 'Anything.' Bibi took a deep breath. She closed her eyes. And that was when she revealed her plan.

32
Lori

A month later, Peter Selznick moved in. Peter was an actor, twenty-seven, recently emerged from the hit show *No Husbands Needed*, in which he appeared as a topless gardener. His first starring role in a movie was due to hit screens early next year, so as far as publicity was concerned there was everything to play for.

Lori had attempted to find him attractive when they'd first met: it would be so much easier. But, she didn't. He *was* good-looking, just not for her. Tall, broad and strapping, with a floppy mop of streaky blond hair and a goofy grin, he was a real Californian jock. Nothing he said particularly interested or engaged her—he seemed fond of the phrases 'Hot chicks', '*Sweeeet!*' and 'No fear, dude!'—and yet nothing about him offended her. He reminded her of a puppy, breathy and enthusiastic and eager to please. Of the many people she could have been made to live with, Jacqueline might have set her up with a great deal worse.

Anyway, they were hardly ever in the mansion at the same time. Lori's shoots often took her away overnight and Peter was in the first flushes of attending every party going, at some of which they arranged to meet and pose for photos together. It was easy, and the press crowed about what a staggering couple they made.

Tonight they were returning from one such event. Peter employed a Hispanic driver called Santo, whom he spoke to like an imbecile. Lori made a point of conversing with him in Spanish and being as friendly as she could, to make up for Peter's rudeness. Perhaps they weren't so unlike a real-life couple after all.

'They were hot for us tonight, baby!' Peter rambled as the car pulled up the drive. 'Jerking themselves right off for a piece of the action!'

Presumably he was talking about the paparazzi. 'Mmm,' said Lori, who was tired and thinking of getting into her bed.

So, it seemed, was Peter. Once inside the mansion, without warning, he pinned her arms behind her and pushed her up against the wall.

'What do you think you're doing?' she demanded.

'Come on, babe,' he crooned, his breath smelling faintly of Jack Daniel's. 'I know this whole virginity thing's a loada horse crap. You *gotta* want me.'

Firmly she drove against him, using the weight of her body because her hands were tied. 'I don't,' she said. 'Get used to it.'

'Aw, don't say that.' He pressed himself closer and she was alarmed to feel his erection straining through his suit pants. 'Little Peter's gonna get upset.'

Little Peter didn't feel that little. Lori managed to pull her hands free.

'I mean it,' she told him, holding them up in surrender. 'Back off.'

He scrunched his face up. 'You *really* a virgin?' His voice went all high at the end.

'Yes.'

'How old are you—twenty-two, twenty-three?'

'Nineteen.'

'Sheesh! And you've never had cock?'

'Good night, Peter.'

He grinned, eyes soppy with lust. 'You know I like a challenge?'

She turned at the stairs. 'I hope you're drunker than I think you are,' she said. 'Otherwise we've got a problem. Sleep on it.'

She was woken by the sound of a handle turning. Sleepily, she consulted the time: two a.m. And the silhouette of Peter Selznick in her bedroom doorway, his outline totally black, only the dim light from the hall illuminating him from behind.

'Go to bed,' Lori said wearily, flopping back on the pillows. It occurred to her that she should feel threatened—what exactly did he think he was doing?—but she couldn't find Peter threatening. Even though he was older than her, most of the time he acted like a kid.

'I can't sleep,' he complained, flicking the light on.

To her alarm he was completely naked—and completely hairless. His entire body had been waxed, it seemed: the smooth golden chest, bursting with pecs, his long, muscular legs. And that part in between…the part of a man she had never seen in the flesh before… Peter's engorged member sprang proud from his baldness, hairless as the day he was born.

Were they all this huge? She found herself mesmerised by it, couldn't stop looking. Of course he read this as an invitation.

'You know you want it, babe,' he announced, striding in buoyantly. 'What are we fighting against? You gotta put out some day, why not with me? I can teach you stuff.' He tugged once at his penis, an odd gesture that was somehow absent-minded. 'All you gotta do is lie back, relax and let me show you a good time. You know how many girls out there would kill to be in your position?'

Lori sat up, trying doggedly not to stare at his bulging groin. She felt as if someone were trying to sell her a cheap holiday. 'Peter, I told you. *No.* I'm not interested. I thought One Touch made it clear to you what the deal was.'

'One touch is all it takes,' he panted, clambering on to the bed. Lori recoiled against the wall, aware her tank top and shorts did little to conceal the swell of her breasts and hips. Peter drank it in and, for a second, as his bulk stood to attention only a matter of inches away, she experienced that arrow of desire she had known with Rico. She had no doubt Peter was a practised lover. Yet, as ever, the arrow missed its target and shot straight into the ground.

'I want you to leave *right now*,' she commanded. 'We'll talk in the morning.'

'Why're you doing it?'

'Doing what?'

'Missing out.'

'Missing out,' she repeated flatly.

'On sex. It's the best there is. More specific, sex with *me* is the best there is. You're only punishing yourself.'

'Go to bed, Peter.'

'You telling me you don't want some of this?' He sat back and gestured to the obscene tower between his legs. She resisted looking.

'Yes.'

'Yes, you don't; or yes—' he winked naughtily '—you do?'

'Go to bed,' she said again, pulling the sheet up to cover her.

For a moment Peter weighed up his chances, before releasing an exasperated puff and bouncing off the bed. He headed for the door, swollen staff leading the way. Lori fought the urge to laugh. It wasn't funny, he was way out of order—but his unabashed attempts at seduction were at least straightforward.

'You know where I am if you change your mind,' he said gravely, turning to award her one final glimpse of what she was missing.

'Sure.'

Sulkily, he closed the door. When she was sure he'd gone, Lori lay back and turned the light off. For a long time she stayed awake, unable to get to sleep. She thought she heard intermittent yelps from the opposite end of the mansion— Peter bringing himself the pleasure he'd promised her? Snaking her hand down past the band of her shorts, she closed her eyes and, to her disappointment, thought of JB Moreau. Nighttime was perilous, dark and sweet, a landscape for dreaming. She wondered what he would look like naked.

'I'm not kidding. He just turned up in the middle of the night! You've got to talk to his management again about whatever it was you agreed.'

Jacqueline was appalled. 'Lori, I'm so sorry,' she said. 'This is awful.'

'It's OK.' She dismissed her concern. 'It's just annoying. And it's like Peter's dead-set on this campaign now to get me into bed. He won't take no for an answer!'

Jacqueline straightened in her office chair. '"No" is the word we made *absolutely clear* throughout the negotiations.' Again Lori thought of the puppy. It was as if Peter were in toilet training—next she'd be teaching him to walk at her heel. 'It's completely unacceptable,' her publicist went on. '*Completely* unacceptable. Leave it with me. I'll sort it out.'

'Thanks.'

'Don't thank me. Just stick with it. It sounds like you handled it great.'

A thought occurred to her. 'Surely everyone else imagines we're…doing it?'

Jacqueline nodded. 'That's the beautiful thing. Peter's a renowned ladies' man and you're a virgin. As far as the press are concerned, he's met the woman he's prepared to wait for… or has he? Peter might have switched you. I guess they'll never know. Him being partnered with you makes everyone see him from another angle; you being partnered with him achieves the same. That's why we were keen to get you together.'

'So long as we don't *actually* have to get together, in that sense, it's fine by me.'

'And it's fine by me, too.'

Desideria Gomez was throwing a dinner party to mark her fortieth birthday. Peter was out of town so Lori attended by herself, the low-key affair marked by just a knot of photographers outside the host's beachfront apartment.

Desideria herself looked stunning in a killer dress and

heels, her glossy black hair caught in a long low ponytail at the nape of her neck. She greeted Lori at the door, enveloping her in sensual musk, and Lori presented her gift: a solid silver bracelet bearing the engraving *DG*. Desideria bit her lip with pleasure when she opened it.

Guests mingled inside. Lori spotted Dante, a gorgeous shaven-headed black man new to the modelling circuit, and Pearl, a six-feet-plus redhead with legs that went on for an eternity. Both were represented by La Lumière.

'Hey, sweetie,' crooned Dante, kissing her. He grinned wickedly. 'How's Peter?'

Lori didn't want to think about Peter. 'Another time,' she said.

'Have you *seen* the face on that?' Dante murmured, nodding over her shoulder.

Lori turned. Dante was known for his catty one-liners and backstage bitching—she wondered what poor soul was on the receiving end this time.

Rebecca Stuttgart.

She was in conversation with a man Lori didn't recognise. Lori's attention flitted anxiously across the room, half wanting JB to be there and half unable to trust herself if he was. The strength of her dislike impelled her to march straight up and chuck her drink in his face.

'You wouldn't think she was bedding the sexiest guy on the planet,' crooned Pearl, licking rosy-pink lips. 'Imagine sleeping with JB Moreau every night.'

'Excuse *me*!' Dante was indignant. 'The sexiest guy on the planet is standing right here.' He sighed. 'But I do kind of agree with you.'

To her intense discomfort, Lori was seated next to Rebecca Stuttgart at dinner. Her husband was nowhere to be seen.

'How's Mac Valerie treating you?' Rebecca politely enquired, placing two fingers over her wineglass when the waiter tried to fill it.

'Great,' said Lori, wondering why a reminder of JB had to be there every damn way she turned. Her conscience buckled each time she tried to meet Rebecca's probing gaze. Did the woman know? She'd certainly had that impression when they'd met at La Côte. Had JB confessed to what had happened? Had he lied to cover his tracks, vowing Lori to be the one who kissed him, not the other way around? Perhaps she *had* been? She could no longer be sure of anything that happened that day. Had they laughed about it, the silly child clinging on for a recurrence? Or was Rebecca suspicious of every La Lumière model she met, knowing the predator her husband had become? 'I'm proud to have the contract.'

'So you should be.' Rebecca eyed her for a moment then said, 'JB thinks a lot of you.'

Lori didn't respond. She had the sensation of being mocked, invited to join a game whose rules she couldn't grasp and which she would never win. She didn't know whether to feel ashamed or embarrassed and so settled for both. Did they have kids?

If I'd known he was married, would that have made a difference?

There was a brief hiatus while their appetisers arrived, followed by a smattering of polite appreciation for the food.

Rebecca smiled stiffly. 'What I mean to say is, he's fond of you all at the agency.'

'I'm sure.'

Gently, Rebecca pressed the back of her fork into the salmon mousse. 'JB's out of town right now,' she said, 'in Europe. With his family.'

Lori wondered why she was telling her this. 'In France?' she asked, to be gracious.

Rebecca took a small, controlled bite and chewed without relish. 'Italy. Capri.'

'I've never been.'

There was an uneasy pause, so Lori enquired, 'Will you join him?'

'I don't think so. I ought to be heading home this week.'

'You don't live in LA?'

'JB has a place here,' said Rebecca. 'But it's not our home.'

Home, with its connotations of safety and warmth and all things familiar, didn't fit with a man like JB. She was surprised he had married at all. What was the point of marriage if you spent your whole time pursuing other people? It was possible they had an open relationship, something she was encountering more and more in Hollywood and which was anathema to her. Marriage was sacrosanct, a bond, a pledge. It was for always.

'Where's home?'

Rebecca looked blank.

'I'm sorry,' she tacked on hastily. 'I'm prying.'

'That's all right,' said Rebecca, sipping from her water glass and leaving a stain where her lips touched. She didn't volunteer the information, so Lori took it the conversation was over.

Fortunate diversion came from Desideria making a toast to her guests. It lasted long enough for the tension of their discussion to dissipate, and for there to be no obligation afterwards for either woman to resume it.

33
Aurora

'Come to Italy.'

A week before term began, Pascale called. Aurora jumped at the invitation. One last blowout before Mrs Durdon sank her vampire teeth back in. And eight weeks in LA had felt like a long time, even in spite of the renewed focus Rita Clay had given her. Rita was working overtime laying the foundations of her so-called comeback: exciting things were planned for when she left school in a year's time and returned here permanently.

Permanently.

The thought freaked her out. What if she didn't want to? What if she wanted to go somewhere quiet and be anonymous for a while? She hadn't told Pascale about her anxieties because she knew what Pascale would say: that she should quit LA for good and do something 'meaningful' with her life. Only it wasn't that simple.

Gisele and Arnaud Devereux had a villa on the island

of Capri. Having never visited Italy before, Aurora hadn't heard of it (though she had heard of Capri pants: not a good look). She flew out to Naples early September, where Pascale greeted her impassively at the airport.

'I missed you!' cried Aurora. They kissed each other briefly on the lips.

Pascale led her through the terminal. 'We've got a boat to catch.'

A cab took them to Naples harbour. The ferry ports were swarming with tourists dragging over-stuffed wheelie suitcases at their ankles. Aurora and Pascale bypassed the crowds, located the Devereux Bombardier Bowrider and climbed aboard with the help of two swarthy Italians. One, clad in crisp white shorts and a shirt with insignia across it, was at the wheel.

'Grazie, signor,' Pascale said, before uttering something else in Italian that was incomprehensible to Aurora.

The rocky peaks of Capri could be made out across the water, the low, thick haze of the midday heat obscuring the crags. As the girls whipped from the quay, abandoning the dirt and dust of Naples in their wake, Aurora breathed deeply the sea-salty air and heard the receding clamour of Italians on the mainland, quickly drowned beneath the humming engine of the speedboat.

'Pretty, don't you think?' said Pascale, slipping on her Gucci shades.

'Totally.' Immediately Aurora wished she hadn't said 'totally'. She needed to get a handle on what Pascale would call 'this crass American thing'. She was in Europe now. With Arnaud and Gisele Devereux. She wished she had just a pinch of Pascale's sophistication.

Twenty minutes later, they reached the island. There

was a queue of vessels waiting to come to ground: one by one, tourists were being assisted to shore on the solid bronzed arm of a young Italian. Open-top taxis, all white, hovered to take visitors to their hotels or apartments, or over the winding, jagged cliffs to the southern, older town of Anacapri. Aurora noticed how the Devereux boat had its own docking space and a flock of men descended as it landed, seizing the ropes, tying them down and helping the girls out with their belongings.

Pascale located her father's driver right away. Aurora reckoned he must have a different one for every place in the world.

Arnaud and Gisele's house was set on a rugged outcrop, a golden three-storey pied à terre sporting a huge, sea-facing semicircular veranda. Olive-green shutters, paint peeling in the warmth, lent an old-world glamour entirely at home on the island. Lemon trees burst with ripe, thick-skinned fruit, and a lagoon-like plunge pool dazzled in the sun.

It was windy. They were at the highest point of the island. Below, the chalky outcrops of the town of Capri, above, wide blue sky.

The villa was empty. Gisele had left a note, penned in flamboyant script, on the refrigerator. While Pascale scanned it, Aurora wandered aimlessly through the lofty, cool space, running her fingers across ornate dressers and cabinets, the frames of paintings and the spines of books, grooves and hollows soft with dust. Inside, the place was more like the English churches she had been forced to go to at St Agnes—quiet and chill, echoey, and smelling of oldness.

'They're out,' said Pascale, stating the obvious. 'Want to go into town?'

'Sure,' said Aurora. 'Where are they?'

Pascale tucked the note into the waist of her jeans. 'Meeting my cousin.'

Aurora's interest was aroused. 'JB's here?' She remembered the conversation she'd had with Gisele in Paris, the photograph of him in Pascale's dormitory.

'Didn't I say?'

'No.'

'You'll get to meet him in the morning. Papa's taking us out on the boat.'

'The one we came on today?'

Pascale laughed. 'Don't be silly,' she said. 'That one's just a toy.'

The boat they ended up sailing was a majestic ninety-foot superyacht with on-board games room, casino and fully stocked bar. They travelled at speed across the glinting sea, hot wind and sun and sparkle on the water. Smaller vessels passed—Italian, French, German flags rippling in the breeze, cresting on the waves the mammoth yacht left in its wake.

Over the bow, a swimming pool was carved out of the deck and framed by plush recliners, several uniformed staff ready to jump at the first signal. Gisele was sunbathing, her dark hair secured beneath an elegant turban headscarf and her enviable figure encased in a cutaway black swimming costume with a cluster of jewels at the cleavage. Pascale was beneath one of the parasols reading a book.

'Mind if I take a look around?' Aurora asked, unplugging her iPod.

Pascale didn't raise her head. 'So long as you keep to this end.'

'How come?'

A shrug. 'They're talking business.'

Aurora wondered if she'd *ever* get a chance to corner JB by himself. Since he'd come aboard, Pascale seemed to be trying everything to keep them at a distance. *'He's married, you know,'* she'd said primly when they had set sail at dawn, yet another smaller boat coming to collect them from the island and take them to where Arnaud's 'princess' was moored, a great white cut-out in a canvas of blue. *'So?'* Aurora had countered, reminding herself she was so over boning whatever guy happened to be there at the right time.

Yet on seeing the cousin in the flesh, Aurora was forced to acknowledge first that JB Moreau was about as far from Billy-Bob Hocker as it was possible to get, and second, not since before Paris had she fancied anyone so much. Plus the fact remained that he was a huge deal: he was one of the biggest names in fashion. When she'd let slip to Farrah— regrettably—that she'd made friends with his family, she'd been barraged with questions. Was he superhot? Was he a weirdo? Was he shy? Was he divorced from his ancient wife yet? Not that Aurora had been able to dispense many details: Pascale was just as cagey about Moreau as her parents were.

'Back in a sec,' she said breezily, choosing to ignore her friend's sidelong glance. If she could catch JB's eye on her way past and tempt him into one of the cabins then what Pascale didn't know couldn't hurt her.

A panel of frosted glass doors opened to the grand saloon. Aurora glimpsed the men at the stern, engrossed in conversation on the L-shape banquettes. JB was wearing a white shirt that was shivering in the wind, open to his navel.

He didn't look over.

Fuck.

She'd get his attention some other way. It was a dead cert he fancied her. How could he not? Weeks in LA had banished the waxy pallor awarded by St Agnes and restored Aurora to the all-American long-legged sweetheart men found impossible to resist. The moment they'd been introduced, she'd caught him scoping her out. If Pascale hadn't been there she'd have ramped her flirt banter into overdrive, but no such luck. His gaze was mesmerising, as unnerving as it had been in the photograph at school—intense, straight on, unblinking, even in sun. It was weird to meet him. She realised she must have been carrying his image in her head all that time without knowing it, because the truth of him was uncanny, as if he were a figure in a remembered painting come miraculously to life.

Below deck, Aurora found herself in a wood-panelled corridor adorned with works of expensive art. She perused at leisure, liking what she saw but not understanding it. She decided that one day, when she had her own place, she'd fill it with stuff like this that would have people coming past and oohing and aahing and drawing conclusions about what it said about their host, even if their host hadn't an idea what that was herself. Yes, she'd be intriguing. She'd be mysterious. She'd be—a word Pascale liked—*beguiling*.

'Hello.'

The voice came from behind. It was deep, and even in those two syllables carried an accent far stronger than Pascale's or her parents'.

'Oh,' she stammered, turning, putting a hand to her

chest in surprise and pissed he had caught her off guard. 'You frightened me.'

'Sorry.' JB smiled. His eyes were the bluest she had ever seen. It looked like he was wearing contacts or something. He raised a hand so it was resting just beneath the picture rail, leaning his body in close. The movement parted the material of his shirt.

'I—I thought you were upstairs,' she fumbled. It sounded like such a dumbass thing to say. Where were her playful one-liners and glittering repartee?

'I was,' he replied. 'Now I'm here.'

'Guess so.'

'Looking for something?'

'Just exploring.' Great—now she sounded like a five-year-old with a bucket and spade. She bristled, on the defence because it was easier. 'What's it to you?'

JB made a very French expression, a sort of shrug. God, he was sexy up close. Especially the scar, which was less pronounced than she'd envisaged but which gave his top lip a malice that was totally and utterly fucking ruinous.

'Making sure you keep out of trouble.'

Bingo! He was flirting. 'Trouble's not such a bad thing.' Aurora glanced up at him through sun-kissed eyelashes, at last hitting her stride. 'Is it?'

'That depends how often you get into trouble.'

Coquettish, she lifted an eyebrow. 'Oh?'

'You know what I mean.'

Abruptly, his demeanour changed. Aurora suddenly felt as if they weren't flirting at all. There was an unsettling awareness about JB, as though he knew every single thing she was thinking, had ever thought, the colour of his stare beaming into her like a laser.

'You should look after yourself better,' he said, drawing back.

The words threw her off course. 'I'm sorry?'

'Your body is a precious thing, Aurora. You shouldn't give it to anyone who asks.'

'Whatever,' she spluttered, unable to fathom that he was now assuming to give her some shitting lecture. 'You're not my dad.'

'Someone ought to be.'

'Ex*cuse* me?'

'Guidance. It's important.'

'How *dare* you? You've never even met my dad! You know nothing about him!'

'I know that you're too young to behave the way you do.'

She was raging. 'What would *you* know about the way I behave?'

'I know when someone wants me to make love to them.'

Aurora opened and closed her mouth, struck dumb by his candour. 'As *if*!' she spluttered, mortified. 'What makes you think I'd want to do anything with you…*Grampa*?'

'I'm thirty-three.' He was amused. She wanted to slap him.

'Exactly,' she spat, certain if ever she'd made a tit of herself, it was now. It sounded like all she'd done was suck off a few frat boys with buckteeth and braces.

'Get back upstairs,' he said. 'Pascale will be wondering where you are.'

'I'm not doing what you tell me.'

'As I thought: astounding maturity.'

'Fuck you. Seriously. Fuck you.'

He smiled but it didn't reach the eyes. 'So much attitude.'

'I wouldn't *have* an attitude if it weren't for you dicking me off,' she lashed. She folded her arms. 'I have to go to the bathroom.' She'd said the first thing that popped into her head and bitterly regretted it. Despite her anger, she had no desire for JB to be imagining her crouched over a toilet. 'To freshen up,' she added lamely.

JB regarded her strangely. Again she had the sense he already knew her: that they had been introduced at another time, maybe, and she wasn't remembering.

'Have I met you before?' She realised she'd asked it aloud.

He smirked. Yes, it *was* a smirk, as if she'd told a joke. Unbelievable! He had to be the rudest guy she'd ever met.

Without answering, JB peeled open the doors to the upper deck and seconds later vanished in a wash of white light.

Aurora visited the nearest restroom, splashing her face with cold water. Classical music piped into the closets; a selection of bottled hand therapies lined a Roman-bath-style bank of sinks next to squat cubes of unbearably soft white towels.

To hell with JB Moreau!

He was insufferable. The worst type of up-himself Mr I'm So Fucking Important. Well, he could shove his stupid *loco parentis* (one of Mrs Durdon's favoured phrases) up his (grudgingly pretty nice) ass and be done with it. What would he know about her life? Nothing, that was what. *Nothing.*

Jerk!

Re-entering the corridor, Aurora turned to make her way back out, but something stopped her: a sealed panel to her left, a gateway to the private life of Arnaud and Gisele

Devereux. Inquisitiveness spurred her on—that and a pinch of rebellion at JB's earlier reprimand. She decided she would try the door. If it opened, then surely it was fair game.

It did. Behind the panel, a giant room folded out, opulent and den-like. Swathes of red curtain were draped around a four-poster bed, lavish black rugs were spongy beneath her bare feet and a curved, gleaming drinks bar faced into the room. So this was where the great French couple slept when they were at sea. Aurora went quietly across to the bed, running a hand over its silky cream linens and the thick iron twists of its elaborate bed-head. Looking up, she caught sight of a huge ceiling mirror lit with tiny spot-bulbs.

She put a hand to her mouth to stifle her giggle. The famed politicians had their kinky scene, who'd have guessed it? Images of Arnaud screwing his wife popped into her head, Gisele's pale legs wrapped round him from beneath as she gazed up at their tangled reflection, at his tight ass, bright below the line of his swimming shorts.

One palm resting on the silken bed sheets, Aurora closed her eyes. In a flash, it was no longer Gisele beneath her husband, it was she entwined with JB… He was kissing her slowly on the lips, deeply and with feeling, his tongue finding hers, his strong arms lifting her from beneath, and then he was chastising her again, branding her an immature kid, and positioning himself above her, steering his cock into her mouth and telling her how to make him come…

Her fantasy was interrupted by the sound of the men's voices. Panicking, Aurora's first thought was to hide. They had found her out. Then she realised where the voices were coming from. In the corner of the bedroom was a hatch, partially open, that lifted on to the stern of the boat, exactly at the point where they were having their clandestine conversation. Indeed they spoke quietly, in a mixture of French and English.

'Of course it is her...' JB's accent was more pronounced than the older man's. 'We never lose sight of any of them.'

Arnaud's voice was cutting. '*The concerned fathers*, I am sure.'

'In some ways.'

A rumble in French that she didn't understand, before Arnaud continued: 'You know how we feel. Gisele, in particular.'

'I never asked you to get involved.'

'We are your family.'

'I have no need of family.'

Aurora moved closer, standing on tiptoes, straining to hear.

Arnaud's voice followed, hushed and urgent. 'What do you think your mother would make of this? Paul, too.'

'Paul supported Reuben unconditionally. They were like brothers. In any case, they cared little for what I did.'

'That was before you became involved in this...*scheme*.'

'Reuben's scheme makes money, vast quantities of it. Do not tell me—' a pause, during which Aurora imagined JB gesturing round the boat '—that holds no interest to you?'

'You would never have been without money.'

'I never wanted their money. I wanted my own.'

Arnaud swore in French. 'How many this year, Jean-Baptiste? Tell me.'

'Three. Selected by me.'

A bitter laugh. '"Selected." You make it sound like picking apples in the market.'

'In some ways, that is all it is.'

'What it is *is wrong*.'

'In my view, we are helping. We are doing a brave thing. It's only wrong in your view.'

What was wrong? What were they talking about? Aurora cursed the wind that kept snatching the words before they reached her.

'In any acceptable view,' countered Arnaud. 'How do you sleep at night? Knowing those mothers are out there, bribed and seduced and...*exploited*?'

'And rich beyond their wildest dreams.'

'But not as rich as you and van der Meyde.'

'It's relative.'

'Does it all come back to money? You can pay for life, trade it like a commodity?'

'You can pay for everything else. Why not that? It's the most valuable thing in the world. There is no reason it should not command a handsome fee.'

'You would think van der Meyde would be more careful after the situation he got himself in with that woman. Imagine! Meant to give the boy away, then, at the last moment, unable to.'

'Margaret Jensen has nothing to do with this.'

'No? I think she captures eloquently my point.'

'Jensen is lucky to be alive,' said JB. 'Reuben could have done with her as he wished.'

'Van der Meyde can do with anyone, any time, *as he wishes*. That's the problem. Did anyone stop to think about the boy? Believing his real mother to be dead?'

'Reuben had no alternative. Jensen was a liability, safer under his roof—'

'With the consolation prize of being able to raise her

own flesh and blood? Madness. What was van der Meyde thinking fathering the child himself? I thought you employed men to—'

'It was a lapse in judgement.' JB's voice was measured. 'It happened once and hasn't again. Today it is a meticulous process, you know that.'

'I'm sure. And you are meticulous in your "selection", are you?'

'Always. Hollywood is rife with possibilities but not all are appropriate. It must be the correct match.'

Aurora's heart was beating wildly. She felt very sick though she couldn't decide why.

'As much of a risk for them as for you?' Arnaud demanded.

'Let's call it collateral.'

Arnaud spoke so quietly she was hardly sure of the words. 'The babies who are not…born right. I know how van der Meyde has…*disposed* of them.'

'You know nothing.'

'You cannot play God, Jean-Baptiste.'

'God and the Devil, are they so very different? Look at the girl, Arnaud. *Look at her.* And tell me she would have been better off staying with her real mother.'

A shiver travelled down Aurora's spine.

Her real mother.

'We will never know.'

'Wake up. She has everything a girl could want.'

'You may imagine so,' Arnaud said softly. 'I see sadness in her.'

'You see sadness in everyone. It says more of you than it does of us.'

'Do you think she never wonders about her mother and father? The ones she never knew?'

Aurora backed away from the hatch, spots of colour bursting behind her eyes.

'Why should she?'

A sharp intake of breath as Arnaud took in smoke. 'That is precisely why you are able to do this.' There was a note of reluctant admiration in his words. 'You simply *do not care.*'

Alarm bells rang loud and long in Aurora's head.

Do you think she never wonders about her mother and father? The ones she never knew?

Tell me she would have been better off staying with her real mother.

Questions shot through her, their edges blunted by fear. She turned and stumbled, knocking a glass decanter from its position on the dresser. It smashed on the floor.

Immediately the conversation above her stopped. Aurora's heart was thrumming in her ears. She was trapped. She would be found. *God and the Devil...* The words resonated, taunting. She heard footsteps approaching, the sliding doors above her being peeled apart.

'What do you think you're doing?'

Quick, too quick, Arnaud was in the doorway. His eyes darted from wall to wall, absorbing the evidence, clocking the open hatch and returning accusingly to her face.

'I...I got lost,' she managed. She felt ill. The motion of the sea was too much.

'You got lost,' Arnaud repeated. His eyes were coffee-brown, his large nose and winking gold chain lending him an air of classic authority, like an emperor in the ring.

'I'm sorry, I didn't realise this was private, and I came in and I started looking around, and then I accidentally…' She gazed mournfully at the glass at her feet. 'My parents will pay for it…' The word 'parents' sounded vacant, absurd.

He considered her for a moment. 'Get out,' he said, not unkindly.

Gratefully, she headed for the open door. On the way past, he stopped her.

'Anything you might have heard,' he warned, his breath warm and smelling of cigarettes, 'forget. It is for your own protection. Do we understand each other?'

She nodded.

Abruptly, Arnaud grabbed her arm. 'Remember, you are on my boat.' He squeezed her so hard it hurt. 'And everything on this boat belongs to me. Every conversation, every word, every whisper.' She tried to pull away but his hold was too firm. 'I will not forget we had this talk. Will you?'

Eyes filled with tears, Aurora shook her head. 'N-no,' she stammered.

'Good.' She was on the cusp of crying out when he released her. 'Now go, get upstairs.'

Aurora's arm ached. It was red where he had gripped it. She locked herself in the bathroom a long time before she emerged.

34
Stevie

Xander's friend, a London financier named Paul Priestly, loaned them the boat. It was modest, a Sigma 35, with a dark blue mainsail and sleek wooden hull. Paul kept it moored in the South of France for most of the year, except during the summer months when he and his family would head down towards Greece and Italy. They had arranged to coincide with the midway point of the Priestlys' trip, when Paul would take to shore and travel back through mainland Europe.

'This is bliss,' Stevie said, arranging her towel across the bow and rubbing on sun cream. She decided there was no better scent in the world: it reminded her of caravan holidays with her brothers and sisters when she was young, getting burned under a Cornish sun and playing cards on a foldaway table. Warm wind filled the sails, inflating them like cheekfuls of air, sending the boat slicing through the water in purposeful strokes. On the horizon, the sharp contours of the isle of Capri could just be made out, the broad back of her sister Ischia sleeping next door.

'We could stay, you know.' Xander was at the stern, hands on the ship's wheel, richly tanned from a fortnight in the sun. 'Hire another boat. Sail around the world.'

There was nothing she'd like more. But there were responsibilities waiting for them back in America. Lives, jobs…friends.

Stevie turned over, resting on her elbows. The hot sun pooled in the small of her back. 'Ask me again in an hour,' she called.

Xander grinned and gave a mock captain's salute. He played it down but she was impressed by the way he handled the vessel, every so often jumping to operate the boom or the jib—'Let's see what she can really do'—and then Stevie would help and at first get it wrong, laughing as she clambered about the deck getting port side and starboard confused, before gradually and determinedly getting the hang of it. He said he'd learned after school, which seemed to Stevie an unusual time to do it, but then she was remembering her own post-school days, characterised by hours alone in her bedroom circling job applications in red pen and drinking horrible whisky miniatures because it made her feel gritty.

Xander brought the boat to rest and dropped the anchor. They were in shallower depths, so it was possible to see the sunlight reflecting off the seabed, making the water green.

'Swim?' Xander climbed over the thin ropes cordoning the boat's flanks. He raised his arms above his head and dived cleanly into the water. Moments later, he reappeared. Droplets twinkled off his mouth and nose and Stevie put her chin in her hands, watching her husband.

'Fish,' he informed her. 'Silver ones.'

'What are they?'

'No idea.'

'Maybe they're sharks.'

'Bit small for sharks.' He dived again. Re-emerging, he asked, 'You don't get sharks in the Bay of Naples...do you?'

Stevie laughed. 'I think you'll be all right.'

Lying back, she shut her eyes. It had been a month since the wedding and she hoped things were moving forward in LA. Back in the Bahamas, Bibi had confided her plans to divorce Linus Posen—and as far as Stevie was concerned it wasn't a moment too soon. Hearing about Linus's increasing demands on Bibi's body was dreadful, and now, at last, her friend was seeing sense: Linus had no intention of securing his wife above-board work in Hollywood, wanted her only for his sick perversions. She'd given Bibi a key to Xander's place in case she needed somewhere to stay, and would be back in time to support her friend if Linus decided to make things ugly. Whatever happened, they weren't backing down.

Stevie raised herself on one elbow and squinted behind her sunglasses. A massive white yacht was bobbing on the water several hundred metres away. It was giant, opulent, with an elevated sun deck. She could decipher two dark-haired women reclining on the bow, a taller blonde one standing. She wondered who they were. A French flag flapped in the breeze.

Xander came aboard, the drips from his body as he hauled himself on to the boat snapping her from her reverie. He knelt and grabbed her from behind, kissing her neck.

'Get off! You're sopping.'

'Sopping…now that's sexy.'

'You're wet, get off.'

He scooped her into his arms and for a moment she thought he was going to throw her in. 'Don't you dare!' she warned. 'If I go anywhere near that water, this marriage is annulled.'

'That's a bit soon, isn't it?'

'Seriously, put me down.'

He did as he was told then he kissed her, softly. His lips tasted briny. She felt his erection on her stomach and his tongue slip into her mouth.

Down in the cabin, they made love. The salt residue stung a bit, as it had when they'd had sex in the water late at night, she gripping on to the silver ladder that led from the boat while Xander entered her from behind. She thought about how phenomenal sex with her husband was, how she would never, not in a million years, get tired of sex with him. And then she thought about how she had stopped taking the Pill, and he had stopped using protection, and how they both knew that was what they were doing. And didn't stop.

Across the Atlantic, Bibi Reiner applied the final touches to her outfit. One of Linus's favourites: crotchless panties, leather bra with the nipples cut out, slovenly school uniform thrown over the top, cropped blonde wig. She stripped her face of the day's make-up. Dabbed fragrance behind her ears and on her wrists—not too much; he didn't like it if he could taste it.

She consulted the time. He would be home any minute, back from an important studio meeting with Dirk Michaels. Perhaps they were in talks about their new action blockbuster. Or perhaps they were in talks about another hopeful starlet desperate enough to appear in one of their clandestine ventures.

Never again could she look Dirk Michaels in the eye. Last week Linus had rolled in blind drunk and ordered her to strip. He hadn't been alone. Dirk was there, and another of their producer cronies, all puffing on cigars, drinking shorts of brandy as their eyes raked across her exposed body. She'd been forced to dance for them, then to get to her knees: first for Dirk, then for his friend, then to let them take her, one after the other, their sagging, aged bodies ramming into every orifice they could find. Meanwhile her husband surveyed all, waiting for his turn, licking his fleshy lips and loving what a swell party he could lay on for his friends. And then that final...*thing* he and Dirk had forced on her—*in* her. She gagged. It was something she could not come back from.

That was the night he had sealed his fate. Divorce was no longer an option.

Cutting Linus loose was too easy, too kind. Why should he be able to walk away when she could not? Was it fair that he could begin a new life when, after the shame she had known, she considered her own to be over? Divorce would be a bruise to his public ego but it wouldn't change him, it wouldn't make him understand the repercussions of what he'd put her through. The hours of torment, the degradation and despair...and now he saw fit to share her with others. Linus, Dirk and their friends had gone through life devouring women, never once stopping to recognise they were dealing with human beings, people with feelings who could bruise and tear and hurt. She hated them all with a passion she'd never imagined was in her to possess. The way they cajoled each other into it, rallying each other on as if she were a toy they could play with and discard, whose sole purpose was to provide a forum for their bragging display, attempting to outstrip the others by making her cry out the loudest.

Linus had robbed her of all respect and dignity. Now, it was payback time.

It was a fantasy she'd cherished for so long, a pipedream that had comforted her in her darkest hours and was now suddenly, beautifully, achievable. Bibi was certain that as long as the director walked this earth, she would never live again. She would never again smile and really mean it, laugh with her friends till her cheeks ached, gaze at the ocean and feel lucky to be alive, right here, today. None of it, ever again.

Linus Posen was a man who would never be made to face justice. Not unless justice came to him.

The front door went, echoing through the quiet mansion to where Bibi was preparing upstairs. She met her reflection in the mirror, totally sober for the first time in months. She had to be, for what she was about to do. Mustering her courage, she stood.

Downstairs, Linus was pouring Scotch, his back to her.

'What is it?' he grunted irritably.

Gritting her teeth, Bibi approached. 'Hard day at the studio?' she crooned, gently kneading his bloated shoulders.

Linus downed the liquid in one. She hated the way the bristles at the back of his head scratched against his shirt collar. 'Every day's hard,' he muttered, dismissing her understanding. 'All I want is bed and a blow job.'

She withdrew her hands and stood back. 'Funny you

should mention that,' she purred. Linus turned, a slow grin seeping across his face. He knew this routine because they'd done it before. Bibi had never initiated it—in fact, he hadn't even known she liked it. That was part of the sport for him, but a dame's enthusiasm had its merits as well.

'Well, well,' he growled, pouring a second drink but not taking his eyes from her body, 'this is a welcome surprise. What's the occasion?'

'Does there need to be one?' Bibi steeled herself for what she was about to do.

One last time... Then it will be finished.

He necked the Scotch, wiped his mouth. 'Bend over,' he commanded.

Bibi thought of what was waiting upstairs. 'No,' she told him, pulling gently at his hand, praying he'd follow. 'I've got something different in store for you tonight.'

Linus was too thick when it came to women to read unusual behaviour, let alone analyse it. He was also too aroused. His bottom half was distended with a raging hard-on.

'Lead the way,' he choked. Bibi's skirt was short and as he trailed her upstairs he grabbed at the exposed flesh like something savage snapping at bait. Forcing a light-hearted giggle, she slapped him away.

On the bed, she tied his wrists, using a silk black ribbon. She tied the knots tight. Straddling him, she removed his clothes, from his tie down to his socks. He was breathing heavily now, all but foaming at the mouth with excitement. It was better this way—being in control. Why hadn't she thought of it before?

From the bedside cabinet, she removed another silk scarf, attempted to blindfold him with it but he resisted.

'I wanna see everything,' he pronounced gutturally, sweat building in the dip of his clavicle and forming a sheen across his meaty chest. She tried to force the blindfold—she had her reasons—but when he began to get angry she knew to cut her losses. Already she had him tied up: that was the most crucial part.

Standing, she slowly and purposefully stripped off. Linus bucked against the ties when he saw her underwear—or lack of it.

'Get over here,' he managed, red-faced, salivating over the scant panties, the soft nest of russet hair peeking through.

She bent to him, bit back bile as she touched her tongue to the sour head of his penis. It tasted of cheese and sweat. She ran her tongue down its length, taking him into her mouth. Linus released a protracted groan, a high-pitched whine, as he raised his hips. Ordinarily he'd be pressing her down, forcing her to choke, but not now. For once, she had the power.

'Keep goin', baby,' he crooned. 'That's the way Daddy likes it.'

Bibi obliged, measuring the potency of his thrashes against the bed frame until she knew he was ready to come. Lifting her head, she mounted him once more. The heat from his cock burned and he attempted once or twice to stab it into her, fruitlessly, aimlessly.

'Not so fast,' she teased, each time evading his grasp. 'I promised you a treat...'

Bibi produced a thin black rope from beneath the pillow. Linus watched, mesmerised, as she weaved it round his neck, bending to graze her tits across his chest, over his mouth, letting him lick them, chew on them, anything to keep him hard.

'Not happenin', baby,' he wheezed. 'I don't go in for that.'

Bibi pouted, pretending to be disappointed, but she'd planned for this—she wasn't as dumb as he thought. 'Come on, Daddy Linus,' she breathed. At the beginning she'd called him that all the time, his favourite. 'For me.'

He was torn. Bibi's practically naked body hovered tantalisingly above him; he was centimetres from heaven.

Taking his silence for consent, Bibi gently tightened the rope, hardly at all at first so he could ease into it and think she was being cautious, playful. He leered as, for his reward, she sank her body on to his. Linus's eyes rolled back in his head. Again, Bibi pulled on the rope, saw it dig more firmly into his skin, then she released.

'Again,' he panted, thrusting into her. She obliged, tightening then releasing, tightening then releasing, tightening then releasing.

Tightening.

Tightening.

Linus's eyes bugged. Deftly Bibi raised her body from his, kneeling over him, thinking of every bad thing he had done to her, every terrible act he had made her do. He was trying to shake his head, strange gurgling noises escaping his lips, his body writhing beneath her as she tightened and tightened, every muscle in her spent with the force of it. The rope cut into him, beginning to draw blood. A bluish hue sprang up around his eye sockets, purple and black.

Die, you fucker! You sadist! You rapist!

'*I hate you!*' she screamed at him, again and again and again. 'I HATE YOU!'

She thought she might cry, or laugh, or both at the same time.

Bibi squeezed her own eyes shut, unwilling to look at him: at the final moment, a coward.

Abruptly, Linus Posen ceased shaking and became still.

Stevie and Xander came into land the next day. Stevie wanted to see Capri, to visit the Blue Grotto and take the cable cars to the top of the island.

It was Xander who saw the news stand first and recognised the face.

'My God, Stevie,' he said. 'Look.'

She had bought them ice cream, *gelati*, from a nearby stall. Catching the strawberry with her tongue as it melted down the cornet, she made her way over. 'What is it?'

He was frowning, pale beneath his tan. Italians bustled around the kiosk, clamouring in their fluid, colourful language.

'Xander?'

He presented her with the paper he was holding. On the front page was a picture of Linus Posen. Stevie didn't know Italian, but she had enough common sense to deduce that the headline beneath his headshot read: AMERICAN PRODUCER DIES AGED 56. Another paper, another headline, this one more shocking, more revelatory: SEX GAME ENDS IN TRAGEDY.

Stevie's smile dropped. 'Oh no,' she said. 'Bibi.'

35
Lori

Lori was in New York, shooting an anti-fur-campaign calendar. July girl, she was hot as the height of summer.

'Beautiful!' the photographer told her, clicking away. 'Another one just like that!'

Lori repositioned the faux-blood-soaked stole. It sounded grosser than it was: in reality the fake fur pieces were dampened with a dark, inoffensive liquid, and only in the finishing pictures would the red sheen be added. Against the models' skin, those textures—the glossy red and sticky fur—made for a reel of dramatic images.

Dante was December. They had the hottest male model in town set against a crystal-white backdrop, his theatrical eye make-up and slim build rendering him near androgynous. The soaking-yet-still-so-lavish artificial bearskin wrapped around his ravishing black form made him resemble a 1940s debutante gone horribly, beautifully wrong.

'Ew!' He tore the material from him the second his shoot was done.

Lori laughed as she got changed. 'It's not real.'

'Yeah, I kinda got that part.'

'I meant the blood.'

Dante touched his fingers to his chest and made a face. 'It sticks, darn it. To think I had a wax done yesterday! *And* I'm seeing you-know-who tonight.' Dante was sleeping with a married actor, filming in NYC on the set of his new movie.

The mention of Dante's wax reminded her of Peter Selznick. Following her chat with Jacqueline, Peter had mostly been behaving himself. He'd slipped a couple of times, usually following a mutual appearance, as if he couldn't get his head around the fact they could pretend to be a couple and then get home and not necessarily sleep with each other. 'Tons of chicks *say* they're virgins,' Peter had announced, rampantly chewing his Big Red gum. 'It doesn't mean they *are*. If it's the press you're worried about…'

'It's not the press,' Lori had said. 'It's a personal thing.'

The whine had crept in. 'How long're you gonna hold out on me?'

'You knew this was the deal, remember?'

'Didn't think you'd actually *meant* it,' he'd snorted.

But if you omitted the sex pestering, Peter was surprisingly easy to live with. Plus Jacqueline had been spot-on when she'd said the world would go nuts for them as a couple. According to the media they had been together over three months now. Was Lori sleeping with him, or wasn't she? Gossip columns raged with speculation.

'Coffee?' Dante asked as they exited the warehouse.

'Can't.' She kissed his cheek. 'I've a flight to catch.'

* * *

Landing at LAX early evening, Lori saw that, even weeks after the event, the city still hollered news of Linus Posen's death. The effect had been less in New York—it was Los Angeles that had made him royalty—but the aftershock remained. At the airport, every newspaper and magazine carried stories on his life's achievements, his contributions to the movie industry, his devotion to Hollywood. Each mourned the great talent that had been taken, too soon, from them.

As her car sped back to the Bay Heights mansion, Lori's thoughts turned to Bibi Posen. She felt for the woman, knew what bereavement was like—and in those circumstances, too... It was a stretch for Lori to imagine what they must have been doing to lead to such a tragedy, but while she was a virgin she wasn't naive: people did that kind of stuff and all it took was one wrong turn. Bibi had been taken in for police questioning but shortly afterwards released. Her husband had been a willing participant in a game that had gotten drastically out of hand.

Lori was surprised to find the mansion shrouded in complete darkness. She was sure Peter had said he'd be in.

The entrance hall was steeped in gloom.

'Hello?' she called into the silence.

Nothing. In the kitchen, she flipped the lights on, dropped her bags and opened the refrigerator. Half-eaten energy bars and vats of homemade fruit smoothies, blueberry pips clinging to the syrupy sides of their containers, let her know Peter had been here recently.

She grabbed a carton of juice and shut the door with her knee. As she poured, something flickered in the corner of her vision. Peering out to the terrace, into the fading light of evening, she saw an orangey glow emanating from one side of the pool. He must be out there, though what he was doing in near-darkness was a mystery.

Padding out of the patio doors, she caught the bleed of music seeping over. It was sultry, sexy, something R&B. What was Peter doing?

Nothing could have prepared her for the sight that met her eyes.

Peter was at the foot of the pool, its water aquamarine and lit from below. He was standing hands on hips with his eyes squeezed shut. Candles flickered. Music blared. He was *wearing her lingerie*. The purple silk set she had treated herself to from Belle Gray a month ago. And shoes. *Her shoes*. Dagger-sharp Louboutin heels donated to her after a shoot.

Between his legs, two naked blondes were on their knees. One was kissing his legs—at one point, yes, his feet—the other's head fixed a little higher, bobbing up down, in and out, like a nodding puppet, as Peter rammed resolutely into her, grim as a soldier marching into battle.

Lori's first urge was to laugh. Then came the certainty that he must be stretching her clothes: his size-twelve feet teetered on the precarious heels; it was only really his toes and the ball of his foot that had managed to squidge themselves in. Inside the lingerie, his frame looked like the Incredible Hulk's, expanses of oiled muscle rippling out of a tiny, futile attempt at discretion. He brought to mind a chair that had had an item of clothing thrown carelessly over it.

Peter climaxed furiously into the girl's mouth.

Lori couldn't help her words. Anger hit. What was Peter thinking, letting strangers into their house? *Her* house?

'What the *fuck* is this?' she demanded. She never cursed.

Peter's eyes flew open. He teetered on the brink of his

heels before toppling forwards, falling headfirst into the pool. The girls went with him, all three surfacing seconds later, Peter's beetroot-red face frantic as he thrashed about, scrabbling to reach the side.

'Oh wow,' one of the girls purred. 'Lori Garcia. Wanna join the party?' She was high.

'Get them out,' Lori said flatly. *'Now.'* She made her way back indoors, blinking back the inexplicable burn of tears. What did she care?

This is what men are about. Get with it. They're all the same.

To think she'd ever believed in the fairytale was a bad joke.

Several splashes later, Peter was at her heels.

'Hey, come on,' he whimpered. 'I'm sorry you had to see that—really, I am.'

She spun on him, could scarcely take him seriously in that lingerie. At least the shoes had come off. 'Is this what you get up to every time I go away?'

He had the nerve to grin at her. 'Jealous?'

'Get away from me, Peter.'

He chased her up the stairs. 'I didn't mean that. I'm sorry! OK? Jeez.'

'You're dripping water everywhere.'

'Lori, *wait* one second, would you?' He grabbed her arm.

'I even told you I was coming back tonight!' At his nonplussed expression, she added in wonder, *'Jesus!'* and turned and continued up the stairs.

He reached for her again. 'How am I meant to hold out?' he protested, wiping his face with the back of his arm. 'You've got a hot-blooded man living here, baby. You knew that all along. And living with *you*, such a prize piece, y'know, sometimes I gotta get a release...'

She gestured at his outfit. He seemed to remember he was wearing it. 'Oh,' he said. 'Yeah.'

She put one hand on the banister. 'I understand you have needs,' she said reasonably, 'believe me, I do. But this is disrespectful. It's disrespectful of my property and it's disrespectful of me.'

He pouted. 'You've been disrespecting Little Peter since the moment we moved in.'

We?

She wanted to laugh. 'Screw Little Peter!'

'I wish you would.'

'That's it. I can't do this any more.'

'Do what?'

'This. With you. We're too different.'

'Hey, it's just one freaking mistake!'

'It's too...' She thought of his feet sandwiched into her shoes. 'I'm sorry, I can't.'

Peter's face hardened. 'You're breaking up with me?' he asked coldly. 'What're we gonna tell everyone?'

'I don't know. That's what PR is for.'

'But we make a great couple.'

'You know we don't.'

He folded his bulky arms. 'I'm not gonna beg.'

'I'm not asking you to.'

Lori couldn't understand. Was the whole of Hollywood set on their sex games? Was it all they ever thought about? She didn't want to be part of it. Couldn't. She'd seen how it might end.

'Try not to take it personally, Peter,' she said. 'Tomorrow I want you out.'

* * *

Days later, Jacqueline Spark gave her the news.

'He's telling anyone who'll listen that you've got a problem with sex.'

Lori's face was burning. She took the phone outside and sat with her back to the pool. 'Just because I'm saving myself doesn't make me some kind of freak.'

'I know.'

'How about if I tell the world he likes dressing up in women's underwear?' She wasn't used to this snappy version of herself, but couldn't take this lying down. Or in any other position Peter might be envisaging.

Jacqueline sighed. 'Lori, hear my advice. I don't want to involve you in an ugly public spat. Better to be dignified and let people make their own minds up.'

'But why's he saying all this?' She couldn't understand his vitriol. 'I mean, we were friends…sort of.'

'He's digging his own grave. The fans aren't stupid; they'll read between the lines. Is Peter telling the truth, or could his ego not handle the rejection?'

'I'd imagine his ego was so huge it could handle anything.'

'Never overestimate a man, honey.'

Lori closed her eyes. 'So I'm learning.'

'Let's keep quiet, ride it out.'

She knew Jacqueline was right. Her publicist hadn't been pleased when she'd learned about the fallout—to her, Peter's behaviour was irritating, but not surprising; inconvenient, but not bang out of order. 'These things happen all the time,' she had counselled. 'It's LA. You're in a bogus relationship. He's an *actor*. You can't be that astonished.'

And maybe she hadn't been. Only, the Posen affair had been a wake-up call. Lori had tested her ethics with Peter but this was one step too far. She didn't want to go down that road, find herself in ten years looking in the mirror and not knowing who she was.

'I didn't think he'd react so badly,' she told Jacqueline. 'It's like I've actually dumped him. Like we were really going out with each other.'

'Well, he certainly thinks a lot of himself.'

'Sure does.'

'It's probably a defence mechanism. He thought we'd get to the press first and he wanted to beat you to it.' A pause. 'Was he *really* in your underwear?'

'I'm not sure "in" accurately describes it.'

Jacqueline laughed. 'I'll call you later.'

Alone, Lori thought about inviting Dante over, but decided not to. She needed to get used to the mansion again and to living here by herself.

A niggling voice told her that now the place was empty she would have to readdress Angélica's threat to move in. It seemed no matter how successful she became, they still had, and always would have, the power to make her feel like a frightened girl.

Exhausted, Lori slid to the floor, cradling her head in her hands.

Later that evening, her cell rang. She had returned early from a drinks party in West Hollywood, where speculation over the break-up with Peter was raging at fever pitch. There were only so many times she could brush off the probing questions, tell the photographers, 'No comment,' before she'd had to call it a night.

She let herself into the house and, without thinking, picked up.

'Lori. It's JB.'

In the darkness of the hall, the moonlight pouring a silver puddle at her feet, the sound of his voice wrecked her.

'Hi,' she said.

'I heard about what happened with Selznick.'

How had he got this number? Why was he calling her? His tone was impossible to read. She didn't think Jacqueline had told the officials at La Lumière about Peter. Had she changed her mind? Or had he found out some other way? His words came back to her, words she had buried deep but now sprang forth with familiar devastation.

You'll be all right... I'll make sure of it... I always will...

'We'd like to get you out of LA while things calm down.'

'That isn't necessary,' she replied curtly.

'You're one of my girls,' JB came back without hesitation.

I bet I am.

'I say what's necessary.'

'This isn't.' Lori refused to back down. She was sick of people making decisions for her: Tony, Desideria, Jacqueline, and now him, the man who'd reeled her in and spat her out. Why couldn't they let her live her life? 'I'm fine,' she said coldly. 'I don't need to go away.'

'We'll fix your appointments,' he finished, in a tone that defied argument.

'No,' she reiterated. 'Thank you, but no.'

'This isn't a discussion. It's an order. My car will collect you at seven.'

The line clicked dead. He was gone.

For seconds, Lori kept the phone to her ear, listening for what she didn't know. All she heard was silence, a world of it, standing alone in the night.

36
Aurora

Returning to St Agnes was worse than Aurora had feared. It wasn't just that winter was settling in, the grey skies of England turning ever darker, the mornings pitch-black when Mrs Durdon rang the breakfast bell and the sun making a grudging effort behind a bank of dense cloud before disappearing completely at about four o'clock. It was that, since her trip to Capri, Aurora had barely slept a night through. She would lie awake in her new dorm, one she shared with Pascale, and listen to the bad weather thrash the old building, rain incessantly battering the windows and wind whistling through the cracks, seeping uninvited through vulnerable spaces and rattling from the inside out. Pascale slept, she dreamed of her faraway planets, while Aurora turned bad thoughts over in her head and stared out at the pale moon.

Of course it is her... We never lose sight of any of them...

Do you think she never wonders about her mother and father?

She was plagued by that dreadful conversation and what it had meant. Every lesson, every prep, every evening spent trying to think of another thing, but it always came back.

What had JB and Arnaud been discussing?

Tell me she would have been better off staying with her real mother.

They had been talking about her. She knew it in her bones and in her blood.

Thoughts of Tom and Sherilyn spooled, chaotic, in her mind—their remote relationship, her mother's unhappiness, the way they had always spoiled her and handled her like a china doll... Her eavesdropping had pulled at threads she had always known were there, hidden, not wanting to be touched, but now coming loose like a giant knot unravelling. Maybe this was what she'd been hoping to express to Rita Clay when they'd met that day. Yes, she felt an enduring emptiness about her charmed life, but she also felt that it was somehow based on one huge lie. As if she were living in a TV show and acting it out and speaking a script, and, at least in LA, so was everyone around her. Fake.

What were her parents hiding? And what did it have to do with JB Moreau?

After her encounter with Arnaud she had emerged from below deck, settled on her lounger, her towel rumpled as she had left it, her bottle of Sun Perfect oozing lotion that melted in the heat, just as if nothing had happened. She'd lain back, shades in place, heart plummeting and stomach turning, waiting for Arnaud to tell them all how she'd misbehaved. But Arnaud said nothing—he remained his usual aloof self for the rest of her stay—and JB departed on business as soon as they returned to the island, presumably none the wiser.

On their first night back at school she had broached the subject with Pascale. 'Your cousin,' she'd said, as casually as she could. 'What exactly does he do?'

Pascale had been folding her clothes, deliberately and with care, feeding them on to the shelves in her closet: pastels in one pile, blacks, whites and greys in another. 'You know what he does,' she said. 'He's the House of Moreau.'

'I know that. But he does other stuff too…right?'

'Like what?'

'That's what I'm asking.'

Pascale had her back to her. 'He's involved in charities.'

'Such as?'

She'd rounded on her. 'You find him attractive, don't you?'

'No.'

'Come on.' A condescending eyebrow shot up. '*Everybody* finds JB attractive. *I* find him attractive and…well, we're family, so it's forbidden.'

Pascale's voice caught her attention.

'You haven't…?' Aurora swallowed. 'With JB, I mean. Have you?'

The French girl had smirked, reminiscent of her cousin. 'That would be wrong.'

'But have you?'

'See? You find him attractive. Jealousy is the first giveaway.'

Since the trip Aurora had felt as if her friend was mocking her, giving her sly looks and deliberately confusing her. Maybe she was paranoid: she'd been smoking too much grass and that sometimes messed with her head. But when she thought about it, *really* thought about it, she realised that Pascale had never been an open book. When had Pascale ever given much away?

Maybe she was more like JB than she cared to admit.

Monday morning came around with its usual sluggish dis-inclination. The bell rang shrill in Aurora's ears. Outside, the sky was still dark. It seemed like only five minutes ago that she'd finally gotten to sleep. Pascale, in the adja-cent bed, rolled over and tugged the sheets over her head. Aurora thought about the motions of getting up, planned in her head the outfit she'd wear (it was own clothes in sixth form) to save time, and rapidly fell back to sleep.

Ten minutes later, Mrs Durdon charged in without knocking.

'GET TO BREAKFAST THIS INSTANT!' she bel-lowed, slamming the door repeatedly against the wall in an attempt to rouse them. To Aurora's fragile head it sounded like gunfire.

Pascale sat bolt upright, the back of her hair a messy black nest where she'd slept on it. She swore in French and pulled a sweater over her pyjamas.

The girls made their way to the dining room without speaking—Aurora had learned a long time ago that Pascale didn't like to talk before ten in the morning. They were ticked off a register by a pinched-faced housemistress in a baffling lemon-yellow onesie, minutes later slumping on to one of the long wooden benches with a bowl of soggy cereal.

Fran Harrington, in contrast, was chirpy in the morn-ings. She'd chosen the hot breakfast option: flaccid curls of boiled bacon, a slippery fried egg and some button-headed mushrooms that looked to Aurora like the inverted cock of a virgin musician she'd once had sex with. English people ate some creepy things.

'Hey, Aurora, want to partner me today?' Fran asked, plopping herself down next to Pascale, who put on her best bitchface and inched down the bench.

'Sure, whatever.' Aurora was taking Art. She didn't excel in anything academic so was opting for the 'general' qualifications that supposedly gave her more choice further down the line but she knew was just a term designed to make thick people feel better. Pascale was doing languages and Science, meaning they hardly had any lessons together any more. Fran attempted to pair with her at every opportunity.

'Great!' Fran sucked buttery fingers as she slathered more grease on to her toast. 'Virginia Pringle-Stoat heard Mr Wade saying we could do life drawing, if we want, for our final pieces. What do you think?'

Aurora couldn't help the expression her face fell into. 'Erm, no.'

'It wouldn't be weird or anything.'

Pascale leaned across. 'I'm trying to stomach my breakfast,' she said, with a swift, practised glance up and down Fran's body. 'Must we talk about such *grotesque* things?'

Fran's face coloured. It was no secret she was afraid of Pascale. Normally Aurora found the regard her best friend was held in gratifying, but today she just came across as mean.

'Thanks for saying,' she told Fran, who seized Aurora's weak smile like a life buoy, 'but let's forget it, yeah?'

Across the table, Pascale fired a sharp look and continued to eat her cereal.

* * *

Friday lunchtime, Tom called. Her parents hardly ever got in touch in term-time so it had to be bad news. Her first thought was that Sherilyn had died. Her second thought was that her first thought hadn't been that earth-shattering. What kind of a daughter did that make her?

'Dad?' She took her iPhone past the hockey pitch to her and Pascale's usual smoking patch: a clearing in the dense bushes that lined the school gate.

'Honey, it's Dad,' he said pointlessly.

'I know.' His voice made her want to cry. She lit the cigarette and sucked. 'What's up?'

'Do I need a reason to call my only daughter?'

Aurora was overcome with the need to blurt her anxieties. See if he could allay them. Get to the truth. But she was afraid of what the truth might be.

Do you think she never wonders about her mother and father? The ones she never knew?

What was it she wanted to ask? She hadn't even figured that out herself. She was paralysed by a million questions, a trillion what-ifs.

'I guess not.'

'As it goes, baby, there *is* a reason. Rita asked me what I thought about you taking a break after college is over.'

'It's school, Dad. How do you mean, a break?'

'Before you come back to LA. She said it might help you get focused, y'know, back in the game in the right frame of mind.' He cleared his throat. 'Make sure, for your mom's sake, we don't get a repeat of the last few years.'

The thought of Sherilyn depressed her. 'Where?'

'You'll sort that out between you. But the idea's a good one?'

'S'pose. How's Mom?'

Tom hesitated, but it could have been the slow line. 'She's fine.'

Normally Tom papered over the cracks with false enthusiasm. 'Amazing' meant 'good', 'good' meant 'average', so 'fine' might just as easily mean 'dead'. Perhaps Aurora's first instincts had been right, after all.

'What's the matter with her?'

Tom sighed deeply. 'What the heck: we've had to cancel our North America tour. Or I might go it solo, I haven't decided.'

'Why?'

'Honey, come on, I'm a professional. I can't let the fans down...'

'I mean why isn't Mom going?'

'Oh. She won't leave the house.'

Aurora was confused. 'What? How come?'

'Panic attacks.' She pictured her father running a hand through his tousled hair. 'She's become a little, well... agoraphobic.'

'Agoraphobic?'

'That's right.'

'You can't be *a little* agoraphobic, Dad.'

'OK, she's a lot agoraphobic.'

'Since when?'

'A few months.'

'And you didn't tell me?' No response. 'Can I speak to her?'

'She's sleeping.'

Aurora chewed her lip. 'Tell her I said hi. And I'll email.'

They hung up. Aurora stamped her cigarette into the ground and folded her arms against the cold. She returned to Main School feeling uneasy.

* * *

'Are they trying to freeze us to death?' Pascale complained in bed that night, yanking the sheets up to her chin. 'I'm colder than I've ever been.'

Aurora turned off the light and lay back. The pillow smelled of hair dye she'd applied on Monday and hadn't had the chance to wash through properly before their ten p.m. curfew. She'd meant to do her laundry that evening but hadn't found the energy. 'Go to sleep.'

'Why don't you come here?' Pascale whispered, and Aurora heard the rustle of covers being lifted. 'Warm me up.' The girls often lay together when it was cold, small toes touching at the foot of the bed. Some nights they'd drift off like that; others, they'd kiss, maybe more, before returning to their individual beds. Pascale said she couldn't sleep touching someone.

Aurora wasn't in the mood. 'No, thanks,' she said, rolling over to face the wall.

Pascale flicked the lamp on and sat up. 'God, you're in a shitty mood.'

'I'm allowed to be in a shitty mood, aren't I?'

Pascale's scowl was useless because Aurora couldn't see it. 'Ever since we came back from Capri you've been acting like a cow.'

Aurora hadn't been called a cow before. She wondered why Pascale didn't ask her what the matter was. But, then, she never did.

'I've got my reasons,' she said sharply.

'Yes,' snapped Pascale, 'like you're too busy fantasising about my cousin.'

Aurora wondered if jealousy over JB belonged more to her friend than it did to her. She didn't reply—it was too complicated. And in a sense she *was* fantasising about JB.

She was inventing all sorts of possibilities to explain what she had heard on Arnaud's boat.

'He'd never look twice at you,' said Pascale cruelly. 'You're not his type.'

Aurora couldn't help her temper. She pushed back the covers and faced her friend. 'I couldn't give a crap about JB, OK? I've got stuff on my mind, really deep stuff, and I've had a messed-up time of it lately and you haven't even bothered to notice! All you think about is sex, Pascale, all the fucking time: sex, sex, sex.' She realised she could be addressing herself two years ago. 'If it's not sex with me, it's sex with someone else.' The words were out before she could stop them. 'It's sex with your own cousin!'

Pascale's eyes flashed.

'I don't know what's wrong with your family,' Aurora rampaged on. 'You're...*weird*. All of you. You act like the rest of the world is beneath you, like you're royalty or something. Well, here's your wake-up call, Devereux: you're not. You're just like me, only you're probably a bit more insecure and a bit less brave because you like to make out like nothing touches you, but *I* know it does because *I've* taken the time to work that out. I mean you hardly know a single thing about me! I'm just something you carry around, like a goddamn handbag. Except if it came down to it I'm not as important to you as all that, am I?'

'After everything I've done for you,' Pascale said bitterly. 'You ungrateful *bitch*.'

'Didn't you stop for even a second to think how what happened in Paris affected me?' Her voice broke. 'That maybe I needed your support—'

'Oh, spare me!' Pascale delivered a mean laugh. 'You think we all have to fawn over you because you got yourself knocked up by some inbred farmer? How do you think that made *me* feel?' Her own voice splintered, just for a second.

'What do you mean?'

She glanced away. 'Forget it.'

'That hurt you?'

'Don't flatter yourself.' Pascale extinguished the light. The room plunged into darkness and silence. Aurora sat still, confused. She wondered if Pascale was crying and listened out for it, but heard nothing.

'Pascale,' she whispered, struggling to make sense of their argument. 'I'm sorry—'

'He lives on an island.' This time the French girl spoke with her customary reserve. 'On the other side of the world, where no one can find him.'

Aurora was thrown. 'Who?'

'Who do you think? JB. It's Reuben van der Meyde's place. Cacatra.'

Aurora blinked in the dark. 'Why are you telling me this?'

'I'll ask to switch dorms in the morning.'

'What's Cacatra got to do with anything?'

Silence. 'Good night.'

'Pascale…?'

Aurora's heart was thumping wildly. Pascale knew something…something about the island and JB and Reuben van der Meyde.

Arnaud Devereux's words swam towards her through the night. *The concerned fathers, I am sure…*

Aurora lay back.

She remembered Rita's offer to take her away.

It was settled, then. She knew exactly where she wanted to go.

37
Stevie

The headlines in London were the worst. SORDID SE-
CRETS OF A SEX MANIAC screamed the UK tabloids.
PERV PRODUCER IN SHOCK DEATH TRYST. Stevie
hadn't realised how intent the British press were on the
gory details. At least in LA they treated the episode with
a modicum of respect, if not for Linus then for poor Bibi.

Her friend had been inconsolable when Stevie returned
from her honeymoon. She had accompanied Bibi to police
questioning—a formality, they were assured—before helping her move out of the Posen mansion and into a small
apartment of her own, close to where Stevie and Xander
were living. Bibi was frail, her body wrung out by drugs
and despair, flashbacks from the night her husband died
circling in her memory. Stevie thought how small she
looked, how fragile, and wondered how anyone, whatever 'formalities' might be necessary, could suspect her

of murder at a time like this. It had been a terrible, tragic accident—nothing more.

Mercifully she'd been tied up the past couple of months on the set of her new film, a biopic centring on a fugitive young woman on the run from the government. She was filming in San Francisco, but made a point of coming home whenever her schedule permitted.

Early Friday morning she flew into LAX, politely greeted a handful of paparazzi waiting outside Arrivals and took a cab straight to the Bel Air place she shared with Xander. The villa, a circular-fronted construction half obscured by lush vegetation, was modest in comparison with its neighbouring counterparts. Xander didn't employ a housekeeper and Stevie was glad: she'd hate not to be able to kick off her shoes when she got in, cook what she felt like or make a mess if she wanted. She fixed coffee and unpacked, knowing she was stalling the inevitable. Bibi would be here in half an hour and there was something she had to do first.

Upstairs in the cool, quiet bathroom, she extracted the pregnancy test. They'd been having unprotected sex for months now—it hadn't been a conscious decision, just what happened. They loved and trusted each other, and, while Stevie had for a long time carried a horror of falling pregnant again, being with Xander had, slowly but surely, begun the healing process. She was content to let nature run its course.

Only nature hadn't delivered.

It didn't mean anything was wrong. Couples spent years trying to get pregnant, and it wasn't even as if she and Xander were trying in earnest. Even so, Stevie could admit to the fear that terminating her first had left her unable. Or, if it wasn't that, retribution for her duplicity.

She remembered the day she'd found out. They'd just spent a blissful weekend—his wife had been away, she hadn't asked where—holed up in a hotel, having sex and ordering room service and showering together and sleeping in each other's arms. He'd told her for the fiftieth time that his divorce was imminent: the affair had been going on for months now and it was she he was in love with. And Stevie had looked into his eyes and believed with the whole of her heart that she had loved him truly, and it didn't matter that there were nearly twenty years between them, or that he was a father or the man she worked for—they were technicalities. So when she'd registered on Monday morning that her period was late, and decided to buy a test at lunch to put her mind at rest, there'd been a part of her that knew that even if the unforeseen were to happen, and even if the timing were impossible, he would be happy. Because wasn't this what he wanted? A future with her, a family? He said he did.

It hadn't happened that way.

In that toilet cubicle on the seventh floor of an office building on Fleet Street, a twenty-six-year-old Stevie had sat alone with the news, letting it sink in, deep breaths, deep breaths, and practising how she'd put it to him, what she'd say.

I'm pregnant, she'd told him late that night. He'd been in meetings and the relief of letting it go was immense. She'd waited for the smile, the outstretched arms.

You're what?

I'm pregnant.

Whose is it?

The question had been a knife to her throat. *It's yours.*

It can't be.

And he'd denied it, saying he didn't believe her and she must have been with other men, and she'd been so stupid, so *weak* back then, that the first thing she'd cared about was that he doubted her fidelity and how she could prove it to him.

I'll get a test when the baby's born, she'd said. *Then you'll know.*

It's not getting born. Which was surely a contradiction, because if he'd honestly thought he had nothing to do with it then why put in the request?

Request. It hadn't been. It had been an order.

I don't want to. I'm keeping it. It's my child, too.

That was the first time he had hit her. His fist came from nowhere, slamming her backwards, and she remembered hearing her head crack against an expensive Escher print he had framed on his office wall. He'd hit her so hard her ear bled. Then came the threats...

Stevie shook her head against the past. She ran a hand over her stomach, brushing off superstition. What would be would be. She had to have faith. With Xander, it would be different.

Last month she'd waited in ignorance, savouring a maybe, her late cycle ripe with promise, before she'd bled into her knickers. Today was the same. She needed to stop using these tests that spelled the damn thing out: NOT PREGNANT.

She stood, washed her hands, unlocked the door (seclusion was weirdly necessary) and made her way downstairs, just in time for the main-gate buzzer to sound.

It was Bibi, clad in a headscarf and huge shades that shrank her already tiny features.

'Talk about *Thelma & Louise*,' Stevie teased, enveloping her in a hug. Bibi was feeble in her arms and so she didn't squeeze too tightly.

'Want to run away with me?' Bibi enquired weakly, at-tempting humour as she stepped inside. When she took off the dark glasses, Stevie could see the haunted look around her eyes, the badge of sleep deprivation and bad nutrition.

'Let me make you a sandwich,' she offered. 'And tea.'

'Tea?'

'Cures all ills.'

'You'd better make a lot of it, then.' Bibi sat at the breakfast counter and unwound her scarf. Underneath, her hair was patchily dyed, alternating clumps of harsh blonde and red-orange—but that wasn't the sole reason she wore the camou-flage. Since her husband's death, paparazzi had been trailing her non-stop. Though she had been cleared of any involve-ment in his killing, at least any involvement with intent, she was fast becoming a black-widow figure, elusive and remote. Nobody considered that perhaps she was still in shock.

'Are you OK, B?' Stevie put two mugs on the counter and settled opposite. 'You look a million miles away. Aren't you sleeping?'

Bibi endeavoured a smile. 'Not much.' Try not at all. At night she lay terrified, convinced she was about to hear a knock at the door, a warrant for her arrest, or that she'd wake to find herself rotting on death row and the time since Linus's demise would all have been a dream. She couldn't believe she was still walking free. People didn't get away with murder...did they?

'Nightmares?' Stevie gently pressed.

'Kinda.' Oddly, not of the night she had killed him. Instead, images from her marriage and the games her husband had sub-jected her to. Perhaps that was her special punishment, her own bespoke hell—because now she was no better than him, just

as morally bankrupt and as undeserving of redemption, con-
demned to a life trapped inside those dreadful recollections.

'B…?' Stevie was concerned. 'You've gone white as a
sheet.'

She sipped the too-sweet tea. 'I'm fine.'

'If you think it would help to talk about what happened…'

'It wouldn't.'

'All right.'

'I'm not ready. Sorry.'

Stevie took her hand. 'You know I'm here, don't you? I'll
always be here.'

Bibi kept her eyes down, afraid that if she met Stevie's
kind, understanding gaze, her confession would fall straight
out of her mouth, thick and scaly as a big ugly fish.

'Talk to me about you,' she said, desperate to put her mind
to anything else. 'I wanna hear how you're doing, Steve.'

Stevie sat back. 'Things are busy.' Such an anodyne
comment in light of Bibi's misfortune felt like a brush-off
so she added, 'We're hoping to get pregnant.'

Bibi's face lit up. 'You are? Any luck?'

'Nah. It's early.'

'I'll say. Why the big rush?'

Stevie frowned, but it was tempered by a smile. 'I met
the right person.'

'That's romantic.'

'Yeah.'

'Xander's been good to me. Since what happened, I
mean. You're lucky.'

'I know.' She paused. 'Although sometimes… No, it's silly.'

Bibi leaned forward. 'What?'

Stevie thought about whether or not to voice what was
on her mind. 'It's not a big deal, it's just…' She put her

elbow on the counter and supported her chin in her hand. 'Sometimes I feel like there's stuff going on with Xander that I haven't got a clue about.'

'What makes you say that?'

'He closes up.' She sighed. 'Not all the time, just occasionally. And it's fine, you know—there're bits of people we never see, and it's not like I have to know everything about him and he about me… I guess it's that he gets this *look*. I don't know how else to describe it. He gets further and further away from me, in his thoughts, I mean, and then he seems like he's about to tell me something but at the last second decides not to.'

Bibi waited. 'Might you be looking too much into it?'

'Possibly.'

'Xander's a trustworthy guy, Steve. Believe me. By rights I ought to hate every man out there but I don't hate Xander. He's decent.'

Stevie smiled. 'I know he is. I expect I'm just thinking of reasons for it to go wrong.'

Her cell rang. 'One second.' She picked it up and went to the patio doors. After a brief conversation, she folded it shut. 'That was Marty,' she said, refilling their cups. 'I was talking to him about you. An agent friend of his is seeking new clients. Can I put you in touch?'

Bibi had been approached for representation a number of times since her husband's death, but the intentions behind the offers were seldom honourable. 'I dunno,' she said cautiously. 'Work's the last thing on my mind.'

Stevie sat down. 'So what's next?'

'I'm taking it a day at a time. Dirk Michaels has booked me in for a week on Cacatra—I know, I know, he's the last person I want to accept favours off, but he insisted, saying it's what Linus would have wanted. So I can get away from it all.' She bit her lip, uncertain. 'I could do with getting out of LA. And after the favours I've done for him…'

'Cacatra?' Stevie had read about it—a remote island in the middle of the ocean. She'd thought it was a rehab spa, at the forefront of a host of breakthrough therapies.

'Dirk knows Reuben van der Meyde,' said Bibi. 'I imagine he struck a deal. There are dozens of treatments I can access while I'm out there, all paid for by him. Though the only things I want to prioritise right now are blue sky, deep sea and doing as little as possible.'

Stevie agreed. 'It sounds exactly the thing you need. But when you're back, let's hook up with Marty's contact, OK? I think it's going to make a difference to how you feel, B; help you get some confidence back. Right now it's all about you being Linus Posen's widow, but it doesn't have to be. You're not Bibi Posen any more, remember? You're Bibi Reiner. And that's who you were all along; you just lost sight of her for a while. So, after a little R&R, soon as you're back on your feet, we'll—'

Bibi cut in. 'Steve, I killed Linus.'

Stevie didn't think she'd heard right. 'What?'

'I killed him.'

It took a moment for her meaning to become clear. 'Oh, sweetheart, you mustn't think that.' She reached across and touched her friend's arm. 'It was an accident—'

'*No.*' Bibi withdrew. 'That's exactly what I'm telling you. It wasn't.'

Stevie searched the other woman's face. 'I don't understand.'

'I killed him, Steve. I lured him into his favourite game and then I took his life. It was planned; it was intentional; it was entirely in cold blood.' She swallowed. 'I *murdered* him.'

38
Lori

Miles from the mainland, Cacatra was a beautiful jewel in a glittering ocean, a destination that was somehow part of the world and yet distinct from it, as if, by a trick of light or a sleight of hand, a curtain had been lifted to reveal a glorious, heavenly secret.

A solitary figure was waiting when the helicopter touched down on the south of the island. Its rotors whipped up a startling wind from which the man didn't flinch. He was wearing a charcoal shirt, tucked in loosely at the waist, and his hands were in his pockets.

Lori's ears were buzzing from the noise of the pistons. The helicopter had dipped and bumped as they'd come in over the cliffs, and she was relieved when finally it met ground. An official in a canary-yellow jacket came rushing over to release the doors and shout a reminder to keep her arms down. He gestured towards the man standing outside the perimeter.

The sunlight was strong, rendering her surroundings hyper-real. Close up JB's eyes were silver, the pupils vanishing.

'Fun, isn't it?' Smoothly he claimed her bag and swung it on to his shoulder. 'I used to fly them myself. Not so much any more.'

'You didn't need to do this.'

'I know.'

'You seem to know a lot of things.'

For the first time she saw humour in his eyes. Warm. She found it hard to look at him.

'Shall I show you where you're staying?' he asked.

'Sure.' Lori took in her immediate surroundings. 'It's beautiful.'

'Good.' He didn't take his eyes from her. 'I think so, too.'

The helipad and runway took advantage of the only level terrain on the island. From here, the rest was hidden behind a steep rocky bank. Vehicles waited beyond the fence to meet new arrivals and a private jet was unloading a short distance away. Lori was surprised by how wild it was. The rugged cliff face, chalky and golden and green, gave way to a sheer, rocky drop, below which the blue ocean lashed angrily, white horses riding into war, the island an unwelcome obstruction in an otherwise unblemished expanse.

JB carried her bags towards a gleaming black Jeep.

'You're going to fall in love with this,' he told her.

Cacatra was enormous. The part Lori had seen in photographs and magazines must have been just a fraction. A winding road was carved from north to south, along which the Jeep now sped, JB at the wheel. Occasionally they came off on to a narrow snaking track, a short cut through marshy patches sunk behind ironed-out golf courses, natural outdoor pools and lush rock waterfalls, tennis courts and diving centres and boats bobbing patiently on transparent water.

To the north, the ocean was calmer. Fanning from the island were twenty or more wooden walkways, at the tips of each the villas where visitors were accommodated. Another, smaller island could be seen further out, on which, just decipherable, stood a lighthouse, thimble-sized in the distance.

'Cacatra is a spa on a mega scale,' JB was explaining. For politeness' sake, she listened, but she'd give him nothing more. The unspoken encounter of almost two years ago sat between them like a forgotten offspring, once demanding attention, now resigned to obscurity. 'It's the highest order of recuperation and leisure on the planet. Anything a client wants, we have it. Everything they are yet to think of, we have that too.'

They rejoined the smoother road and slickly he changed gear. 'Many use it like a club or a holiday retreat,' he continued. 'A week of fresh ocean air, concentrated workouts, time away from the spotlight—that is what they pay for. Others come for different reasons.'

Lori watched his hand on the steering wheel, the way his Rolex flashed in the sun and the muscles in his forearms as they pulled and relaxed.

'Therapy?' She had heard about troubled stars sent by worried management—addictions, depression, anxiety, Cacatra treated it all.

'The island accommodates every mode of recovery. We employ a team of specialists from across the world. Time spent here has proven results.'

'Like rehab?'

'Everyone in LA goes to rehab, it's a given—especially for girls your age.' She resented the observation. 'Months later, the problems remain. Cacatra is different: you visit once and you don't need to again. It makes you see life with new eyes. That is the key. Rediscovering nature can be like an epiphany. This is the dearest place in the world to me.'

Lori was touched by the expression.

'When we're children,' he elaborated, 'we are full of amazement at the miracle of life. We want to find out, we want to know. We must know everything—all the secrets there are, even if we would be happier in ignorance.'

She looked at him sideways. 'And when we're grown?'

'When we're grown we see that ignorance is precious.' His jaw hardened. 'Once you know a secret, you can never go back.'

They mounted a steep incline. 'What about me, then?' she asked. 'Why am I here?'

'Escape,' he answered. 'The third reason they come. People who are known the globe over pay vast amounts for privacy. It interests me how treasured loneliness can be.'

'Who says I need privacy?'

The Jeep came to a halt. They were on the highest point of the island. From here Lori could make out the landscape's sweeping contours, the patches of different terrain and clusters of chalky-white buildings.

'I do.' He slammed the door and came round to her side. 'The attention over Selznick—' was that a grimace as he said Peter's name, or had she imagined it? '— will worsen before it improves.' On the warm wind Lori caught the aroma of JB's skin, the same as it had ever been: the same

as that first day, the same as La Côte. 'A fortnight of troubling publicity, then it's over.'

He seemed certain. How many other La Lumière girls
had JB offered this to?

They were parked outside a low-lying structure with
an ornamental front. Steps led up to a grand entrance, on
either side of which were poised two stone-carved sea monsters, Oriental in style, with ridged heads and tongues like
fire.

'Follow me.'

Inside, the air conditioning was prickly cool. Behind a
marble counter, a smiling woman in a blue uniform greeted
them.

'Welcome to Cacatra.'

'Lori will take Villa 19,' he informed her. The woman
appeared fleetingly surprised before vanishing wordlessly
into an adjacent room. JB put one arm on the counter. Lori
caught his eye. They watched each other a moment.

'Enjoy your stay, Ms Garcia.' The uniform reappeared
and a card was passed to Lori. She reached to take it but JB
claimed it first, slipping it into the top pocket of his shirt
and patting it once as if to make sure it was there.

Set apart from the rest of the accommodation, Villa 19 was
positioned yards from Cacatra's easternmost tip, where the
rocks ended abruptly and plunged into turbulent sea.

JB brought the vehicle to rest a short distance away.
'Dramatic, isn't it?'

To Lori it was the perfect word. 'I love it.'

The villa was sparsely furnished, rustic in style and
charming for those reasons. Lori felt inexplicably at home,
and, entering the master bedroom, she saw why. The win-

dows at the foot of the bed were thrown open, crisp white curtains dancing in the breeze. From here, high up, there was nothing to see but endless ocean. As she gazed out at the view she knew it from her fantasies. This was the place she had visited when she was a girl, immersed in her books, wishing for a future…quite simply, it was the same. The likeness was irrefutable, a cousin of déjà vu but with none of the shadows that cast it into doubt.

'We used to stay here when I was a boy,' said JB. 'In this villa.'

She turned, taken aback by his honesty.

'Every summer.' He had his eyes open but something in him was dreaming. 'My parents came. They would let me join them.'

It struck her as an odd way of putting it.

'Some years I'd bring a friend. A girl I knew from our village…' His gaze refocused. 'It was a long time ago.'

Lori waited. 'Are they happy memories?'

He blinked, looked away. 'I'll leave you to settle in.'

The moment was lost if ever it had been there. JB tapped the doorframe once, with his knuckle, an absent-minded, affectionate gesture. The ghost of a smile played on his top lip, pulling gently at the scar like a child tugging his mother's arm, pleading for a game.

Reuben van der Meyde's mansion was in its own territory, positioned above a private horseshoe of pale sand, metres from the beach. Lori recognised it from the pictures she had seen.

'Cacatra is Reuben's base,' qualified JB, 'as it is for me. The rest of the time, he travels.'

She wanted to know where JB lived on the island. Was it

on a cliff edge, like Villa 19? Or less imaginative, like here: a gentle gradient chosen over a sudden drop? Was Rebecca Stuttgart there too, waiting for her husband to return?

At the top of the winding stone steps, an irate-looking woman appeared. Small, flinty eyes, pinched with suspicion, flitted between JB and Lori. A boy of about six trailed at her heels.

JB's face broke into a grin, an easy sort she'd never before seen him wear. 'Hey, buddy—' he ruffled the child's hair '—what's happening with you?'

The boy looked up at him adoringly. 'I went swimming.'

'Yeah?'

'And I saw fishes.'

'What kind?'

'Whales.'

'Seriously? I don't think you're being serious.'

The boy laughed, high and excited, and bobbed a little dance, which Lori noticed made JB's eyes light up. 'I did see one,' the boy said. 'It was big as a house!'

'Not this house, I bet.'

'Bigger.'

'Mr Moreau.' The woman cut in, her accent clipped English as she wiped her hands efficiently on her skirt. 'Can I be of assistance?'

JB rested a hand on the back of the child's small neck, his thumb fondly stroking the skin there. 'Reuben's expecting us.'

'Mr V!' Inside, the woman bellowed into the mammoth atrium, sending the last letter bouncing violently off the walls. The boy was clearly accustomed to such a summons. Unfazed, he was fidgeting with the sails on a toy boat.

Lori bent to speak to him. 'What's your name?'

He gazed up at her, unsure.

'I'm Lori,' she offered.

'Don't frighten him,' said the woman, placing a proprietorial arm across his narrow shoulders and pulling him close. 'He's shy.'

'JB.' Reuben van der Meyde charged into the lobby, his bulk and vigour a marked contrast to the prim manners of his housekeeper. He was shorter than Lori had believed, and wider, with pink calves and freckled forearms. His chest was bare and round like a barrel, covered faintly in coils of silvery-red hair. He didn't look like one of the richest men in the world: he looked like a kid with attitude who'd got lucky. She remembered having the same impression when she'd seen him at the Frontline Fashion event in Vegas.

'Meet the one and only Lori Garcia,' JB said. 'She's one of ours.' There was a sliver of a pause before he tacked on, 'At La Lumière.'

'Glad to meet you.' Reuben's lizard eyes raked her up and down. Lori was hot in her jeans, had been wishing she'd worn something cooler, but was now glad of the extra layer.

'Likewise,' she returned. Over his shoulder, the housekeeper was regarding her frostily.

'Tell me what you make of Cacatra,' Reuben puffed, readying himself for her eulogy. His South African accent made the word sound like someone sharpening carving knives. 'First impressions are everything.'

'It's stunning.'

'Isn't it.' It wasn't a question. He grinned and she saw he'd had his teeth capped, an expensive, subtle job. 'Whatever you need while you're here, let me know.' He winked. 'Anything for a Valerie Girl.'

She noted the implication she wasn't the first he had welcomed.

'Join us tonight.' Reuben threw the next bit over his shoulder, not bothering to address the woman directly. 'You got that, Margaret?' Lori caught the prickle of dislike between them.

'Do you want to see my sailboats, Daddy?' The little boy stepped forward, tugging on Reuben's shorts. 'I've got ten of them, all reds and yellows.'

Instantly the woman called Margaret softened. 'Not now, sweetheart,' she said, steering him back. 'Your father's working.' But she threw a glance at Reuben, like it was a test.

If it was, he failed. 'Later,' Reuben informed the boy, with an awkward pat on the head. Sensing this was insufficient, he added, 'We'll go hunting on the beach.'

'For turtles?'

'Whatever you like.'

The boy looked sad. But as Reuben ushered them both across the lobby JB must have said something, made things better, because the child emitted a burst of laughter.

Outside, Lori was momentarily blinded by sunlight.

'You haven't seen the island till you've seen it from the water,' Reuben was saying, rubbing his hands together as he gestured to where a sleek speedboat was moored in the shallows. In true entrepreneurial style, she saw he was able to jump from one thing to the next instantly and without reflection. He led the way.

The Frenchman didn't follow. 'I'm needed elsewhere,'

he told her. 'The boy's name is Ralph. He's quiet, but give him time.'

'You're good with him.'

'He reminds me of someone.' JB backed away. 'Don't let Reuben take you too far out.'

Lori lost track of time on Cacatra. A week passed. Then another, and another, until she woke one morning and realised she had been on the island for over a month. Minutes, hours, days had lost their meaning. She was swimming, walking and diving, enjoying the yawning blue sky and fresh salty sea. She slept deep, untroubled sleep and woke feeling alert and contented.

The conversations she was obliged to have with Desideria and Jacqueline were unwelcome interruptions to her routine, reminders that this wasn't real life. Desideria was keen for her to return. LA missed her, she said, and so did Dante and Pearl. But right now she could imagine little that appealed to her less than returning to the thrust and noise of the city—not when she could be here, a capsule of perfection in an imperfect world.

There was no Rebecca Stuttgart. JB's wife was in Canada visiting her mother. Lori told herself it was irrelevant: no matter where the woman was, she was still JB's wife, and no matter how much time had passed, JB had still lied to and humiliated her in the worst possible way.

Yet, as the days mounted, the island cast its slow, creeping spell. She felt herself breaking through the vine of her defences, the one she'd grown, remembering reading a tale with her mama when she was little about a prince who'd slayed foliage dense as wire, thick as a wall, to reach the castle of his sleeping love. All the uncertainty of those first months with JB, the wonderings and the what-ifs, returned, more demanding of answers than ever. Life became a basic dichotomy: the hours he spent with her and the hours he didn't.

Once, Lori had been exploring a deserted cove and cut her foot on a rock. Bleeding, without shade, and dehydrated in the heat of the midday sun, she'd called for help, aware the likelihood of being heard was minimal. And yet she knew, simply, he would come.

JB's boat had slipped into view, closing in till expertly he dropped anchor, jumping into the shallows and even though the bottoms of his trousers were rolled above the ankle they got wet. He'd handled her foot lightly, cradling it like a damaged bird, and had removed his shirt, binding the wound tight so the cotton turned red.

'It's going to scar.'

He'd helped her up, one solid arm round her waist. 'Is that OK?'

Lori could feel his muscles, his skin. Yes, it was OK. It was OK.

Now, as Lori fingered the promised scar on her ankle, she hoped it would always be there. A reminder of the time they had shared, a mark on her body to prove it.

39
Aurora

Clearly her name still carried currency where it mattered. Aurora was pleased at how easily Rita had been able to secure their place on the exclusive island. 'Cacatra?' Rita was surprised when she suggested it. 'Why? I was thinking Barbados, the Maldives…?'

'Why not?' she replied easily. 'It's the hottest place to be right now.'

'It's a rehab spa, Aurora. You don't need that.'

'I know I don't.'

'So why are we doing it?'

'You asked me where I wanted to go, and now I'm telling you.' She sounded snappish—it was an easier, lazier way of getting things done. The fact remained that Rita was her agent and she was the one calling the shots.

'What do your parents think?'

Aurora shrugged, irritated by the reference. The less she thought about them, the better. 'It's cool.'

Tom and Sherilyn would be too distracted to enquire after her plans anyway—her mom was now house-bound, unable to leave the confines of her bedroom, while Tom was in the thick of it on tour—and that was exactly how Aurora wanted it. Several times since returning from school she had talked herself into voicing her fears to Tom, only to talk herself out of it again. It didn't occur to her to broach it with Sherilyn, because they'd never really been close about stuff. It was she and Tom who shared that bond: Tom who she told when she'd started her periods; Tom she ran to when she'd had a fight with her friends; Tom whose shoulder she cried on when things got tough. But this wasn't just a boohoo moment, nor was it anything she could accurately label and go to him with. She needed to find out more. She needed to get the facts.

She needed to see JB Moreau.

They arrived on Cacatra at the weekend. Aurora was tired and tetchy after the journey—a mask for her nerves—and, now she was here, started to wonder if it was all a mistake. What exactly was she looking for? What did she expect to find?

The women were taken across the shallows to a tranquil villa, raised on stilts of wood. Rita thought it about the most peaceful place she had been. The view of the ocean was wide and uninterrupted. Below, in clear water, tiny fish darted across the alabaster sand.

Aurora seemed too distracted to take it in.

'Are you all right?' asked Rita. 'You haven't stopped fidgeting since we landed.'

'Sure.' She wandered on to the veranda. 'I'm fine.'

'Do you like it?'

'Yeah.'

'Is that all you're going to say? "Yeah"?'

Aurora didn't seem to hear. 'Yeah.'

Surreptitiously Rita rolled her eyes. Having kids had never been on her agenda. It was easy to remember why when dealing with belligerent teenagers. 'I'm going for a swim.'

'Cool.' Aurora turned her back on the view. Rita thought how very pretty she was, even when she was frowning. Maybe she needed this trip more than either of them realised.

'Why don't you take a look around?' Rita smiled. 'See what van der Meyde's hiding.'

Never mind big fat sweaty Reuben van der Meyde. It was JB Aurora had to find.

The island was bigger than she'd pictured. It wasn't going to be easy. But, then, how had she thought it would unfold? Had she imagined she'd just turn up on Cacatra, be shown straight to him and then demand he tell her what he'd been discussing in a conversation he'd had some months previously and which he'd believed to be private? The idea was laughable. Not to mention how foolish he'd made her feel last time they'd met.

As Aurora crossed the walkway she spied a pleasure cruiser departing the shore, manned by an actor couple, A-list sweethearts who had recently got married. They didn't look like newly-weds—both sat to the rear of the boat, a gaping space between them. The woman had her chin cupped in her palm, deep in thought as she gazed at the water.

'Do you need anything, Ms Nash?' She almost ran

straight into the guy. He was dressed in a blue uniform and was grinning fixedly at her, robotic in his willingness to please. *For morons like you to leave me alone*, she wanted to retort. Instead, she decided to take advantage of the offer. 'I'm here to see JB Moreau. It's important I speak with him.'

The man was charmed by her beauty. Hundreds of gorgeous famous women came to Cacatra, but rarely were they more captivating in real life than they were in pictures. Still, it didn't change the fact that Mr Moreau was unavailable—no matter how pretty Aurora Nash was or how she rated her chances. 'If there's anything I can help you with…?'

'I'd prefer to see him.'

'Of course.' The girl's resolve, the obstinate set of her mouth, told him she was here on personal business. It wasn't the first time a cast-off lover had come to Cacatra to corner Moreau. He'd pass on the message. 'I'll ask him to contact you directly.'

She nodded, mumbling her thanks and padding off up the beach.

Cacatra was the world's most opulent playground for grown-ups. Aurora surmised from the accommodation that there couldn't be more than fifty or sixty people staying at any given time, including staff. As well as the blue uniforms she saw others, too, wandering between the white-block buildings: balding, bespectacled men reminiscent of Dr Lux, and women with tight-wound buns and serious expressions. But the expanse of the island made it easy to become lost and to feel entirely alone. Celebrities paid for solitude. It was impossible to get it anywhere else.

Settling on a patch of sand, she listened to the gentle waves rippling lazily on to shore. The sand was damp and compacted between her toes. She breathed in deeply through her nose and for a moment wished Pascale were here. Rather, she wished they could erase the past six months and be as they used to be. The friendship with Pascale had been the closest she'd ever known. She'd never had a friend like that before and doubted she ever would again: someone integral in every way, an ally, them against the world. But like all intense things it had burned itself out. In the final weeks of term the girls had barely said two words to each other. Aurora had suspected Pascale was keeping things from her, paranoid because Pascale had *always* kept things from her, hadn't she, so why was this any different? But it *felt* different. Ever since Capri.

Privacy, retreat, loneliness. Looking out across the liquid distance, Aurora had never before felt so by herself.

She was distracted by activity at the other end of the beach. A couple were rounding the cliffs. Or maybe they weren't a couple. The woman, she couldn't see who it was, held her arms round her as if she were cold, or self-conscious. Wild black hair whipped in the ocean breeze. She was wearing a pair of frayed denim shorts and a thin vest, no bra. And the man…

Aurora put her hand to her forehead to counter the glare. It was him.

She sprang to her feet. As they came closer she realised the woman was Lori Garcia, the Valerie Girl. Back at St Agnes everyone banged on about how glamorous she was, but in real life she was less glamour—the word didn't do her justice—and more raw, absolute beauty. The sun was dipping, casting her skin a rich brown. Her eyes, as they met Aurora's, were raven-black.

JB seemed taken aback when he saw her, managing in time to produce the conceited grin he had accosted her with on Capri. She wanted to slap it off his face. She hated his smugness, the fact he was always making out as if he was privy to a joke she didn't get.

'Aurora, this is a surprise.' He kissed her on both cheeks. 'Reuben didn't tell me to expect you.'

'It was spontaneous.'

'Lori Garcia, this is Aurora Nash.'

'Hi,' said Aurora.

'Hello,' said Lori.

There was an uncomfortable pause. Aurora smiled but the other girl didn't return it.

What a rude bitch! thought Aurora. Didn't she realise JB was married? Anyone would think she was a jealous psycho girlfriend.

Is she one of his lovers? thought Lori. Envy surged, despite her efforts to hold it down. JB was a player. She'd confronted that months ago.

'How long are you staying?' JB asked. 'A while, I hope.'

'A few days.'

'Is Pascale with you?'

Aurora noticed Lori Garcia's expression. So she *was* a jealous girlfriend, no doubt freaking that JB was screwing Aurora *and* her friend. Ha.

'Nah,' said Aurora, deciding to have some fun. 'She should have come. She's missing you like *crazy.*'

Clearly JB thought it a weird thing to say. 'I'm sure,' he said drily.

Aurora shifted her weight, thought about how to word it

and wished Lori Garcia weren't standing right there, hanging back but so obviously listening in. What a loser.

She spoke quietly, hoping her tone conveyed sufficient urgency. 'I have to talk to you.' She tossed a glance Lori's way. 'In private?'

Concern—unease?—clouded JB's expression, but only momentarily.

'Of course.' He had enough discretion not to ask what it was about. 'Tomorrow?' He appraised her a moment. 'Come up to Reuben's house.'

What, too busy now with your Spanish friend? Why don't you get back to your wife, you fuck.

'Fine.' Aurora nodded. 'Tomorrow.'

That night she and Rita dined on their veranda. They ate freshly caught crab and sautéed shrimp, swordfish steak and fries and salad. It was some of the most delicious food Aurora had ever been served but she could stomach none of it.

'Weren't you hungry?' Rita raised an eyebrow at Aurora's barely touched plate.

'Not especially.'

Rita sighed. 'Come on, honey, the whole point of this break was to relax. LA's not gonna be an easy ride. Make the most of it while you can.'

'I'm tired is all.'

Rita sat back, breathed in deeply and closed her eyes. 'Second that.' The food and the sea air were taking their toll. 'Think I'll hit the hay, read for a bit.'

'OK. Night.'

'Aurora?' At the door Rita glanced back, fighting the

uncharacteristic urge to put her arms round the girl. She looked so young, so unhappy…so lost.

'What?'

'Get some sleep.'

An hour later, Aurora was still awake. She felt queasy with fear. What was JB going to reveal when she challenged him? Up till now she'd been able to pretend her worries were unfounded, convince herself they were based on nothing but an overactive imagination that had spiralled out of control. But he had the power to confirm them. He, this man she had met only once before, had the ability to transform everything about herself and her family that she believed to be true.

At midnight she gave up, threw on a pair of jeans and a sweater and made her way out on to the walkway, barefoot. It was bright, the moon a crisp orb that spilled metallic light on to the black water. Never had she seen so many stars. Thousands of them, millions, countless, puncturing the canopy: clusters, constellations, billions and billions of light years away. Pascale had told her about the time it took for starlight to reach the earth, how the stars they saw tonight could already be dead, extinguished in a soundless faraway combustion. The universe was infinite: observable space, alone, more immense than she could imagine.

'Have you seen Aurora Borealis?' Pascale had asked once when they were leaning out of their dorm window on a rare clear night.

'Who?'

'The Northern Lights, stupid.'

'Oh.'

'It's your name.' Pascale had smiled her secret smile. *'Your name means light. Aurora was the dawn.'*

The dawn felt a long way away now as she crossed to the island. She needed a walk, a diversion. Cacatra was dotted with lights that flickered and splintered like torches in the dark, people still awake, guests and staff, the faint waves of conversation and music drifting over. It was warm, the air filled with the soothing wash of waves coming to land.

Aurora kept away from the lit paths, putting her trust in the glow of the moon. The sand was cool underfoot but the rocks were sharp and she wished she'd slipped on her sneakers. By the time she reached the south of the island, when the gathered aircraft came into view—Reuben van der Meyde's VDM helicopter crouching like a giant dragonfly—her feet hurt badly.

Back in the direction from which she'd come, Aurora spotted a smaller islet. On it was a lighthouse, its searching beam flashing and receding, flashing and receding, the rhythm hypnotic. The sightline drew her attention to a private inlet, concealing the arms of a building that was scarcely visible from this angle—in fact it couldn't be properly visible anywhere but from the water. It was huge, imposing, whitestone, with a grand semicircular front. It was the van der Meyde mansion: she had seen it before on an instalment of *MTV Cribs*.

Intrigued, she located a steep rung of half-overgrown steps leading down to the beach. They had once been painted white, and the chipped, just-visible coat shone to show her the way; they were crookedly laid, like a row of uneven teeth. Evidently this route to the house was no longer used. She felt like a trespasser. It occurred to her she *was* a trespasser.

Distance here was deceptive and it was some time before Aurora reached the mansion, which had appeared closer than it was. A window on the ground floor was fractionally open, light emanating from inside, partly concealed behind a stone wall. She caught sight of a couple, their backs to her, heads bent together as they examined something in their laps. She recognised them as the couple she'd seen earlier in the pleasure cruiser: the newly-wed actors. Afraid of being seen, she ducked and skirted round to where the wall became shallower. The positioning of the house created a vacuum and Aurora found she was able to hear what was being said.

'We *understand*.' Reuben's voice was softly persuasive. 'Partnerships like yours are different. You have special requirements. Rest assured we discuss each individual case at length before an arrangement is made. Some couples choose to participate in the process, either the mother's or the father's genes, where others wish to keep it fifty-fifty, a clean severance. You'd be surprised at how many opt for the latter. An equal stake in the product, shall we say.'

The man spoke. 'It could take some time.'

'Sign the agreement with us this week and we can set the wheels in motion right away.'

Aurora leaned closer, straining to hear. She lost the start of the next bit.

'…following a more in-depth meet we will offer you a choice of pairing. My scouts recruit women from all over the world to deliver our needs, and to provide authentic matches. After that, of course, a nine-month wait.'

'Authentic matches?'

'For instance, you are both dark…a fair-haired child might raise eyebrows.'

'So if we were black, say, or Asian...'

'We would match you with a black or Asian surrogate.'

It was the woman's turn. 'And the mothers?' she asked. Her voice was anxious. 'What happens to them?'

Reuben's answer was immediate. 'This is a humanitarian outreach. The women sourced—and I ask you not to call them mothers, because they are merely hosts, *vessels*, if you will, to the opportunity of your own motherhood—all have one thing in common. They seek a better life.'

'A better life?'

'And a better life is what we offer them. Don't get me wrong: these are healthy women—our checks are rigorous—and naturally they are physically superior. But their lives might not have taken turns altogether... fortunate.'

'And you help them how?' the actor queried.

Reuben laid it out. 'Perhaps these women need money,' he said. 'Twenty per cent of your initial fee goes directly to them. We're talking volumes of cash these girls have never come close to, never *dreamed* they would come close to. But, hey, not everyone's set on being rich, which is why our insurance, not just for the surrogates but for their families, counts for, in some ways, a great deal more.' There was another pause. 'Tell me: given the opportunity to immeasurably improve the lives of those you hold most dear, simply by providing a service and keeping quiet about it, wouldn't you seize it with both hands? Happily, women do. Women have.'

He elaborated. 'The family might be in difficulty. They need medical care, say, or they've lost a loved one to crime or drugs or prostitution. The scheme promises to look after not only the individual but also her family—and not just financially but with employment, housing, education, over generations to come. We're talking immense wealth in the short term,' he concluded, 'and assurance, *in*surance, in the long.'

'And you sustain the payments how?'

Reuben didn't miss a beat. 'By regular instalments from clients such as yourselves, paid quarterly until the child reaches twenty-one. That way we guarantee discretion, now and in the future.' A meaningful pause. 'In doing so, my friends, *you* are making lives better.'

Aurora couldn't make sense of it. Another man spoke. There must be four of them now. The actor's manager?

'Our concern is with confidentiality,' the second man said.

'Naturally.'

'If this ever came out... The risk is immense, Reuben.'

'There is no risk.' Reuben's voice was measured, assured, each question anticipated, as if he'd had the same conversation hundreds of times before. 'That is the beauty of our service. Couples like you have many and varied reasons why they are unable, or choose not, to have a child. Those reasons do not concern us. What we do is give you the opportunity to present the infant as *biologically your own*, depending on your needs—be they personal, professional, public—without the mess and speculation of adoption. You announce the pregnancy, take a break from publicity or, as some couples choose to, plan appearances where you can show off the bump.'

Realisation hit. The knot fell free, its length slipped round her neck, quiet as a noose. Aurora clamped a hand over her mouth to stop herself screaming.

'What bump?' It was the woman again, irritable this time.

'There are ways. We offer several cosmetic possibilities ourselves.'

'Surely people would ask questions.'

'Not if your term was convincing.'

'And if the...*surrogates* do break confidentiality?' the manager demanded. 'What then?'

'That would not happen.'

'You can't possibly guarantee—'

'I can and I do. All surrogates are made aware of what it means to enter business with Reuben van der Meyde. I am a very powerful man and I will not be crossed. There are consequences. I can benefit their lives immeasurably or, if I see fit, I can destroy them.'

'But what about the child?' interrupted the woman. 'The lying!'

'It depends where your conscience sits,' countered Reuben. 'A simple transaction, that is all. Making one life to save countless more. My conscience is clear.'

'What about the fathers?' the actor asked. In a smaller voice, he clarified: 'The biological fathers.'

'The men, too, are vetted—' Reuben cleared his throat '—but their situation is different.'

'How?'

'They receive a handsome payment, as you would expect, but the process, from their perspective, is anonymous. They enter a gene pool, a sperm bank, if you will. They receive no information on the woman they have been paired with and there is no further contact from us.'

A long silence followed. Aurora held her breath.

'Put simply,' said Reuben, 'you must try to think of this as a surrogate agency.'

The actor: 'A top-secret surrogate agency.'

'It goes without saying.'

'An agency that is fooling the world.'

'An agency that offers a solution to all.'

'Discretion *guaranteed*?'

'More. Satisfaction guaranteed.'

Aurora turned. She could hear no more. Blood raged behind her eyes.

She wanted to vomit. She bent and heaved, retching till her stomach hurt but nothing came up. Staggering back down the beach, half running, half stumbling, she groped in the dark for something to hold on to and found only black air.

That was it, then.

That was it.

40
Stevie

A week on Cacatra and Bibi Reiner could have been the girl who'd opened the door all those months ago in New York, her hair in rollers, one hand flapping in an attempt to dry freshly painted nails that got smudged anyway when she came in for a hug. The place reached into the soul and shook it to life.

'Back later.' Bibi kissed her. 'I've got a hot date with a spa. Want to join me?'

'Thanks, I'd rather stay here.'

'Suit yourself. Don't miss me too much!'

Alone, Stevie passed the morning in their villa, reading, and every so often drifting into weightless sleep, lulled by the sound of gently lapping waves. She was trying not to dwell on Xander and the unhappiness of their parting. The way he'd reacted when she'd told him her plan to accompany Bibi to the island had left her dumbfounded.

'Why would you want to go there?' he'd asked stiffly, his back to her at the patio doors.

'Bibi needs me, Xander. She's been through things you or I couldn't imagine. I don't see why it's such a big deal.'

'I don't want you to go.'

'Why not?'

'I can't explain.'

'Try? Because you know I can't bail on my best friend because my husband's decided he doesn't want me to go to Cacatra for some reason he "can't explain".'

Stevie had attempted to make sense of their argument. She knew Cacatra Island was owned by Reuben van der Meyde, and dim recollection prompted the image of him sitting at JB Moreau's side at the Frontline Fashion event she'd been invited to in Vegas, the one Xander had refused to attend. *Old adversaries*, he'd said. How he was whenever the fashion magnate was brought up in conversation, like he'd seen a ghost. Was that it? Was this something to do with JB Moreau?

Xander had turned on her, gesturing between them. *'It's not about...this, is it?'*

Their phantom baby. Nothing, still.

'Why would it be about that?' She had taken his hand. *'This isn't about running out on you, all right? I love you.'*

'Then go someplace else. Anywhere else. Please.'

The last thing Stevie wanted was a marriage of secrets, even though they were under a year in and already seemed to be building up an arsenal of the things. For, despite Xander's evasiveness, she had to admit she hadn't been honest with him, either: the truth about Linus Posen's death hung over her like an axe...but she had to respect Bibi's confidence. She began to wonder if they might have rushed into the wedding. The more she tortured herself, the less convinced she became that she knew her husband at all. What if their relationship was a fake? What if she'd signed on to spending the rest of her life with a stranger? Whatever Xander was hiding, it clearly had to be enough to compromise their relationship—his behaviour was too bizarre for it to be anything else.

Around lunchtime Stevie swam in the sea, floating on her back with her palms in the air. The sun was blazing and the water was cool, lightly rocking her body. The current was stronger than she'd thought and when she went to put her feet down, expecting to meet sand or rock, she was surprised to find that she'd drifted out. Her limbs felt tired and the distance back to the villa, against the tide, was disheartening. Behind her, further out, was a lighthouse island, closer to her than the main beach. She let the current wash her towards it, deciding to rest there till she had strength to swim back.

The shore was rocky and sharp, painful on the soles of her feet, and because of the lone building's sheer walls there was little if any shade. The lighthouse itself dated back, she guessed, to the sixties. It was typical of its style and fairly well preserved, given the battering it must have received over the years, its white-hot walls only slightly chipped, flaps of paint peeling away. She felt thirsty and a bit sun-sick, and hammered her fist on the door once or twice in the hope someone might hear. There was no response. Raising a hand to ward off the midday sun, she spied a small rectangular window at the very top. It was impossible to see clearly but she thought she saw the dark outline of a person back away from it.

'Hello?' she called. A seagull swooped overhead with

a lonely cry, coming to rest on the chalky tip. It flapped its wings once or twice. Stevie squinted at the window, wondering if the island and the heat were playing tricks on her.

There was a docking space and a landing rope on the south of the islet. She touched the tip of the rope with her toe and felt it was still wet. Obviously the building was still in use, though for what she couldn't imagine. It didn't look like a working lighthouse and, anyway, from what she could gather, visitors typically arrived by air. She attempted to peer into one of the lower windows but they were too high. With a little jump she could catch a gloomy glimpse of its interior, but all she could decipher were piled-up boxes and what looked like paperwork. Folders and files, too many to count, and a system of shelves that would have been more at home in a library, with large initials at the end of each row: A, H, M... P, S, W...

She was relieved when a speedboat approached, its tail of white foam looping as the vessel came to rest. A man in uniform was at the wheel.

'Everything all right?' he asked. He helped her on to the boat and close up she saw that he was young, with a broad, flat face that brought to mind the back of a wooden spoon.

'I came out further than I meant to,' she said. 'Thanks.'

'I'm afraid the lighthouse is off-limits,' he told her. 'No access here at all.'

She found his expression curiously blank. 'Like I said, it was a mistake.'

They travelled back to Cacatra in minutes. Stevie looked behind her, the lighthouse diminishing, smaller and smaller, in their wake.

* * *

'Where've you been?' Bibi asked when she got back. Her friend was relaxing on a wicker lounger, legs tucked under her, magazine in hand, a long-forgotten smile on her face. Dirk Michaels had advised her to see a therapist while she was here—Cacatra had the best, he promised—and while Stevie knew Bibi wouldn't be revealing the final details of Linus's death, it seemed like the appointments, however they were being used, were having a positive effect.

'Long story.'

'I was getting worried!'

Stevie sat down. 'Good session?'

'I think so.' Bibi shrugged. 'I got so relaxed I fell asleep!' She surveyed the lunch menu. 'I'm starved.'

'Me too. Let's order a feast.'

After they'd eaten, Stevie went on to the veranda to hang her bikini to dry. She noticed a couple of maids cleaning out the adjacent villa, efficiently stripping sheets and carrying bundles of linen across the walkway. That was strange. She had seen Rita Clay there only this morning—the women had met through Marty King—and could have sworn Rita told her she planned to stay another week.

Confused, Stevie checked the villa on her other side. No, she was positive it had been that one. Never mind, maybe something came up and Rita had been obliged to return home.

She made her way back inside. 'Take a walk with me?'

Bibi yawned, stretching her arms high. 'I'm kinda tired. Might sleep for a bit.'

Stevie hesitated. She'd wanted to broach the subject since they'd got here but hadn't found the right time. Was there ever a right time to discuss what they needed to?

'B, what are we going to do?' she asked softly.

'About what?'

'You know about what.'

Bibi started packing a bag with beach things, even though she'd said she was staying in. 'I'm not thinking about it. It's over.'

Stevie was unsure whether to go on. 'You can't pretend it didn't happen,' she said.

Bibi snapped. 'You feel sorry for him or something, is that it?'

'Of course not. Never.'

'Because it's not like what I did to him even came close to what he did to me.'

'I know.'

'You can't possibly know.'

'I'm trying. I want to help you.'

'Then let me forget it.' Bibi was shaking. She vanished into the bathroom. 'I don't want to regret telling you, Steve,' she said through the closed door.

After a moment, Stevie knocked gently. 'Let me in?'

'No.'

'Telling me was the right thing. That isn't in question.'

'You're saying I should confess.'

She chose her words carefully. Was it possible to live life by a moral compass when other people didn't? Wasn't everyone equally at sea?

'No, actually, I'm not.'

'I'm a murderer.'

'Linus was evil,' she said. 'I'd have done the exact same thing.'

The lock on the door clicked. Stevie pushed it open and saw Bibi on the loo with her head in her hands.

'But I do think you're going to have to try and work this

Victoria Fox

through,' she continued, 'if you want to get your life back. Otherwise it's going to destroy you.'

'You said you owed me,' Bibi said quietly. 'Do you remember? When you won the Lauren audition?'

'Yes, I remember.'

'So this is it. This is when I get to cash in.' She looked up. 'Please, Steve, I want to forget it happened. I want to *forget*. That's why I'm here, in the middle of the goddamn ocean, in the middle of nowhere. I'm praying that by the time we go back—' she gestured around, as if the bullshit of LA were something she could clear, like steam '—people will have moved on, and it won't have to be the first thing I see or hear or think about every single day when I wake up. So leave it,' she finished. 'All right?'

Stevie rested her head against the doorframe. 'All right.'

That Friday, she got her period. It happened unexpectedly, when she was swimming. She'd been late, just a few days but wondering all the same...*if*. If she was, it meant being able to have a family. If she was, then there was nothing the matter with her. If she was, then she could go back to Xander with the news and that would make everything all right. But she had known, really, the moment she'd woken that morning and felt the scrape in her gut.

She was hurrying back to the villa, wrapped in a towel, when, eyes down on the beach, she ran straight into JB Moreau. Embarrassingly she sort of collapsed into him and he had to gather her, holding her at arm's length like a puppy brought out of a box.

'My fault,' he said. 'Didn't see you coming.'

Stevie's mind was blank, aware of the pressure of his touch on her shoulders. At the Vegas event she had thought him handsome, but in proximity he was magnetic in that way so particular to dangerous men. There was a look in his eye that reminded her of her first day working at Simms & Court. How she'd entered his office, primed for direction, and he'd turned from the window to face her and everything in his expression had said: *This is inevitable.* Once you gave away an innocent heart, you could never get it back.

'I don't think we've met.' JB extended his hand. 'Jean-Baptiste, call me JB. I'm a business partner of Reuben's. We look after the island.'

Stevie found herself drawn involuntarily to his eyes, which were of a startling, unusual blue. She shook his hand firmly, registering the quiet strength of his grip.

'Stevie Speller.'

'Yes, I know.' That smile again—it was killer. 'Xander's wife.'

The observation struck her as blunt and a little rude. 'I prefer not to think of myself as just someone's wife,' she said, aware she sounded stuffy.

'Xander's not just someone,' JB countered, dark humour in his voice that she couldn't account for. Stevie had the sense he was feeling his way, aiming to grasp how much Xander might have told her. 'He's an old friend of mine.'

Old adversaries.

JB waited for her to confirm or deny her knowledge. She decided to do neither, though it was beyond tempting to ask him to elaborate on their relationship.

'How is he?' he asked smoothly. 'It's been a while.'

'Fine,' she said carefully. 'We're very happy.'

He smiled. Stevie saw his teeth were very nearly straight but not quite, the imperfection, as with the scar, adding to his weird beauty. His canines were slightly sharp, giving his mouth a malevolence. 'I'm pleased to hear it,' he said. 'We used to know each other well.'

Stevie returned the smile, close-lipped.

'Well, it was good to meet you,' she said, backing away.

'Likewise,' JB said. 'Perhaps we'll run into each other again?'

'Perhaps.'

As Stevie crossed the bridge to the villa she sensed his eyes on her back. Despite the searing heat, cold seeped down her spine like syrup dripping from a spoon.

41
Lori

Lori was due to return to LA the following morning. She had been on Cacatra for eight weeks.

Island life suited her. 'It better had,' said Jacqueline when she told her she was coming home. 'Your schedule's back-to-back.'

'And Peter?'

'Gone quiet. Moreau was right about this break—it was for the best.'

Lori hadn't seen him for days. He had been tied up in meetings with Reuben van der Meyde. She wasn't sure what the connection was between the men but recalled Desideria telling her JB ran a number of pursuits separate to the fashion house and decided this must be one of them. While it was tempting to read more into his attentiveness during her stay on Cacatra, as she was a Valerie Girl owned by La Lumière it stood to reason he would make the effort.

But then she would think of the time he had taken her

out in his boat and caught a fish the size of a violin, slipping his thumb into its mouth to kill it; or when he'd dived with her, moving through underwater shadows and across knuckles of pink coral; or the way he was with the child Ralph, like an elder brother, how it lit him like a flame in a glass; or how he'd held on to her that day she'd hurt her ankle—and all the longing would seep back in, under the door she'd closed on it, insistent and everywhere, like trying to hold back a furious river with only her hand.

He invited her to dinner that night. One of his assistants came to Villa 19 just as the light was fading behind Cacatra's serrated silhouette. Lori was pulling her bags together for the early-morning departure, holding close items of clothing and breathing them in, wanting the scent of the island to travel with her. But clothes, like memories, would be washed clean: replaced, renewed, until they forgot the places they'd been.

It was a relief to know she would see him one last time before she left. She fully expected him to withdraw the moment they were back in America. It was wise. JB Moreau was unavailable, in every sense of the word.

'Give me an hour,' she told the assistant, even though she could have returned with him. It was an hour to sit at the window of her villa and embrace the view that had become over the past two months as familiar and beloved as the one from her childhood bedroom, when her mama was still alive and life was laid out ahead of her in its glory. What it was, she saw now, was possibility. Chances. A view, plain and simple.

She made her way to JB's villa along the beach. His had a wide veranda carved out of the rock—she'd been up once

before when he'd taken her on a tour of the island—and, up
on the terrace, she was surprised to find a table set for two,
covered in long white linen and overlooking the sea. An
ice bucket was positioned to one side, chilling champagne.

JB was standing at the balcony, his back to her, head
tilted towards the stars. He was smoking a cigarette.

'It's not meant to be romantic,' he said, without turning
round. 'Chef must have thought I was dining with my wife.'

Lori wasn't sure what to say. 'I didn't think it was.'

He ground out the half-smoked cigarette on the chalky
wall, where it left a smoky grey smudge. 'Sit down.' He
gestured to the table. His eyes were changed, she saw, the
pupils large so they swallowed the blue, as though staring
down infinite distances had at last absorbed the dark im-
mensity of sea and space. 'Relax.'

The food was delicious: tender pale mussels and hunks
of salted bread, raspberry and chocolate fondant that dissolved on her tongue. They shared a bottle of Krug and
Lori began to feel drunk. The sky was in limbo of deep
purple. Water contained them like glittering ink. Candles
were lit and the glow accented each contour of JB's face:
near-blackness around his mouth and eyes, through which
she would occasionally capture a flash of sapphire, glinting
sharply like treasure on the ocean floor.

'Come for a walk,' he said when they finished. He saw
her hesitate and held out his hand. 'There's nowhere like
the beach this time of night.'

Lori took it, but only to stand, and released his grip
before he had the chance to do it first.

The sand was wet between her toes. Firm, compacted, solid
ground, yet comprised of grains so tiny that alone they

were invisible. She loved how the sea came in on its rhythmic tide, smoothing it over again and again like a mother's palm across a fevered forehead.

'You see why I choose to be here,' he said. They walked in quiet, only the sound of the lapping waves for company.

Lori turned, unable to make out any detail. He was nearest the shore, against the moon, so that its light was absorbed by the side she couldn't see, drawing him a blank shape.

'It's not hard to imagine,' she said.

'No?'

'Living on Cacatra. Being happy. It's the first place I've felt that way about since my mother died.'

She thought he moved closer, walking so their arms would touch, could touch, if she wanted them to. In the same moment she remembered JB's own parents, Paul and Emilie Moreau, who had both died so horrifically when he was a child.

'I'm sorry,' she said, 'that was insensitive.'

'Because I'm an orphan?' The word conjured images of filthy abandoned children, weak and shivering and alone—not JB, with his wealth and sex and the cold fire that burned in his eyes. 'Your pain is no less legitimate.'

They continued in silence, but it was comfortable, understood, as when confidences are shared and each tentative word valuable. Lori looked behind her. The house they'd come from was a twinkling cluster in the distance.

'I was fourteen.' JB stopped and turned to the ocean. 'I never wanted to see water again. Now, I can't imagine any other way than to be surrounded by it.'

'Fourteen is young.'

'Any age is difficult.'

He crouched, picked up a roughened stick and carved a wide arc in the sand, from left to right. Lori lowered herself down next to him.

'We lost control of the boat,' he said, his voice strange, too low, as though he was trying to get far enough beneath the words to support them. 'One minute we were together. The next, they were gone. I lost them.'

Lori closed her eyes. She pictured the jumping, steaming waves. Grey, brown, violent.

'There was nothing I could do. I watched them both drown.'

She put her hand on his arm. Once upon a time she might have thought better of it, but now it came naturally. Whatever misunderstandings and embarrassments had gone between them in the past, she wanted to be his friend. She owed him that.

'I'm sorry,' she said. 'I'm so sorry.'

JB looked up. There was sadness in him, such deep loneliness, deeper than Rico's that day in the parking lot, deeper than her father's, deeper than her own.

'Do you believe in God?' he asked. His expression was determined, as though he sought not just her faith but the absolute answer. He needed to know.

'I used to,' she said. 'Didn't everyone?'

Reclaiming the stick, JB swept through the arc, completing the circle around them. He had to lean across her to do it and his proximity was hard to bear.

'Afterwards, I lay on deck,' he said. 'The storm had passed. The sky was purple, like a painting. They were the worst hours. Me and God, with nothing to say.'

'Were you alone?'

'Our boat had been reported missing. They came for me.'

She studied his face, knew the truth before she asked for it. 'Were you hurt?'

JB raised a finger to the scar on his mouth. 'Only this. I slipped trying to reach them and it cut right open. The wound was deep. It took a long time to heal.' He shook his head. 'Sounds dramatic, doesn't it? But it felt like they were reminding me.'

'Who?'

'My mother and father. Even after the stitches were out, every time I went to smile, it hurt. It felt like they were reminding me of what I'd let happen.'

'But you didn't let anything happen,' she said. 'It wasn't your fault.'

'Maybe.'

A wave rinsed up to Lori's feet. 'Do you feel close to them on Cacatra?' she asked.

'Close?' The word was acutely, painfully intimate.

'Here more than anywhere. Because you used to—'

He took her chin in his hands and kissed her.

It happened just like that. She must have turned at the exact same moment because they were sitting side by side and then they were kissing, and there wasn't anything else in between.

JB's lips were soft and inquisitive, sure and firm, and when he broke away Lori felt like a parched desert-wanderer given a thimble to drink. She needed more. She had to have more.

This time they went for each other, his hands running down her body, mouth on mouth, body against body, aching with burn. Switched like a light, flooding her with glow. She was thrown back on to the sand, JB's fingertips trailing a line down her neck as he kissed her earlobe and her chin and then her mouth again and his hand moved lower. Lori felt him cross her breast and her body shook. She shivered with heat.

'Do you want this?'

'Yes.' Such a small word for the emotion it betrayed: months of devotion, of hatred, of confusion, of dreaming of this. She yearned for all of JB Moreau, his entirety, his body and soul.

His hand was on the inside of her thigh. Damp in her knickers. The sand was still warm and Lori imagined her body was fire, scorching the earth beneath. When his touch disappeared inside her she moaned, spilling on to him, reaching down to grip his forearm and clasp him to her. She could not see his face, a black outline against the sky blacker still. Only the wide eye of the moon gazed down at her, full and brimming with light.

He kissed her again, his tongue in her mouth. Water washed between them, the tide coming up, thick with salt and cold and raw. She unbuttoned his shirt, running her palms across his chest, the smell of him accompanying the parting of the material, as if he were a window she had opened on a summer's day.

'Are you a virgin?' he breathed.

She could barely speak for the blood in her voice. 'Yes.'

His hardness pressed between her parted legs. Never had a sensation been so consuming, the promise of euphoria that was too much to bear.

The instant he entered her, Lori came alive. Light-headed, she swam in infinite depth, JB's strong arms pulling her to him, saving her, holding their bodies together. The pain was searing and momentary, followed at once by immeasurable pleasure. Feeling him inside, joined with him, as one, riding his rhythm, she would be content to die right here, now, on this island, and float out to sea, her body spent, this union spelling all it had ever been and ever would be.

Pleasure and pain...

He drove into her on the cusp, obliterating the line between the two. Lori was going to orgasm, faster than she knew she could. Sea water rushed up to shore, more of it, swelling around the point where they locked, getting her wetter and wetter, stinging with saline, and now his pace was increasing, his breath in her ear, the heat between them soaring till she thought they were ablaze, and he was going in deeper, more painful and more pleasurable both at the same time and it flared her like a striking match and suddenly she was ignited, climaxing with the scream she had been holding on to for years, out and absorbed into the boundless sky.

Another thrust and he joined her. She felt the release and the liquid and his face buried in her shoulder, his back rising and falling, sticky with sweat and salt water.

He rolled off, one hand across his chest, eyes closed. She could see the pulse flutter in his neck. For seconds, she watched it, waiting for her own to slow.

Lori matched her breathing with his. She touched the leather band on his wrist, because now she could. 'Thank you.'

JB kept his face turned away. 'What for?'

'You know what for. What you did that day. You saved me. You never gave me a chance to say it, so I'm saying it now.'

'You don't need to.'

'Yes, I do.'

He faced her. His eyes, in the moonlight, appeared softer to her now. At last, human.

'It was wrong,' he said. 'I shouldn't have been there.'

'But you were.'

'It was wrong.'

'Don't say that.'

'It's the truth.'

'Why did you pretend it never happened?' She put a finger on the hollow of his elbow, where the skin was so soft it was like silk. 'When Desideria brought me back. You killed a part of me that day.'

He averted his gaze, looking unblinking up at the sky. 'There are things you don't know, Lori. Things I can't tell you.'

'You can tell me anything.'

He laughed, but there was no mirth in it.

'You can,' she insisted. 'Nothing you say could change a thing.'

She saw his throat rise and fall. 'When you came to this island,' he said, 'I told you that ignorance was precious. I meant it.'

'I've spent my whole life in ignorance,' she countered. 'Don't love me like a woman then treat me like a girl.'

Sitting up, he ran a palm across the back of his neck. He brought his knees up and rested his arms across them, head dipped.

'I'm leaving my wife,' he said quietly. 'It's over between us. It has been for a long time. We never loved each other, not in the way it's meant to be.'

She waited. The guilt she'd felt previously over Rebecca was a useless instrument now. Lori knew she'd passed the point of no return and the last thing on her mind was an apology.

'The way I feel about you…' He struggled for the words. 'I'm not used to feeling…' He shook his bowed head. 'I'm not used to feeling at all.'

She reached out to touch him. 'It's OK.'

'I want it to be.' He gave her his profile. 'I swear it, Lori. I want it to be.'

The words she wanted to say, she held tight to. She wanted to save them. And when she finally let them go, she wanted to be sure he'd say them back.

They had sex again in his bed. And again, and again—Lori lost count of the number of times. JB explored her, taught her how to explore herself, with a touch that brought her to the brink of paradise and had her drowning in pools of ecstasy.

It was a shock when he told her that protection wasn't necessary—at least not for fear of pregnancy. Lori was shattered that he would never be a father. He'd accepted it a long time ago, he said, but for Lori, knowing the breadth and scope of his heart undiscovered, and how he was with Ralph, and how much love was missing from his world, it was an especially cruel misfortune. She realised what she felt for JB was real because she thought not once for herself or what his admission might mean, only for his loss and how brutal a lottery was life.

At three a.m., he showered. Lori slipped on her dress and padded to the room's shutters, opening them and letting in sea air. She admired the unbroken view of the lighthouse: a pale beam thrown back and forth, searching, searching, leaning out and resting her arms on the sill. Her wake-up call was in four hours but she wouldn't sleep. The moment she was alone she knew she'd play out every second of tonight and it would keep her from sleep for a hundred years.

On the other side of the window frame was a tiny carved-out nook. It was invisible to the eye and Lori only noticed it because she was running her hand across the wood and her fingers disappeared inside. Curious, she felt about and came into contact with a small key, which she extracted and looked at, puzzled. The shower continued to pound.

There was a desk by JB's bed. It was made of thick, worn wood and had two panels of drawers running down either side. On a whim, she crossed to it and knelt. She didn't know what she was looking for, or why—but something compelled her.

The key jammed against the first panel of locks. She began to think it wouldn't fit any of them before at last it slid into one of the holes and released a neat *click*.

Inside the drawer was a large black file. On the front in capital type it read: ABORTED.

Lori fingered its edges and met a sheaf of escaping paper, which she tugged at gently. She wasn't expecting it to come free and must have torn it from some fastening.

*LORIANA GARCIA TORRES (17)—ref. LA864 (cont'd)
...surviving father, Antony Garcia (40) m. Angélica Ruiz (43), 1996. Stepsisters: Rosa Garcia Ruiz (24); Anita Garcia Ruiz (22). Mother: Maria Valeria Torres (deceased age 31). Household income per annum c. $38,000: see p11 of this doc + employment detail. Boyfriend Enrique Arrio Marquez (20); connections to San Pedro El Peligro street gang—*

The shower stopped. She heard the panel slide across.

Confused, fumbling, Lori grabbed her purse from the floor and stuffed the paper inside, in the same movement returning the file, closing the drawer and locking it. She replaced the key seconds before JB emerged from the bathroom.

She saw his eyes absorb the scene, look over the desk as if he'd known where she'd been though that was impossible. 'What are you doing?'

Lori swallowed. She linked her hands behind her back. 'Nothing,' she lied. 'Only waiting for you.'

42

Present Day
Island of Cacatra, Indian Ocean
Two hours to departure

Reuben straightened the knot on his tie and checked his reflection. He was set. He was Reuben van der Meyde and this was *his* party. Nothing—*nothing*—was going to go wrong.

So why did he look so bloody peaky? Beneath his tan, his skin was yellowish and damp, waxy as cheese. He had the shits—he always got the shits when he got nervous. Five times he had visited the bathroom since Jax Jackson and his entourage finally departed: there surely couldn't be that much left to come out. His ass certainly felt like he'd shat out a truck.

I'm one of them. Tomorrow the truth comes out.

It was a practical joke, he kept telling himself. He ought to be less concerned over the message's content than the fact some clown had managed to hack his account. That was the real threat. Not what the message said.

Not what the message said.

Reuben was due on the yacht, scheduled to brief this evening's crew and make sure they understood they were playing with the big boys now. It wasn't his style to employ a new agency but it was for a charitable cause, disadvantaged kids needing a break, and wasn't his island all about rehabilitation? He had to at least be seen to be giving back to the community.

I'm one of them.

In the air-conditioned solitude of his office, Reuben logged on. There the message was, just as it had been yesterday, mocking him.

I'm one of them. Tomorrow the truth comes out.

JB hadn't understood the implications. This person was bluffing, he'd said. Reuben might have thought the exact same thing, were he in the Frenchman's position. But he wasn't. There was a lot JB didn't know about the scheme. He didn't know about the vast cheques Reuben pocketed each month. He didn't know about Reuben's failure to wire the money to the poverty-stricken surrogates to whom it was promised. He didn't know about the insurance Reuben had to take out against the paupers, threats to their livelihood and their families in case one saw fit to blab. He didn't know that to get to where van der Meyde was you couldn't always play Mr Nice and sometimes that meant playing Mr Downright Fucking Evil.

Reuben didn't lie awake sweating it out. Business was business.

But this was different.

This was a revelation he knew he had to take to his

grave. It ran deeper than the surrogate agency, deeper than the fortunes not exchanged and the broken guarantees. It was the only thing that, from time to time, made Reuben stop whatever he was doing, heart racing and breath caught, and think, just for a moment: *I've gone too far.*

Oh, there was a lot JB didn't know.

I'm one of them.

As if this could be any child. As if this could be one of the standard set who'd been placed and bought and sold and paid for. Christ! That would be bad enough.

But not this...

I'm one of them.

Reuben was the only man alive who knew what that could mean. Not JB, not Rebecca, not Margaret, not any of his scouts. This was a secret he had kept entirely to himself.

Only now it seemed that someone else knew it too.

Rebecca Stuttgart ran her hand over the gowns laid out on the bed linen, jade and cobalt and crimson, like a cast of exotic butterflies. She slipped one over her head and brushed her red hair loose around her shoulders.

JB was fastening his tie at the window. He was normally adroit; she could tell he was distracted.

'Do you want me to do that for you?'

He didn't say no and so she went to him, looping the ends over each other and tightening the knot. Up close he smelled of an aftershave he'd worn in the early days, one she hadn't known in a while. Patting the tie smooth, she fought down a swell of tears. If only things had been different for them. In another life, at another time, perhaps...

But that was like wishing black were white, and God only knew she'd done enough wishing over the years.

The way her husband's jaw was set betrayed his anxiety. It was Rebecca's own fault. It was the lie she'd told, the horrible lie. She'd been acting out of desperation, a last-ditch attempt to rouse her marriage from the ashes. Now she saw it had lain there too long for rescue.

'You're more beautiful today than you ever were,' JB said, with a tenderness she hadn't heard since the beginning. The compliment was unexpected. Over the past few months they had barely spoken to each other at all.

Rebecca ran a hand over the crisp shoulder of her husband's suit. She looked up at his face, into the blue eyes she knew would haunt her till the day she died.

I'm not beautiful. I've done a terrible thing.

But in him she saw the resignation that matched her own: an unspoken understanding that they had reached the end and that tomorrow it would be over. It would all be over.

'So are you,' she replied.

And before she could change her mind, Rebecca reached up and kissed JB's mouth. Only briefly, but enough to remember.

Enrique Marquez, known back home as Rico, slipped out on to the megayacht's main deck the instant his cell beeped.

'What the fuck you doin' callin' me?' he demanded, ducking behind an abandoned crate of table centrepieces. 'I thought we agreed no contact!'

Margaret Jensen sounded nervous. 'I wanted to make sure you'd arrived,' she hissed, barely audible as she endeavoured to keep her voice down.

'Course I've fucking arrived. Where the fuck else am I gonna be?'

'Is everything set?'

'Jeez, lady, you sound like you're dealin' with an amateur.'

'Just answer the question.'

'It's set.'

He heard her expel breath. 'Mr V's on his way.'

'You think I don't know that?' A uniformed man approached the crate and Enrique made off, talking loudly so it sounded legit. 'It's what I was waitin' on when you *called me*.'

'You'd better go.'

'No shit.' He hung up.

Returning the cell to his pocket, Enrique made his way through the galley and into the saloon. A group of identically dressed crew were milling anxiously, awaiting instruction and straightening their uniforms, determined to make a good impression.

Enrique had struck gold when the employment agency secured him the van der Meyde gig. It was his knowledge of boats that had swung it. That and the false ID he'd had an acquaintance supply him with. Prison had been good for at least something.

A sharply tailored white suit, gold braiding at the collar and cuffs, concealed the hardened, heavily tattooed body beneath. Two years behind bars for a crime he had never wanted to commit had changed Enrique beyond recognition. Finally, his appeal had been granted—he had been acting on behalf of his brother, the notorious Diego Marquez, whose ever-elusive whereabouts had been exchanged for his own release in a backhanded deal set up by the LAPD, whose drugs squad had been tailing Diego and his crew for nearly a decade.

Enrique didn't feel bad about it. Had Diego taken the rap when it all went to shit? Had Diego come to visit and say he was sorry and pay his fucking respects? No. Instead he'd set his only brother up, quitting town and sending word that a rival gang was planning a hit on their mom. Sure, he'd done it. Sure, he'd gone down for his trouble. What else was he going to do?

Only, now, gone were the gentle eyes, the ready laugh and the dimples of humour. In their place, hostility against the world that had wronged him since the day he was born. Anger—no, too weak: *rage*—at his betrayal by the woman who had promised she was his.

Loriana Garcia Torres. Once so innocent, a virgin. Not any more. These days her body was there for the taking, a hooker masquerading as something else but a hooker all the same. He'd seen her parading her boyfriends, splashed across magazines like she hadn't a care in the world. Didn't she give a crap? Didn't she think of him? Clearly not.

He'd heard what happened at Lori's salon—Diego had made one lame attempt to get him out, at least. He and his gang had paid Lori a visit and asked for the alibi that would set Enrique free. Had she given it? Course not. The woman who'd vowed she loved him had turned her back and walked away, without a second thought, leaving him to rot like an animal in a cage. And, more—*worse*, because he'd always suspected it to be the real reason she was holding out—her boyfriend had shown up, some sharp suit with a fist and an attitude.

Prison had been agony for a whole host of reasons, but those first few weeks were easily the lowest. Imagining

Lori—his girl, his *woman*—with another man, one she'd chosen so swiftly over him, was torture. No wonder she had always refused to put out, she'd been getting it elsewhere the whole time. She'd broken his heart, and instead of waiting for it to mend he had done away with it altogether. He didn't need a heart any more. All it caused was pain.

Reuben van der Meyde was descending the spiral staircase into the atrium. A hush fell over the crowd as he surveyed the assembly with jumpy eyes.

Enrique despised him on sight. Van der Meyde was exactly like the rich bastards he used to work for at the harbour at San Pedro: arrogant, limp-dicked creeps who expected the world to bow and kiss their feet. Van der Meyde was sweating, mopping his brow like a kid who got caught jerking off. Enrique felt no remorse. It would bring him pleasure to witness this man's demise. Along with all the other Hollywood sons of bitches without a clue how real people lived, suffering, struggling, every day a mountain. No damn clue. Well, they were about to get a lesson in that suffering. A very fucking serious one.

With their money and fame and vanity, those people could never understand what it felt like to be locked up. Enrique's cold stare was a badge of the horrors he had faced. Incarcerated with monsters, it had slowly turned him into one of them. Days and weeks and months of abuse and pain and loneliness had stripped him of pride and dignity and the faith that, beneath the layers of hurt, the world was fundamentally a good and forgiving place. Like hell it was. The world had showed him nothing but cruelty—and it was about time he paid some of it back.

Lori Garcia.

He twisted the silver band on his finger.

So much for promises.

She had forsaken him when he had needed her most.

Tonight, she would pay. They all would.

'No mistakes, no excuses,' van der Meyde was saying. For the Very Fucking Powerful Entrepreneur he was meant to be, the guy looked like he was cacking himself. 'Every drink you serve, every smile you give, will be observed...'

Enrique wanted to laugh. He'd be giving them more than a smile tonight.

Van der Meyde closed the brief. Enrique had scarcely listened to a word of it. He didn't need to. He had his own brief. And the big man's rules counted for nothing.

BOOK FOUR
2011-12

43
Lori

'At least meet him, would you?'

Lori came to a halt, bent and put her hands on her knees, catching her breath as Jacqueline Spark slowed up next to her.

'What's the point?' She drank from her bottle of water. 'I'm not interested.'

A jogger passed, the first they'd met, his dog leaping in the spray. It was early and Venice Beach was deserted, the lilacs of dawn still hazy in the sky.

'Maximo Diaz is a *nice guy*,' promised Jacqueline. 'He's not like Peter.'

'I thought Peter *was* a nice guy. Until he stole my panties.'

Jacqueline smiled and tamed a strand of blonde hair that had escaped her ponytail. She was determined to get Lori to say yes to the meet. A bounce back after Peter was exactly what her profile needed, and no one better fitted the bill than the new kid in town. Maximo Diaz was from royal stock, the cousin of a nephew of a prince or some such, and last year had played the love interest in two acclaimed movies (he was good to look at but he wasn't exactly versatile). Jacqueline understood they'd been burned by Selznick, but the fact was that if Lori wanted to stay pure as driven snow, someone had to make sure, at least romantically speaking, that other things were getting driven—namely, her PR machine.

'All I'm asking,' she said, 'is that you let me set you up. And I'm doing it as your friend, not your publicist.'

'Thanks, but no.' Lori resumed the run. Jacqueline moved to catch her up.

'Come on, what's the problem?' She came level and they slowed the pace. 'In honesty, it's a bit of both—the publicist/friend thing, I mean. I really think you'll like him, I really do. And, yeah, while it wouldn't exactly be *bad* for you to start dating one of the most handsome men I've *ever* laid eyes on—'

'He's still an actor, and it's still in the interests of his career.'

'You're right on both counts. But what I'm saying is you might find you want to see him again regardless of anything else.'

'I doubt it.'

Jacqueline appraised her sideways: the wild black hair pulled back in a ponytail, gaze fixed on the beach with a contained sort of determination. What was going on? If she didn't know better she'd say Lori had a boyfriend hidden away. She certainly had that glow—the first flush of a new affair?—and kept zoning out while they were talking, her eyes misting over, remembering some past encounter. If this were true, they were going to have to work harder than ever to protect her virginity—or the illusion of it. Her innocence went hand in hand with her appeal. If the press caught on that she was jumping into bed with an unsuitable man, most likely someone working down the local minimart (for judging by Lori's distaste for celebrities, it had to be), they'd have a nightmare on their hands. Deceptions like this one were magic tricks. They needed to be practised, managed and delivered with precision timing. They also needed to exist under a controlled environment, meaning her wild-card lover, whoever he was, had to take a step into the wings. And enter Maximo Diaz.

'Just say you'll meet him for coffee.' Jacqueline slowed to a walk, forcing Lori to do the same. 'Please? For me?'

Lori put her hands on her hips. She kicked gently at the sand.

'Fine,' she said, 'I'll meet him. But only so you'll quit hassling me.'

Jacqueline was pleased.

'And just once, OK? I meant it when I said I wasn't interested.'

Her publicist nodded. 'Understood. You won't regret it, Lori.'

At Jacqueline's beachside apartment, Lori showered and changed before taking a car downtown. She and Desideria were meeting with a global fragrance company. Lori's contract with Mac Valerie was coming to a close and several brands were queuing to sign her.

It was Tuesday, a little after eight a.m. Twenty-nine days, two hours and seventeen minutes since she had last been with JB Moreau.

In that time, her weeks on Cacatra Island had acquired a dreamlike quality, soft-edged in her memory like the melting contours of a surrealist painting. She thought of him incessantly, wanting him more than she knew she could. Their lovemaking didn't feel like something that had happened to her, too perfect, too passionate, too long-time her fantasy so that when it materialised she didn't altogether trust it was real.

Yet it was. Those hours in JB's bed had been the truest she had known. She remembered his honesty, his vulnerability: the things that had brought him within reach.

I'm leaving my wife...

And then she would recall the document she had found in his villa. Part of Lori wished she'd asked him then and there what it meant, what he was doing carrying information about her life—private, personal details—but she had stopped herself. She'd been prying, and to be caught in the act would have risked his trust, everything she had in that moment cherished. The most exquisite night of her life hadn't been one she was prepared to blemish.

But the mystery continued to bother her. Whichever way she turned it, it made no sense.

LA864. The number stayed in her mind and troubled her most. Lori played it over and over, like a pin she had been given to wear: her name, her identity.

Perhaps La Lumière kept details on their girls; it wouldn't be unheard of. But that sounded feeble, even to her. Why the secrecy? Why the hidden key? Why *her*?

Lori resolved to ask him direct. If their acquaintance had proved anything, it was that she could not be kept in the dark. Were they to make a go of things, they would need to be truthful with each other, right from the beginning.

In the meantime, she decided to put it from her mind. To conclude that what she had found was in any way sinister was to commit to a suggestion she could not begin to understand—and to believe it was to think badly of the man she adored.

She loved him and her love made her blind.

'You were phenomenal,' enthused Desideria when they emerged on to Olympic Boulevard. 'Want to celebrate? I know a gorgeous little place…'

Celebration was the last thing on Lori's mind. After her run she had started to feel ill, a gradual sickness that had over the past couple of hours reached debilitating heights. All through the meeting she'd been primed to make her excuses and dash to the bathroom. Funny, because after Cacatra exercise always made her feel better, as if she could run so far or so fast that she could end up back in his arms, running across oceans, if that's what it took. Now, out in the heat with the sunlight searing, nausea rushed at her like a tidal wave.

She stopped. Her mouth stung with saliva, like she was about to puke.

'Honey?' Desideria leaned in. She smelled of cigarettes and sour musk that turned Lori's stomach. 'Are you OK?'

'No.' She blinked back panic. 'I—I don't feel well. I need to go home.'

'Here.' Desideria steered Lori into a nearby café. 'You're going nowhere.' She was deposited at an outside table, where several diners turned to stare. 'I'm going to go get you some water, sweetheart. Don't move.'

Beneath Lori's feet, the ground had turned to mush. Pinpricks of stinging colour scattered behind her eyes. Perhaps she'd overdone it. She'd had a lot on her mind, wasn't sleeping more than a few hours a night and her schedule meant she'd taken to skipping the occasional meal.

When Desideria returned, Lori sipped with caution. What was wrong with her? With every drop she thought she was done for.

'You really don't look good,' observed Desideria, her face creased with worry. 'What's the matter? What can I do?'

'I'll be fine,' Lori managed. 'It's just a bug.' She was due her period. Actually, she was overdue. Maybe that was it, finally arrived. She didn't think she had ever before felt so wretched.

Desideria frowned, full of concern. 'Are you sure…?'

'Sorry.' Lori pushed her chair back. 'I have to leave.'

'You want me to come with you?'

'No.'

'But what if you—?'

'I'll call you. Sorry.' She fled the café, catching her bag on the back of someone's chair and apologising, wishing for today she were invisible.

London was going through a heatwave. On Charing Cross Road, tourists sweated in shorts and sun hats, drowning under maps of the Underground and swarming outside Leicester Square like bewildered children on a school trip, blinking into the light as moles emerged from the earth, waiting for direction. Most people were waiting for direction. They craved the certainty. He'd seen it enough times. He knew the susceptible ones.

JB Moreau passed through the crowds like a stream across the desert. He took a left on to Shaftesbury Avenue and up towards Soho, the destination clear in his mind. In possession of a memory so honed that he need only ever glance once at the facts, in his mind was a chart of the area, street by street, the address he was heading for a red pin to which he was edging ever closer. He moved quickly but without haste.

The woman he was meeting showed potential. A scout had sourced her some time ago, compiling the file that JB had spent the past month studying. Eighteen years old, a runaway from the south of the country, hitting the big city in hope of a brighter future when what she was really heading for was a struggle on a bigger scale. He'd explain all that. London, like any indifferent metropolis, exacerbated things. Without money, without prospects, it was a lost cause.

It shouldn't be difficult. From her photo he knew she was a perfect fit. Their clients, Arizona politicians, would be pleased. The prospect would be hardened, of course—but when he set forth the proposal he felt certain she would take the bait. It was win-win. The politicians got their child and the runaway got her happy ending. More money than she knew what to do with: a new start in life and one she deserved. JB knew she deserved it, even if she didn't.

As he made his way through Chinatown—dark meat hanging in windows and the deep aroma of spices, red and gold lanterns blowing in the warm breeze like paper gourds—he considered what might have happened if he had ever reached this stage with Lori Garcia. He'd have approached her in the exact same way, an examination of her profile and then in at the optimum moment, targeting her alone at her family's salon. Two days before he was meant to move, Lori had been paid a different visit and the rest was history.

JB had been there every day that week. He'd been with Lori for months, under the guise of awaiting opportunity when in fact it was because he could not tear himself away.

Things would change. Lori Garcia made it so he could turn back the clock, back to before things had moved beyond his grasp, and however illusive that might be it was enough to console what he'd decided was inconsolable. A part of him closed, a part he'd never thought he'd get back, glowed now as hesitant as an ember, smouldering from a core, willing to catch light.

He would leave Rebecca and then he would come clean: about his past, about the island, about it all. If Lori was truth, if she was loyalty, then he had to match her intentions. It was time.

The building, tucked into a sidestreet, was derelict. Most of the windows were boarded and a guy was crouched in the entrance, rolling a smoke with cracked, blistered fingers.

JB stepped past him. Inside, a couple of mattresses on which were slumped the dreaming or the dead. Concrete steps led up to a second level, and as he reached the top he saw her straight away, in the shadows, crouched with her knees under her chin. He recognised her from her photograph, but more than that he sensed her desperation, glinting like a beacon.

Green eyes, whose light had been extinguished. Lank, matted hair that had once been blonde. Sadness that he knew he could take away.

'Hello.' He went to her, held out his hand. 'You don't know me but I know you.'

* * *

The mansion was quiet, cooled by the air con.

Lori dumped her stuff, headed to the kitchen and fixed herself a soda, concentrating on each mouthful and the sole aim of holding it down. She felt odd, sick and ravenous at the same time. It was an alien sensation and she hoped she hadn't got food poisoning—she had a busy few weeks and couldn't afford to spend them with her head stuck down a toilet bowl. Every so often she experienced a twinge in her belly and decided to go see if her period had come.

On her way through the hall, a plain white envelope, slipped or pushed under the door, caught her attention. In her haste, she must have walked straight past it.

Confused, Lori bent to retrieve it.

There was nothing written on the front. Running her thumb along its seal, she peeled it open. Inside was a note pressed into precise quarters, which she unfolded and flattened.

Individual cut-out letters covered the sheet from left to right.

On E d AY A V Ir G In
N e XT d A Y A WH O RE

She examined the letters, some of them matte, black and white, from a newspaper; others were glossy, a variety of types. The letters were different-sized, arranged haphazardly across the page, some mashed up close and others set further apart.

Lori had received weird mail in the past. It went hand in hand with her celebrity. But this one bothered her. First, it had been hand-delivered. Second, most of what she saw was dirty, sexual, some more twisted than others, but rarely was it personal.

Disgusted, she ripped it to pieces and threw it in the trash. A fan who had got carried away; it wouldn't be the first time. She would talk to her security, have them look into it.

The buzzer on the gate went. Lori kept her nerves in check. Hollywood was rife with tales of stalkers, women afraid to step outside their house and more afraid to stay in it, ardent fans whose fantasies spilled into warped realities by the spotlight of their fixation.

To her relief, it was only her father. She and Tony had been seeing more of each other since his last visit, forging a new relationship that to her happiness was separate from Angélica and the girls. Thanks to Lori's regular contributions, *Tres Hermanas* was slowly getting back off the ground. She knew what it symbolised to him—her mother's legacy finally restored. If that was the only thing her modelling was good for, it was enough.

But relief was quickly replaced by unease when she saw Tony looked as bad as she felt.

'I've had some news.' He shook his head, taking her hands. 'I'm sorry, Loriana. Your grandmother passed away last night. Corazón's dead.'

44
Aurora

Aurora breathed in smoke, prickly warmth seeping up from her toes. She leaned back. Next to her was a guy with sleeve tattoos, a few years older, and he raised one of the sleeves now and slid it behind her shoulders. He was Casey Amos, the twenty-year-old son of Roland Amos, the renowned music producer who had soared to fame by spearheading a host of TV talent shows. The skin in Casey's armpit was pale and papery, with lots of soft chestnut hair, and she found herself staring at it for a long time, stoned.

This was the way it went, ever since Cacatra. Aurora was so far out of it she hardly knew where she lived. She was unable to face reality; the hours rolled into days rolled into weeks as she bottled her emotions in, suppressing her fears and suspicions and shattering them with a cocktail of narcotics. It was like her old life, all over again. Except now, as far as she was concerned, her parents no longer existed. The word itself meant nothing. *Mom. Dad.* Nothing.

'Casey, over here.' Farrah Michaels was dancing in a pair of frilly knickers. The party was at her parents' Malibu apartment. Dirk and Christina were in New York and had left their only daughter to her own devices. Currently their lounge was packed with OC royalty getting smashed and taking each other's clothes off.

Casey obliged, clearly disinterested. Farrah's perky tits bounced as she wound to the soundtrack of Rihanna. 'Want summa this?' she purred.

Bored, he turned to Aurora with a lascivious grin, said 'Hey' by way of a greeting then abruptly moved to kiss her. She let him. Out of the corner of her eye she saw Farrah stomp off.

Casey was a good kisser, but Aurora was too high to notice the details.

'Bitch!'

Sudden, freezing cold. Before she knew what was happening, Aurora was drenched. An empty bucket dangled from Farrah's arm, dregs of icy water dripping on to the parquet flooring.

'What the *hell*?' Aurora blinked once, twice, totally soaked through.

Farrah had the nerve to laugh. 'Whore!' she snarled, her mouth an ugly coil of jealousy. The rest of the room had gone quiet, numbly observing the spat.

Aurora stood. 'Fuck off,' she told Farrah, in an infuriatingly reasonable voice. 'It's not my fault Casey's got taste.'

Farrah was scowling so much her eyes were like slots in a pinball machine. 'Get yourself a towel,' she said menacingly. 'You're ruining the place. But I guess you're used to ruining things, huh, Aurora? Nothing much matters so long as *you're* all right.'

The room awaited her response. Someone turned the music off.

Aurora felt tired. She always felt tired these days, as if her bones had got old and she couldn't be bothered to do anything. Sometimes it was too much effort to even get out of bed so she just stayed there, all day, in a dark room, her thoughts taking her to a dark place. But Farrah's moany bitchface ignited her wrath. Her so-called friend had no idea what she was dealing with—or not dealing with, as the case may have been—and instead had the nerve to whine like a piglet about some jock she could frankly take or leave.

She slapped Farrah. It was sharp and satisfying and left a pleasing pink blotch. Then, with the weird dragging lethargy of a slo-mo action scene, Farrah went for her, grabbing Aurora's sodden hair and pulling her to the ground, where she began attacking her with her nails. Distantly Aurora realised she was in a fight. She hadn't been in one before, which in itself was surprising. Farrah's knee was pressed to Aurora's chest and her bare tits jiggled violently with the effort.

'Get off me!' Aurora managed, as Farrah dug in and scratched, sharp as a cat. She shoved her with force, sending her careening back into a glass coffee table, which duly smashed.

There was a horrible silence.

'What the hell is your problem?' Aurora was breathing hard, her body flushing hot and cold. She realised her friend was sitting practically naked in a pool of broken glass and reached out to take her arm. 'Get up, come on.'

Casey seized Aurora's hand. 'Let's split.'

Clearly no one else here was going to help Farrah. They

were all looking on, dazed: lobotomised onlookers at a tasteless pantomime. The life she was living.

Farrah was a pathetic figure in her underwear. 'Get up,' Aurora said again. 'I mean it.'

'Fuck you,' came the response.

Aurora wasn't fussed about leaving with Casey but the look on Farrah's selfish little face more than made up for that.

'Suit yourself,' she said, and grabbed her stuff and left.

Aurora woke with the mother of all headaches. She felt as if someone were skewering her brain through her ear-hole. Her room was trashed. Empty bottles and overflowing ashtrays littered the floor, clothes strewn all over the place. She had no idea if it was night or day.

Fuzzily, she rolled over. Casey Amos was fast asleep, his mouth parted, emitting a ragged but gentle snore. He'd kicked the sheets off and his cock was exposed, curled like a dormouse in a nest. His chest was covered in tattoos: naked, big-breasted women, mostly.

Aurora groaned. She felt sore in her stomach and between her legs. Her chest and mouth and eyes hurt from the stuff she'd put in her body but she couldn't remember what any of it was.

Shrugging on a T-shirt and knickers, she hauled herself off the bed, slowly because she felt faint, and got to her feet. The room swayed. As she tentatively fingered the blind, a jet of scorching sunlight shot in. She felt like a vampire and half expected it to set her skin on fire and she'd just stand here burning like some effigy until there was nothing left except a tiny pile of stinking ash. Who knew, maybe she'd get lucky.

Downstairs, the phone rang. Aurora was tempted to ignore it but the incessant tone was splitting her head in two.

'Hello?' she answered groggily.

'Aurora, what's the time?' It was Rita.

She had no idea what the time was. 'Ten?' she hazarded, rubbing her eyes.

'It's past midday.'

'Um…' Vaguely she recalled having to be somewhere.

'I've been calling your cell all morning. Where are you?'

'At home.'

'And you've only just picked up? I thought something had happened!'

'My battery must've died,' she offered weakly.

'Not only have you pissed me off, Aurora, but you've pissed off the guys at Strike.'

The record label. They were meant to have met to discuss her next album. Crap.

'Sorry,' she muttered. 'I'm really sorry.'

'You gotta get it together, kid. This is bad.'

'I know.'

'No, I don't think you do. There's only so much damage limitation I'm prepared to carry out. You know you'll get another meet because of your father, but this reflects badly on you and on me. I'm putting my ass on the line with this and it seems like you don't care.'

'I overslept.'

'Like every other day? What about that *Princess Perfect* shoot you were meant to make last week? Or that interview I set up with *USay*? It's embarrassing.'

'Sorry.'

'Stop saying sorry and clean up. I thought you wanted to

avoid all this. Drugs, partying, guys only after one thing. You're going down a dangerous road right now and I can't follow.' Rita exhaled, exasperated. 'Ever since we came back from Cacatra you've been a damn liability. I thought that place was meant to sort people out!'

The name of the island throttled her.

It's not happening. It's not real. Don't think about it and it's not real.

But still she caught it in flashes. She remembered how she'd rushed back to the villa that night, demanded of Rita that they leave first thing. She ought to be kissing Rita's feet for not giving her the Spanish Inquisition, not throwing her efforts back in her face.

'Never mind,' said Rita briskly. 'It's done. We've rescheduled, so just make sure you show up next time. Don't let me down again.'

'I won't.'

'You won't let me down or you won't show up?'

'I won't let you down.'

As she hung up, Casey's arms circled Aurora's waist. His odour was of smoke and cooking meat and his hard-on was jutting into her back. She leaned forward on the dresser and parted her legs. What was the point in resisting? What was the point in any of it?

Sherilyn Rose peeled open the luxury box of chocolates and ran her bitten, baby-pink fingernails across their dark, smooth shells. Belgian, her favourite.

The housemaid brought a box up every couple of days. She couldn't go without. They were her only pleasure, her darling treasures. Caramel, raspberry, cappuccino… She'd pop the chosen one into her mouth and let it melt on her tongue till it burst with silky flavour and awarded her the brief moment of ecstasy that made everything all right. Just for now, everything all right.

In the gloom of Sherilyn's bedroom, she could scarcely make out which she had chosen. That was part of it, and about as much of a risk as she was prepared to take these days. The blinds were drawn against the LA sun, the TV rampant with garish commercials and game shows.

She had been ensconced here for months. It had started with the panic attacks that prevented her leaving the house, then the mansion itself became too much, too unknowable, to bear, each corner a reminder of the sham she was living with her husband and daughter.

As if! But what else was she going to call them?

Her bedroom was the only safe place. Secure. Enclosed. She and Tom had always possessed individual rooms, blaming her restlessness and Tom's supposed snoring. To the public they'd laughed about that. Ha ha ha, she couldn't get a wink once he got started! Except in truth they were laughing at the world's biggest goddamn joke of a marriage that ever there was.

Sherilyn flicked the remote and settled on the shopping channel. She watched as a woman sold her a swan-shaped pendant. She could buy it. Hell, she could buy a thousand of the damn things, ten thousand: a million! She could be sitting right now in a swimming pool neck-deep with swan-shaped fucking pendants and it still wouldn't make things right.

She ramped up the decibels when she heard Aurora mount the stairs with her boyfriend. Half the night she'd lain awake listening to the soundtrack of their shrieks and

yells. She wasn't about to risk a reprisal now. A nympho-
maniac *devil*: that was the beast they had raised.

The volume got so loud it hurt.

Sherilyn clamped her hands over her ears and the chocolates scattered from the bed, a spherical one rolling across
the floor, arcing at the last minute and rounding on her.

It was turning on her. Everything was turning on her.

She didn't know how much longer she could pretend.

Two thousand miles away, on a sprawling stage somewhere
in Tennessee, Tom Nash replaced the microphone, took a
bow and heard the roar go up. The grand finale of his sell-
out tour was an uncontested triumph. He'd sounded better
than ever. He'd set the crowd wild with his gyrating dance
moves and lilting croon. He'd delivered the most sensational run of gigs of his career. Tom Nash was riding high
on the big time. Oh yeah, the magic was still there.

'TOM! TOM! TOM!' Women chanted his name over and
over, weeping into their sleeves at the certainty he would
never be theirs. A few panties got thrown on to the stage,
several red roses and the usual knots of paper containing
phone numbers and email addresses. Camera phones glittered throughout the auditorium, feet stamped and a new
incantation began:

'More! More! More!'

Beneath his leather slacks, Tom was trembling. But this
time, it wasn't with fear, or self-doubt, or a slinking conscience. This time it was with euphoria, plain and simple.
Pumped with adrenalin, he let their adulation wash over
him and cleanse the anxiety of the past few months.

Who needed Sherilyn Rose? If anything, Tom was more
bankable without her. He had worried he could no longer

do it by himself. Now, he'd proved he could. The thought of Sherilyn decaying in her agoraphobic state depressed him, but not tonight. Tonight he was a free agent, the one and only Tom Nash.

He needed this. Just to be him, without a wife, without a daughter, without a goddamn family. Aurora was in a bad place, he'd heard it from Rita Clay: she was going off the rails and he had to intervene, because when had her mother been any help? But he couldn't, he hadn't been able to deal with it. He'd wanted some time…away. Just some time. Worry for Aurora had characterised the last three years and had almost butchered his career. Now, Tom had to be the pop star they all relied on, the man who made the money and kept things on an even keel. Shit, he knew Aurora had called, she'd called countless times, and to his shame he hadn't picked up. But that was for the greater good, right? Where were any of them without the Tom Nash reputation? In the gutter, that was where. He'd sort her out when he got home.

'TOM! TOM! TOM!'

The crowd got what they wanted. As the encore began, his number one smash 'Lady Knows the Way', the house-wives' screams reached fever pitch.

Tom strutted across the stage, grinding to his audience, living every word and every beat.

He was king of this world. Nothing was going to jeopardise that.

45
Stevie

Marty King called to say the role was hers. It was a British film, a novel adaptation by an acclaimed writer. She would be shooting on location in London.

'You sound relieved,' he said.

'I am. LA's driving me crazy.'

But it wasn't LA that was driving her crazy as much as her husband. Things with Xander had deteriorated since she'd returned from Cacatra. He had barely spoken two words to her, not even to enquire after Bibi and their trip, and delivered only vapid chitchat whenever they did speak. He'd been in Vancouver on and off for the past month and Stevie was forced to admit that time apart might be for the best.

The suspicion he was having an affair crept up quietly, insidious, until she woke one morning and was faced with the realisation that this was how it felt to be on the other side. It was the fact she was going to bed alone most nights,

Xander stumbling in hours later amid a cloud of alcohol with no justification for where he'd been. It was the freezing out, the rejection, the finding excuses why they couldn't spend time together. It was his refusal to meet her eye.

She didn't know what to do. She'd tried again and again to get to the heart of it, pleading with him to open up, because whatever he told her she'd try to forgive. Yet every exchange went the same way, ending in one of them stalking out, unable to continue the dialogue, same as the ugly fight they'd had before she'd left for Cacatra. She was running out of ideas, and of patience.

Hollywood looped vulture-like over the apparent separation, not helped when Stevie was obliged, when Xander was in Canada, to attend parties by herself. Gossip columns flaunted news of SHOTGUN WEDDING HITS THE ROCKS and SINGLE STEVIE...ALONE AGAIN! She tried to ignore it but it was difficult. 'We'll get you together for a long weekend,' encouraged Wanda Gerund. 'Tip off the press and you'll be front-page next morning.'

Tonight was the annual Actors League Awards. A month had passed since the notorious Vegas *Eastern Sky* premiere during which Lana Falcon, an actress whom Stevie had met once or twice and liked, had been attacked by a crazed fan. The industry was feeling vulnerable and tonight would be missing a few key faces.

Stevie hadn't wanted to fly out to New York but was nominated for a Supporting Role and her publicity was looking weak enough as it was. She didn't win and would have preferred to return to the hotel, but instead got lynched by Christina Michaels, Dirk's wife, who, with trademark insensitivity, ploughed into a Dom Pérignon-fuelled rant about failing marriages.

'Husbands get bored,' she counselled, shooting Dirk a sidelong glance as he celebrated his triumph as Best Producer. 'That's when the girls move in, pretty blondes with juicy tits and asses you could eat sushi off.' Xander didn't like sushi but it was a waste of breath to say so.

'Xander's not like that.' It was a mechanical response. She didn't know any more.

Christina raised an eyebrow, as much as her Botox would allow. 'They're *all* like that. Take it from someone who knows.'

It was debatable which was worse: hanging out with Christina or with Dirk. The man of the moment made a beeline for Stevie as soon as his admirers dispersed. He was drunk.

'Life's tough without the guy,' he confided, swaying gently. 'Linus and me, we were tight.' A trio of photographers jumped in and Dirk and Stevie posed together, smiles fixing then vanishing the minute they'd gone.

'It was sudden,' she agreed.

'No kidding.' Dirk regarded her shadily. 'You liked Reuben's place?' he asked.

It made sense Dirk and Reuben would be cronies. Linus, too. They were the same type: chauvinist, unreconstructed, thought money could buy everything. Maybe it could.

'Very much. Cacatra's a beautiful place.'

'Seems it's done Bibi a world of good,' Dirk went on. 'Heard she got an audition with Sammy Lucas.'

'It's about time she had a break.'

Evidently it struck him as an odd thing to say. 'Getting with Linus was her break.'

'That depends.' Stevie wanted to add: *If you mean it nearly broke her then I guess so.*

He came closer. 'Wanna know something?'

She raised an eyebrow.

'There's some of us thinkin' Linus's death might not have been an accident.'

Stevie kept her face perfectly still. 'Oh?'

'Ms Reiner should watch herself. Because rest assured we all are.'

'Don't try intimidating me, Dirk. It won't work.'

He spat the words. 'It's always attitude with you women, isn't it? Attitude that gets you into trouble. If you know what's good for that bitch you'll bring her straight to me.'

She wanted to hit him, turned before she could and he grabbed her arm.

'Tell her that Linus's pals aren't as boneheaded as the cops,' he hissed. 'And you can bet your bottom dollar we're not gonna rest till we get to the truth.'

The following morning she was back from LA, sore-headed from a sleepless night. Dirk's threat bothered her more than she cared to admit. He was powerful enough in this world, but if 'Linus's pals' included Reuben van der Meyde then they were up against a colossus. But, she reasoned, what could any of them know about Bibi? What could they prove? Absolutely nothing.

She hadn't expected Xander to be home till the weekend and was surprised to find him waiting for her back at the villa.

'What's this about?' she asked, bemused as he deposited an enormous bouquet of flowers in her arms, followed by a swift kiss to the lips, the first in weeks.

'I came back early,' he said. His hair had grown to just below his ears. It suited him.

Stevie put the stems in water, taking her time, watching as Xander made his way out to the terrace pool and stood with his back to her, hands on his waist. He looked like an orator about to address an assembly.

She followed him out.

'Xander…?'

He turned. Written all over his face was confession.

'We need to talk,' he said. Those four words among the very worst there were. She could see it in his eyes and hear it in his voice. Guilt.

'I need to be upfront with you,' he said. 'I thought a lot about this while I was away and I've realised I have to tell the truth. It's only fair. I want to be fair to you, Steve.'

Don't be a cliché. Please don't be a fucking cliché.

Who was it? Some debut actress he'd fallen for, in the same way he'd fallen for her? Some older woman, someone she knew?

Lowering herself into a chair, she held her hands in her lap. Xander crouched next to her.

'You asked me once if I knew JB Moreau,' he said quietly. 'Well, I do.'

She blinked. It took her a second to adjust, the notion of his affair still fresh in her mind.

'This is about him?'

Xander released a lungful of air. 'I don't know where to begin, honest to Christ. It's complicated, Steve, there's so much to—'

'Begin with why you didn't want me to go to Cacatra.'

He ran a hand across his unshaven jaw, trying to find a way into the labyrinth. 'OK.' He cleared his throat. 'Paul and Emilie Moreau, JB's parents... I was there when they died.'

'What?'

'I was there.'

'But what's that got to—?'

'Listen to me. *Please.*'

She struggled to remember, a story finally surfacing. 'The boating accident,' she said.

'That's right.' Xander watched her carefully. 'What I'm trying to tell you, Steve, is that it *was no accident.*'

'We attended the same school, JB and I. The international academy in Switzerland. I hated it.'

The too-tall Jewish kid who nobody liked. He'd told her before, laughed with her, even—ostracised in his school days for having bookish, boring parents and a bookish, boring life and always doing his bookish, boring homework.

'This French kid turned up in the middle of semester. He was different from everyone else, kind of detached. He seemed older than thirteen, like the world had shown him all there was to see, and he was weary of it. He didn't care for rules or authority; he did things his own way. All the boys wanted to be him, me included. All the girls wanted to date him. But he never looked at anybody, just kept himself to himself.' Xander narrowed his eyes, drawing the memories into focus. 'You can imagine my surprise when he singled me out, decided maybe I was worth making the effort for. And when JB made an effort, you knew about it. He could make you feel like the most important person that ever lived.'

'You became friends?'

Xander nodded. 'He only had one other friend, he said. Nicole, her name was, this girl from his village back in France. He was fond of her, the way he talked about her. She was the only thing that made him happy, over there at least, because his parents didn't give a thought to him, they never had. Weekends and half terms came about and all the other students were picked up, full of excitement about the holidays. They'd forget to send someone to collect him, because they never came themselves, and he'd stand outside the academy, this lost, lonely kid with his cases, just waiting, and nobody came.'

'What was it about you?' she prompted. 'Why did he pick you?'

'I think he saw himself in me. A part, however small. I was smart, I was quiet…and I was alone, too, in my way.' A ghost of a smile. 'Every decision JB makes is a definite one. He doesn't bow out of it. If he decides it's you, it's you.'

Xander became animated. 'And I found him inspiring and exciting and all the things I wanted to be. He knew stuff I couldn't work out *how* he knew, about history and politics and people… How people work, you know? How they feel, which is harder to learn than equations and biology and conjugated verbs, complexities that come with the wisdom of age. He knew what people wanted, what they feared and loved and valued—and how far they would go to get it.' Darkness crossed his face. 'Our friendship became intense. Quickly.'

There was the shade of a question on Stevie's tongue but she didn't know how to ask it.

'End of the first year, I found out he'd started dating Nicole. He didn't tell anyone except me. But JB changed.

He became brighter. He started to pull away from me, letting the other boys in, and I didn't like it. Of course everyone was impressed he had a girlfriend and whenever he spoke about Nicole he got this look and this manner that the rest of us were too young to identify. He was happy, for the first time. He lost his heart to Nicole. As far as I know, it hasn't happened since. He's never lost his heart, not in that way, to anyone else.'

Xander stood. He put his hands in his pockets, facing the pool and the sun so that all Stevie could see was a black outline.

'His family were rich, it goes without saying. It seemed like every summer his parents would experience a pang of conscience and realise they hadn't seen their only son in a year, and so they'd take him on a brief vacation in St Tropez, or to a castle in the French countryside, or on one of their fleet of boats. I couldn't believe when he invited me out one time. It felt like the golden ticket. I'd been scared he was extracting himself from the bond we'd shared, like I might get replaced, but JB was loyal. Is loyal. He doesn't do stuff like that.'

Xander turned to face her. One of his fists was caught in the palm of the other.

'We took the boat out early one morning,' he said. 'There was bad weather forecast, but JB's father didn't listen. By the time the storm hit, we were helpless. Paul and Emilie were torn from each other, the wind howling and the waves pounding, and I hadn't a clue what to do though they were shouting instructions I couldn't understand. JB was an able sailor, he'd spent his early years thrust out of sight on every activity going, but even so it was a lost cause.

'Paul went over first, then Emilie.' Stevie saw her

husband's knuckles tense, geared for impact, the bone cauliflower-white as it pressed against his skin. 'It was suicide, JB and I both knew it, but Emilie was the stronger swimmer and she believed she could save him. Next thing their arms were in the air, reaching and stretching, and their mouths were filling up with water.

'They drowned. Lives, memories, everything, snuffed out like a candle flame.'

'You were so young,' Stevie murmured. 'Poor JB…'

Xander looked at her directly. 'That's where you're wrong,' he said. 'It's not "poor JB", it never has been.'

'I don't understand.'

'He was watching it happen, Stevie. While I was trying to save them, he was *standing there and watching it happen*. His parents begged. *Help us, please, help us.* And I was shouting at JB to do something, because he was the one who knew boats and time was running out, the water was getting higher and the rain thrashing so it made me blind, thinking I saw them then losing them, till I didn't know what I was seeing any more. I grabbed what I could—a rope, jackets, the lifebuoy I knew they kept on the underside of the cabin—but nothing made any difference. He didn't help me, Steve. And I couldn't see fear in him, though I looked for it. He just stood there. He let it happen.'

'That can't be right,' she said. 'He was only a boy!'

'That's what they thought,' agreed Xander. 'And it's what he relied on. *It's the shock*, they all said. *Poor child.* He didn't speak for days. He went to stay with his aunt and uncle in Paris and I went, too, for a while, but by then he frightened me. And it wasn't till we returned to school in the fall that he told me what happened.

'He vowed that his father was a cheat and a liar, and

that he was glad he was dead. Because he'd walked into Paul's office a week before the boating trip and found a fourteen-year-old Nicole on her knees. He told me Paul had been forcing the girl's head into his lap, the girl JB loved, the only person he'd ever loved and who had loved him back, the only thing that belonged to him alone and not to his parents. And if Paul was forcing Nicole then, how many other times had he forced her? JB believed he should have done something sooner, to help her, prevented it from happening in the first place. She stopped coming by. She stopped holding his hand. She stopped everything, after that. So it was for Nicole that he'd let them drown. Well, his father was for Nicole. I believe his mother was for him.'

Stevie recalled the furore over the couple's deaths. 'You're saying he let them die?'

'You do believe me,' Xander insisted, 'don't you?'

'Of course,' she said, and she did, even if something wasn't right. The story didn't seem entire. There were so many questions. 'Why didn't you tell someone?' she asked. 'Why didn't you admit what happened?'

'How could I?' protested Xander. 'Anything I said would have been dubious at best, malicious at worst. JB had lost *both his parents*. What kind of person would accuse him of that?'

Stevie examined him. 'You should have told me,' she said. 'I don't know why you didn't.'

'I wanted to.'

'So that's why you didn't want me to go to Cacatra?'

Xander held her gaze for a fraction too long.

And then he lied. The coward JB Moreau always told him he was.

'Yes,' he said. 'That's why.'

46
Lori

Lori and her father flew to Spain for the funeral. Despite her repeated offers to pay their fare, for Tony's benefit more than theirs, Angélica and her daughters elected not to come.

The black-clad procession winding through Murcia was filled with mourners for Corazón. Lori was amazed at the number of lives her grandmother had touched. She would always treasure the precious few months they had shared. If Corazón had done half as much for these people as she'd done for Lori, their affection ran deeper than she knew.

The following day she and Tony had the difficult task of sorting through Corazón's belongings. Trinkets, diaries and photographs; string-bound bundles of brittle letters laced with faded ink; drawers packed with clouded silver. Lori remembered how frustrated she'd been last time she had visited, how desperate in the aftermath of Rico's arrest. How caught up she'd been in her lust for another man…

Corazón had given her a way out and in doing so had given her everything.

Now, more than ever, she needed her grandmother's counsel.

She needed her mother. She needed a woman she could trust. Turmoil couldn't come close to describing the state she was in.

Pepe the dog lay on the stone floor with his chin on his paws, his eyes sad, every so often pricking his ears and sniffing the air, either mistaken in believing the old woman was with them or the only one, perhaps, who could sense she still was.

'What'll happen to him?'

Tony was at the table, sorting through papers. 'Mama organised him to go to a friend.' The afternoon light was fading, a burned, Spanish light, and bathed him in its glow. Lori saw what he might have looked like as a boy, as Corazón would have seen him in her kitchen.

'I should have been with her,' he said. 'After Maria died, I didn't come back as often as I should, and now—' he shook his head '—it's too late.'

Lori rested her hands on his shoulders. They felt thin and small. 'There is too much death in the world,' Tony said sadly, 'isn't there?'

Taking her silence for assent, he reached round and took his daughter's hand.

'Death makes way for life,' she replied, feeling his fingers entwined with hers. 'You can't have one without the other.' Releasing him, she eased into the chair opposite.

'I have something to tell you, Papa,' she said, allowing

him a moment before she broke her news. She steeled herself, strong as she could be.

'I'm going to have a baby.'

JB returned to Los Angeles in the same week that Lori
departed for Spain.

He found out about her grandmother's death. Since the
moment of his intervention he had stood by his vow to
keep watch over her. The scouts he employed to source
for Cacatra were, from time to time, engaged in other pur-
poses. Moreau had his own methods. They knew enough
not to ask questions.

By the same manner he discovered her pregnancy. Or,
rather, the suspicion of it. Lori had been forced to cancel
several bookings through La Lumière and had been sighted
incognito in a downtown pharmacy. It wasn't long before
word reached him that she was being moved into an arrangement with aspiring actor Maximo Diaz.

Wednesday lunch, JB met with a global clothing chain
interested in acquiring a customised Moreau range. He ordered well, and ate and drank with apparent enjoyment. To
look at him it would be impossible to know that anything
in him was altered.

It was. As plans were laid before him, proposals set forward and pitches anxiously articulated, he listened with the
same removed expression, the same still blue eyes that had
become his trademark. Personnel elected for the meeting
had been briefed that this was a practice designed to draw
associates into saying more than they wished to: silence
was a powerful negotiator. In reality it was nothing of the
sort. It was the guard going up, the hatches slowly batten-
ing, the armour reassembled. A door ajar pulled shut.

'Let us talk you through stock changes,' chattered a nervous buyer, fumbling to retrieve her paperwork. 'We'd anticipate an autumn-to-winter range,' she babbled. 'Chunky-knit coats, leather accessories, the works—let's call it country chic with the Moreau signature twist.'

He supposed she had been with Maximo just after they had been together on Cacatra. Her dates would suggest as much. But then Lori's declaration that he had been her first was no guarantee, for when had a word counted for anything? It was actions that mattered. If anyone should know that, it was him. And if she had been able to lie about her feelings then she would have lied about that.

But, then, what feelings had she admitted to? None. Lori had given an impression, certainly, but she'd never confirmed it. The rest had been his invention.

JB wasn't a man who indulged in imagination. He dealt in facts. And he hadn't realised till now that he'd started imagining again. He'd started dreaming.

The buyer was arranging a stack of documents on the table. It was awkward, she should have waited till coffee had been served, but enthusiasm or pressure was getting the better of her.

'As you can see—' she indicated the charts '—our yield at this time of year is streaks ahead of our competitors...'

If there was one thing JB Moreau could not abide, it was being made the fool. He himself had not been with another woman, not even his wife, since the night with Arabella Kline in Vegas. Wrongly he had expected the same of Lori—he'd *assumed* the same. He'd taken for granted that she would wait for him, when in truth during those first few months of their reacquaintance he'd given her no reason to do any such thing. Who knew how long she'd been with other men? He'd understood the agreement with Peter Selznick, much as he'd hated it, to be platonic, but, then, who knew how far they had gone behind closed doors? Had she been with Peter in the way she had with him? And now, with Maximo? Pregnant with another man's child when she *knew* the painful truth? When he'd confided the sad, sad reality that he was unable to ever become a father himself?

And at the centre of it all, the fact that he had made an error of judgement. JB was not accustomed to being wrong. He knew people, he was able to work for Cacatra by knowing people, and the discovery that he had misread Lori Garcia so dramatically did not sit easy on his mind. He'd been blinded by emotions, reeled in by imagining her to be reminiscent of somebody else when she wasn't. She was an entirely different person.

Emotions, as he'd always known, were the dominion of the weak.

'So—' the buyer was flushed in the face, exhilarated following her presentation '—do you have any questions for us?'

For the first time since the meeting began, JB smiled. He suppressed a sensation that for any other would have been heartache, but for him was a silent thunderstorm, breaking over distant hills.

When Lori landed in California ten days later, she had a deluge of voicemails waiting. Three were from Maximo Diaz. On seeing the blinking lights, she'd hoped JB might have got in touch. She knew he'd been in Europe on business but would now be back in town. It was imperative she spoke to him.

To her disappointment, it was a different voice that emanated from the machine.

'I haven't stopped thinking about you,' the first message said. *'I must see you again.'* The second was a direct invitation: *'I'm having dinner with friends on Saturday. Join me?'* The third, Maximo seemed to remember the reason for her absence: *'Anything you need, I'm here.'*

She and Maximo had met just once, as promised to Jacqueline, days before she left for Spain. Maximo had been courteous, friendly, and as incredible in the flesh as One Touch had promised. But Lori had felt nothing. How could she, when every waking moment was consumed with memories of JB Moreau?

And how could she, when she was carrying his child?

Oh, she had battled it. Pretended it wasn't happening. Buried it and unearthed it and dusted it off and tried to find a way of handling it that made any kind of sense.

Even now she could scarcely believe it was true.

Tony had taken the news badly. He had imagined his daughter to still be the good Catholic girl he and Maria had raised. The irony was, for a long while, she had been.

'How could you do this?' He had charged across his mother's kitchen, reeling from the blow. *'What were you thinking?'*

Lori had fought to restrain her own temper. Her concern was for JB and their unborn child. She had neither time nor inclination for trial in her father's court.

'I found what I was waiting for.'

'Which was?' He had been unable to comprehend why she would even consider keeping the child, jettisoning her career in the same sweep as shaming herself.

'Love.'

'You know nothing about love—and even less about this man. And yet you're prepared to throw your life away for him?'

'I don't see it as throwing my life away.'

'He's married*, Loriana.'* Tony could barely spit the words out, he was so furious. *'He has a* wife. *Are you mad? How could you be so thoughtless?'*

But, in spite of how Lori feared the discovery of her pregnancy, she had never before been thinking more clearly. Her time on Cacatra had been the most lucid of her life.

Now she was back in America, it was clear what she had to do. If Tony didn't want to help her then she was not going to beg. It hurt, but what choice did she have? She was a woman now, not a girl. JB had shown her that. Once she spoke with him, everything would be OK. They were meant for each other and this child was proof. She wanted to tell him that Rebecca Stuttgart had been wrong. That he could and would be a father. That their union had resulted in the miracle she had no doubt he longed for. That she loved him.

How would he take it? What would he say? He'd be shocked at first, but then what? He'd be overjoyed, she was sure, but he'd tread carefully, too—the timing was far from ideal and there were people, commitments, to consider. Lori moved between states of ecstasy and unease, knowing her news would change both their lives beyond recognition.

Lori managed to put it off for most of the day, returning Maximo's calls and politely declining the invite to dinner. She swam and fixed lunch. She spoke to Desideria about the fragrance brand she'd been signed for. She welcomed her assistant, a fresh-faced, efficient girl named Anne, who talked through her schedule for the week and brought her mail.

'Most I've sorted,' she said, 'but it's really piled up since you've been away.'

By evening, Lori had exhausted all avenues of diversion.

She dialled JB's number and it rang and rang. She considered trying the agency but knew the chances of him being there were minimal. Perhaps she would leave a message.

Hello, it's Lori. I'm pregnant with your child. Call me.

She'd try again in the morning.

Sleep evaded her that night. Lori's mind fevered with thoughts of Corazón and her father, the island of Cacatra, the feel of JB moving inside her and the feel of a life growing, now, where he had been. The mystery number— LA864—that insisted on surfacing though she tried to keep it down. She dreamed of the Indian Ocean littered with torn pages and woke needing water.

At one a.m., she padded downstairs in the gloom. The stack of mail Anne had left caught her eye and automatically she sifted through it.

Immediately, she spotted them.

Three sealed, plain white envelopes, identical to the one she had received weeks ago.

Quickly, before she changed her mind, she tore them open, one after the other. Presumably an order had been intended, but her absence meant they had lost their sequence.

dEs er V et O be PU ni s H e d

P r E Tt y Gi R L s w H o bRea K Pr Om I Se S

R e M em be r Th a t

Rigid with fear, Lori read the notes a second time, then a third.

All possessed the same quality that had concerned her about the first. They were somehow knowing, somehow familiar. Messages meant only for her.

Temptation was to send them the same way, but sense told her to keep the evidence. Whoever this person was had crossed a line. They had been to the house...more than once. They knew where she lived. They might be on her right now.

Lori shivered. She crept back upstairs but it was hours until she got any sleep.

47
Aurora

'Fuck Strike Records,' announced Casey Amos, drawing on a fat joint before offering it to Aurora. 'I'll talk to my dad and he'll talk to his people, piece-o'-cake.'

They were in the basement home-movie-theatre at Roland Amos's Venice Beach pad. Casey was sprawled across a leather couch, his hand buried deep in a bucket of gummy bears. Aurora had only known him a month but had learned already he was as addicted to them as he was to his bags of white powder and pills.

Nepotism, one of the words Pascale had taught her, sprang to mind. Above, she felt the weight of Roland Amos's success bearing down on them: framed platinum discs adorning the walls, all those photographs of the famous mogul grinning alongside hallowed names of the music industry, going way back to the big guns of the seventies and eighties.

'Forget it,' said Aurora. 'Rita's on the case.'

Casey raised an unconvinced eyebrow and she didn't blame him. Strike Records was pissed off. She had aborted on three meetings now and clearly they deemed her too much of a liability. OK, so the first time was her fault, she accepted that, but the second occasion she swore Rita hadn't even told her about (even though Rita claimed she'd been drunk and hadn't remembered). The third she turned up at the wrong address and spent an hour in traffic across town. Everyone had left by the time she got there and all she had to show for it were several fuming messages from Rita on her iPhone. *'You're falling apart,'* her agent had blasted. *'What's going on, Aurora? What's the matter?'* As if she could tell Rita. As if she could tell anyone.

Nepotism. What was the difference between pulling favours from Strike because of Tom Nash's kudos, and Casey's promise that his dad would help her out? Absolutely nothing.

'Good luck with that,' said Casey, groping in the bucket of gums.

Aurora toked heavily on the joint and sat back. Justin Bieber's new music video filled the screen and Casey snorted in a derogatory way and ate more bears.

'Who gives a shit anyway?' she muttered. 'I can't sing.'

'Since when's that got anything to do with it?'

'It's kind of the point, isn't it? I can't dance, I can't perform. I haven't got a musical bone in my body.' Bieber's hair was mesmerising.

'Crap,' said Casey. 'It's in the genes.'

She gulped. *Genes.*

'Success, the right connections,' she conceded. 'Not talent.'

'Who gives a rat's ass about talent?' Casey gestured

to the screen. The sound of him chewing on the gummy bears was all of a sudden intolerable. 'My pop looks out for me. Sure, he'll bring me in on the big time. I'm hardly the schmuck who's gonna complain.'

'What if you wanted to do something else?'

'Like what?'

'Something different.'

Casey shrugged. 'What'd be the point?' He retrieved the roll-up and sucked on its end, lying back to eject a thin stream of smoke.

They sat in silence for a bit. The Bieber video ended. Aurora asked, 'How do you separate who you really are from the person you're supposed to be?'

Casey screwed up his face. 'Huh?'

'Imagine you were born on the other side of the world, to different parents, in a whole other life... What then?'

'Fuck all.'

'How can you be sure?'

He reached for her. 'Wanna gimme a blow job?'

'Get screwed.'

He was unoffended. 'Quit complaining. Enjoy what you got. Millions would.'

Aurora had an unexpected longing for St Agnes. Much as she'd whinged about it, right now she wanted nothing more than to sit up in her dorm talking to Pascale after lights-out. She wanted to ask Pascale everything she knew about JB and Cacatra and Reuben van der Meyde, but at the same time was loath to acknowledge that Pascale might have been privy to the facts all along and that made her as deranged as her cousin. Fran Harrington had messaged her last week saying that Pascale had been accepted into a top college in Geneva and had acquired a boyfriend twice her age who played in a folk band. That part of her life seemed now like a daydream, which was ironic since it was the only part of her life where she'd felt engaged. Her friendship with Pascale had been the anchor she'd never known, one that forced her to assess things where she'd never assessed things before. LA, the people here, they ate her up.

'Casey, can I tell you something?'

'Shoot.'

'I don't think Tom and Sherilyn are my real parents.'

He turned on her with red-rimmed eyes and laughed before realising she was serious.

'I think they adopted me when I was a baby, but I don't know how or from whom.'

He struggled to ascertain if she was for real. 'Get fucked.'

'I think they couldn't have kids of their own, for whatever reason, and they wanted to cover it up so they had to get a baby they could pass off as theirs.'

To her surprise, he scoffed. 'Bullshit.'

'You couldn't possibly know.'

Casey ran a hand through his hair. 'Look, man, it's natural. I've wondered before. Hasn't every kid? Parents suck. You'll get over it.'

'This is different,' Aurora persevered. 'I feel it. I feel it's the truth. But if I face the truth then that means the whole of my life's been a lie.'

His eyes were stoned.

'Casey...?'

'Hmm?'

'Please say something.'

He held out the bucket. 'Wanna candy?'

Aurora summoned her courage for where she was headed next.

'I think they ordered me.' She checked his reaction. 'Like, in a catalogue or something.'

He laughed with good humour. 'That's crazy.'

'Is it?' Her hands were shaking so much she could barely light her cigarette. 'I mean, supposing…supposing someone really, really rich had this idea to make money, and set up this agency to get kids and have people pay for them. Famous people. People like our parents.'

'They'd never get away with it.'

'But what if they pretended they were something else?' She paused, wondering how close to the line she could go. 'Like a rehab facility. Because that's how they'd target the vulnerable ones who thought there was something missing in their lives.'

Casey had zoned out. 'Pretty cool idea,' he said.

'It is, though, right? That's the point. It's *clever*. Massive sums of money. Couples who are so loaded they're prepared to pay anything. What else are they going to spend it on but the one thing they can't buy? Except now they can, Casey. Now they *can buy it*.'

Casey raised a disbelieving eyebrow. 'And you think *you're* one of these kids, that it?'

'You make it sound like I just told you I got abducted by aliens.'

'That's about as weirdass as it sounds.'

'I knew you wouldn't understand.'

He nodded to the screen, where another young starlet was flaunting her new single. 'She could be one, too?' Seconds later, another, from elite Hollywood stock. 'And him?'

Aurora pictured the parents. 'Yeah...' she said, considering it. 'Yeah, maybe.'

'Why would *your* folks do it?'

So many times she'd been over it, trying to think of a reason. What could possibly be worth that level of deceit? What were Tom and Sherilyn concealing?

'I don't know.'

Casey snorted. 'You're funny.'

'*Listen* to me,' she pleaded. 'Mom and Dad are like strangers. They don't do things together, they don't even *see* each other; they have zero in common and it's like we're stuck in the same house and none of us know how we got there! I'm telling you, their marriage is *weird*—'

'Every marriage is weird.' He peeled open his bag of tobacco. 'Don't get married.'

'It's more than that. It's my life. This—' she waved her hands about '—it's all wrong!'

Casey cocked his eyebrow. 'You *positive* you've gone through puberty?'

'You know what?' She bit back tears. 'Forget I said anything.'

He scooted up next to her and planted a wet kiss on her cheek. 'Sorry,' he said, 'but I gotta tell you straight. It sounds nuts.'

Aurora angled her body away from him and concentrated on smoking. She knew her claims ran out of steam at this point, unless she had the proof to back them up. Even when, next year, she saw the couple she'd witnessed at Reuben van der Meyde's house parading a baby to the press that wasn't theirs, it wouldn't make the slightest bit of difference.

'I guess so,' she said emptily.

* * *

Across town, Tom Nash was enjoying his fortnightly spa session at the Springs Central Resort in Beverly Hills. He liked to relax, sweat it out in the sauna and steam before being pampered, having his hair treated and his skin peeled. He deserved it. Thanks to a string of acclaimed concerts, he had single-handedly secured the Nash name as the most bankable in the business. He'd worked his ass off to make the fans, and the label, happy. This was where he got to cash in—a little rest, a little recreation. A few of the treats he liked best.

'Nearly goddamn killed me,' he told Stuart Lovell, his producer. The men liked to unwind in each other's company. 'Don't know if I've got it in me to do it again.'

Stuart had been a high roller at Strike Records for years. He was mid-forties, heavy-set with dyed jet hair and a fleshy, pale face. A poor surgery job had left his complexion stretched and mask-like, on a bad day, to his alarm, like the hovering apparition of Michael Myers in *Halloween*. He was a family man, a regular john, with a model wife and two teenage sons. He reeked of money, hard earned by others and kept safe in his pocket.

'You won't have to once we get Sherilyn back on track,' he replied, reclining against the wall of the men's private room. The air was so thick with eucalyptus that it was impossible to see further than a few inches. He could barely make out Tom's outline on the bench opposite.

'That's what I'm worried about,' said Tom, breathing in deeply through his nostrils, the mint stinging. He could feel his hairline melting, beads of perspiration gathered on his scalp, making it itch. 'I'm not sure she's going to *let* us get her back. She's in a bad way...'

'We can't afford to sustain dead weight,' said Stuart

bluntly. The men had known each other intimately for years and could talk candidly. 'What we want is the Nash family package. That includes Sherilyn *and* Aurora.'

'I know,' said Tom, weary of the women in his life. 'We'll get there.'

The other man stood. Beneath Stuart's white towel, a rock-hard erection sprang.

Tom's breath caught. He always felt the same, no matter how many times it happened. Like the kid he used to be checking out copies of *Mr Gay America* in his bedroom when he was twelve, hearing his pop's tread on the stairs as he bundled the magazines beneath his mattress, pulse racing, fumbling with his open fly, praying they'd never be discovered because you just *couldn't* be a guy who liked guys. It wasn't an option. He had to like girls, with their skin too sweet and their stupid laughs and their sticky lips.

Gays were sick. They had an illness. That was what he got told. An affliction to be cured.

Now, he felt once more like that terrified boy. As if he was about to be discovered, that queasy feeling in his stomach, a mixture of disgust and thrill.

'Come to me,' he croaked, licking lips that, despite the steam, had gone dry.

Stuart obliged. Kneeling between Tom's legs, he peeled away the towel and dipped his head. Tom always took a while to get hard. Even after the many years this routine had claimed, the fear of their being interrupted stalled his abandon.

Both men knew there was much at stake.

As his dick vanished into the record producer's mouth, Tom surrendered to a surge of pleasure. He grasped Stuart's head and closed his eyes, forcing his swelling hardness against the back of the other man's throat. This was his only release, the only discreet way. He came quickly, in abundance, heart hammering, sweat pouring. A tear seeped from his eye.

Like clockwork, always the same, Tom rose from the bench and turned. He raised his ass and spread his legs. Seconds later, a piercing ecstasy.

He vowed to savour every second. Night and day he craved cock, a non-stop preoccupation with the thing he was denied. Instead he was forced to play happy families, all-American nice-guy, straight as an arrow. Ever since his career took off twenty years ago...

It was a long time to deceive the world.

His palms slipped on the bench with the force of Stuart slamming into him.

For now, at least, his wife and daughter were the furthest things from his mind.

48
Stevie

Bibi Reiner, for a short while Bibi Posen, emerged from the Truman Associates offices on Sunset, just in time to spot a woman hurrying past on the opposite side of the Boulevard with her face buried in the pages of a gossip magazine. For once, Bibi's photo wasn't front-page news.

Lunch with Phyllida Colt, the agent with whom Marty King had put her in touch, had been inspiring. As Bibi breathed the warm noon air, thick with the heady fumes of ambition, she replayed Phyllida's kindness when she had confessed her work in Linus's pet projects. To her relief, and just a pinch of alarm, the woman hadn't been surprised. Bibi wasn't the first actress in LA to come equipped with a difficult past and she undoubtedly wouldn't be the last.

As Bibi hailed a cab she realised that life, just at the point where she'd been ready to give up on it, had got suddenly, incredibly, better. Since her break to Cacatra, she'd felt more like herself with each day that passed. It was true what they said: the place did work wonders. Dirk Michaels, in spite of an aversion to him that would never abate, had been right about the breakthrough spa treatments. They had left her relaxed and reinvigorated, ready to retake control.

Quite why Dirk had been willing to organise it with van der Meyde in the first place continued to baffle her, but she wasn't about to turn down a favour from a man who ought for ever to be in her debt. She preferred to imagine Linus's death had stirred a realisation in him, made him repent the nature of his professional sideline and private kicks. Though, she doubted it.

Bibi's apartment in Westwood was a million miles from the grandeur of Linus's place, but she loved it all the same. She hadn't been able to consider staying in the Beverly Hills mansion, even though her lawyers had told her she was entitled to it. She would sooner have one untainted room than a hundred filled with bad memories.

A brown square package was waiting in her mailbox, addressed in a neat block of precise, handwritten capital letters. Puzzled, she shook it. It made no sound. Tucking it under one arm, she fumbled for keys with her free hand.

Once inside, she tore the parcel open.

It was a disc, packed tightly in cardboard and bubble wrap, catching the light like a jewel presented on a velvet cushion. There was a typed label across the front that read: PLAY ME.

Mystified, Bibi fed it into the stereo and listened.

In London, winter was approaching. The days were getting shorter, the nights edging in, the dark snap of November crackling in the air. Stevie missed the British weather. She missed rain and hot tea and fires and crumpets and the smell of the tube when it was wet.

Coming back after all this time was strange. The capital seemed smaller than it had when she'd left, three years ago a towering, oppressive, inescapable city, something she realised now had been more to do with her than it.

Wednesday morning she was filming at St Paul's. They'd closed the roads from Aldwych and from Bank, but that hadn't stopped fans crowding around the square's perimeter, craning their necks to catch a glimpse of the action, though Stevie suspected it was less for her than for her romantic lead, a tortured RADA disciple who had a reputation for brooding shyness but had actually taken more women to bed over the past six months than anyone could count.

Her character was required to run down the famous cathedral steps, setting the pigeons aflutter, into the arms of Impatiently Waiting RADA. Pigeons didn't sound poetic, but they lent a lack of fuss to the scene. The grey birds against the grey sky against the celebrated grey dome, in which Stevie's buttercup-yellow coat glimmered like a lucky penny. But the pigeons were sent AWOL by crowds and crew, leaving the space atypically empty and more post-apocalyptic than die-hard romantic. Cue take after take, waiting for the birds to land long enough for her to incite their dramatic departure.

It meant she was running late by the time she left for her appointment on Great Portland Street. As Stevie's car pulled up outside the private clinic, nerves sharpened. She had deliberately waited till London to get checked out because her doctor was a friend, a woman she trusted, and if it was bad news she wanted to hear it from a source she knew over a jaded LA physician who saw more women with fertility problems than she'd had hot dinners.

'It's good news, Stephanie,' said Dr Hayashi, putting her out of her misery straight away. 'You're functioning normally. There's every reason you can conceive a child without treatment.'

Stevie raised her eyes briefly heavenward, which was hypocritical since she was atheist. 'Thank you.' She sat down.

'Like we discussed, I recommend your husband gets checked.' Dr Hayashi regarded her kindly over horn-rimmed glasses. 'Which means you're going to have to talk it over with him in the not-too-distant future...?'

'I know.'

Xander wasn't even aware she'd made this appointment. Following his admission about JB Moreau, Stevie had found it difficult to communicate with him at all. When the time came for her to fly out on location, she'd been secretly relieved. She needed time away to think. For, while Xander's story was one she had to trust, she couldn't help feeling there was something about it that didn't add up. She was tired of secrets. Marriage was meant to make you feel secure and safe, if in nothing else then in the knowledge of your partnership. Right now, indeed for the past six months, she'd felt anything but. And Xander knew it.

'Remember you're young,' advised the doctor. 'Don't rush or put yourself under unnecessary pressure. Stress does funny things to the body.'

'You mean if I want it too much, it might never happen?'

Dr Hayashi linked her hands in front of her. 'Relax, stay healthy and get together as often as you can. But if you end up waiting several years—' she shrugged '—so be it. Your results indicate there's no risk in postponing.'

'But his might?'

'I can't comment on his.' She spread her hands flat. 'I would suggest, for your own peace of mind, he seeks his own advice.'

Xander called on the cab ride back to her hotel.

'Hi.' She was surprised to hear from him. 'Is everything all right?'

The taxi passed Euston Station, where they overtook a double-decker bus. Lori Garcia's image was plastered to its flanks, advertising a make-up giant, her eyelashes impossibly long.

'I'm coming to London,' he said.

'What?' She sat up straighter. 'Why?'

There was a long pause, during which she thought she'd lost him. At last, he said: 'Because I have to see you.'

'Xander, you're scaring me. What's the matter?'

Dark clouds gathered. It looked perilously like rain.

'I'll explain when I get there.'

49
Lori

Every opportunity she had, she attempted to make contact with JB.

In between shoots in Europe, at departure lounges throughout Asia, during a string of galas in South America... Delicately worded messages had been left at La Lumière. She'd even tried to contact Reuben van der Meyde directly, but his army of personnel made it impossible.

Where was he? Was he still on business? If so, what? What could possibly take him away for this long? She couldn't understand it. It had been three months since Cacatra and he knew where she was. Time was running out. She was paranoid people could tell. The swell in her belly was minimal but she knew from the books she'd read that when change happened it would happen swiftly. She couldn't bear the idea of him finding out from someone else, but if he didn't get in touch soon she'd be left with no choice. And what was she meant to tell everyone? She couldn't possibly announce to the world that she was carrying JB Moreau's child, especially when the father himself, not to mention his *wife*, had no idea.

It was as if he had received none of her messages. At first, Lori had been ambiguous, wanting to save the revelation. *Call me, I have to see you...* Then, in recent weeks: *JB, it's vital we meet... Something has happened... We've got news...*

He travelled. Perhaps he was in a far-flung country, in a different time zone. Perhaps he had lost his cell or changed his number. Perhaps he had tried calling but her own phone was broken and swallowing up the data...

She wasn't stupid. Every way she looked at it, the facts were clear.

The next day, they're history...

Between you and me, he's an asshole...

You know nothing about love—and even less about this man...

It was what everyone had warned her about: Desideria, Jacqueline, even her father.

And though it broke her heart and ripped her to shreds, the fourth reason for his silence was the most feasible. He was with Rebecca Stuttgart, busy making amends.

The inevitable snub. Lori had always pitied the women in romance novels who believed they could conquer the rogue or tame the savage, certain that with them he was different, the things he'd said and the way he'd made them feel, the fact they knew him as nobody else did: they knew him *better*. Couldn't they see he was stringing them along? Wasn't it obvious? Yes, to everyone else. To the person it was happening to, an irresistible delusion.

For a while, she followed suit. She refused to accept that

JB had done that to her. What they'd talked about on the beach on Cacatra, the things he'd shared, how he'd touched her and kissed her, how he'd looked into her eyes like it meant everything...

Lori was terrified.

She was terrified of raising this baby alone, for even if JB had the nerve to ask her to get rid of it—would he attempt to offer her money? Would he stoop that low?—she had no intention of giving it up. She was terrified of the repercussions, for how would she explain it? How many lies would she need to tell? She was terrified that it would shatter the life she had built for herself, the life her grandmother had given her the courage and the means to pursue, and then where would she be? She was terrified of ending up back in *Tres Hermanas*, all this a dream, just as she'd feared in the early days, with absolutely nothing.

But none of this came close to the biggest terror of all. For, much as she despised his selfishness, much as she could scarcely get her head around his cruelty, much as she was unable to fathom how one human being could treat another so callously, she was terrified that she would never be with JB Moreau again. Terrified that whatever they'd had was over.

The following month, Lori said yes to dinner with Maximo Diaz. Jacqueline had been on her back about it, not to mention the man himself. Maximo was persistent, haranguing her with calls, inundating her with flowers and having his management chase hers near enough every day for a meet. After they ran into each other at a gathering in Boston, she finally accepted.

What harm could it do? Maximo was pleasant enough

company. He was forever telling her how beautiful she was, how special, and right now that was what she needed. Lori was desperate, lonely and frightened. She was used and ashamed and betrayed. Her body was giving her away. Beneath the loose-fitting tops her shape was getting harder to conceal. She needed a friend—and naively told herself that, for now, it was all he wished to be.

Tonight was the third occasion they'd been out. Maximo had suggested Sands, a popular eatery overlooking the beach, and came to meet her early evening, the sun hot-pink over the water. He was dressed in a pale linen suit, and smiled and waved when he saw her.

In another life she would have found Maximo attractive. Tall, lean and brooding, he was vampirically pale with liquid dark eyes and full, soft lips. You could tell he was from royal stock because everything about him looked and smelled expensive. He had modelled on and off before entering the acting fray and was so ravishing on the eye that it didn't much matter what he got up to on-screen. Teenage girls were wild for him.

They sat outside beneath a wide cream canopy that rippled in the ocean breeze.

'How was your audition?' she asked. Maximo had gone for another romantic lead but this was a mega-bucks project, one that could propel him to the big league.

He looked self-conscious. 'It was OK.'

'Just OK?'

Maximo deflected the question by ordering drinks. When Lori went for San Pellegrino he observed, 'Still not drinking? Gotta admire you.' She'd told him she was avoiding alcohol because it was bad for her skin, and her sense was that he was impressed at this, in a way that made her uneasy, as though he appreciated the preservation of looks above all else.

When the waiter had gone, she pressed him. 'When will you hear?'

He pretended not to know what she was talking about and returned her gaze blankly. If this acting was anything to go by, the answer was never.

'About what?'

She raised an eyebrow. 'The audition?'

'Oh, right. Yeah. Not sure.'

'You don't seem very enthusiastic.'

The drinks came. When the waiter had gone, Maximo checked about him and blushed at the tips of his ears.

'I gotta get my—' he shrugged '—y'know, I gotta get my junk out.'

Something about his countenance made her want to laugh, which was an alien sensation. 'OK…' she said, reining it in. 'You're uncomfortable with that?'

'Wouldn't you be?'

'It depends on the context,' she admitted. 'Probably.'

He sat back. 'It's the real deal. Full nudity.'

'Is it important to the part?' She suspected it wasn't. Maximo was hardly going to be working on an arthouse movie, though they'd probably dressed it, so to speak, that way.

'Yeah,' he mused, 'I'm pretty sure it is. I mean, they said it was.'

His discomfort surprised her. 'I would have thought you'd be used to people swooning over you by now.' She'd meant it in a conspiratorial way but he took the compliment face-on.

'Guess so,' he said. 'But I'm not sure…' He looked up at her as though trying to convey a hidden meaning. 'I'm not sure they're ready for it.'

This time Lori did laugh, her troubles fleetingly forgotten. 'Really?'

He nodded. 'It's just that…' The waiter came back to take their food order. Maximo muttered, 'Never mind,' and, though she would try to steer the conversation back on to it, he resisted and the subject was lost.

Afterwards, they headed back to Maximo's apartment. He'd regaled her over dinner with anecdotes from his privileged childhood and Lori had expressed interest in seeing some photographs. Following the poisonous mail she'd been receiving, she had also become hesitant about returning to the mansion alone late at night, especially in her condition.

Maximo's place in the Hills was a bona fide bachelor's pad, all chrome and leather and enormous flat-screen TVs mounted on the walls. Lori perched on the edge of a couch.

'Want a drink?' he called from the kitchen.

'I'm all right.'

He stuck his head round the door and made a face. 'Seriously? I was thinking brandy.'

'I'm not drinking.'

'One won't hurt.'

'No. Honest, I'm fine.'

He shrugged. 'Suit yourself.' Moments later he emerged with a bottle of Courvoisier and two goldfish-bowl glasses, 'In case she changes her mind.'

Lori noticed there was little if any personal memorabilia. The way Maximo had been going on she'd imagined he had photos all over the place.

'Let's see these pictures, then.' She smiled. 'I'm dying to see this castle you grew up in.'

Maximo sat down next to her. He poured the amber liquid, taking his time, and his silence unnerved her.

'You know, Lori,' he said at last, 'I really like you. You must realise that.'

His voice was very calm, very measured. He didn't look at her.

'I'm enjoying your company, too,' she said carefully.

He ran a pale finger around the rim of his glass. 'And I think you know what I want.'

Lori made the mistake of taking his hand. 'Max, I have to be honest with you,' she began. This wasn't going to be easy. 'The way things are for me right now, it's complicated.'

He held her hand tightly. She realised for the first time how big his were.

'When isn't it complicated?' he returned.

'No, you don't understand, it's more than that. It's—'

Without warning, Maximo's lips were on hers. She could feel his hard white teeth and smell the musk in his hair. His tongue darted into her mouth, warm and slick.

'I'm hot for you, Lori.' His breath was strangled as he buried his hands in her hair, forcing her backwards. 'Say you want me too. Don't fight it.'

'Wait,' she managed, attempting to fend him off, 'please—'

He pinned her down on the leather, driving her legs apart and jamming himself between. Lori anticipated his erection but could not feel it.

'Max, *don't*!' But he was biting and pulling and as she pushed against him with all her might, panicking, he unzipped his fly, holding her chin tight with his other hand. She couldn't speak, her chest and lungs filled with fear as she felt him tug down his pants and the thin, abrasive fabric of his jockeys rub against her. Again she felt nothing, just the chafe of his flat groin on hers. His grip darted to her breasts, fumbled with the buttons and freed one nipple, taking it between his teeth and tugging so she cried out in pain. His fingers were inside her knickers, tearing them down, clumsily stabbing at her dryness.

'Get off me!' She hit him. It was useless. He was driving against her, a starving rhythm, as though he were already inside.

And then she realised, with horror, he might be.

'*Stop!*'

'You want it, Lori,' he spluttered in her ear, 'I know you do. *Relax.*'

This time she raised a knee and ploughed it into his groin, eliciting a shriek of pain as he lurched backwards, off the couch and on to the floor.

His erection, compact as a pink lipstick, was no bigger than her little finger. He was hardly wider than a straw. She hadn't known any that small existed.

'*Bitch!*' he rasped, pushing himself up. 'That's how you want to play it? Huh? You like it rough?'

'Get away from me.' She attempted to struggle back into her clothes, turning and groping on the floor. But he was on her again, this time from behind, wheezing and moaning, his miniature prick pestering for entry. He rutted against her, once, twice, three times, before he released a high-pitched wheeze like air escaping from a balloon, and withdrew.

Seconds passed before he said, quite happily, 'That was amazing.'

Lori couldn't speak. Her tongue was bloated. Her heart was pounding.

'You sure are a wild one, Lori Garcia.' He was kneeling at the foot of the couch and admiring his diminutive manhood. 'I know it's tiny,' he crooned, 'but it can work wonders. So many girls get put off, you know? It's not what they're expecting. But once they've sampled the Maximo magic they always want more. Do you want more, Lori?' He reached down and stroked her back. 'I can go all night...'

Quick as a tiger, she rounded on him, balling her knuckles and punching him squarely in the jaw. Or she'd thought it was the jaw but it could have been higher, because as Maximo was propelled backwards a flash of red shot out of his nose. Naked, he came to rest on the floor, cradling his face with one hand and his balls with the other.

'You sicken me,' Lori raged, stumbling to her feet. She was shaking but determined to control it, refusing to give him the satisfaction of another hushed victim. All the agony of the past few months possessed her entire being, and she didn't know where the words came from but that she meant every one. 'If you come within a hundred feet of me again,' she threatened, 'I swear I'll take your pathetic excuse for a cock and I'll rip it off and nail you with it. But don't worry—you'll scarcely feel a thing.'

She gathered her stuff and headed for the apartment door.

Maximo's pitiful cry echoed in her wake. 'Wait, Lori, come back—'

But she was gone, out on to the empty dark street, stumbling, unseeing, heading for home though she had no idea where that was or if it even still existed.

50
Aurora

The words went something like: *'Oh baby, what you do to me, yeah, baby, why can't we be free,'* but she couldn't remember what happened after that. It was a crappy, repetitive song, so perhaps if she just spat that part out again and again no one would notice.

In the studio, Stuart Lovell shook his head. 'This is bad,' he said. 'Real damn bad.'

The sound engineer agreed. 'We can up the quality on the record, but if the lyrics aren't gonna stick…'

Stuart slurped his latte. 'Can't we take samples and piece them together? Get her to sing those bits separately?'

The engineer, bearded in a Guns N' Roses T-shirt, sighed, exasperated. Starlets like Aurora Nash were good for one thing: spending Daddy's money. The less the world had to hear about them, the better. Except now she was making another record. Hadn't one been enough?

'She don't look good,' he supplied, removing his head-phones. 'Someone oughtta hit rehab and fast.'

Stuart gritted his teeth. You'd think Aurora was Tina freaking Turner for how they'd been chewing their own asses off to get her in the studio. The girl didn't seem to give a shit. Didn't she care about Tom's legacy? She was a car wreck.

Aurora removed her own headphones and waited for them to tell her what to do. On the outside looking in, she could see the men in heated discussion but couldn't hear what they were saying. A bit like her life, really. They appeared to her like two fat parasites, leeching every last drop from her celebrity. She hadn't even wanted to do this album. Tom had made her. It was his idea of 'sorting her out'. Maybe she wouldn't need sorting out if he hadn't lied to her, the worst, most despicable lie ever told, since the day she was born.

No wonder she couldn't summon a single iota of enthusiasm.

Stuart Lovell was eyeballing her. He'd been friends with Tom for ages but she'd always found him gross, like he was ready to jump her bones any second. All men that age were the same. She had no doubt Stuart had reaped the fruits of his power before now, pop-tart sweethearts queuing up on their hands and knees with their mouths hanging open.

His voice drifted into the recording booth. 'Let's wrap it for today, Aurora.'

'Fine.' She was only too happy to.

Rodeo Drive was, or had been, her favourite place to shop. On the way over to Casey's she hit the boutique she and Farrah used to spend their Saturdays in, cooing over chic pieces and lying about what looked good for fear of being upstaged by the other.

A handful of paps followed her and she gave them the finger, prompting the inevitable shower of flashing bulbs. People were staring. What had happened to the blue-eyed golden girl of Aurora's youth? Her hair had grown out, dry and limp with bleach, orangey at the roots, and her pale complexion was hidden behind oversized black shades. She looked forty, an unhappy has-been Hollywood divorcee attempting to conceal bungled surgery beneath too much make-up.

Inside, she drifted between rails of designer gear. Every piece could be hers. Fuck it, she could afford the whole entire store! Nothing to save for and no reason to try… nothing whose acquisition would ever mean anything. *Pretty please can I have it, Daddy?* Of course she could. She could have anything. Take it all.

Except the truth.

Aurora felt like sitting down in the middle of the store with her head in her hands and just waiting for them to carry her away. This wasn't living; it was surviving—and only just. She could see no exit. Her confession to Casey had been a waste of time. All it did was prove that no one was ever going to believe her. The island's story was too far-fetched, too much like fiction.

And yet it was real.

Tom was too busy and important to bother with her. He hadn't even cared when he was away on tour, supposedly fending for the family but what he didn't realise was that she needed him at home. She didn't need his cash or his fame or his credit card. She needed answers. She needed explanations. She needed *him*. Her father.

Her father…

She choked on a sob.

Stupid! Don't cry. They're nobody to you, remember?

Aurora fingered the collar on a thousand-dollar vest. She slipped it from its hanger, checked the tag and held it against her, like any ordinary shopper. Without caring who saw, she wandered with it casually draped over one arm, pretending to browse the other items that caught her eye. Then she slid it quietly into her bag and made her way out.

Easy.

Too easy.

'Hold it there, miss.'

Approaching the doors, she quickened her pace.

'Miss, you need to stop right there.'

She turned. Security loomed over her.

The big guy took her arm. 'I think you've got something that belongs to us.'

'What the hell were you *thinking*?' Tom Nash signed the release papers with an angry flourish and yanked Aurora's elbow. She'd never seen him so mad.

'It was an accident,' she mumbled. 'It sorta fell in.'

'Don't insult me, Aurora,' he warned. They emerged from the police station and headed towards Tom's Escalade. He'd recently had his highlights touched and the effect was a kaleidoscope of flashing honeys and coppers. Beautiful hair. Girls' hair. 'I'm this close to snapping right now.' He pinched a sliver of air between finger and thumb.

She got in and slammed the door. 'Sorry,' she muttered.

'Sorry doesn't cut it. You know I'm up to my neck in it defending you to the record company. First your mother and now you! Don't think Stuart didn't call me. Jesus H,

Aurora!' He banged the steering wheel. 'Some days it's like I'm the only one keeping this family afloat.'

Family, my ass.

For the gazillionth time she opened her mouth to confront him but no words came out. How was she meant to begin? What was she meant to say?

'I thought that school had finally sorted you,' Tom ranted on. They crossed the street at speed via an illegal manoeuvre. Car horns blasted. 'But *theft*? What next?' He turned to her. 'Sometimes I don't know where we went wrong!'

Aurora stared out of the window, biting down hard on her lip.

'Well?' He was waiting for the attitude, the backchat. It didn't come. 'What have you got to say for yourself?'

'There's nothing to say.'

'Don't you see how lucky you are?' His voice trembled. 'I *never* had what you have when I was a kid. I had nothing. Less than nothing. I never even knew kids *had* lives like yours! You've got it all, everything you could ever want or need, and *I've* given it to you. I've given you everything! But it's still not enough, is it? *Theft*? When all you had to do was *ask* me for the money? What would make you do such a stupid thing as that?' He ran a red light. 'When have we ever deprived you, Aurora? Go on, when have we?'

She spoke so quietly that he had to ask her to repeat it.

'I said,' she mumbled, 'who's *we*?'

Tom didn't understand. 'Your mother and me, who else would I be talking about?'

She snorted. 'Mother. Sure.'

They drove the rest of the way in silence. Tom's knuckles were white on the wheel. When they arrived at the mansion, he told her she was grounded.

* * *

Being grounded for a day was one thing. Being grounded for a week was entirely another. Seventy-two hours in, Aurora was going out of her head.

The house was empty. Tom had back-to-back interviews and Sherilyn, for once, had ventured out. Trips to see her Lindy were the only incentive she had to leave her bedroom. She was a complete state, a brittle-boned doll. Like mother, like daughter, Aurora thought wryly.

Sherilyn's room was predictably locked, but she knew where the key was kept. It was in the same place she hoarded all the drugs she imagined no one had a clue about.

The bedroom door opened, releasing a musty, lived-in smell. It was a mix of the cloying scent Sherilyn used to wear and a staleness like breath. Four or five empty chocolate-box trays were strewn across the floor around the bed and it was dark, the blinds drawn.

Aurora sat on the unmade bed sheets. A packet of pills had been attacked on the cabinet, next to a half-drunk glass of water. Aurora examined the packet, some kind of sedative. She felt defiant touching things, as if she were disturbing artefacts in a museum.

Getting a taste for snooping, she padded into Sherilyn's bathroom and rummaged about. Painkillers, sleeping pills, Valium, Xanax…there was a whole pharmacy in here.

Back in the bedroom she began opening drawers, pulling stuff out and tossing it on the floor. What she was searching for, she wasn't sure. A birth certificate? A letter? A contract?

A photo of baby Aurora in the arms of a woman who wasn't Sherilyn Rose?

Ridiculous. Of course her hunt threw up nothing. Real life wasn't like the movies.

Sherilyn hadn't updated her walk-in closet in some time. It was a separate room, wall-to-wall with hanging garments, mostly from the eighties in peach and pastels, the underwear compartment filled with baggy, shapeless panties, some of them stained. Whoa. Aurora was pretty sure they didn't have sex any more, but even so. Morbidly fascinated, she rifled through.

At the back of the space her hand touched what felt like a card. She pulled it out. White on one side, gold on the other. There was script on the front but because it had been torn, the edges papery and ragged, it was impossible to make out what it said.

Aurora felt about for the remaining pieces, just two more. When she pieced them together, she saw what the card was.

Bingo.

Reuben van der Meyde was having a party. On Cacatra. This summer.

It looked like the mother of all parties.

The mother.

No doubt Tom and Sherilyn were very special guests. Except they, or at least she, had elected not to go. Surely it was only right their daughter should take their place.

Aurora held tight to the card, so tight that the tips of her fingers deadened, as if she had found herself in a strange unfamiliar country and this was her passport home.

51
Stevie

Stevie could spend hours watching boats on the Thames. One came into view under Waterloo Bridge and she didn't take her eyes from it till it passed Blackfriars and disappeared off towards Canary Wharf. It was all she could do. If she watched the boats, she didn't have to look at her husband.

And if she didn't look at her husband, she didn't have to acknowledge what he had just told her.

'I didn't want you to know,' Xander said. 'That's why I didn't say anything. Because once you know something like this, it's impossible to go back. I wish I could.'

She said nothing.

'You have to understand I couldn't keep it to myself. It's a part of my past and I can't suffocate it and pretend it didn't happen. Not with you.' His gaze pleaded with her but she refused to meet it. 'I don't want this marriage to fail. I can't lose you. Please, Stevie.'

The anonymity of London was what she loved. Not because she and Xander were seated in overcoats on a bench on the South Bank, unrecognisable as they clutched polystyrene mugs that steamed in the freezing wintry air, but because English people were too proud to let on that they'd noticed. They might glance over once or twice, bury their chins in their collars and scarves and mention it later: that they'd seen someone famous, but it was no big deal. She was rarely approached in her home city. Now, especially now, she was grateful.

'What you're telling me,' she said, and her voice didn't sound like hers, 'is that there are kids in Hollywood whose parents aren't really theirs?'

'Yes.'

It sounded absurd. A joke gone too far. 'How many?'

'I'd say fifty.'

'You'd say?'

'Fifty I know about.'

The world turned on its head, reflections of buildings in the grey line of the river switching things the wrong way round. Terrible, terrible.

'And you helped make this happen.' Finally she looked into his dark eyes, wondering at the person she'd given herself to, and the way he shook his head suggested she was wrong but they both knew she was right.

'I was starting out in Hollywood,' he said for the second time. 'I came into contact with dozens of potential couples, hundreds. It was easy.'

Stevie wanted to laugh.

Instead she got to her feet and started walking, thinking only of getting away. She had to be alone. She had to try and process this and work out what to do.

He followed. 'Moreau needed me,' he said.

'To feed back valuable information?' she tossed angrily over her shoulder. 'How resourceful.'

Xander kept pace. 'I was a trusted asset. Imagine approaching the wrong person. Prospective couples had to be observed over long periods of time.'

'Meanwhile Moreau sourced the surrogates and van der Meyde stuck them all together to make a pretty picture?' she lashed.

'Stevie, wait. *Slow down.*'

'What a happy family you must have made.'

'It wasn't happy. That was why I got out.' He reached for her, forcing her to stop. 'And I did get out. That has to count for something, doesn't it?'

A cyclist rode past, head dipped against the cold.

'Moreau took over?' His name was ghoulish to her now; everything about him was. 'That's why he spends so much time in Hollywood? *Finding people?*'

'And other cities.' The wind was stinging, rain turning to sleet. 'They've got scouts all over the world, retrieving the men and women who can make these children and carry them.'

'You make it sound like a damn production line.'

'It is, in a way.'

Unable to conceal her disgust, she turned on her heel.

'Don't walk away, Stevie. Listen—'

'To what?' She whipped round. 'It's one thing you kept this from me, but, hey, we all have stuff in our past we'd sooner forget. What I can't abide is the idea you were involved at all in something this...*evil.*' Her voice broke. 'Who are you? I just don't know any more.'

'I'm me.' He went to touch her but she pulled away. 'And

I believed I was doing a good thing, OK? Helping people. That's what JB always said. That we were helping people.'

'La Lumière,' she murmured, the pieces fitting. 'It's a foil. It gives him an alibi, a day job. It makes him a businessman. What was yours, then? Actor by day, child farmer by night?'

Xander went to the river and put his elbows on the railings, rubbing his hands together against the cold. A boat horn sounded.

'How could you?' she whispered hoarsely. 'How *could* you?'

'JB and I, we were close at school. He was my best friend. I worshipped him. And after his parents died, I suppose that worship turned to fear.' Xander stared flatly at the water. 'I went along with whatever he said. I always did. This was no different.'

'What were you afraid he'd do?'

But he didn't need to answer. Stevie could tell Xander hadn't been afraid of a temper or an act of violence. He'd been afraid that the friend he'd adored would freeze him out, as JB had done that last term before the tragedy, and Xander would never be close to him again.

'He makes it so you don't question things,' he said. 'You trust him. You put your faith in him. *Not once do you question things.*'

'You question everything.'

'But I didn't. What started out as a favour, because it was dressed in a way that made it sound unimportant, inconsequential—just keeping an eye out, a quiet word after a drink or two—became, before I knew it, the most clandestine operation Hollywood has ever known.'

A tube rattled over to Embankment. Red buses over

Waterloo, the chimes of Big Ben and the spires of Parliament...
Life carrying on as normal.

Stevie let his words sink in. 'And I'll bet it makes money.'

Her husband bowed his head and she could see where his hair was cut above his collar and wanted to reach out and touch him but didn't.

'Van der Meyde discovered in the nineties that two of his close friends couldn't have kids.' He named a celebrated Hollywood couple. She was an actress, he, a screenwriter. Between them they had over sixty years in the industry, a wealth of Awards, and three children: two sons and a daughter, now in their twenties. All had followed their parents' path into show business. The daughter was enjoying an especially lucrative career.

'They were devastated,' said Xander. 'It was the only thing they had ever been denied. How could it be they had everything and yet the one thing they truly desired evaded them?'

She pictured the family. 'You're telling me those children aren't theirs?'

His silence answered her question. A short, hysterical laugh escaped her lips.

'The kids look like each other,' he explained, 'because they're from the same surrogates.' He was peeling the layers back gradually, with care, so she understood. 'These days it's unheard of to do as many as three from the same foundation. The risk is too great. But the money van der Meyde's friends were prepared to pay, way back then, sowed the seeds of a revolutionary idea. It was realistic. *Supply and demand.* And it was lucrative, highly lucrative. We're talking tens of millions of dollars—and that was twenty years ago.'

'And now? What do they pay now?'

'I haven't been in it for years. I don't know. When I stopped, a child could fetch anything between—and this is the whole package, from the initial fee to the twenty-one-year guarantee—thirty million and two-hundred million, dependent on the couple's means.'

Stevie said, 'Jesus.'

'Van der Meyde saw an opportunity and he went for it.' Xander returned to the water. 'He's made a fortune. More than he's made on any of his other schemes.'

'These people pay for fake children? How can they? How can they live with themselves?'

'You'd be surprised at the reasons.'

'Would I?'

'Remember the riches these clients possess. Money corrupts. There's a black irony in having it all, you know, everything you ever wanted, but no legacy and no one to hand it to. Some enter into this because they can't conceive naturally. It really is as simple as that.'

His voice shook. How she wished it hadn't.

'Others do it because they're afraid to fall. Years they've spent building and growing a career based on assumptions of heterosexuality, or sexual potency, or family values, when those things couldn't be further from the truth. But they'd die before they let the world discover that. They want to show the fans *their own kids*.'

'Can't they adopt like any normal person?'

'Adoption defeats the point, Stevie. Imagine if—' here he named a hard-man action hero '—had to tell the world he was firing blanks? If the service is there and they can pay for it… What better thing is there to blow a fortune on?'

'Can they be specific about what they want?'

'How do you mean?'

'I mean, this is Hollywood. If you're going to spend on a baby it might as well be the one you've always dreamed about, right? Boy, girl, blue eyes, brown hair? Whatever they want, they get? It has to be happening.'

He nodded, confirming her fears. It was like some nightmare dystopia come to life.

'And what about the ones that don't come up to scratch?' Her mouth was dry. 'Disabilities, syndromes, complications, stuff like that?'

'Van der Meyde lets them go.'

'Explain,' she demanded, sickened. 'He *lets them go*?'

'It's mercifully rare.'

'Mercifully? Don't make me laugh.'

'The ones he can use stay on the island. They work for him.'

The island... She and Bibi had been there, the epicentre of this grim machine. Bibi had been vulnerable, as so many seeking the spa's remedies. Was that how they spotted the ones most likely to cough up? Get them into therapy; have them admit to something missing in their lives...? She'd put nothing past van der Meyde, or Moreau. They were capable of anything.

'Those with more obvious defects are abandoned.'

'Abandoned?'

'It's too risky to re-engage them in an adoption process. The couples receive a full refund unless they wish to proceed again, but, should the supposed birth already have been announced, it may be that a new child needs to be supplied with immediate effect. In those cases, couples will stall while a suitable alternative is sourced, informing the press they don't yet wish to share images. People buy that. New parenthood commands that extra degree of privacy.'

'I've heard Hollywood conspiracy theories before,' Stevie choked, 'but this is…'

'I know.'

It made a horrific kind of sense. Stevie thought of those bizarre LA couplings, marriages she wasn't convinced were real or had heard wacky rumours about but had put down to tattle.

Fifty? Who were they?

'Who are they?' she asked.

He named a few. She was stunned.

'No wonder she's such a mess,' Stevie commented sadly.

'She doesn't know,' Xander reminded her. 'None of them do. The kids never find out.'

'And that's meant to make it better? That's the worst part of all, surely. How could they, how could *you*, know this when they don't? People's lives, their core, toyed with like—'

'It was an error of judgement. I'm not proud.'

'And the surrogates? How could they give up their own baby?'

'Ethics are the luxuries of the well off. You lead a lucky life, Steve.'

'Don't patronise me.'

'I'm not. I'm saying that desperation does strange things. We're not talking fifty-dollar bills here: we're talking *millions*. Safety, security, insurance, a *certainty of future*.'

'And they see the money, do they, these surrogates?'

'Why wouldn't they?'

'Come on, Xander, what's to stop van der Meyde pocketing the cash himself? I shouldn't imagine there'd be much the average woman on the street could do about it.'

'I'd have known if that was what JB was doing.'

'But not if that's what van der Meyde was doing.'

Silence.

Stevie rubbed her forehead. 'Fucking hell.'

'You don't need to tell me.'

She wrapped her coat tighter, watching as the world carried on, ignorant of its change, as though every person that passed, every car and dog and smiling child, were flipped inside out, colours reversed like the negative of a photograph.

'That's the real reason you didn't want me to go to Cacatra,' she said quietly. 'Isn't it? Not because of Moreau or your friendship or his parents or any of that, but because of this.'

There was a long pause, before, at last: 'You think I'd want my wife going anywhere near a man who makes a living from couples who can't have babies?'

She rested a hand on his back. A small gesture, but she felt him crumple beneath it.

'How could you imagine I would ever, ever in a million years, consider something like that?'

Xander turned to her. His eyes were tired. She hated what he'd done, the fact he'd been part of it, but she could not hate him. They were on the same side. It was what being married was about. 'I came here to tell you I'm sorry,' he said gravely. 'You're the best thing that's ever happened to me, Stevie. Please, give me a second chance.'

She looked at him and took in his sins and felt her love cling on despite it all. She leaned into the warm solidity of his shoulder.

Everything he'd said, the promises he'd made…from here on in, it was about trust. A fresh start. A new beginning.

'You have to keep it to yourself,' Xander murmured. 'Do you hear me, Stevie?'

'Yes.'

'I mean it. Promise me. You *have to stay quiet.*'

She looked out at the water and didn't say a word.

52
Lori

'We have to go out with it,' said Jacqueline Spark. They were at the One Touch offices on Pico Boulevard. 'There's no other way.'

Lori nodded. She sat at her publicist's desk with her hands in her lap.

Jacqueline got up. 'I'm sorry,' she said, coming round to join her. She might have hugged the Lori she used to know, but not this one. This one was harder, fossilised by the depth of JB Moreau's betrayal. 'I did try to tell you.'

'And I didn't listen,' Lori replied. 'Don't worry—I've been through it a thousand times. I know everything you're going to say.'

Even if her client was steeled against her emotions, Jacqueline was incensed enough for both of them. Who the *hell* did Moreau think he was? He had a wife, a business. He was one of the most important men in Hollywood. And he thought he could knock up a poor sweet girl like Lori

Garcia and leave her to deal with the consequences? She had always thought him a cold sonofabitch, but this? It was unbelievable.

She touched Lori's arm, deciding what she needed now was a friend, not a colleague. 'If I were you I'd have left it on his voicemail. That's what he'd do.'

Lori put a hand on her stomach. 'I've made it clear enough. He has to know, or at least be able to guess, what's happened.'

'That would explain the silence, then.' With each revelation, Moreau plunged in Jacqueline's already low expectations. 'He messed up. He was probably counting on you getting rid of this kid, but, seeing as you haven't, he'll have to pretend like it never happened.' She winced. 'What a bastard.'

'He told me he—'

'Pulled out in time? Was allergic to condoms? Couldn't have kids?'

Lori grimaced. 'How did you know?'

'I didn't, till half a second ago. Guys like him don't use protection. It's a slight on their ego or some shit. He fed you a line, honey. I'm so sorry.'

'Don't be. The last thing I need is people feeling sorry for me.'

'You don't want to try him one last time?' Privately Jacqueline thought Moreau would deserve everything he got—or everything he didn't get, as the case may be—but she had to keep her opinions in check before they made the call to go it alone. She didn't want Lori turning round months down the line and resenting her railroading them into a decision.

'Why?' Lori challenged. 'I agree JB ought to be told the

kid is his, but what am I hoping for? That it's going to make everything OK? That he's going to say, "Wonderful, now let's run off into the sunset and play house"?' She looked down. 'It's a fairytale. It's not real. It's time I realised that and moved on.'

Jacqueline frowned. 'He's done this before, you know, just vanished for months on end. He can, because he's got Kirsty running things at La Lumière and an army of subordinates wiping his ass all across America. And before you tell me you thought you were special or different or whatever, don't let yourself walk into the biggest cliché that ever there was.'

'I know.'

'So—' Jacqueline stood, back to business—this was one approaching shitstorm if they didn't take cover now '—let's get to the facts. Your baby is due in a matter of months and it's clear to me Moreau has no intention of being involved.' She faced the window, arms folded, circling through options. 'If I felt for one second that it would be any use to you—and you alone—to admit this child is his then I wouldn't hesitate in advising it. But, I don't.' She turned round. 'I think it will make you appear a marriage wrecker, a tramp and, worst of all, a girl who's cheated her fans into believing she's a virgin sweetheart when in reality she had way too much to drink one night and ended up sleeping with the boss.'

Lori moved to object, but Jacqueline held a hand up.

'I'm not saying that's what happened, just that's how it will be perceived.'

'And it's exactly what he wants,' Lori conceded. 'To keep the whole thing quiet.'

'I don't give a crap what he wants. You're my priority

and fessing up to a one-night stand with a married fashion mogul, when you're deep in the industry yourself, is a very bad idea. We have to keep this to ourselves or it's game over.'

'So what do we do?'

'We hit the press with it now. Or there'll be too many unanswerables.'

'And say what?'

Jacqueline hesitated. 'Two words,' she said. 'Maximo Diaz.'

Maximo Diaz was an unthinkable option. And yet it was the only one they had. It made sense. Lori had been dating him, they'd been photographed together; he'd been harping on in the press—at least before last month's encounter—about how much he admired her. Was it so out of the question that he'd been the man to at last claim her virginity? If they spun it right, it was the perfect story. Girl from the wrong side of the tracks weds (for there would have to be a wedding) into aristocracy when finally she meets her prince, and he was worth waiting every second for, because everyone knows a prince doesn't accept sullied goods. It was a lesson for young girls everywhere. Lori shuddered to acknowledge its farce.

How could she confide in Jacqueline—in anyone?— the humiliation of what had happened at Maximo's apartment? In any context, let alone the one she found herself in after the debacle with JB? There was no way. She detested Maximo and yet acknowledged he was the only one who could save them from the questions that would arrive at her door. She was at his mercy.

And so she was forced to go along with it, hands tied,

496 Victoria Fox

belly swelling, like a witch led head-bowed to the river. She found herself swept along in a plan she had no alternative but to follow, a scandalous, fraudulent plan born out of sheer desolation.

JB had put her in that position. She despised him for it.

Tony had been attempting to get in touch. She didn't want to hear from him. It was too little, too late. At the point she had needed her father's support he had turned her away. She would do this by herself. It was her body, her child and her decision. She had become a fortress, gale-beaten on an outcrop, standing resolute, old as time. She'd need to be for what lay ahead.

In bed, at night, Lori felt the scale of the mansion, vast and open with emptiness. She pictured herself inside its floating space, as her baby was now inside hers, a being within a being within a being, like she was trapped inside a Russian doll and running out of air.

Late March, Lori gave birth to a boy. She named him Omar.

Everyone told her that all babies had blue eyes in their first months of life but she knew this type of blue like the back of her hand. Pale, silvery: the eyes of JB Moreau.

'He's beautiful,' they crooned, and she and Maximo Diaz, proud parents, showed him to magazines and TV cameras and all the while Lori wished she had no part in this parade.

Maximo had taken the bait. He couldn't believe his luck. For a while he'd feared Lori would do something stupid like go to the cops—he'd never known a woman to react so unreasonably to his advances—so to have her come crawling with such an epic request was deeply rewarding. He was told the father was an ex-boyfriend, someone Lori had made a mistake in sleeping with, and that the man was happy to stay out of the child's life.

For Maximo, the offer was the answer to his prayers. It meant he no longer had to prowl the beds of single actresses and see on their faces, regular as clockwork, the disappointment and disgust when finally he unveiled his shrivelled member. It was also a dream move for his career. Who knew, maybe he'd get bored in a couple years' time and sack her and the kid off, but for now he was on the threshold of the big league. Stepping into Lori's world was all it took.

Lori could neither love nor respect him. She refused to leave Omar with him for even one second. She existed, numb to the pain. She got through one day and then the next. It was enough. It had to be.

How she wished she could close her heart to JB Moreau. She loathed him, yet she needed him. She hated him, yet she could not let him go. She wanted to hit him till her fists bled, yet she wanted to kiss him more.

How could she abandon the man who was half the child she adored?

Motherhood propelled Lori to megastar status. Having a child qualified her to enter a community of women interested in more than just fashion and glamour.

'A woman in your line of work must feel pressure to shed the baby weight.' Petra Houston, queen of the talk show, was chatting to her on the *Saturday Fix* sofa. Petra was known for her incisive lines of questioning.

'I'm realistic. Health is the most important thing.'

'How's Maximo as a father?'

'Great.' As *a* father, not necessarily Omar's, he was fine. 'We're settling into it well.'

'People were surprised by the pregnancy,' Petra suggested.

'None more than us. It happened quickly but it felt so right.'

'Was it love at first sight?' She raised an eyebrow. Cynically, Lori thought.

'If you believe in it,' she replied, 'yes.'

'So you always wanted kids.'

'I did after I met Max.'

She found the deception astonishingly straightforward. If anything, it was easier to read a script, play a part, than it was to be real. For the public, it was nothing. None of these people, these millions of viewers, knew anything about her. She was a product, an idea.

After the show, Lori was obliged to mix with Petra and several TV notables before making her excuses. All she could think of was returning home and seeing her baby, looking in on him while he was sleeping and marvelling over his tiny parted lips and soft dark sweep of hair. Every night the nanny spent with him was one she missed.

Maximo was out of town on a junket and the mansion was quiet when she returned. The nanny updated her in hushed whispers and exited the house with practised gentleness.

Upstairs, Lori stood at the door to her son's nursery, the light from the hall illuminating his cradle. His tiny head was turned to one side, fists curled by his ears like seashells. Her heart ached with love, pure and uncomplicated. She watched him till she began to feel sleepy herself.

It was only when Lori went to fix a drink that the envelope caught her eye, propped up in the hall by the nanny. It must have been delivered while she was out.

Plain white, like the others.

Opening it with care, she peeled out the paper inside.

NOT LONG
I'M COMING FOR *YOU*

Lori stood, mind ticking over while she held it, until she reached a conclusion.

Slowly, she folded the note back and pressed down the seal.

It was obvious.

How could she have missed something that was staring her in the face? Her obsession, her single-mindedness, her devotion to the wrong man...

There was only one person who could hate her this much.

They had given themselves away. She knew exactly who it was.

53
Aurora

The trouble with a grounding sentence was that the instant normal life resumed, she hit it like there was no tomorrow.

As far as Aurora was concerned, there wasn't. Hours merged into days, days into weeks, a glass-eyed paralysis that had her living for the brief respite of night when she would hook up with people she disliked and get high with them and have sex in somebody's apartment who she didn't know and wake up the next afternoon before she did it all again. Paparazzi chased her wherever she went, incessant bulbs snapping like jaws at a piece of meat. Her image was plastered across the tabloids, synonymous with everything wrong with Hollywood kids: proof that it was only a matter of time before the evils of excess spat out the monsters they had made, and the world looked on in smug complacency as their theories about the corruption of money were gratified and they were able to think, *I might be poor but at least my kid's not like that.*

Rita Clay did everything to try and get through to her. *Aurora, you're losing control. Aurora, this isn't what you wanted. Aurora, don't let it happen to you.*

But the point was she wasn't letting anything happen. Life had happened to her and there was fuck all she could do about it.

She woke in a house in Malibu. Couldn't remember how she got there.

The room was shrouded in semi-darkness and she was lying on the floor, her head on someone's crumpled-up sweatshirt. When she sat up, a sliver of acute, disabling pain splintered behind her eyes.

Casey Amos was on the couch, asleep with his shirt and pants off but with a grubby sneaker slung off one foot. A blonde not dissimilar in appearance to Aurora was sprawled across him, naked from the waist down.

She took a cab back to Tom and Sherilyn's. She didn't care that the driver spent the entire journey ogling her in the rear-view mirror and absorbing every detail so he could cough it up in a magazine deal, like a cat with a hairball, soon as she was out. Whatever turned him on.

'Roadblock up ahead,' he informed her as they turned into the street.

Aurora tossed a wodge of dollar bills into the front of the cab and opened the door. It was hot, the sun blinding, and she realised she hadn't properly seen daylight in a while. She groped around in her bag for her Ray-Bans but couldn't find them.

As she got closer to the mansion it became clear what the roadblock was.

A barrier of cop cars was wedged together, front wheels

up on the sidewalk, their blue and red lights pulsing. Cops were talking urgently into their radios; one, thriving on the drama, stood with his foot resting inside the passenger door, a lean, tanned elbow on the roof of the car.

Up ahead, the flash of an ambulance.

The ambulance was right outside her house.

Aurora increased her pace, held back momentarily by the cop, who was older in the face than he'd appeared from behind, and who didn't realise, such was her shambolic appearance, who she was, before he told her to wait and stand back and not go any further, but she didn't listen. The house and the ambulance came towards her in dislocated, shivering images, like an old movie. Her bag was thumping against her leg and she felt it drop to the ground.

Tom was there. A stretcher was being loaded into the back of the ambulance. Aurora caught a flash of white-blonde hair as the rear doors slammed shut.

'Dad?' The word she hadn't spoken in months was the only logical thing to say.

'Baby.' Tom held her. 'Baby, I'm sorry.'

'What's happened?' Against his chest, her voice came out little more than a squeak.

Behind the ambulance, she saw a second raft of police cars. Beyond that, a crawling swarm of ravenous photographers clicked aimlessly, shouting things she couldn't hear. Aurora in Tom's arms sent them wild.

'It's bad news, honey,' he said, stroking her hair as he had when she was little, 'real bad news. It's your mom.'

They had to wait hours at the hospital. Tom's PR arrived on the scene, his management intermittently issuing statements to the press outside. Yes, Sherilyn Rose was still alive. No, they had no further news. Yes, they were expecting confirmation of a suspected overdose.

Stuart Lovell, Head of Production at Strike Records, turned up. Aurora watched him shake Tom's hand and the men pulled each other into a swift, efficient embrace.

Aurora wanted to brush her teeth. It was all she could think about to stop herself going crazy. The private clinic smelled of antiseptic masked with air freshener and the smell of it turned her gut. Voices, low and concerned, hummed meaningless as white noise.

Casey tried calling but the hospital didn't allow cell phones. She noticed he didn't bother coming in person.

'Aurora?' Rita Clay was crouching next to her, full of concern, and for a moment she felt like a kid at a party of grown-ups who were all too busy with themselves to take any notice of her, except one, and that person's kindness made her cry. Rita gave her a hug. A tear spilled from her as if it had been wrung out, a wet towel twisted over an empty basin.

At last, the news came. A doctor with a grave, sympathetic expression, one well worn, approached the gathered party. She addressed Tom directly.

'Mr Nash, we were unable to resuscitate Sherilyn,' she said. 'We did all we could. I'm sorry. Your wife is dead.'

Over the next seventy-two hours, Sherilyn Rose's overdose dominated the media. Was it suicide? Speculation raged. The cocktail of drugs found in her body was certainly excessive by any normal person's standards, but then this was LA, and, for a woman relying on prescription medication, accidents did happen. Moreover, there had been no suicide note.

At least not one that was ever made public.

Tom
It is over for me. It was over a long time ago.
I cannot live this way.
Tell her the truth—
I'm sorry I could not.

Tom Nash had found it alongside his wife's body. He had known at that moment that she would never pull through. Sherilyn had no intention of waking up.

Nash and Rose. They had been married over twenty years. In happier times, in the beginning, they had been genuinely fond of each other, best friends, allies who had conquered the charts and reaped the fruits of their celebrity, their success ample antidote to the difficulties of their arrangement. For her, admittedly, it was harder. She took lovers, ever discreet, but she would never be able to live an ordinary life, with an ordinary family. For Tom, in the industry he had embraced, he accepted there would always be an element of sham. He did everything to throw them off the scent: the macho ranch, the overt lyrics about women, his vociferous political conservatism... But rumour was a persistent beast. It rumbled on, speculating over his hair, his clothes and the light surgery job he'd pursued in an ill-conceived moment of vanity.

It was harder these days than ever to conceal a secret.

Sherilyn had needed greater persuasion from the outset. It was easier for him, she had argued: he'd probably never have a kid of his own. She, in another life, with another man, a life where she hadn't expectations to meet and records to sell, might have. For a while they'd discussed either one of them being involved—neither had any desire to pool their genes, it felt too much like conceiving with a sibling—but in the end decided an equal share, a mutual disassociation, was the prudent route. Perhaps that was where they had gone wrong.

Tom struck the match. The amber flame lit the shadows of the yard, bringing the trees into looming frame like onlookers at a masked ball. He held it to the corner of the paper, watched as it licked the edges and curled them brown, then black.

It burned till the words had vanished, dissolved into the air until nothing was left.

After the funeral, Aurora travelled alone. She told them she needed to get away, was going to Europe to stay with a friend. Nobody questioned her desire for change.

Her jet arrived in Paris early morning. Aurora checked herself into a hotel on the Rue de Rivoli, unpacked her small case of belongings, drank several cups of coffee and consulted a map of the city. She didn't know how long she would be here but was prepared to wait.

The apartment in Montmartre was as she remembered. It was winter and the sky was slate, threatening rain. She sheltered in the wide porch, watching as the doors swung open and residents came and went, as the showers came down, bouncing off the cobbled sidewalks and spraying under car tyres. Bodies, impatient to reach the dry, hurried past beneath umbrellas.

Aurora was without security, without friends, in a city she barely knew. No longer recognisable: her hair was wet and plastered down her cheeks, her eyes tired and sad and fearing things hidden in shadows.

That day, they didn't come.

Nor did they come the next. Hours she was inside that porch, scanning every face that passed, now and then being moved on by the building's security, pitying her as they would an orphan child. She sat against a wall, knees under her chin, and waited.

On the third morning, she thought they might have gone away. Perhaps they had moved. Perhaps the trip had been a bad idea. She had committed on a whim and there was every chance they weren't in Paris at all. They could be halfway across the world.

Then, as daylight was fading on that third, final day, the man materialised, approaching through the driving, incessant rain. He was wearing a long black coat that went right to the floor and a brimmed, formal hat.

Arnaud Devereux.

Rainwater trickled down her hairline and into the hollow behind her ear. She was shivering, her skin laced with goose bumps.

For a moment he did not recognise her.

When he did, his features changed.

'I want to know everything,' Aurora told him. 'From the beginning. *Everything.*'

54
Stevie

'I wouldn't go if you paid me.'

The matter wasn't up for discussion. Stevie had no intention of setting foot on that godforsaken island ever again.

Xander turned the card over in his hands. Gold on one side, white on the other.

'Don't tell me you're considering it?' Disgustedly she took it from him.

60

VDM Communications in partnership with La Lumière

invite

Stephanie Speller

Xander Jakobson

60 years of Reuben van der Meyde

'"Sixty years of Reuben van der Meyde"? They make him sound like a political regime.'

It had arrived by courier that morning. Just when they had been back in LA sufficient time to feel as though things were slowly getting back to normal, their marriage gradually back on track, here it was: a reminder of her husband's past. On Xander's return from London, Wanda Gerund had been straight on the line, informing Stevie that the papers were running a story about the UK being the scene of crisis talks between them. London *had* been the scene of crisis talks, of course, the irony being that the press had no bloody idea how critical.

'They want to keep me sweet,' Xander commented. 'It's in their interests.'

'I bet it is.' She threw the invitation down.

Reuben van der Meyde turning sixty was no big secret, but exactly what he had planned was fuelling plenty of theories. Stevie, for one, could quite happily never find out a damn thing about it. Knowing what she knew, anything and everything that man did was of the lowest order.

Xander took her hand. 'It's over,' he promised. 'Van der Meyde's party is the last place we're going to be this summer.'

Bibi Reiner had landed a part in a candyfloss rom-com. It wasn't the starring role, but her ex-girlfriend-scorned was funny and original and there was plenty of scope for Bibi to take it in the direction she wanted. Finally, the role she had always dreamed about.

She and Stevie had spent the morning at a spa in Beverly Hills. For Stevie, it was a chance to celebrate her friend's happy news.

'I'm overjoyed for you.' She'd squeezed her when they'd met that morning. 'No one deserves it more.'

But for Bibi, relaxation, never mind celebration, was impossible. Any thrill she'd felt at landing the part was quickly replaced by panic, because it meant only that now there was further to fall. For weeks she'd kept the threats to herself, pretended it wasn't happening. But the facts were inescapable.

He'd been biding his time to take her down, to expose her as the criminal she was…

The murderer.

Back at the house, Stevie fixed lunch. 'Stop worrying about something that might never happen,' she teased, clocking Bibi's worried expression. She went to chuck salad wrapping in the bin and caught sight of van der Meyde's ripped-up invitation. She slammed the lid shut.

Bibi was checking something on Stevie's MacBook. Her head snapped up, imagining for a second that her friend had read her mind. 'What?'

Stevie sucked the end of her finger where she'd lightly cut herself. 'It's like you're scared of messing up, and I get why, because it's a big opportunity, but you have to believe in yourself, B. *We* all do.'

'Oh. Yeah.' She closed the laptop. 'Guess I've been a long time out of the game.'

Stevie brought the plates over. 'But it's never too late to get back in. You're the proof. This is *your* chance. No one's going to take it from you.'

Bibi found she had suddenly lost her appetite.

'Steve, can I tell you something?'

'Sure.' She passed her cutlery.

'Someone's been…' Bibi hesitated.

'What?'

'Someone's been blackmailing me. I got the recording

just after you left for London, but I didn't say anything then because it's not as if you haven't been good enough to me already—'

'What recording?'

'I've got it here—' Bibi twisted her hands '—if you want to listen.' She went to her bag and rummaged through its depths. 'I thought I could deal with it myself,' she said, struggling to keep her voice easy. 'But now I'm not sure I can. When I heard about the part I realised that's what he'd been waiting for. So I could get a taste for recovery only to have it snatched away.'

Alarm bells were ringing. 'Hang on, B. Who's "he"? What are you saying?'

Bibi held up a small disc. 'Can I play it?'

Anxious, Stevie led the way into their office. On the desk was a script Xander was editing, papers strewn across its surface. She took the disc and slipped it into an adjacent stereo.

To her surprise, it was Bibi's voice that filled the room.

'I had to do it...there was no other way...'

'What is this?'

'Listen.'

With mounting horror, Stevie realised what she was hearing.

'I hated him... It wasn't difficult because I hated him... everything he had put me through. It was payback time...'

'What the—?'

'Shh!'

'I lured Linus into his favourite game, he had plenty of favourites, and I tied him down. I wanted to make him suffer like he'd made me suffer. I wanted him to know confusion and pain and humiliation... I put the rope around

his neck and I pulled it hard. I wasn't about to show him the mercy I had always begged for and he had never given me...'

The voice sounded drugged, lethargic. It was indisputably Bibi's, but spaced out and distant, as if she was half asleep.

'I'd do it again if I had to. I'd kill him again...'

The recording ended, leaving only furry silence. Stevie's heart dropped like a stone. Into the quiet, to her immense dismay, emerged the unmistakable gravelly baritone of Dirk Michaels.

'So you see, Ms Reiner,' he said, *'I have interests to protect. Linus was a friend of mine and I am loyal to my friends. I am also loyal to my enemies. I never forget who they are or what debt I owe them. Remember that.'*

The recording clicked off.

The women stared at each other. Bibi's eyes glistened with tears.

'I thought I was free,' she rasped, 'but I'm not. And I don't deserve to be.'

'How did he get that?' Stevie demanded. 'How did he get you to say all that?'

'It was recorded on Cacatra.' Her voice cracked. 'Those spa sessions I went to.'

'What fucking spa sessions? You went in for a massage and ended up in a confessional?'

'I've been trying to work it out, OK? I'm as confused as you are. I've listened to it a thousand times and what scares me is *I don't remember saying it!* Any of it! It's like they drew it out of me without me knowing!'

'But that's impossible.'

'Is it? Don't you remember those cutting-edge "methods" Dirk was telling us about? How Cacatra was at the frontline of remedial breakthroughs? How their rehab therapies were second to none?' She closed her eyes. 'I was set up.'

'By who?' Stevie's mind was staggering from one explanation to the next. 'By Dirk?'

'Yes.'

'Why?' Even as she questioned it she knew the answer. Dirk's warning at the Actors League returned with gruesome clarity. What with Xander's revelations, she'd totally forgotten.

Ms Reiner should watch herself...

'The spa sessions,' elaborated Bibi. 'Dirk booked them all. I mean, shit! He booked me on to the island in the first place!' Her hands were shaking. 'He kept calling it their "initiative", this curative approach they use on stars who've undergone trauma. It had a name. He called it "Rooting". They use hypnosis to draw out the base cause of the disturbance.'

'Hypnosis?'

'Of course I didn't know that before I went,' she babbled. 'I just knew I was getting special treatment and that Dirk understood and that maybe he felt bad because of what he and Linus had done to me...' She bit back a sob.

Stevie wrestled her disbelief. The deceit. The trickery. *The island.* What more was it capable of? Would Reuben van der Meyde stop at nothing?

'I *did* feel better on Cacatra, Steve. Couldn't you tell?'

Numbly, Stevie nodded.

'I felt great and have done ever since. That must have been why. The release!'

'Who did you tell it to? Who was there?'

'A woman,' she said tremulously. 'We were in a white room with a couch in the middle of it and I lay down and shut my eyes and...' Frustration stalled the memory.

'That's all you remember?'

'Yes.'

'So the implication,' said Stevie, 'is that you admitted all this while you were under?'

Bibi collapsed into a chair. 'Naturally it's meant to be confidential. But Dirk...he must have organised it so the whole thing got recorded. But, then, how could he?'

Everything was starting to make sense. Stevie felt as if she were underwater, her ears and throat and head full of liquid.

'B,' she said, 'when I was last in NYC I bumped into Dirk Michaels. He told me he suspected Linus's death hadn't been an accident.'

'*What?* Why didn't you tell me?'

'I thought he was bluffing.'

'But Cacatra? How?'

'Dirk is friendly with Reuben van der Meyde. Linus was, too. My guess is Dirk called in a favour from the man himself, got the place to use its "remedial breakthroughs" to draw a confession out of you and then get it all on tape. Believe me: van der Meyde has no scruples whatsoever. He's powerful beyond the law.'

'This is why Dirk organised for me to go to Cacatra and not someplace else?'

'I'd say so.'

Realisation hit. 'How could I have been so stupid?'

'You couldn't have known. It's not your fault.'

'What do I do?' Bibi jumped up, started pacing the room,

wracked with fear. 'I'll never be free of it now, *never*! I've got to confess, I'll go to the cops, it's the only way—'

'It's not.' If Bibi fessed up it would almost certainly mean life imprisonment—if not worse. Stevie could not let it happen. It was too gross an injustice. 'I've got an idea.'

The main door opened and closed.

'Hello?' Xander called out.

After a few seconds he appeared in the doorway, went to kiss Bibi on the cheek with a fond 'This is a nice surprise,' then, on seeing the women's expressions, stopped. 'What's happened?'

Stevie's eyes flicked between the two. Bibi gave a brief nod to acknowledge it was OK.

'Do you want to or shall I?' Stevie asked.

Bibi gestured to the stereo. 'The recording says it all, doesn't it?'

Xander was baffled. 'Can someone tell me what's going on?'

'I've got an admission of my own,' Stevie said gravely, 'and you're not going to like it.'

Her finger hovered over Play.

'We might be accepting our invitation to Reuben van der Meyde's party after all.'

55
Lori

Lori hadn't returned to *Tres Hermanas* in over three years. She barely recognised it.

For starters, it was busy. As she peered through the once-murky windows, expecting to see that half-forgotten palette, as usual deserted, maybe Anita examining her nails over an abandoned counter or Rosa through the back with a cigarette, nothing could have prepared her. It was positively bustling. Two women she didn't know, about her age, seemed to be managing things. The decor was changed, rustic in style, warm and welcoming but with a polish missing in its previous incarnation.

She hadn't been back since the day she'd met JB Moreau.

Lori didn't believe in ghosts, but here she was surrounded.

Out front, gone was the battered *Tres Hermanas* sign. In its place was a modest *Maria's*.

She smiled. For once, remembering her mother, she felt at peace.

At Tony's house, she knocked tentatively. Omar was asleep in his pram and she rocked him, waiting for the discordant song of her stepmother's instructions, or of Anita and Rosa arguing about who should get the door, and when they didn't come she assumed he must be out.

Without warning, it opened.

Her father looked altered, sharper and healthier. The last time they had spoken had been in anger, but as soon as she saw him she knew he felt the same regret.

'Hi, Papa.'

Tony was unable to take his gaze off Omar, who was awake now, blue eyes curious, tiny hands reaching out and grabbing fistfuls of air.

When he didn't speak, Lori gestured inside. 'Can we…?'

'Yes,' he said, standing back. 'Of course you can, of course, of course.'

The house was tidy and organised and calm, all the things her stepfamily wasn't.

'Where's Angélica?' Lori asked, taking a seat at the kitchen table. Everything looked smaller than it had three years ago, as if she had grown.

Tony made them drinks. He was nervous, determined to get things right.

'Angélica isn't here.'

'She isn't?' Lori took Omar from his pram and held him.

'No.' A beat. 'Have you seen *Maria's*?'

'I stopped by on my way. What can I say? It's wonderful.'

'It's thanks to you,' he said, joining her. 'I don't think

Angélica could handle that.' Omar's fat hands reached for his grandpa. 'She never supported your success. She hated it. Especially when things were so different for her own daughters.'

Lori frowned. 'Anita and Rosa don't work there any more?'

Tony sighed. 'There's much to tell, Lori. After you left, they could no longer manage *Tres Hermanas*. And since then...well, Rosa got pregnant by a local boy. She's living in Glassell Park with twins, another on the way. Anita—' his face clouded '—she thought she could follow your footsteps into modelling. She hoped your name would carry her.'

'Did it?'

Tony stroked the child's cheek, mesmerised. 'Did what?'

'Did it carry her?'

Tony pulled away, not wanting to contaminate Omar with his news. 'Anita got in with a bad crowd. The type of work she was doing wasn't good; it wasn't legitimate. She was promised things would change but...' He trailed off. 'This is the last I heard. They refuse to see me now Angélica's gone.'

Lori was surprised. 'Angélica left as well?'

'Actually, I asked her to.'

She experienced a moment, fleeting but all the lovelier for its brevity, of joy.

'We fought,' Tony explained, 'about your pregnancy. I told her your situation after we came back from Spain. I was confused and angry, Lori, but most of all I was worried.' He searched her face. 'This was the sort of thing you needed your mama for, not me, and I didn't know what to do. Angélica said some unforgivable things—things that weren't true and I knew I could never forget. I could not keep her under my roof.'

What her stepmother might have said no longer affected her. 'How did she take it?'

'She begged to stay but I told her no. Because it wasn't only her bitterness, it was the fact *Maria's* was doing so well and she couldn't embrace its success. It made me see that she never understood what was important to me and never wanted to try.'

'Papa, I'm sorry.'

'No. I am sorry.' He met her eyes. In that glimpse he told her more than words ever could. 'I realised something I should have realised a long time ago.'

She looked to Omar. 'Do you want to hold him?'

Tony's face lit up. Lori passed the child into his arms and watched as he gazed down, with total absorption, at Omar's matching inquisitive expression.

She and her father smiled at each other, the wonder of the baby between them. Lori's smile turned into a laugh, and, with it, the lump in her throat ruptured and exploded into beads of relief.

It was late by the time she returned home. Maximo's Lexus was in the drive, alongside another car that she didn't recognise.

'Max?' The hall was in darkness, a lonely glow emanating from the lounge. She parked Omar's pram and scooped him into her arms, following the light.

In the lounge, Maximo was seated with a woman. He stood when Lori came in, as though he'd been caught out, though judging by the woman's countenance it was a formal visit. The woman was dark-haired, her pale knees held together in a crimson pencil skirt.

Shock was pursued by fear.

Rebecca Stuttgart.

The woman who had sent her those filthy notes. Here, in her house.

'What's going on?' Lori demanded.

Rebecca's eyes fell to Omar, affection and desire ripe in her gaze, and all Lori could think was: *She wants my baby. She wants to take my baby.*

'What are you doing here?'

Omar began to cry.

'I must speak with you.' Rebecca got to her feet. Her eyes kept switching back to the baby and Lori held him tight. She remembered JB's regret.

'Rebecca and I tried for years for a child... I'm not able to...'

Her words were out before she had time to check them. 'I want you gone,' she said. 'I don't want you here.'

Maximo intervened, confused by her outburst. 'Darling, aren't you being—?'

'What? A concerned mother? You have no clue what this woman is capable of. I don't want her anywhere near my son.' She backed away, attempting to soothe the infant's cries. 'She's been sending me letters. Despicable, horrible letters.'

Rebecca frowned. 'I have no idea what you're talking about.'

'Don't pretend. I know it was you.'

'What was me?'

'Get out. And don't think about coming back.'

'I'm not going until you hear what I have to say.'

Lori passed the screaming child to Maximo. 'Take him upstairs,' she ordered, he being the lesser of two evils. 'And promise me you won't leave him, even for a second.'

The instant they were gone, Lori turned on the woman. 'Whatever it is, Rebecca, make it quick. And then leave me, and my son, alone.'

Rebecca matched her defiance.

'Lori,' she said simply, 'I know Omar's his.'

'Did you honestly think I wouldn't be able to see it? I've been married to the man for *ten years*—do you think I haven't imagined a thousand times what his child would look like? In such detail that when I saw your boy I knew instantly, without a shadow of doubt, that he was JB's?'

Lori had slept with a married man. For the first time she saw the devastating result, woman to woman, of her selfishness. She sank to the couch in a gesture of surrender. 'I'm sorry for what I did,' she said. 'It was wrong. Believe me, I see that now.'

The apology was final proof, a confession that quashed any shoot of hope Rebecca might yet have had, and it broke her. Her neck fell, the knots of her spine white as sand-blown pebbles.

'You know we can't have our own?' She emitted a short, harsh laugh. 'I told him it was his fault. I told him the problem lay with him, not me. It was a lie. He's perfectly able, as you well know.'

Lori didn't reply. In her mind, gears were starting to shift: slowly, grinding, gaining momentum.

'That's why he has no idea about Omar,' Rebecca continued grimly. 'As far as JB's concerned, it's a physical impossibility.'

The facts began to settle, like mist on a dewy morning. 'You lied to him?'

'I was losing him.' The older woman's voice was snappish, switched on the defence. 'I could feel him slipping away. Come on, Lori, you must know what that's like. It was wicked revenge: I admit it. It felt too unkind that I should be the one struggling. Why should I? So I turned it round on him. One lie after another, mounting and mounting, till I no longer knew how to unpick it.' She looked up. 'He believes Maximo is the child's father, Lori. Why shouldn't he?'

Pieces of the past year slipped over each other, rearranging themselves into a new picture. She blinked.

'But I tried to tell him,' she murmured. 'I tried to get in touch—'

'And I made sure he never heard a damn word.' Rebecca turned to face her adversary. There wasn't a note of regret in her words and Lori wasn't expecting one. 'I instructed my contacts at La Lumière to disregard every missive you attempted.'

'But his cell, what about the messages I left—?'

'Do you really know so little of JB?' Rebecca laughed incredulously. 'You're nobody to him now. He'd have blocked you as soon as he realised.'

It made sense. It made complete sense.

'Is he back?'

'JB's never back. He's always absent, one way or another.'

Lori saw the key. The key was Rebecca: it had been all along. She went to turn it, fingers outstretched, afraid of what she'd find behind the door but knowing she had to look.

'Where has he been?'

JB's wife poured herself a drink. 'On business.'

'What business?'

The liquid vanished down Rebecca's white throat and her next words were soft, a low rasp, so that Lori had to strain to hear.

'You were just a number...'

She leaned forward. 'I'm sorry?'

Rebecca's bloodshot eyes were red-rimmed, their emotion closer to pity than anger.

'You were just a number,' she repeated. 'You were meant to be just a number. One of them, that was all, no different.'

It flashed through Lori's mind. *LA864.*

Rebecca smoothed her skirt and Lori noticed her fingers were shaking. In her head was a rushing sound, like water being poured from a great height.

'I knew about you long before I met you, Lori Garcia.' She nodded, as if to confirm it was still the truth. 'You were perfect. JB had been seeking a Hispanic woman for a long time, the remit was so particular, and then, suddenly, there you were. The first time he saw you, at the harbour with your boyfriend, he knew. Both of them did: he and Reuben van der Meyde.

'Van der Meyde brought his boat there once, to the San Pedro harbour. JB and I were with him. That was it. He saw you and that was it. He knew you were the one. JB chased you down, he had his people find out everything they could and he came back and he told us you were the answer.' Rebecca looked to the floor, unable to meet Lori's stare. 'My husband found out about your poor dead mother, and your father and your stepfamily, and how unhappy you were, and how little money or means you had, and about your boyfriend and his brother and how desperate things had become. All of you, crying out for help. Help the organisation could give.'

Lori's voice cracked. 'The organisation?'

'He became obsessed by you. And, do you know what? I should have seen it coming. So many women, *so many* he'd tracked over the years but you…you were too special to let go. I never incited that passion in him. No one did.

'For a long time he watched over you, under the pretence of making sure you were viable but I knew it was more than that. He wanted to take care of you. He told me you reminded him of a girl he used to know. And the saddest thing? That's one of the only times my husband has ever come close to confiding in me. Oh, I've tried to join the dots. Hasn't everyone? Unhappy childhood, distant parents, accident child, solitary upbringing… Only he couldn't help himself. He got too close.'

'But La Lumière…'

'JB sent Desideria Gomez. He feared for you. He wanted you near, even if it killed him. And it did. In the end, temptation was too hard to resist.'

Lori couldn't get her head around it. 'What are you telling me?'

Rebecca rolled the empty glass between her palms.

'I'm telling you that you were meant to have a child,' she said, 'but not this one. Not Omar.' Her tone was measured. 'You were meant to carry a child for a couple who wanted to pay you for it. They would have paid you a fortune. More money than you have today.'

Lori waited for the punchline but it didn't come. She burst out laughing.

'A Spanish couple,' Rebecca went on, 'one of the enterprise's most exacting to date. Willing to pay the highest rate yet. But no woman was good enough, no woman fitted their specifications… Until you.'

'That's enough.' These were the ramblings of a crazy woman. 'You should leave.'

'*Listen to me!* You were meant to be a surrogate to these people, Lori, *for God's sake*. That's why JB found you. That's why all of this happened!'

Lori grasped the woman's error and clung to it, grappling for any explanation other than the one she was hearing. 'But JB didn't find me,' she countered, fumbling for an alternative, 'Desideria did.'

Rebecca slammed her glass down. 'Aren't you hearing me? JB *sent* Desideria for you. He's been looking after you since day one!'

She was desperate to refute it. Yet Rebecca Stuttgart's story, parts of it, shades of it, rang appallingly true.

'LA864…'

She didn't realise she'd said it aloud, but Rebecca nodded sadly.

'You did end up having a baby for him,' she said softly. A single tear escaped down her cheek. 'Only not in the way he had planned.'

'I have to see him,' Lori mumbled. 'He has to know.'

'Then come back to the island.'

'I can't.'

'You can. I've told you because I can't keep living the lie— not about what's going on on Cacatra and not about your child.' She took a step closer. 'Now, it's your turn. You have to tell him. *You.* At Reuben van der Meyde's party, a month from now.'

Lori's eyes were hollow. She raised them to the other woman's face.

'I need to know the whole story.'

'And you'll get it,' Rebecca said gravely. 'But after this, there's no going back.'

56

Enrique Marquez was smoking: a still, solitary island amid the tumultuous waves of organisers, caterers, planners, managers and assistants, all rushing and darting like wasps to sugar, desperate to be involved and important. Enrique regarded them with ill-concealed loathing.

He'd had to escape the yacht; the atmosphere there made him sick. Morons fawning over what van der Meyde was going to like or not like, what was good enough or not good enough, each and every one of them falling over themselves to please a man who couldn't give a crap, had *never* in his privileged fucking life given a crap, about pleasing other people. Enrique was here for one reason and one reason alone. Revenge.

The sun was setting. Apricot light spilled on to the water as if a great fire burned beneath the surface. Had Enrique not known better, he'd have said this was what heaven looked like.

A trio of sharp-suited caterers were loading crates on to the boat, pursued by a big, moustachioed bald guy, head of the company organising tonight's event.

'Are you gonna put that out, or do I have to make you?'

Enrique dragged deeply. 'A man's allowed a smoke—it's a free country.'

'You're in van der Meyde's country now, son. Put it out.'

He extinguished it on the web of skin between first finger and thumb.

Disgusted, the man pushed past. 'I'll be watching you like a hawk tonight, Romero.' It was the name he'd given the agency.

Enrique grinned. Sure. Let the whole world watch and they'd still be facing the wrong way. Where they ought to be looking was right beneath their feet, to the blinking device he'd fixed earlier in the lower deck. The detonator clipped to the inside of his shirt. One button, one contact, one second was all it took. He closed his eyes and pictured it now, the small black box awaiting his instruction, time running down like sand through a glass.

Shouldn't he be on that boat?

From the top of the van der Meyde mansion, Margaret Jensen shivered in her plum-coloured evening gown. She glared down at the beach and wrung her hands. Enrique Marquez was a risk—and he had to be, for who planned to execute a stunt as ambitious, as grisly, as this, if they weren't prepared to lay it all on the line?

'Can we go see Daddy now?'

Ralph was in the doorway, dressed in a tux and with a toy boat dangling from one arm.

'In a minute, darling. Your father's busy.'

'He's always busy.'

Margaret crouched, holding him close and inhaling his soapy smell and the softness of his hair. Her son. Beloved.

'I know,' she told him. 'But this is a special night for him. Tomorrow, everything's going to be different. Just you wait and see.'

Through the open doors of the van der Meyde mansion, Rebecca Stuttgart could hear the bustle and flurry of preparations down below. In less than an hour, four hundred VIP guests would be shown on to the most opulent yacht the world had ever seen.

She and JB were awaiting Reuben's emergence in the mansion's lobby.

As she watched her husband, his hands in his suit pockets, his blue gaze cool on the marble floor, she braced herself.

I'm one of them, Lori had warned: for who else could have sent the message?

The truth comes out.

The girl was braver than Rebecca had given her credit for. She wasn't content with bringing JB the truth about her son... Now she wanted to blow the lid on Cacatra.

Rebecca should have been immobilised with fear. It had been her disclosure, after all.

Only tomorrow, she knew, she'd be long gone. Her destination was set, her new beginning planned. Her husband and his fury, the island and its secret—come the morning, they'd be distant memories, carried on the wind.

* * *

'You look amazing.'

Maximo Diaz looped his arms around Lori's waist and kissed her on the lips.

She could not stand his touch. 'Don't.'

He raised her hand and kissed her fingers instead. His eyes were framed by soft lashes and his skin was porcelain. She thought of him growing up in his European castle, Gothic spires buried deep in a pit of ferns, and imagined herself to be trapped there, chained to an underground wall, hearing his vampire tread and the long, lonely cries as he consumed his women, knowing he would live on and on with no end to her suffering, locked in till the end of time.

'You know the pretend thing turns me on,' he said. 'Sometimes I can't help myself.'

Lori removed herself under the pretext of adjusting her dress, a simple, elegant fishtail silhouette in blazing ochre. Her dark hair was loose, tumbling in jet waves.

They departed their accommodation shortly before six. She had already seen some faces she recognised. Jax Jackson, the Olympic idol, months from London 2012. Stevie Speller and Xander Jakobson. Aurora Nash, the contact of JB's she had met once and hadn't liked. Brock Wilde and Fiona Catalan, Hollywood power agents. Clusters of faintly familiar British celebrities, royalty or politicians or both. All had one thing in common. They weren't him.

'Come on, Lori,' said Maximo as she resisted taking his hand, 'aren't we meant to be a couple in love?'

'I'll never love you.'

'Sure you will.' His top lip curled. 'You'll learn. And if you don't, I'll teach you.'

* * *

JB Moreau was calm. Unlike Reuben, he had all his life possessed a capacity for peace, and the more the world around him trembled with fear or unease, the quieter his centre became, like the silent funnel at the heart of a tornado.

He did not want to see Lori Garcia. He did not want to witness her beauty and be forced to turn away. He did not want to watch her on the arm of another man. Yet sometimes life had a way of imposing the unwanted, and in doing so it revealed a new objective.

Despite the hurt she had caused him, despite everything, he could not allow Maximo Diaz to go unanswered. JB knew what he had done to her. He saw the unhappiness in her eyes.

Maximo might be father to her child, but he wasn't and never would be a lover of women. He was a manipulator, a bully. And he had chosen to fight the wrong battle.

JB knew what he had to do. The man hadn't known over whose threshold he stepped.

Reuben van der Meyde descended the staircase. His son raced past, arms stretched wide like the wings of an aeroplane with accompanying sound effects, the housekeeper in close pursuit.

'Get that boy under control!' he boomed at Miss Jensen, who nodded meekly and grabbed hold of the child's elbow. She muttered something as they melted into the kitchen quarters. He thought he heard the kid snivelling.

Reuben didn't have time for this. He needed to get his head down and concentrate on reaching the morning without any major hiccups.

Distilling what was at risk to *a major hiccup* was laughable.

'Drink?'

JB was in the lobby with his wife. The Frenchman held out a glass of thick liquid.

Reuben nodded. He downed the poison in one. 'Let's do this.'

Stevie and Xander's Jeep approached the beach, slipping into the procession of waiting glitterati snaking its way towards the giant vessel. A navy-blue and shimmering-gold VDM emblem crowned the magnificent yacht. Tiny bulbs were strewn along its enormous flanks and across the bow, beginning to glow with the fading light. Uniformed staff, tiny from this distance, moved across the decks like blood rushing through a vast, complex organism.

Xander took her hand. 'How are you feeling?'

Stevie gazed straight ahead, cool and collected in her dove-grey Elie Saab pantsuit.

'Focused,' she replied. 'We're here for a reason, and that reason is B.'

He nodded. 'I don't know how far we'll have to take it. The things we know…'

'As far as we have to.' The decision was made. 'The truth sets Bibi free.'

Preparation was everything, and Aurora Nash was leaving nothing to chance.

Concealing the seven-inch hunting knife in the band of her knickers, pointing it down in the way Billy-Bob Hocker had taught her one summer on Tom's ranch, she dropped the silver floor-length gown over her head. It rippled down the length of her body. At the ruched waist she had slivered an opening, concise as a paper cut.

She swallowed back the sickness that had been plaguing her for years.

Was murder all it was cracked up to be?

Was there really such a difference, was there *really*, when it came to that moment of action, that instant of do or die, between sinking a knife into meat and killing a man?

Feelings, she supposed. Compassion. Empathy.

She had neither of those for Reuben van der Meyde.

Arnaud Devereux hadn't taken much persuading. His conscience had buckled a long time ago. By the time Aurora had arrived in Paris, it was as if he had wanted to tell her. As if he had wanted to give her van der Meyde's private details. As if with confession came catharsis, and, perhaps, forgiveness for the part he had played.

I'm one of them. Tomorrow the truth comes out.

Sending the message had been easy. Aurora wasn't afraid. She knew she was taking on a giant, that a nineteen-year-old girl was no match for a man in Reuben's position— and it didn't make the damnedest bit of difference. She had an army behind her, even if they didn't know it. All the kids like her, the ones who had their suspicions but whose suspicions were too shadowy to pinpoint, the ones who had always sensed something was wrong but couldn't be sure what, the ones who didn't know and maybe never would. Tonight she was leading them all into battle.

Crossing to her waiting car, the salty breeze whipping her white-blonde hair and the sun dipping to the ocean like a final farewell, Aurora touched the reassuring contours of the weapon. She hoped that in the last twenty-four hours she had given Reuben van der Meyde a taste of the uncertainty that had hounded her for nineteen years.

Arnaud hadn't known who her real parents were. One man definitely did. Once she had taken the information she needed, she was going to make him pay with his life.

No punishment she could inflict on Reuben would ever equal his crime.

But Aurora had always been willing to try.

BOOK FIVE
Departure

57

Reuben felt better the instant he set foot on his 400-foot-long triumph. Like a castle, his defence, it was a rock-solid reminder of his supreme wealth and influence.

And it looked bloody impressive.

'I gotta say—' a grinning TV exec, first on the boat, clapped him on the back '—she's a beautiful thing.'

'Ain't she?'

'You're a lucky man, van der Meyde.'

'Sixty years of luck.'

'And sixty more, I don't doubt.'

Guests continued to arrive, seeping on to the vessel like contagion. Reuben focused on showing them the great man they were expecting: cool, calm and unflustered, the entrepreneur who had made billions and eclipsed them all for money and power ten times over.

It was a novelty, for one night only, for these VIPs to be made to feel inferior. He had realised some time ago that they embraced it.

* * *

Obscene in its adornments, the grand saloon was a lofty half-oval space, strung with lights and filled with the tinkle of polite discourse. A marriage of classic romanticism and contemporary design, it combined gleaming wood panels, a traditional fireplace, an old ship's clock on a conventional mantelpiece—nods to the intrepid ventures of Columbus and da Gama, notions of discovery and breakthrough—and charcoal parquet, aluminium porthole windows, a spotlit canopy and current, clean furnishings, which brought the van der Meyde vessel to the cutting-edge of modern interiors. It was a clever mix, a fusion of past and present, and typified everything Reuben imagined himself to be: integral to history and at the same time making it.

Stevie was sickened when she considered what had paid for it.

Lori Garcia was at her side. The supermodel was full of sweet conversation, innocent of the place and its evils.

'I loved *Goodbye, Vegas*,' she was saying. 'Was that your first project with Xander?'

'It was how we met.'

'I saw you there at the Frontline Fashion night. Before things took off for me,' she prompted. 'You might not remember.'

Stevie smiled. 'Of course I remember.'

Maximo Diaz joined them as the yacht eased from its station with a gentle tug. Severed from the shore, Stevie felt the menace of their floating island, a capsule, adrift, the clink of crystal and merry voices concealing a reality that was treacherous as the ocean beneath.

'Let's hope it's smooth sailing,' he said cheerfully.

'Let's hope,' she replied.

* * *

Aurora disliked the feel of Reuben van der Meyde's sweaty palm in hers. She had disliked it when she had first been on Cacatra, but she disliked it more now.

'Champagne,' he commanded.

A dark-haired Hispanic waiter, dressed in white and oddly familiar—perhaps he'd modelled—materialised. Reuben thrust the flute of Rémy into Aurora's hand.

She enjoyed watching him struggle, no doubt surprised she had put in an appearance in the aftermath of Sherilyn's death, and felt like she had when she was seven and playing Squash the Bug with Farrah by the pool. Reuben was the beetle, fat on its back, lolling on a broken shell.

Revoltingly, he touched her arm. 'We were sad about your mother,' he wheedled. 'Sherilyn was a wonderful woman.'

The champagne tasted like acid.

'Thank you.' She had to force any scrap of gratitude from her mouth. With a tight smile, all she could muster, she adjusted her stance, feeling the handle of the knife press against her skin. Security had been rigorous, but not for her. What danger could a teenage girl pose?

If only he knew.

'Happy birthday,' she told him, raising her glass.

Reuben raised his in return. 'It's gonna go with a bang.'

Enrique Marquez passed the gleaming baby grand piano, a tray of golden flutes high on his shoulder. Guests swarmed, plucking drinks blindly and without thanks, their rich, powdered faces scouting out others of their kind with practised ease, never once deigning to glance his way. Little did they know he had all their lives, each and every dirty-rich one, in the palm of his hand. Given a sniff of his intentions, they would be down on their knees and begging for mercy.

It was a glorious thought. Enrique remembered the device, buried in the engine room, and imagined for a thousandth time the instant before detonation. It was too quick... He wished it could last longer so he could savour it more.

He presented champagne to a cluster of women dripping in diamonds. Just one of those rocks would have been enough to feed his poor dead mother for a year.

Several times, he caught a flash of her hair—maybe, once, the shimmer of her gold-black eyes. He had to keep his distance. Though he looked different now, he could not risk her recognising him. It wasn't hard to defy temptation. After all, she had taught him well.

Lori.

He glimpsed the bronze of her skin not ten feet away, the curve of her shoulder, the body he had been denied. As her male companion slid a possessive arm round her waist, Enrique's resolve hardened, as cold and absolute as stone.

Lori abided Maximo's touch because as far as the rest of the world was concerned, they were together. They had a child. They were passionately in love.

'How's your son?' enquired Stevie. 'He's gorgeous, such blue eyes.'

Lori's smile faltered. 'He's an angel,' she replied. Out of the saloon's wraparound windows she could see the retreating line of golden sand and the contours of the island they were leaving behind. 'Do you and Xander want to have kids?'

Stevie was cut short by the appearance of her husband at her side.

'Lori, Maximo, have you met Xander Jakobson?'

'A pleasure.' Xander extended his hand and Maximo shook it enthusiastically.

'I was just telling Stevie how much I enjoyed your joint venture,' Lori told him.

'It was certainly the start of something special,' he said. Stevie kissed his cheek.

Lori wished life were as simple for her. Love, marriage, a family. Stevie and Xander were so happy. How had she herself wound up embroiled in this web of unthinkable deceit?

Her gaze travelled fleetingly across the room, searching but not finding: blind to every face but the man's who could save her.

On the shores of Cacatra, Margaret Jensen watched as the gargantuan yacht peeled silently off into the wide, blue ocean. Her brief commission to present her son at Mr V's side was over.

She turned back to the house. Despite the balmy warmth of the evening, she shivered.

'Are you cold?' Ralph lifted his face to her, cute as a button in his custom-made suit.

'No, darling,' she lied. 'Come on, let's get you inside.'

Ralph clambered ahead up the white stone steps. Margaret hung back, glancing across the water at the doomed boat as it set sail on its final, gruesome voyage.

Damn Reuben!

If he hadn't been such a selfish, neglectful user, she would never have had to resort to such desperate methods.

To have a son who knew her only as a housekeeper, a whole life hidden from the public eye because she wasn't good enough for Mr V's billions of dollars and with that kind of money he could—and did—buy anyone he wanted.

She had been left with no choice. Mr V deserved to die. *And those people...*

She gulped. Those people were the reason he did what he did. They were just as corrupt, taking advantage of young women the world over. Judgement Day had been a long time coming.

Margaret entered the ghostly hall, like the house of someone who died. Ralph was shouting for her to join him upstairs, where he wanted to watch the boat from the roof because he could see it better from there.

Xander knew he was drinking too fast. Being in proximity to JB Moreau had the familiar effect. He was running hot and cold, his heart skipping. Would JB be pleased he had come? Would he greet him like an old friend? After all it had been Xander's decision to keep his distance. JB wasn't good for him. JB wasn't good for anyone.

He pretended to be interested as Maximo Diaz blathered on.

'I'd love to collaborate,' Maximo plugged. 'How about working something out?'

Xander knew how it went. He slugged back the last of his glass.

'I'll have my people call your people.'

Always better that way around.

Whoever had failed to update the guest list would be fired unceremoniously at dawn. Reuben had assumed that *none* of the Nash family would be present and that suited him just fine. So why had no one informed him Aurora Nash was coming?

I'm one of them.

The message haunted him. Through the smiles and laughter and autopilot salutations, Reuben was sweating like a twelve-year-old in a brothel.

If Aurora had written it, he knew his very worst fears were confirmed.

A senator's wife air-kissed him on both cheeks. He grimaced through it.

Someone must have informed her. It was the only explanation.

As soon as Reuben found out who that was, he swore it would be murder.

Enrique Marquez deposited his tray in the galley and waited stoically while the chefs, frantically moving and yelling at one another to keep up, loaded the platters. Steam and sweat obscured their faces. Their pace was astounding and Enrique mused on the sheer futility of what he was witnessing. In less than three hours, these people would all be dead. The painstakingly prepared food would be blown to trillions of pieces, the lobster sundae and squid-ink nests returned to the depths from which they'd come. Nothing left. Carnage.

The canapés were arriving, teeny-tiny creations that had taken hours to craft but would vanish in a greedy half-second down the gullets of the wealthy and privileged. Enrique was presented with a board of smoked salmon, each paper-thin sliver arranged like a rose with a nub of slick caviar at its centre. Lifting it, he departed the bustle of the kitchen and made his way back up the narrow staircase and into the saloon.

Lori was nowhere. Enrique cursed himself for daring to look. Supposing she saw him? He had to stay low or it was game over. Fixing his eyes to the floor, he focused his mind.

The plan was perfect.

He knew this kind of vessel like the back of his hand. Van der Meyde's yacht boasted six dinghies attached to its stern, each lowered to the water via a system of pulleys. At midnight, while van der Meyde received his gift in front of the crowd—a two-hundred-year-old bottle of brandy ship-wrecked on its way to a king, today the most expensive drink in the world—Enrique would slip to the rear, where he'd descend the aft platform. There, he would board one of the boats, drop to the churning swell and, under thirty minutes later, as he approached the shore…

Click.

Boom.

Even if his escape were witnessed, it would be too late for them to do anything about it. *Carnage. Perfection.*

The two things weren't so different, after all.

58

The girl in the cake was predictable. Reuben grinned through it: she was pretty enough, young, eager to please and entirely fuckable, but his attention was elsewhere.

'Happy birthday to you,' she sang husky-Marilyn-style, dressed in a corseted playsuit, the nipped-in waist an extreme contrast to the generous spill of near-escaping cleavage. These days they called it Burlesque. As far as Reuben was concerned, a stripper was a stripper.

She concluded by sending him a kiss. On an ordinary night he'd have her waiting in his cabin for their journey back to shore: a quick blow job between engagements.

People were clapping him on the back and congratulating him, glasses raised and toasted as the night moved into gear and celebrations formally kicked off. Reuben charmed his way across the saloon and towards the stage, mingling with ease as he introduced unfamiliar faces and reacquainted old ones. The consummate host was both a king and a man of the people.

Once the welcome was done, he'd find Aurora. And when he found her, he could end it.

So where was she?

Stevie was sickened by the show. It was the twenty-first century and yet performances like this still got put on. Reuben van der Meyde had smirked lecherously for the duration, crocodile eyes raking the woman's body. Stevie sensed the dancer would likely drop her knickers soon as the birthday boy decided on an added perk. That's what wealth could achieve. When had the world become such a sinister playground?

Dirk Michaels appeared in her vision. He was at the opposite end of the saloon, standing next to his miserable-looking wife and chewing enthusiastically with his mouth open. Stevie deposited her glass on a passing tray and moved off.

'Wait.' Xander stopped her. 'What are you doing?'

A couple in front shot them a look to be quiet. Reuben had taken to the mic, was tapping it for sound as he prepared to welcome the assembly on board.

'…to see so many of you here,' he began, 'so many faces from over the years…'

Stevie's voice was barely a whisper. 'The sooner this is over,' she told her husband, 'the sooner we can leave.'

'We're on a boat,' Xander reminded her. 'We can't just *leave.*'

'Don't be facetious. You know what I mean.'

The woman turned again. *'Shh!'*

'I'm speaking to Moreau first.'

'Why? There's no point.'

But Xander held on to her tightly. Maybe he was right.

She had to be patient. They weren't here to start a revolution; they were here to help Bibi.

Reuben was perspiring in his suit. 'When I acquired Cacatra,' he was saying, 'I had no idea how important it would become. Not only to me but to everyone here...'

I'll bet, Stevie thought bitterly.

'Tonight is as much about the island we love as it is about me...'

'Fine,' she muttered to her husband. 'But when this is over, you're tracking him down.'

Lori visited the bathroom on the upper deck. It was quiet, just a few straggling guests returning from a brief exploration, disappointed to have missed Reuben's address.

The bathroom was decked in gold and mahogany. Mood music piped through invisible speakers and classic leather armchairs adorned the marble floor.

Lori met her reflection. She wondered how many women had stared themselves down in these waters. How many hopeful mothers had visited Cacatra and heard of van der Meyde's solution and looked so deep into themselves and their conscience that it hurt.

JB's involvement was atrocious. How could he consent to such a thing? The treachery, the dishonesty, the brutal deceit... And yet it accounted for so much. For how he had come for her that day, for how he had seemed to know her in a way no one else did, for how he'd been forced to retreat when she'd arrived at La Lumière. And once Lori had overcome the impact of Rebecca Stuttgart's revelation, it became clear that this was Reuben's business and his alone. Involvement was not the same as initiation. It made sense that JB would seek refuge with the man who had been his parents' ally. Could she punish him for that?

When JB had stepped into *Tres Hermanas* all those moons ago he *had* been there to save her—and not just from Diego Marquez. Women sourced were paid and protected for life. If JB had approached her with the offer, helping immeasurably her father, Rico and, yes, herself, could she honestly promise that, hand on heart, she would have refused?

He became obsessed by you, Rebecca had said. *You were too special to let go.*

It clouded Lori's mind, intoxicating her with sweet promise.

She thought of Omar and his beautiful blue eyes.

The family they could be.

Aurora drank in the fresh air like a desert wanderer stumbling across water. The sheltered aft deck was host to a handful of guests, smoke from their cigarettes snatched by the breeze as they talked animatedly beneath heat-lamps. She made her way up to the bow. It was empty.

The sun was slipping away. A canopy of tentative stars winked overhead.

Aurora leaned on the bow, one foot on the bottom tread. One move would be all it took, just one, a leap of faith. What would it feel like? Cold and salty and going down for miles. She pictured the endless fathoms, the mammoth great white sharks that prowled these waters.

Cacatra was far behind them now. Amid open sky and open sea, halved by the horizon, the earth revealed its curvature.

Down in the cabin, Reuben had finished speaking. She

had not felt able to be part of his audience, grovelling over his phony magnificence. It was the last audience van der Meyde would ever have, the last speech he would ever make. He had entered the last hour of his life and he hadn't got a clue. For once, the man who knew everything knew nothing.

Aurora set her jaw. She stared ahead, the power of the vessel in line with her intentions, driving her forward and confirming her fate.

She fingered the knife, adjusted its position so the tough handle was ready to grasp.

Like killing a deer, a clean quick slice to the throat.

Almost too easy. Almost unfair. He would not have a chance to beg for his life.

Lori exited the bathroom and ran straight into Maximo Diaz.

'I've been looking for you.'

She backed against the wall, fending him off. Every time he came close she was swamped by dread.

'We should go back,' she said tightly.

'Should we?' Maximo attempted to kiss her but she dodged his lips. 'Relax, Lori, it's a beautiful night... We'll be married soon...'

A fashion editor in L'Wren Scott passed, smiled awkwardly and disappeared into the restroom. Lori managed to dilute her look of reluctance before it was noted. Maximo ran a thumb across her chin. 'I *am* going to ask you, you know.'

'You wouldn't dare.'

'It's what everybody wants.'

'Except me.'

'Hey,' he teased menacingly, 'I know you don't like to rush things, Lori. I mean, you walk out of my life one day and ask me to be a father to your child the next…'

'Keep your voice down, please.'

'There's no one here.'

'We've talked this through a thousand times. You said you understood—'

'I know, I know.' He held his hands up like he'd only been kidding, but Lori was noticing he referred to the pact more and more. It was as if the longer she held out on Maximo physically, the greater risks he was prepared to take with their discretion.

The beauty editor re-emerged and he took the opportunity to kiss Lori full on the lips, knowing she wouldn't be able to pull away. She let him, even tolerated his tongue in her mouth. When she was sure the woman had gone she shoved him off.

'You're making a mockery of me.'

'No more than you of me.'

And with those words Lori knew she had signed her life away for ever to Maximo Diaz.

He insisted on holding her hand. As they passed down the corridor, Lori felt compelled to turn back. Someone had been watching them; she had sensed it at her neck.

The figure disappeared out of sight, so quick she could have been mistaken. It was a man, hidden in shadow: just a movement, there and then vanished, like the dark wings of a bird.

As far as the patrol on the island was concerned, Juan Romero, aka Enrique Marquez, had never boarded Reuben van der Meyde's boat in the first place.

As Enrique stepped into the lower deck quarters for a smoke, he reflected on what an easy gig Margaret Jensen was getting. All the old lady had to do was stick to a story.

'Three minutes, Romero.' His supervisor collared him on the way past.

With a smirk, Enrique blew out smoke. He'd been playing truant all day, taking breaks without permission, making eyes at the women and giving attitude to the men, anything that gave trouble to the organisers. Later, when he appeared bleary-eyed amid claims he'd fallen asleep on the job, they'd decide it was little wonder he had missed his cue when finally the yacht departed.

Grinding out the cigarette, he made his way back inside. In the galley, signature cocktails were being prepared in sparkling V-shaped glasses. The V formed part of a VDM silver stirrer, on top of which was a *60* made of edible jewels.

In reality, Enrique would have worked his ass off like never before to get to dry land. His part required both mental and physical vigour. First, the disposal of evidence: the detonator tossed over the escape boat, the airplug released on the dinghy, his own clothes stripped off and flung wide so they looked like debris thrown from the wreck. Then the final, critical push. He would imagine the gathered panic on the beach as, on the distant horizon, the world's glitterati perished in pieces on a bomb-wrecked ocean. Margaret Jensen would come rushing, the child's hand in hers, feigning shock, screaming and crying like the rest.

Under cover of darkness, Enrique wouldn't be heading to the northern shore. Instead he would swim east, towards the dry, duplicate uniform Margaret had left for him.

It was almost a pity there would be no one to congratulate him on his genius.

Enrique barely noticed as his serving trays were loaded and he turned to re-enter the fray.

JB Moreau passed him on the stairwell. Enrique had to flatten himself against the wall to stop being knocked into. Invisible to the end.

59

Lance Chlomsky was terrified of slipping up. A fortnight's intensive training might have prepared him for the physical work, but being around all these famous people and not tripping or spilling or making an ass of himself? Forget it.

Tonight was a chance to make something of his life. Six months in a correctional facility for bringing an armed weapon into school…well, his mom had told him then that his future was as good as over. *How could you be so stupid, boy?* But he'd only done it because the other kids told him to. They'd said he could be in their gang if he passed the initiation and Lance had never had any friends. He was lanky, scrawny, with a face full of red spots: a loner and a loser.

One night working for Reuben van der Meyde was his big break. It had been a lottery, too many underprivileged kids to pick from, but for once Lance had been lucky.

He put forward his tray and watched as it was filled. Tiger prawns, swordfish and calamari; fish roe, scallops and lobster.

JB Moreau himself was in the galley. Lance felt the stickiness on his brow, the way he'd felt at school when the big boys ganged up on him.

The Frenchman surveyed the space with sharp, appraising eyes that eventually settled on Lance. The kid looked away, embarrassed.

Moments later he heard a voice, an accent, close to his ear.

'You're going to do me a favour,' it said. 'You're going to listen carefully to these instructions, and then you're going to execute them. Do you understand?'

Stevie needed air. She pushed open the doors to the rear deck and emerged straight into the satisfied regard of Dirk Michaels.

It was cold now, almost totally dark. They were alone.

'I was hoping you'd come,' he growled, a wedge of tobacco between his fleshy lips.

'Lay off Bibi Reiner,' she told him. 'I don't want a fuss; I don't want a scene. And trust me, neither do you.'

He chuckled, a horrid, humourless sound. 'Trust you? That's funny. Seems like you know exactly what the broad's been up to.'

'I know what you and Linus did to her.'

'I admit nothing.'

'Really? I'd have thought it was in your nature to brag about it.'

Dirk leaned in so she could smell his breath. 'The whore deserved everything she got. She loved every second, was begging us for more.'

'You and Linus abused her. You made her suffer.'

'And?'

'You made her life hell and you know it,' Stevie spat. 'Linus tricked her into starring in those movies, then you and he imagined it gave you rights to assault her.'

'She's still alive, ain't she?'

'You would have ended up killing her. If she hadn't killed herself first.'

Dirk eyeballed her. 'I'd watch what you say. There're plenty people here who'd be *very* interested to know what happened the night Linus died. So much for a heartbroken widow! The bitch is a *killer.*'

'You blackmailed her.' Stevie stood her ground. 'Here, on Cacatra. Van der Meyde allowed it to happen. We know everything, Dirk.'

'That's an interesting theory.'

'Don't fuck with me.'

He grinned, enjoying himself. 'Far as I can tell, there's only one way out of this.'

She shot him daggers. 'And I'm not going to like it.'

'Ever since he saw you in New York, he wanted you both. Bibi was only ever half his vision. It was the package he craved.'

'Linus was sick,' Stevie told him. 'And so are you.'

Dirk moved closer. Above, the stars froze like spectators at a death match. 'We're businessmen,' he said. 'We're commercially minded. You know he wanted you as well. I made it clear to the mourning widow when we were last in touch. She stays involved in my...projects—' he shrugged as if it were simple '—and she promises to bring you in, too. There, you have my word. The recording is destroyed.'

'Fuck you.'

'What option do you have?'

'I've got dirt on this place you're too thick to even guess at.'

He smirked. 'I'm sure.'

'You'd better be. Don't make me use it, Dirk, because I don't want to. It affects too many people, innocent people I don't want to bring into it. You might think you're tight with van der Meyde but you're not in on the half of it.'

'I'm giving you an opportunity.' He ignored her words, heard them for diversion. 'I'd take it, if I were you.'

'Thank God you're not.'

'Then be prepared to face the consequences.'

Stevie slid open the door. 'Likewise.'

'It's awful, isn't it? To lose your husband so soon.' Christina Michaels lowered her voice. 'And under *those* circumstances... Bibi Reiner must still be in pieces!'

It was a relief to Xander that Christina appeared to know nothing of her husband's ploy, though not a surprise. Dirk would hardly want to advertise his extramarital curriculum.

'I suppose she's destined for the trash heap,' Christina mused, with a shade of glee. 'Imagine that! Burned out and washed up in Hollywood before she's even begun.'

Xander spotted JB Moreau entering the saloon. He had known this man long enough and well enough to be sure when JB had things on his mind. It was in the way he stood.

Summoning his courage, Xander made his excuses and threaded through the throng. JB possessed radar for incoming challenges, and his eyes landed on Xander's in accordance.

'We need a word, Moreau,' he said when he came close. 'In private.'

* * *

Aurora travelled to the lower deck and through a wood-panelled corridor. It wasn't anything special and she decided it led to the crew's quarters. Beyond, through a glass partition, the lavish guests' accommodation opened out.

Handmade wallpaper, intricate in design, adorned her route. She pushed one of the cabin doors and was surprised when it opened. Inside, a white-silk four-poster bed sat amid ornate bamboo furniture, at the foot of which was a retractable plasma-screen TV. Two gold-framed portholes looked out to night. She stood at one, unable to see through impenetrable darkness.

Aurora lowered herself on to the bed. It was deathly quiet.

She caught her image in the porthole and glimpsed her mother—the woman she had believed to be her mother—before her own, tortured reflection replaced it.

Feeding a hand into her dress, she grabbed the blade and extracted it. It was long and glinting, the grip made of bone.

Aurora pressed the point of it into her fingertip until the soft pad flowered with blood.

Then the tears came, at first because it hurt and then because it seized a deeper ache, one she could bleed out for years and years but never be rid of, and once she started, her head in her hands, she found she was unable to stop.

Lori noticed the kid. He was short and scrawny with a mean-set jaw and a rash of toxic pimples. He'd been hanging around her and Maximo for ages, as if he wasn't interested in attending to any of the other guests, and it was starting to make her uncomfortable.

She knew why van der Meyde had hired staff from an unconventional source. It was acknowledgement that he, too, had come from nothing and that chances in life were few.

Or was it guilt?

Did a man like van der Meyde have a conscience?

Certainly the move had been publicised enough: Reuben was shrewd to the last. But this kid was like a bad omen. Each time she steered Maximo away, he followed.

Memories of the hate mail swamped over her. What if that person was here tonight?

What if he was watching her now?

Lance Chlomsky could not stop staring at Maximo Diaz. The actor reminded him that he had been dealt one of life's great injustices: ugliness. Since his boyhood, Lance had never understood why some people got it all: the face, the body, the height, and how, as if that weren't enough, those very things fed into life's twin triumphs—girls and money. While others, like him, spent their lives squeezing pustules in the mirror and pleasuring themselves by their own hand, the accompanying lack of confidence and self-esteem meaning they would for ever be that way.

Maximo alongside Lori Garcia—they had to be Hollywood's best-looking couple. With dead certainty, Lance knew he would never, not in a million years, know what it felt like to love a woman like that.

It was impossible to take his eyes off them, but all the same it hurt, like trying to look at the sun and catching it only in brief, dazzling bursts.

'Is everything OK?' Lori appeared at Stevie's side.

'I'm looking for Xander,' she said, scanning the saloon for her husband. She thought she spotted his dark head moving among the sea of bodies but was mistaken. 'Have you seen him?'

'Not since earlier.'

Stevie crossed the cabin and followed a winding spiral to the upper level. A couple were embracing where the stairs ended and pulled apart self-consciously. Quickly she dipped into the smaller salon and checked the upstairs bar. Nothing.

As a last refuge she travelled to the lower deck, making her way through the guest quarters, marvelling at and repelled by her surroundings. No wonder van der Meyde wanted this part open. He was a show-off and this was about as impressive as you could get.

She was about to turn back when she heard, faintly, the sound of someone crying.

It was a woman. Stevie halted, sharpened her hearing. A girl. The person was young.

Following the sound, trying to trace it, she pressed her ear against each cabin door in turn. The acoustics, all those pockets of space, played tricks, like chasing a feather on the wind.

Eventually, she came to it. Curious, she knocked. The crying stopped and she listened for a response. When none came, she pushed open the door.

At first she didn't recognise the figure. The white-blonde hair was dishevelled, the dress crumpled and torn and a thin line of blood ran from the girl's hand and trickled down her wrist.

But the instant she looked up, frantic and bleary-eyed, Stevie knew who it was.

'Aurora,' she exclaimed. 'What's happened?'

60

Margaret picked a path through the dark. The ground was prickly, her shoes impractical. She kept off the lit trails, for people were fickle in their memories. When they were questioned later tomorrow, next week, they would be desperate to find a detail they could cling to.

Fortunately Margaret knew this island better than anyone.

The weight of material was reassuring under her arm: Enrique Marquez's replacement uniform. Now she understood how men like van der Meyde and Moreau could become addicted to wielding power. She'd had access to everything that made tonight's stunt possible, from the schedules to what the staff were wearing. Mr V underestimated her. He always had.

At last the east shoreline came into view. Waves crashed in, white froth pummelling the rocks. She hoped Enrique had been right when he'd said he was a strong swimmer.

Wedging the uniform in its designated place, Margaret inhaled the night air. Calm.

She turned and headed back to the mansion, humming softly to herself.

The library was like something from the valiant ships of old. Battered, bruised books and maps crowded the walls. A giant compass, suspended above an arc of glass, pointed out to sea. An impressive antique globe sat alongside a gently flickering fireplace. A clock ticked delicately, matching Xander's heart, two beats to every second.

JB stood facing out of the window. He held his hands behind his back.

'You must do something,' said Xander. 'You owe me that much.'

The other man neither moved nor spoke. It struck Xander that JB might, in another life, have been the captain of such a ship. Always he'd had that way about him: timeless, his waters unperturbed by the passing sands of ages.

'Reuben fights his own wars,' he said. 'I cannot help you.'

Xander had laid it all on the line: Bibi's abuse, Linus's murder, the subsequent threats. 'You must,' he said. 'It's not too late to put things right.'

JB laughed softly. He turned round. 'Things?'

'You know what I mean.'

'I'm afraid I don't. You'll have to explain.'

Xander slammed his fist on the table between them. 'Don't fuck with me, JB. Have Reuben rein Dirk in and do it now, or I swear to God I'll tell the world what I know.'

'About Cacatra? Go ahead. I'm sure they'd be happy to hear about your involvement.'

'It's not the same.'

'No? You made a great deal of money from it, as I recall.'

'And every cent of that's gone to charity.'

'You always were a paragon of virtue.'

'Compared with you, I'm not about to argue.' Xander pulled his trump card with a flourish. 'Let's cut to the chase, JB. This isn't about Cacatra. It's about you and me. It's about what happened the last time we were at sea.' There was a loaded pause. 'If you want to take this up to the wire, believe me, I'm right there with you.'

Maximo Diaz put down his glass and struggled to find his feet. Was he seasick?

'What's the matter?'

Lori's face was blurry in his vision. 'Nothing,' he managed thickly, thinking he'd never been seasick before, 'I'm fine.'

He felt weak. His stomach was in knots like he had to do a crap.

'I need to lie down.' He swayed, biting back nausea. 'Now.'

'Max—'

Abruptly the floor rose up to meet him. The last things he saw were the flinty eyes of that kid who'd been trailing them all night. The last thing he heard was smashing, shattering glass.

'We'll get him to the guest beds.' Rebecca Stuttgart kept her voice down as she and Lori shouldered Maximo between them. A handful of guests turned to observe the minor disruption.

'I'm OK, I'm OK.' Maximo was slurring. A trail of drool seeped out the side of his mouth and spooled to the floor.

Lori glanced up. She looked once, then again. A classic double take.

It couldn't be.

There, across the saloon, plain as day, she could have sworn she saw...

She would know those dark eyes anywhere, even after all this time.

Rico Marquez.

Reuben checked the situation with security. Lori Garcia's boyfriend, a model-slash-actor he'd scarcely heard of, had taken on too much drink. They had medics on board but he was loath to use them for bums. What were they at, a school disco?

'I told you these potions were lethal,' breathed Christina Michaels, licking her lips. 'If I didn't know better, I'd think you were trying to have your wicked way with us.'

Reuben shuddered. Christina had indulged in so much surgery she had the complexion of a bowl of jelly.

He took security to one side.

'Find Aurora Nash,' he murmured, 'and take her to my cabin. Do it now. When it's done, you and you alone notify me. Are we clear?'

'Yes, boss.' The man disappeared.

Reuben felt the same sense of satisfaction as when he caught a fish and gutted it. If Maximo Diaz getting wasted was the extent of tonight's damage, he could well live with it. In the end, kids like Aurora were the same: frightened, needy, wanting reassurance. He'd talk to her, spin her a story. He'd tell her whatever she wanted to hear. It was what he was good at.

His party was going to go without a hitch, after all.

Reuben sucked a salty anchovy from his finger. For the first time in twenty-four hours, his appetite had returned.

'Should we get a doctor?' asked Lori as Maximo's bulk swung into her.

'Let him sleep it off,' answered Rebecca. 'No point getting everyone in a panic.'

With difficulty, the trio descended the stairs. Rebecca opened the first cabin they came to and the women dragged him inside. Maximo collapsed on to the bed and promptly passed out.

Rico Marquez...

Lori shook off the memory. There was no way it could have been him; the concept was preposterous. And anyway, wasn't he still in prison? It had been so long since she'd even thought about him. She was nervy, that was all. That creepy kid waiter had put her on edge, made her think she was seeing things that weren't there.

She returned her thoughts to Maximo. 'I don't know what's wrong with him,' she told Rebecca. 'He really hasn't had that much to drink.'

'Have you been with him all night?'

'No, but...'

'He'll be fine in an hour.' They removed his shoes and socks, revealing the long pale feet that Lori found repellent but she couldn't say why. Seeing Lori's fretful expression, Rebecca added kindly, 'Honestly, he'll be OK.'

Lori pressed a hand to Maximo's forehead. It felt sticky

and hot, his breath ragged. She wanted to see him properly. 'Can we put the light on?'

'Let's leave him to sleep,' advised Rebecca, pulling her away. 'He'll thank you for it.'

Enrique Marquez had been hit by a train. At high speed.

Right now he was thrown on the tracks, the wind knocked out of him, stars dancing in front of his eyes and a buzz like fury echoing through his brain.

Lori had seen him. He had looked her dead in the eye. It had only been a split-second but a split-second was enough...

Fuck!

The spark of old had passed between them. He hadn't counted on it—he'd counted *against* it. His feelings for her hadn't changed. She was beautiful, more beautiful than she had ever been, more beautiful than he remembered.

Enrique went to the bathroom, splashed his face with cold water. His hands were shaking.

It had been straightforward so far: the plotting, the stalking. The hate mail. But somehow the simplest thing, laying eyes on her, having her return his gaze, had pushed him over the edge.

Black-hearted hatred was easier to pursue than shades of grey.

He twisted the silver ring on his finger.

What had he seen in her? Recognition, yes. Affection? Did she still love him? Might she? Maybe she did. Maybe she had known all along it was he—her old Rico, her first love—who had sent those letters. Maybe she was waiting for him so they could be together again. Maybe she was wracked with guilt over her betrayal and wanted nothing more than a second chance...

An image crashed in of her beauty strewn across the ocean, pieces of her he had kissed and touched when they were young... Like a boy dared to take the wings from a butterfly, he wondered at destroying perfection.

No!

Enrique saw Lori not as she had been the past three years, but as the girl he had adored, the feel of her arms around his waist when they rode the freeway on his bike, the sight of her in her scuffed sneakers and string vest as she came down to the San Pedro harbour after a long day's work, how he would shield his eyes from the lowering sun to see her face more clearly.

The smell of her skin. Enrique had thought he'd buried it, stifled beneath the layers of betrayal but there it was, bright as a spring flower pushing through earth.

Why hadn't he thought of it before? It was obvious. To-night wasn't about destroying Lori—it was about reclaiming her. She had always belonged with him. She just didn't know it yet.

Lori was certain she heard voices coming from next door. As she and Rebecca quietly exited Maximo's room, she put a finger to her lips.

'Someone's down here,' she said.

Intrigued, they followed the sound. The voices were female, animated: one of them hysterical, the other one soothing. Lori recognised the second as Stevie Speller's.

She frowned at JB's wife. 'What's going on?'

Rebecca put her hand on the door and pushed.

* * *

The worst part was Ralph's expectant face at the upstairs window. The boy was gazing at the distant yacht as if it was the most exquisite thing on earth.

Margaret peeled him away. 'Time for bed, my darling.' She lifted him and tucked him in, pulling the sheets up tight around him, making him into a caterpillar, the way he liked it. She kissed his forehead. It was important everything ran as normal.

'When will they be back?' he whispered. 'When will JB be back?'

She smoothed his hair. 'Not for a long time.'

61

Aurora's mouth was dry, her throat fit to burst. She felt like she had been talking for hours. The past had come tumbling out, everything that had happened with Tom, with Sherilyn, with JB and Reuben and the island, with Rita and Casey and Farrah, with Pascale Devereux and her family. Everything she knew—and everything she still didn't know and wasn't sure she wanted to.

Stevie Speller had one arm across her shoulders. Aurora was amazed when, even as Cacatra's sordid revelation came, she did not move away.

The room was plunged into silence. Stevie was the one to break it.

'I want to know who the hell they think they are, playing with people's lives like this.'

Aurora turned on Rebecca. 'You're his wife!' she sobbed. 'You knew. You knew everything!' Her face crumpled. *'How could you?'*

Rebecca accepted the accusation. The girl deserved honesty, even if it was too late.

'I'm sorry you found out this way,' she said. 'From day one I feared it would emerge. Secrets as big as this don't stay hidden.'

'No shit,' cut in Stevie.

'Arnaud Devereux told me everything he knew.' Aurora's lip trembled. 'Except he didn't—' a tear plopped out of her eye '—he didn't know who my real parents were. Are.' She shook her head, chasing despair. 'See? I don't even know if they're still alive, dead, what!'

Rebecca moved closer. 'I don't know, darling. That's the truth. Reuben's the only one—'

'How can you be so matter-of-fact?' Aurora lashed. 'Don't you care?'

'Of course I care. I did from the start, I hated it, but what difference did that make?' The shiver in Rebecca's voice betrayed the long years of misery. 'I'm leaving JB. I'm leaving the island. It's over for me.'

'And the others?' Aurora wiped her nose with her wrist. 'The other kids and the other families? *Me?* It's not over for me. It can't ever be! How dare you say it's over when there are all these people whose lives you've ruined that can't *ever be free*?'

'I never wanted a part of it. I swear on all that I am. Never.'

'It came with the territory of a happy marriage, though, right?'

'No. JB's and my relationship has never been happy.'

Aurora choked on a laugh. 'Do you think I give a *shit* about your marital problems?'

Stevie squeezed her shoulder. 'Come on. It's not Rebecca's fault.'

'Isn't it? She let it happen—she was too much of a coward to make it stop!' Aurora leapt from the bed, ready to claw Rebecca's eyes out. She would have had Stevie not pulled her back.

'Let's not fight each other,' she counselled. 'We've got a common enemy here.'

Rebecca shot Lori a glance that spoke volumes.

'Oh, I was forgetting that.' Aurora landed on Lori's dark gaze. 'When I met you on Cacatra you couldn't keep your hands off him. So much for a common enemy!'

Stevie turned to Lori, puzzled.

'Lori was sleeping with Moreau all along.' Aurora's attention swung to the man's wife, waiting for a reaction, kamikaze-style: if she was going down she was taking them all with her.

Instead, Rebecca was calm. 'I already know about the affair.'

'You have to be kidding,' Aurora spluttered. 'You're into trading men now as well as babies?'

Lori stepped in. 'It's complicated—'

Aurora rounded on her, cutting her off, spoiling for a fight. 'How does it feel to find out the guy you've been fucking sells kids into Hollywood, then?' she yelled. 'That he's a liar and a cheat and a fraud and a criminal? Well? How does it feel?' She wanted to hurt them: Rebecca, Lori, anyone she could, to make them feel a sliver of the pain she had experienced.

Lori didn't waver. 'It's not a shock. Rebecca told me before tonight.'

Bewildered, Aurora turned to Stevie, chaos etched across her face.

'I'm sorry, Aurora,' she said softly, 'I knew, too.' She glanced between the three women. 'And now I think we need to talk.'

* * *

'I must admit, I'm finding this very entertaining.' JB made his way to the door. 'But, if you'll excuse me, I have more pressing matters to attend to.'

Xander grabbed his arm. 'I'm asking you a favour because you owe it.'

'I don't owe you a thing.' JB shook him off, straightened the arm of his suit jacket. 'Paul and Emilie's deaths have nothing to do with this.'

'They've got everything to do with this.'

'It's in your head, Jakobson,' JB countered, the untouchable boy he'd been at the academy, eliminating an adversary with a look or a word. 'It's always been in your head. If I didn't pity you I would have silenced you a long time ago.'

'It always comes back to threats with you, doesn't it?'

'And it always comes back to the same repetitions with you. I was tired of it then and I'm tired of it now. You're fortunate I'm not a man who takes offence. What kind of animal do you think I am? You believe I let my mother and father die?' His eyes glinted. 'Wake up, my friend.'

'I know what I saw.'

'You saw a child,' JB stated. 'You saw a boy in shock. *That's what you saw.*'

Images flashed across Xander's mind. The Moreaus reaching for help, his own arms flailing over the sides of the boat while JB stood back and did nothing. Shock did not describe what Xander had seen in that empty blue stare.

'You don't frighten me any more,' he said. 'Once upon a time, you did. Not any more.'

JB made to go then changed his mind. 'You know what? I put up with your suspicions over the years because I felt sorry for you. I did since the first day I arrived at the academy. That's why I let you be my friend, not because I wanted you but because I felt sorry for you. Deep down you knew that. You worshipped me, you wanted to *be* me— maybe you still do. Honestly? It was creepy, the way you followed me around copying how I acted and what I said, behaving like some jealous fucking girlfriend. Everyone used to laugh about it behind your back, lovestruck, desperate Xander Jakobson. You never knew me, not really. You never knew what it took for me to be the way I was, what I had to give away. You still don't. When you begged to come to France that summer, I let you. When you begged to follow me to Hollywood, I let you. When you begged to come in on Cacatra, I let you. You were nothing before me. *Nothing.* I made you. Everything you have now, it's because of me. Including your beautiful wife.'

Xander took a swing. JB dodged it, in a heartbeat grabbing Xander's lapels and pulling him up close. The men's faces were inches from each other.

'You were a kid with an imagination,' JB said. '*That's all.* And I bet it's suited you. I bet it's helped alleviate your conscience. Cacatra gave you a fortune. Reuben gave you a fortune. *I* gave you a fortune. And it was easier to reconcile yourself by imagining the man who'd opened the door was a killer, bad through and through. Sound about right?'

Xander was shaking. 'I know the facts—'

'The facts? Fine, let's talk facts. You're asking me to help conceal a homicide.'

'I'm asking you to help me save my marriage.'

JB released him. 'Your marriage is a sham,' he said.

'Don't you dare tell me what's real and what isn't. You wouldn't know the difference.'

'I know you're trying to conceal a murder. And if what you accuse me of is true, it makes you just as bad as I am.'

'Destroy the evidence against Bibi Reiner,' Xander commanded. 'And I walk away.'

'Or what?'

'I've got enough to sink you for good.'

'Enough to sink me?' JB looked round at the library's grand interior: the boat, robust and solid and incontestable. 'I'd like to see you try.'

Maximo Diaz rolled over. His stomach was cramping. He felt himself whirling down, down, into a deep black pool. He tried to move but couldn't. His body felt heavy, his mind delirious. He thought he could hear voices, women's voices close by, winging into corners like bats.

'Lori,' he spluttered through dry, cracked lips. The air was thick and pitch-dark.

Where was he? His feet were cold. He was freezing all over. His chest hurt.

Maximo reached out, imagined she was there and stroked her face.

With a final grimace, outstretched fingers tensing once and then relaxing, his entire body became still.

'You're wrong.' Rebecca was adamant, leaping to contest Stevie as soon as her story was done. 'JB is guilty of many things but he would never let another person die.'

'You're saying I should doubt my husband over a man who's ruined this girl's life and countless others?' Stevie could scarcely entertain it. 'You must be joking.'

'Rebecca's right,' Lori agreed. 'He isn't capable of that.'

'How can you defend him?' Stevie cried. 'What's wrong with you both?'

'I'm the last to defend him,' said Lori. 'His plans for me were…' It defied articulation. 'But he's not a murderer.'

'You hardly know him!' Stevie blasted. She couldn't doubt Xander and she didn't. Frustration at their shortsightedness made her launch a petty shot. 'But then I suppose he lobotomised you just like he does every other woman who has the misfortune to cross his path.'

Lori fired back. 'If I don't know JB, then you know him even less.'

'What's the matter with you?' Stevie wanted to shake her. 'He tracked you down as a *surrogate*, Lori! He's been leading a double life you knew absolutely nothing about. He was prepared to pay you millions for a…for what should be a priceless thing!' The injustice became personal. 'Money for a baby! How can you even begin to—?'

'He's not the man you think he is,' Lori answered. 'I can't hate him.'

'Then you're a damn fool.'

Rebecca spoke. 'Let's not argue. You said so yourself—'

'No, come on, let's.' Stevie gestured to Aurora, sitting in a red-eyed daze, unable to take in the accounts she had heard. 'There's a teenage girl here who's been to hell and back, and all you two can do is reaffirm why JB Moreau's got away with so much for so long. You're standing up for him! You're standing up for the man responsible!'

'We're not standing up for him,' said Rebecca. 'He should never have got involved. But the way JB sees it is different. Parental love, at least in the biological sense, means little to him. Why should it? My vote is he'd have been better off with strangers from the start. I'm not excusing him, God knows he's no saint—'

Stevie laughed harshly. 'Good one.'

'But he didn't let his parents die,' Lori interjected. 'Xander's mistaken.'

'How in hell would you know?' Stevie countered.

'I just do.'

'You *just do*? Come on, Lori, here was me thinking you were intelligent.'

'Shut up.' Aurora's voice was small. No one heard because they were too busy bitching.

'I've heard him talk about that day,' maintained Lori. 'It was real.'

Stevie grimaced. 'Nothing that man has ever told you has been real—you can rest assured of that. If for one second you're imagining a happy ever after, let me tell you now it'll be the biggest mistake you ever made. It's not a fucking fairytale, Lori.'

'You're jealous,' Lori flared.

Stevie burst out laughing. 'Please! I've heard a lot of strange things recently but that has to take the cake.'

'Shut up.' No one noticed the knife appear from Aurora's dress, the glinting blade.

'You're jealous because JB's never looked twice at you and you wish he would. Because you've got all this passion against him; I can see it in your face. I bet you've thought about being with him. Every woman has—what makes you immune? I've been with him and it sickens you.'

Stevie was shaking. 'You're right. Why? Because men like JB Moreau hurt and cheat and lie. They do terrible things and back out of the consequences. They leave you with nothing. Lori, I don't want to fight with you. I want you to listen. I want you to believe me. Men like him—'

'SHUT UP!'

Aurora brandished the knife. Her eyes were stormy.

The cabin plunged into silence.

'Give it to me, Aurora.' Rebecca held her hand out. 'Nice and easy. Give it to me.'

'Never.' The knife wavered. 'I've wasted enough time. I've wasted nineteen years.'

'If you use this,' Stevie pleaded, 'they've won.'

'They've won anyhow.' A tear coursed down her cheek. 'And I've lost. I've lost so much I've got nothing else to lose.'

'You'll throw away the rest of your life. Don't let them take any more of you.'

Lori spoke. 'She's right.'

A hollow sound escaped Aurora's mouth, between a sob and a moan. 'You know what? I'm not sure life's all it's cracked up to be.'

'This isn't the way,' soothed Stevie. 'I promise you, it's not.'

Rebecca reached out. 'Give me the knife and I'll bring Reuben to you. OK, Aurora? I'll bring him. Before the night is through, you'll get your answers.'

Reuben hated this song. They'd hired a rock band, a chart-storming four-piece with stupid hair and jeans so tight they could barely stand with their legs apart.

He scouted the room for security. Surely Aurora Nash had been tracked down by now. If he could just get her out of the way before the midnight address, he'd be laughing.

He checked the time. Half past eleven. The end was in sight.

For the beauty of a boat was there were only so many places a person could hide.

62

Chill seeped into Aurora's bones, the stinging slap of water audible as it lapped the flanks of the boat. Black air hung like an inky curtain. It was cold on the main deck. Empty.

'Wait here,' Rebecca told her, pocketing the knife with care. 'Don't move. I'll be back.'

Lori checked on Maximo Diaz before returning upstairs. In the dark she could make out his prostrate form, one arm flung over the side of the bed. There was a strange smell.

Quietly, Lori closed the door.

Only a couple of years existed between she and Aurora, close enough so Lori knew that such a discovery, at so tender an age, would have shattered her world. How many other kids had JB put in the same position? How many lives had been torn apart? Up till now she had considered only the aborted prospect of her own involvement. Was that better, or worse?

She closed her eyes against his deception. She had to do what she came for.

She had to face him.

One truth in exchange for another.

Stevie ran into Xander on her way back to the saloon.

'Where have you been?' he demanded. 'I've been looking for you all over.'

'Later.' She refocused on the task. 'Any luck with Moreau?'

Xander shook his head. JB's words clung to him like weeds, throttling, shaming. 'No,' he said. 'We're on our own.'

'Fine.' Stevie led the way. 'Just how I like it.'

Dirk Michaels checked the microphone. Tonight's guests were gathered, four hundred eager faces flushed with drink and anticipation as they waited for him to take to the stage.

'You know what you're going to say?' his wife had asked him earlier as she'd quaffed her twentieth drink. He'd swatted her away like the irritating fly she was. If a man of Dirk's stature couldn't speak off the cuff about the life and times of an old friend, who could?

He hoped Reuben wouldn't mind him using the occasion for a further purpose, once the accolades were done. Unleashing the truth about their beloved Linus's death: how Bibi Reiner was a cold-blooded murderess, and award-winning Stevie Speller her accomplice.

Retribution on his friend's behalf was going to taste sweet.

Reuben slapped him on the back. 'All set?' he asked jovially.

It was what Linus would have wanted.

* * *

'I have to speak with you. It's urgent.'

Reuben was pissed off. JB's wife had been casting about for days with a face like a slapped ass. Her attention now was the last thing he needed.

'So is this.' He returned his attention to Dirk and readied himself for a litany of praise.

'I think you should listen,' said Rebecca.

'I think you should beat it.'

'Reuben—'

'What?'

'It's Aurora Nash. She knows.'

The yacht was stationary. Ocean stretched for miles and miles, its distance immeasurable. Water and sky, all there was. Aurora wrapped her arms around herself.

'Ms Nash?'

She was surprised to see a guy with a radio in his top pocket and a wire coming out of his ear. The man had been searching for over an hour and was relieved to finally locate her.

'Would you come with me?'

'I'm meeting someone,' she replied.

'Not any more, you're not.'

'Excuse me?'

The man took her arm. She tried to shrug him off but his grip was strong.

'Don't fight, Ms Nash. We wouldn't want to keep Mr van der Meyde waiting.'

Xander grasped his wife's hand. 'Steve, don't. He could be bluffing.'

'He isn't.' Stevie eyed her nemesis. Dirk was preening

beneath the stage lights. As far as she was concerned, one trace, one *suggestion* of Bibi Reiner and she was going up there. She'd hoped to resolve it privately, save the devastation, but if Dirk wanted to play nasty then she had no choice but to follow. She would reveal everything about what Cacatra was hiding.

After what she'd witnessed tonight, every person present was going to want to hear it.

Rebecca checked both flanks in case Aurora had ducked down one side. She hadn't.

'I don't understand,' she said. 'I left her right here...'

Reuben had his hand on the doorframe, his shoulders stooped like a man at the end of a long race. His knuckles seeped white.

He lifted his head and narrowed his eyes.

'How did she find out?'

Rebecca met his eye. 'She needs the truth, Reuben. She needs to know who her parents are. You owe her that. I told her I'd bring you to her.'

'What the hell for, you stupid dumb bitch?' Spittle flew from his grimace.

She was shocked. 'Because I had to—'

'It was you, wasn't it?' He rounded on her, eyes rolling maniacally. 'I should have guessed it was someone on the inside, but *you*? Fuck!' His face was puce, his nostrils flared. 'Jesus H, woman—you've got some balls.'

'You're wrong. I don't know what you mean. I never told Aurora a thing.'

'Oh yeah?' Reuben advanced closer, hemming her in, forcing her on to the bow's metal railings. 'How else did she hack into my account, then? Tell me that. How else did she pen me that twisted little note that's had me shitting fear the past twenty-four hours?'

Rebecca had held Lori Garcia responsible for the note. She hadn't known then that the others knew—but, of course, they did. Aurora Nash did. It had been Aurora all along.

Roughly, Reuben grabbed her hair. 'Cat got your tongue?' he snarled, yanking it loose. She struggled fruitlessly against his bulk. He was holding her jaw so tight it made speech impossible. Lashing free, she spat in his face.

Reuben was momentarily stunned. He blinked, wiping the residue. 'Silly girl,' he taunted. 'Silly, silly girl.'

'It's not what you think,' Rebecca managed. 'It wasn't—'

He slapped her. The force flung her back over the bow of the ship. Rebecca's thoughts darted to Aurora's knife, still concealed in her dress. Terrified, she reached for it.

Reuben chuckled dementedly as the blade rose between them, glinting in the moonlight.

'What're you gonna do with that?' he jeered, swiping for the weapon and instead snatching her wrist, twisting the point back towards her, closer, closer.

Rebecca pushed against him with all her might. The knife entered smoothly and cleanly.

At first, it was painless, blood dripping to the wooden deck like the petals of a crimson flower.

Enrique Marquez caught a flash of dark hair and the ripple of a woman's dress. Delirious, he'd been hunting for Lori all over. Round every corner, in every glimpse, he thought he saw her, only to be mistaken. Finally, here she was. He had found her.

But what was she doing on-deck with Reuben van der

Meyde? It was almost midnight. Wasn't the guy meant to be down in the saloon? Enrique pressed closer against the threshold, straining to see through the shadows. It looked as if they were arguing, but with Lori's body concealed behind van der Meyde's bulk, it was difficult to see clearly.

Enrique didn't move for fear of being seen. For one shocking moment he thought they might be making out, before Lori emitted a scream that pierced the night and with it his heart.

There wasn't time to think about it. He pulled open the door and started to run.

Reuben's cabin, the great yacht's master suite, was astonishing. Stretching from port to starboard, it was decked in gold and brown, home to a massive bed with sumptuous gilt headboard, a pearly ceiling lit with tiny bulbs and a zebra-skin rug.

Alone, Aurora explored. She was reminded of the trip to Capri and shrank from her memories of the Devereux boat, the French couple's cabin as she'd stood beneath the hatch and listened in on that shocking conversation that had turned her inside out.

An old photograph on the dresser caught her eye. It was black and white, a bare-chested boy in shorts holding up a caught fish that was nearly greater in length than he was.

Reuben as a child?

Her anger was refreshed. How could he advertise his youth when he'd stripped so many of theirs? Blindly she kicked the bed, then the wall, so hard that she bit her lip and drew blood. The taste of it matched the red of her fury and she was fired with a destructive energy, the urge to obliterate everything in sight.

Aurora ripped off his bed clothes; she smashed his *objets*

d'art; she punched a gilt mirror till it smashed, cracking her frantic reflection; she slashed his curtains, wrenching them from their fastenings; she hauled a chair and sent it crashing into the window; she flung open drawers and closets and tore out their contents, flinging them to the floor and trampling them, with each movement imagining it was him beneath her feet, hand, fist.

That was how she found it.

A smooth .357 Magnum revolver.

She reached into the cabinet, fingers locking round the grip.

Dirk was getting impatient. Where was Reuben? It was his gig and he'd only gone and done a vanishing act.

A sea of faces looked up at him expectantly. He caught sight of Stevie Speller. Her eyes were locked on him, daring him to do the impossible.

Fuck it.

He'd have preferred to offer the information as a small farewell, an *adieu*, but the main man's absence left him with little choice.

'I'm afraid I have some troubling news,' Dirk began. 'It pains me, but this is a truth I feel the good people of Hollywood should be made aware of.'

'It's now.'

Xander attempted to pull her back. *'Stevie,'* he hissed. *'No.'*

'I'm an honest man,' Dirk was saying. 'And ours is an honest town…'

The crowd was murmuring. A frisson of interest rippled round the room.

'And so it is my duty to reveal to you what I've been holding back for some time.'

Stevie fought her way through the bodies. The stage seemed a million miles away.

'This is going to come as a shock to many of you. Even, I'm sorry to say, my wife. You'll be aware that this has been a tough couple of years for those of us in the industry...'

Rage was boiling, hot anger that had simmered in Stevie ever since Bibi had become involved in their venture. It spilled over in a scalding rush.

'We've lost friends, loved ones. The impact of that has been considerable.'

She wasn't going to make it in time. He was going to blurt it out before she could—

'So it is with heavy heart that I am forced to tell you—'

'That's enough, Dirk.'

Stevie stopped. Dirk blinked, confused, as though he'd been woken from a dream in which he wielded absolute supremacy, reminded now that he hadn't and never would.

JB Moreau was next to him. Smoothly he claimed the mic.

'I'm going to have to stop you there.'

His blue eyes found Xander's in the crowd and held them.

'Reuben's on his way,' he said. 'Show's over.'

The sky somersaulted. Rebecca's wound was seeping, sticky, gushing through her fingers.

Reuben pushed her. Once was all it took.

Her body tumbled over the edge of the ship like a rag doll, hitting the waves tens of feet below with a fierce slap. She was dead on impact.

She didn't have time to see the man running at her from inside the boat. Screaming a name that wasn't hers.

63

Reuben whipped round as the man came charging. Distantly, he recognised him.

The man took a swing, punching him hard in the face. For a moment Reuben was dizzy, immobilised, and felt a trickle of blood escape his sinus and course a line through his nose and out his nostril. He crumpled to the deck.

Enrique threw himself against the metal bow. Down below, her body drifted like wood on the waves, moonlight gleaming off her skin.

Lori.

There was only one thing he could do. He jumped.

As Lori hurried past the main deck, she thought she heard a splash. The rest of the ship was so empty that every sound was wide open.

JB was walking too fast.

'What was that about?' she demanded.

'Go back downstairs, Lori.'

'No. Not until you talk to me.'

He turned on the stairwell. His gaze was ice on fire. 'Go downstairs,' he repeated. 'I don't want to see you. I never want to see you. Get back to your boyfriend.'

She was undeterred. 'Wait.'

He waved a dismissive hand.

'Don't walk away from me.'

They emerged at the top deck, elevated above the rest of the ship, totally deserted. An oval pool shone aquamarine beneath a starlit sky, on the bottom of which gleamed the VDM crest, magnified through the water.

JB was looking for Reuben. He checked round the side of the ship. Where the hell was he? He was meant to be in the saloon thirty minutes ago. Guests were becoming anxious, especially after Dirk's curtailed display.

Lori stopped. 'You have to give me this much.'

'I don't have to give you a thing.' He spun to face her. 'What happened between us, it was a mistake.'

'A mistake,' she repeated flatly.

'Forget it. I have.' His voice made her sad. She'd lost him.

'You really have no clue, have you?' she whispered.

JB's eyes were glass, azure as the pool behind. 'Leave,' he told her. 'Leave this island and don't ever come back. You're not welcome here.'

'How dare you?' Lori's hair billowed in the wind. 'How *dare* you after the way you've treated me?'

'The way *I've* treated *you*?' At last, he reacted. Thrusting his hands in his pockets, he turned to go, thought better of it and turned back. 'You're pretty unbelievable, you know that.'

'Coming from you?' she sputtered. 'You've played me since the moment we met. You lied to me from day one!

Everything we had was built on a lie. And if it wasn't a lie it was cowardice. I'm not sure what's worse.'

'I wouldn't know how to be a coward.'

'Give me a break. Where were you, JB? It's been *a year*. How do you think I felt, endless months trying to contact you and all you gave me was a wall of silence?'

'You know nothing,' he growled. 'You're a baby.'

The words flew free. 'I know about Cacatra. I know what you've been doing on this island and I know what you meant me for.'

His expression was blank.

'Don't deny it,' she said. 'Don't even try. I know everything.'

'Wrong. You could never even guess.'

Her dress rippled like liquid gold. 'Then have the decency to tell me.'

'There's no point. You wouldn't understand.'

'I've understood everything else you've told me. I've believed everything you said and I still do. Maybe I'm wrong about that. Some might tell me I was.'

'Keep away from this,' he warned. 'You're not involved.'

'I am. Because all you said about the way you felt—' her voice faltered but she caught it '—I have to know if that was true. That I wasn't just...*merchandise*. That I wasn't just an opportunity to make money.'

'Women in your position are precisely the reason I do this.' She had never seen him so full of passion and in spite of her temper she wanted him. 'They need intervention. They need someone to answer for them because no one's ever bothered before. Are you saying if I'd offered you this you would have turned it down?'

'It's wrong.'

'It's a humanitarian project, the first of its kind. It changes people's lives. It gives them hope. It makes things right.'

'It doesn't sound like the first time you've justified it to yourself.'

'I don't lose sleep over it.'

She laughed. 'Why doesn't that surprise me?'

He took a moment to scrutinise her. 'Did someone tell you?'

'It doesn't matter.'

'That's for me to decide.'

Lori thought back to the discovery of her documents on Cacatra and the uncertainty that had vexed her since. She realised she had known long before Rebecca Stuttgart had visited.

'The night we spent together. Afterwards, in your villa. LA864. Except my file shouldn't have been there. It should have been with the others, the women you have lined up but for whatever reason the prospect falls through.'

In a flash she envisioned where the paperwork was kept. An image of the island lighthouse sprang to mind: abandoned, paint cracking, sea-washed walls thick and hard with salt.

'In case you want to reopen further down the line,' she murmured. 'But I was the exception…because there was no further down the line.'

JB's suit jacket flapped in the cold. It was a while before he spoke.

'Not for me,' he said quietly. 'There was no way I was going to watch you carry another man's baby.'

The statement hung in the air between them. Lori was

shaking. Her breath was visible in the night, escaping in short, hard bursts, blooming then dissolving.

JB spoke. 'I've never found anyone who does to me what you do to me.' His voice slipped. 'But I cannot forget what you've done. You betrayed me.'

She could hold it in no longer. 'I didn't.'

'It doesn't matter how you express it. The evidence is there.'

'What evidence?'

'Don't make me say his name.'

'Let me explain. You need to hear this—'

'*No!*' He sliced the night air with his hand, the word soaring up into the universe. She'd never heard him raise his voice before and the volume of it frightened her. 'How could you do it? How could you be with him? After us?'

'I—'

He was on her, his lips on hers, his hands in her hair.

Kissing her like it was the last kiss on earth.

The waves hit Enrique with a stinging slap. Salt water rushed into his lungs, making him choke. He was a strong swimmer but not against this tide. The ocean tossed him like a child's plaything, fathoms of space below and around him as empty as they were full. He gasped for air, with each undulation battling to keep his head above the surface.

He caught sight of Lori's body, not fifty strokes away. It was impossible to tell through the pitch if she was moving. An arm thrashing, a hand in the air—or was it a trick of the swell? In the next flash, utter stillness, as if she was dead or drowned, facedown on the oil-black sea or faceup to the charcoal sky, cracked with stars, observers to the moment of her expiry.

Arms slicing, crawling through the distance, Enrique swam. The waves buffeted and rocked, throwing him off course, and it seemed with every stroke she only drifted further away.

The yacht was behind them now. His chest was burning, his limbs on fire. By the time he reached the body, he clung to it like a raft.

Reuben van der Meyde staggered indoors. He was dazed, catatonic from an assault beyond his comprehension. Somehow, his inbuilt sense of purpose found a way through. He was meant to be somewhere, doing something.

Oh yes…there were guests. This was a party. His party.

Better patch up quick.

Thoughts whirled through his mind, hot and fast like flames licking up a chimney. It felt like his head was exploding. Maybe he had concussion.

Shock numbed him as he lurched to his private quarters, veering into walls and stumbling as he fought to regain his balance.

He reached his cabin and opened the door.

And came face to face with the barrel of his own gun.

Enrique rolled the body. Dark hair was plastered across the face, obscuring her features. With a wet groan he realised she had been long dead: her skin was pale and she was cold, freezing cold, to touch. He put two fingers to her neck and felt nothing.

Lori.

He pulled her into his arms, a slopping pocket of water between them, and the movement brought a rush through his parted lips. It was not the saline that stung but a new taste: the unmistakable iron of blood. Her corpse floated like an empty sack, a wreck of driftwood, and his hands travelled down till they dipped into the still-warm puncture in her soft, yielding flesh. For a second his fingers disappeared and he gagged, shoving the body away.

The motion washed the hair from her face. Straining to see through the darkness, Enrique saw a woman he did not recognise. He thought he must be wrong, reaching out to touch her, the chin he had cupped so many times before, and felt it was entirely different.

Blindly he thrashed, twisting back towards the yacht, whose lights seemed now immeasurably far away. The coast, ahead of him, an equal distance.

A shape slid across his vision. It came out of the night, several feet away, then swiftly vanished. He blinked. Fear crept up from his toes.

There it was again, unambiguous this time.

A fin, black and huge. Enrique whipped round, caught sight of another. Two fins, three, four, circling him and the body.

Enrique's legs pushed uselessly at the depths, numb and bone-tired. Around him a cloud of red blossomed as he hung suspended in the tepid residue of a stranger's blood.

They kissed frantically, each second of their months apart driven to this point and now his hands were on her body and her face and the smell and feel of him was heaven. He held her body to his, drawing her into his heat, arms encircling her waist so he could kiss her better. Lori fell into the hardness of his chest, the stiffness of that part that told her his want was as real as hers. Moving blindly, peeling off his jacket, unbuttoning his shirt, they reached the rim of the pool and, in a flash, felt the ground disappear. Cool water erupted as its silver sheet was shattered.

Underwater, JB's white shirt came away like sails filled with wind. He carried on kissing her, their mouths slipping over each other, their tongues entwined.

They surfaced in a crash, sparks of blue water exploding. Fiercely Lori pulled at his hair, wrapping her legs around him, her body wet inside and out.

With a piercing thrust he entered her. She clasped his shoulders, held him to her as his length drove deeper, his mouth on her neck and her breasts.

Throwing her head back, she met the endlessness of space.

The first tug pulled him straight under. Quick, sudden, total submersion, before he was released.

Horror surged. Enrique whipped at the water, creating a storm, and heard a high-pitched moan, thin as air, seep from his throat. He pushed forward, veering inexplicably and abruptly left, and it was only when he thrust a hand beneath the surface, groping desperately, palm open, that he realised his right leg was missing.

Another tug. No pain. This time his torso seemed to surge, light as a buoy, and a gush of viscous metal washed from his mouth.

He choked. Something bumped against him, more solid than a wall. He kicked out; thought he was kicking because his mind said he was but there was nothing to kick with. Using his arms, he propelled himself forward but he was drained and his head was full of blood and terror. Reaching down, he felt the stumps. The left was cut above his knee, the right at his hip. A trailing softness was coming from them, gummy and tough and by some warped instinct he drew on the entrails, feeling the same satisfaction when they gave as for a stubborn knot loosening.

One last cold slug of raw night air and he was taken.

'Why didn't you wait for me?'

They were spent. Two lovers washed up on an abandoned beach.

'I did,' she gasped, recovering her breath, the water sparkling and washing around them as it had the first time. 'There hasn't been anyone else.'

His beautiful face right there, the groove on his lip she had remembered kissing a million times. She knew that story. He had trusted her with it.

'No more lies,' he whispered.

'I'm not lying.'

'Maximo Diaz. Your child.'

Lori reached for his hand and he let her take it, her fingers enlaced with his. 'I tried to tell you,' she said. 'I swear I did. Rebecca wasn't honest with you.'

There was a flicker of doubt in him. Pain.

'When she said you couldn't have children,' Lori continued softly. 'You can. My child is proof. Our child is proof.'

He didn't take his gaze from hers.

'It can't be.'

'It is.' She stroked his thumb. 'No more lies.'

There it was; she could see it. Trust. Newborn, fragile: full of fear and hope.

'Omar's yours.'

She pulled him close so he could feel her slow beating heart and know it was the truth.

'He's your son.'

* * *

'Put the gun down, Aurora.'

'Sit.'

'Give it to me—'

'*Sit!*'

Reuben collapsed into a chair. His head was splitting from where he'd whacked it on the deck and he couldn't think clearly. What was happening? He needed to get his shit together and fast. This was bad. This was real fucking bad.

'You're going to tell me everything.'

All across the cabin, his belongings were strewn, smashed, shattered. It looked as if a bomb had gone off.

'My real parents.' The gun wavered in Reuben's vision but he couldn't tell if it was his skewed perception or her trembling aim. 'Come on! *Who are they?*'

'Please...' It came out a sputter. Wretched. He had never begged before in his life.

'You'll get no mercy from me,' Aurora spat. 'Don't even try, you pathetic old man.'

Reuben liked to push himself. It was how he'd got so far in life. He'd think of the most outrageous idea he could and then test himself, *dare* himself, to go right ahead and do it.

But he'd known at the time he had gone too far. He had taken the secret one step further. This was his knowledge to carry and his cross to bear.

The weight of it threatened to crush him.

'Relax.' The barrel of the gun drew in and out of focus. 'Please—before you do something stupid. Security,' he mumbled, 'you'll be taken down—'

'*Who are they?*' Aurora screamed. 'Tell me now before I blow your fucking brains across the room and I swear to God I'll do it and I won't even think twice.'

Reuben gulped. 'She was...' His mind felt like mush. 'She was from Finland. Poor. Desperate. Young.'

Aurora thrust the gun. 'Where is she now? Is she still alive?'

'I—I think so.'

'You *think so*?'

'I don't know.' He held his hands up. 'I can find out.'

'You can *find out*? Something's not right here. Aren't you meant to be sending this woman a fortune every other month? No? What, then?' His words that night on Cacatra floated back to her. 'So much for a *humanitarian outreach*, you evil fucking *bastard*.'

'Aurora—'

'You repulse me.'

It was as if Reuben were sitting next to his own shadow, and he watched his shadow get up and fight her, a silly thing, wrestle the weapon and tell her she was talking nonsense and have her committed because what sort of a kid came up with a story like that? But the real Reuben sat very still, unable to move, his head pounding and his body weak. Every day his sixty years.

'What about him?' she choked.

'Who?'

'My father. *What about him?*'

In the recesses of Reuben's curdled mind, alarm bells rang. He grasped at the truth.

'Tom Nash... He...'

'What?'

'I can't—'

'Say it!'

'Tom Nash is gay,' he croaked.

Aurora blinked.

He said it again. 'Tom is gay. He's gay.'

She laughed.

'You wanted to know why?' Reuben thrashed, desperate to throw her off the scent with the scandal he'd vowed never to expose. 'There, that's your reason. Tom Nash is gay and the world can never find out. That was why they did it, him and Sherilyn. They wanted a child they could call their own—a sweet-as-pie American family and you were the key. Kind of takes the sheen off when you learn he's busy fucking asses from here to Timbuktu—'

'I don't believe you. It's not possible.'

But it was. It was. Tom's and Sherilyn's separate bedrooms, their odd relationship, their distance...that one Christmas on the Texas ranch when Aurora had walked in on her father and Billy-Bob Hocker in the stables, half dressed, buckles undone, but she'd been too young at the time to properly remember or trust what she saw...

Calmly, single-mindedly, Aurora pressed the barrel of the gun into Reuben's forehead.

'If Tom isn't my father—' she released the safety catch '—then who is?'

Lance Chlomsky was swept into a moving current of people coursing to the lower deck. Reports from above claimed that Reuben van der Meyde was missing. There was wild talk of an armed assassin, a psychopath who had boarded the ship and was holding the billionaire for ransom.

Fiction. Staff inventing stories to pass the time.

Nevertheless, true to form, Lance panicked. He had always been of a fretful disposition. *Weak*, they called it. He hung back, waited till the line of frantic gossip had passed and pushed open the door to one of the guest suites. A bad smell assaulted him. He flicked on the light.

Maximo Diaz was facedown on the bed, one arm flung over the side, a contorted expression on his bloated face. His eyes bugged open and his tongue hung loosely out the corner of a grey-green mouth.

Lance gagged on bile, staggering backwards into the corridor.

At first he thought it was someone else shouting, someone else taking control.

But no. It was him.

'Man dead,' he was yelling. *'Raise the alarm!'*

'I named you Aurora,' Reuben said. 'The light. Because you were my first.'

No, no, no, no, no.

'I'd done it all. I was bored. Bored with everything. Bored, even, with what we were doing on Cacatra: the surrogacies, the babies, everything. It made money, but it wasn't testing my ambition. I needed to find another way...'

Aurora's body went slack. She crumpled against the wall, dripping down it like paint.

'It felt like a fucking revolution. A shot at the next big thing.'

The gun was hanging from her grip like a dead fish.

'Not difficult,' he said. 'Not after the first time.'

'Don't say it. Please, don't say it—'

'I don't know why I picked her.' Reuben's tone was resigned to the inevitable. 'I'd travelled to Finland to see her...there was a complication with the exchange and I never expected her to be so pretty. So I had an idea, a genius idea, and I told her this was the request. That Tom and Sherilyn had asked for it.'

Aurora thought she was going to faint.

'The Northern Lights…you were conceived beneath them. I felt like God,' he blathered, deranged, 'the beginning of a new order. Put on this earth for a single reason. *Procreation.*' He licked his lips. 'The second Adam! My children becoming part of the world…you don't get more powerful than that.'

Reuben was trembling, cold at his fingertips and his toes. 'Not unless you do something unprecedented… Don't you see?' His eyes snapped to her, insane. 'Kids born into families right across the world, rich, influential families, who will go on to achieve great, important things that change the world and write history… Kids with *my blood running through their veins…*'

It came at her like a train down the line.

She leapt for him, clawing.

'Don't do it!' he roared. 'I'm the only family you have left!'

She scratched at his eyes, his hair, anything she could grab hold of.

'It's me, Aurora. I'm your father. Welcome home.'

64

A little way down the beach, a small boy was hunting for sea turtles. His father had told him they came in to lay their eggs at night, leathery things whose shells shone white in troughs of sand. He was supposed to be fast asleep by now—Miss Jensen, the housekeeper, would murder him—but it was boring waiting inside the mansion. He squinted at the yacht, hundreds of miles away, it seemed, and wished he could be there instead of here. They told him that one day it would all be his: his great inheritance. Crouching at the water's edge, the palm of one hand cradling his chin and the other blindly raking the beach, it was hard to believe. His knees were damp from where he'd been on them, combing the smooth, still-warm sand for that final, important discovery.

His fingers curled round it instinctively at first, like a baby's around its mother's thumb. It felt like net, the ones he caught crabs in, but it clung to him too unhappily for that, as if by holding on it could force him, maybe, to look.

* * *

Margaret Jensen packed methodically. Something had gone wrong. What? Had Enrique been discovered? Had he been forced into confession? Had he revealed their plan? She knew he would not think twice before giving her away.

Enrique Marquez was as good as dead. And so was she.

The yacht was still out on the water, inching ever closer. It was past midnight. There wasn't much time. She had to get them off this island.

Battling horror, Margaret dashed to Ralph's bedroom. His door was ajar and she pushed it, flooding the room with light.

Panic hit. Her son's bed was empty, the sheets thrown off and the window flung open. She bolted to it, searching hopelessly, and saw where he had climbed down to the beach.

It was then she heard the rupturing scream. His: unmistakably his.

Margaret raced down the stairs and into the night. Every gulp of air froze in her windpipe. Down to the sand as fast as her legs could carry her, not fast enough, never fast enough. Flying wouldn't be fast enough.

Relief struck in a blinding flash. There he was, her boy, crouching at the shore, a tiny figure alone in the dark.

Only, he wasn't alone.

Washed up next to him, like a slippery seal, was a woman. Her dark hair was tangled and matted. Her dress was soaked. One arm, below the elbow, was missing, torn, as though...

Margaret held Ralph tight to her chest and turned his sobbing face away. With her foot she rolled the woman, a huge perished sea-creature. The body made a slipslop sound.

When she saw who it was, she seized her son's hand and ran.

Epilogue

The ceremony was held beneath a clear blue, sun-scorched sky. Spring was here and with it the first warmth of the year. Guests gathered under a canopy of twisting vines and pink blossoms shaken gently by the ocean breeze.

The bride was barefoot, radiant in a floor-length gown that pooled at her ankles, her hair loose and her skin glowing. Countless times she had imagined this day, what she would wear, how she would feel—and who, always who, would be waiting to take her hand.

'Are you ready?' Next to her, her father smiled and patted her arm.

The moment had arrived. She nodded.

Together, they made their way down the aisle. Heads turned to admire her approach. For each recognised face, she remembered one that was absent.

Maximo Diaz's funeral took place a little less than a month after Reuben van der Meyde's sixtieth birthday party. The autopsy had gone on longer than expected, with van der

Meyde's people keen to maintain the man had suffered an extreme allergic reaction and the Diaz clan making waves in the press about suspected murder. It came as almost a relief when they were proven right and the killer was found. Poor Maximo could finally be laid to rest.

The funeral itself was sombre and protracted, a turnout of stooped figures hulked in black around the hole in the ground, dark yews soaring behind. It rained non-stop.

Lori Garcia lost a part of her soul that day.

Enrique Marquez.

Murderer, terrorist, assassin. Evil, through and through.

The boy she had known a lifetime ago, the boy with the kind eyes and the gentle laugh and the ambition and drive and heart had ended up in this wild and lonely place. That boy had died long before she'd met those pitiless eyes across the yacht's saloon.

As summer moved into fall and the world kept turning though Lori couldn't turn with it, life was agony. Hours, days, weeks of uncertainty before the final revelation that the man who had been responsible, who had followed her, stalked her, sent her that filthy hate mail, was the same man who had laced Maximo's food with poison and, in a tragic case of mistaken identity, taken Rebecca Stuttgart's life. He was the man the media labelled an obsessive psychopath, a narcissist and a savage animal, the man who had tracked Lori right on to what was intended to be the scene of her death and countless others.

She couldn't believe it. It was too shocking, too macabre, too like a nightmare.

Questions raged. How had this criminal been permitted on-board, in this day and age when security was rigorous to the point of intrusion? How had a man like van der

Meyde even considered hiring help from such a controversial source? How had nobody picked up on Enrique's behaviour? It seemed Reuben's plan to give back to ordinary people had miscarried. Ordinary people weren't interested in being given back to. Wealth and power changed a man: they made him a pariah. Reuben had thought he was invincible. Turned out, he wasn't.

On the ship's lower deck, the bomb was eventually uncovered. In the beginning there had been too many other lines of pursuit. No one guessed at the magnitude of Enrique's plan and it was only by chance, the last of the CSIs exploring below, it was located.

Lori believed God had been watching over them that night. The device hadn't detonated. But, while it was found, what wasn't found was any trace whatsoever of Enrique Marquez—or, as he'd been known that night, Juan Romero.

Months later, sometime before Christmas, a great white shark would be caught off the South African coast and brought into Port Elizabeth. When its stomach was slit, among its contents glinted a plain silver band. Lori shook to her core when she saw it.

A kid from the wrong side of the tracks, driven to destruction by desire for a woman he couldn't have. It made a good story.

Desideria Gomez joined her at the funeral. 'If there's anything I can do...'

'I'm taking a break,' Lori told her. 'I'll call when I'm back.'

'Where are you going?' Desideria searched her eyes for need but was left wanting.

'Spain. Just me and Omar. The two of us.'

'You know I'm here for you, Lori. If you ever—'

'I know.'

Desideria watched through the driving rain as Lori returned to her car.

By winter, still shaken by events and unable to sleep soundly in LA, Desideria quit her role at La Lumière and moved to the East Coast. She was tired of California, its egos and vanities, the secrets it carried. There, she began work for a charity helping victims of natural disasters and, on her third day, met a photographer named Polly.

Even so, when she heard Lori's news, she still couldn't quite bring herself to attend.

Angélica Ruiz and her daughters watched events unfold on live TV. They were at the mall, shopping for Rosa's fifth child, queueing with their hair removal creams at the pharmacy counter, trying to ignore the images of beautiful Loriana every way they turned, when, passing an electrical store and catching a glimpse of the boy she had known as Rico, Anita came to an abrupt halt. Rosa and her quadruple buggy slammed into her.

'Watch it, fatass!' she crowed.

Sensitive to her ballooning weight, Anita snapped back, 'At least I can keep from getting knocked up every five minutes.'

'Yeah, like anyone'd wanna knock *you* up. Do me a favour and bleach that moustache.'

Angélica intervened, pulling them apart. The screens were filled with news of the island murders, Rico Marquez taking centre stage.

Afterwards, they'd be smug about it, treat themselves to shoes and cakes and bitch about how Loriana's life would never be as perfect as everyone made out.

But, later that night, as Angélica gritted her teeth in bed with her rich, octogenarian lover, praying, as she did every time, for a heart attack, as Rosa changed her fourteenth shitty diaper of the day, as Anita stared miserably at her naked reflection, trying to block the savage taunts of her pimp photographer boyfriend, they'd wonder if their own lives were so much better, after all.

'Two minutes, Ms Reiner.'

Bibi Reiner looked up from her dressing table on Broadway and nodded to her assistant. Her audience was waiting. Bright lights gleaming. She imagined the stage and the rows of captivated faces. At the close of the final act, the thunderous applause rushing at her like a tide, roses being thrown to her feet and her name clamoured from the ranks.

Bibi was a new woman. Not because she was famous, or free, or doing what she loved, but because, for the first time, she was in control. She had the power, and nobody, no matter what they promised, would ever be able to take it from her.

Days after Reuben van der Meyde's notorious party, a courier had arrived at Bibi's home and delivered a parcel. In it was a disc identical to the one she had previously received from Dirk Michaels. Except this time, it was a recording of him in conversation with Stevie Speller, presumably on the night it all happened. Dirk's words incriminated both him and Linus categorically. She knew he would not dare come near her again.

On the front of the disc was a label, in Stevie's handwriting, which read:

SECURITY—NOW AND ALWAYS.

Awaiting her cue in the wings, accustomed by now to

that potent mix of fear and adrenalin, Bibi couldn't help her smile. She had friends, she had family—save for her brother, admittedly, who had moved overseas and was terrible at staying in touch—and at last she had a future. It had been a long, difficult road, but she had made it.

Fame was everything Bibi had dreamed it to be.

No one understood more than her the cost at which it came.

The curtains parted and the roar went up.

'Ladies and gentlemen, I give you...*Bibi Reiner*!'

Dirk and Christina Michaels lasted until the end of the year before embarking on a very messy and public divorce. Dirk had been caught in a prostitute's car on Hollywood Boulevard and was remanded in custody ample time for the press to catch wind of the episode and broadcast it across every newspaper in the country, along with his sorry mug shot.

His wife had long been acclimatised to a marriage of infidelity: Christina herself had three concurrent lovers and possessed a fulfilling and adventurous sex life, the difference being she was clever enough to hide it. When Dirk's latest misdemeanour emerged, she knew, and so did her PR, that to stay with America's most notorious love rat was a point-blank bad idea. Especially since their wild-child daughter Farrah had been arrested by turns for drug possession, indecent exposure in a moving vehicle and assault on a police officer. Christina's filing for divorce spoke volumes about which party was to blame.

Dirk hit back with a series of ill-advised transmissions on social networking sites about the couple's bedroom antics. His bizarre, drunken near-confession to the affairs at Linus's birthday party was, apparently, just the beginning. Each was met with stoic silence from Christina's side and seemed to chip further at his credibility while only boosting hers. He began to drink, fired his spokesperson and embraced a lifestyle of partying, Playmates and pill popping. It wasn't long before the board at Searchbeam Studios rose against him and drove him out.

Some nights, a blonde's head bobbing in his lap, Dirk imagined he was living the life of Riley. Others, he caught sight of his fat, ageing body and was filled with a blank sort of terror.

Mostly, he was too out of it to care.

Pascale Devereux was in a Swiss ski-chalet when news of the island deaths ricocheted through the world's media. Her boyfriend, a forty-one-year-old musician named Benoit, wandered on to the terrace in a red and white Argyll sweater, scratched his beard and asked, 'What's up?'

Pascale put down her novel and squinted into the distance. 'She found out.'

Benoit frowned. He was stirring a mug of tea, spoon tinkling against the sides. 'Who found out what?'

From her position on the wooden swing-seat, Pascale took in the icy mountains, the ski lifts beginning their slow descent to the summits.

'Pascale?' He cocked his head. 'Is everything OK?'

The French girl reached into the pocket of her jeans and removed her cell phone. She scrolled until she found Aurora's number and let her thumb hover over the call button.

Maybe it wasn't too late.

'Never mind,' she said. 'It's nothing.'

* * *

Casey Amos found out while in a friend's condo in Santa Monica. Had he not been there, he probably wouldn't have heard for months. Casey didn't do news.

'Man, that's deep,' his companion diagnosed through a haze of weed.

Even in his addled state, Casey sensed something was missing from the reported accounts. He'd neither seen nor heard from Aurora Nash since her mother died, and rumour had it she was considering 'divorcing' Tom Nash on the grounds of an 'irreconcilable family matter'.

Casey wasn't bright. He was self-seeking and idle, content to disregard anything that challenged or compromised his easy, listless way of life or his steadfast pursuit of gummy bears.

Exactly why it was inconvenient to remember, just once in a while, what Aurora had told him that day in his dad's home theatre. His eyes flicked uncertainly to the lovingly mounted family photograph on his friend's wall. He thought of similar ones at his own mom and dad's: proud parents with their adored, immaculate children.

He sparked up another joint. 'Yeah,' he said. 'I guess so.'

'Can you believe it?' Rita Clay insisted on updates every hour following the scandal. She sat up, scrolling through developments on her BlackBerry. 'All down to that one maniac. To think of the people who could have died...'

Marty King plumped the pillows behind his head. He reached out and stroked Rita's back, thanking everything good in the world that his woman hadn't been on van der Meyde's boat that night. Rita was the one for him: she knew her own mind, she didn't take shit from anyone and that was exactly the kind of broad he needed. Not that he *needed* anyone, but, hey.

'What about your kid?' he asked.

'Aurora?' Rita leaned into his arms, concern clouding her face. 'She'll be back. She hit a dark place…a very dark place if the reports about her and van der Meyde are to be believed.' She frowned. 'They found her in his cabin, did you know? The room was turned upside down. I know she's been all over the place lately, but *him*? He's old enough to be her father.'

Marty pulled her to him and planted a kiss on the top of her head. 'It happens to kids her age,' he said gruffly. 'She'll get over it.'

In the aftermath of Cacatra's devastation, Tom Nash disappeared from the public eye. He holed himself up on the ranch in Texas and spoke to no one. His only visitor, Stuart Lovell, came to Creekside under the guise of discussing Tom's new venture. Only then did Tom experience a whisper of peace, lying safe in the cocoon of Stuart's loving embrace. The men stayed in bed for days on end, content to be alone, together.

Tom had been forced to retreat. The memory of his confrontation with Aurora still brought him to tears, and he knew it would be a long time before he earned the right to look her in the eye. His daughter. His sweetheart. The wrong he and Sherilyn had dealt would never be made right. But Aurora was his daughter, damn it. She always would be.

What kind of a word was sorry?

Aurora had uncovered the secret he and Sherilyn had battled their entire married life to silence. She had found out in the worst possible way. Everything there was—and more.

What Tom hadn't known. What none of them had known.
Reuben van der Meyde was her real father.

Never had Tom imagined a person to be capable of such vile
trickery. All the meetings they'd had, all the cheques they'd
sent, and it had been van der Meyde all along... He supposed
it was justice of a sort. Tom had consented to any guy taking
on the job, so what difference did it make if it was Reuben or
the next jock? They were all liars, each one as bad as the next.

'I don't hate you,' Aurora had whispered that day she
returned, shaken and feeble, weak and tear-stained, his
baby. She'd regarded him with pity, knowing he was living
a falsehood so tightly wound it was impossible to escape.
'But I can't see you. Not yet.'

He had to understand. There was so much to explain, so
much he couldn't yet fully articulate, but he had to respect
her wishes. Waiting was all he could do.

She'd been in Europe. Assumptions about her absence in
the press, not least concerning the supposed divorce, were
distressing. In January, she wrote for the first time. Aurora
promised to see him when she got back. There was just one
last thing she had to do before she came home.

Home.

Tom clung to it: the first step.

There would be many more. However long, whatever it
took, Tom Nash vowed he would never stop climbing.

The boy's voice was tentative, the word a stranger to his lips.

'Mummy?'

Margaret Jensen followed Ralph out on to their Covent
Garden roof terrace. The sun was shining. From here she
could see across London, from the rooftops to the glass
tower of Centre Point, the river and the gold spire of Big Ben.

'What is it, sweetheart?' She knelt to Ralph's level and touched his cheek.

It hadn't been easy. Telling her son the truth was the hardest thing she had ever done.

'You have to listen to me very carefully.'

Ralph's little face had been so frightened and confused. The way she'd held him tight as she could and found the only words that made sense. That she loved him, that she'd always been here and always would be here, that she'd never stop loving him as long as she lived.

The words she had imagined saying so many times, but never had the right before now.

Mr V had been forced to publicly confess his housekeeper's significance: that she was mother to his child. The admission was small fry compared with accompanying revelations in the press, but it was enough. Margaret could not forget the panic of that night; she never would. Even now she would wake in the small hours convinced she was back there, trapped on the island, terrified nothing had changed. And then she would remember. Things were different now.

Margaret had run from that place as if her life depended on it—and it had. As soon as she reached the mainland, she had contacted her lawyers, moving quickly because Mr V had his means: it would only be a matter of time before he tracked them down. But, as Margaret started to build the case against the man who had made her live a lie for nearly a decade, so her confidence swelled. She elected to keep Cacatra's secret to herself, instead maintaining to her lawyers that Reuben had enjoyed what he deemed to be an ill-advised night of passion, and Ralph was the result. Reuben had been too ashamed to admit the boy's mother was his lowly housekeeper and so he had forced her anonymity, threatening her with taking the child away if she objected.

Unsurprisingly, the moment her lawyers approached with the terms, Mr V was the epitome of cooperation. Only he understood the weapon Margaret possessed. Only he knew its impact. And only he knew that at the slightest rumble or objection, she would not be afraid to use it. Mr V's cheques came in regularly and always on time. It was the perfect arrangement.

'Can we go to the park?' Ralph asked now, bobbing up and down on his toes.

The boy would never know the inheritance he had lost. It was better that way. If Margaret had learned anything from her time on Cacatra, it was that no amount of riches, no amount of celebrity, or power, or possessions, was a passport to happiness.

'Of course we can, darling.'

It wasn't Margaret's fault Enrique Marquez had got distracted. The trick was you always had to focus, never lose sight of the prize. Even if it took you eight years.

They went back inside. Yes, they could go to the park. Now, they could do anything.

Reuben van der Meyde exited the Washington space observatory. His assistant returned with a giant hot dog and Reuben shovelled it into his mouth, sausage bursting with grease and yellow mustard trickling down his chin.

Turning to the great dome, he shielded his eyes against the sun. VDM Communications was pursuing a new frontier in interstellar space travel. Reuben had wasted no time in investing several billion dollars into a project that brought man to the brink of the unknown. He'd conquered this world, damn it. Now it was on to the next. He knew when to cut his losses. And Cacatra, though it broke him, was lost. He could never go back.

The jewel in his crown was tarnished irreversibly; Reuben's name, as long as it was associated with the place, synonymous with death and violence. The events of that summer night would haunt him till the day he died. Even now, months on, he could scarcely fathom what had been at stake…how close he had come to the end.

Reuben shuddered, crumpling the wrapper and shoving it into his assistant's hands. The man was taking a call and had to clamp the cell under his ear to receive it. He turned to re-enter the observatory.

Fine, he'd pushed a line with the damn surrogates. Reuben had always known it but he'd done it anyway—that was how he'd got to where he was today, and he sure as shit wasn't going to apologise for it. Reuben was born a leader: it was in his blood.

No, what appalled him was that Aurora Nash—he could hardly bring himself to think her name—had so nearly brought him down, so nearly exposed Cacatra's secret and so nearly put a bullet in his head. Reuben wasn't sure which would have been worse.

He had always imagined himself to be untouchable. Now, he realised he wasn't. Aurora had demanded answers, and to get them she'd put a revolver to the most powerful man in the world. That was his kind of girl. He was almost proud. But then she was his, after all.

Reuben was lucky. It was in the stars. His and Aurora's revelation stayed hidden, was hidden to this day, overshadowed by a murderous psychopath who had stolen the limelight for himself and, as a result, the world was none the wiser. Aurora was sensible enough to know that to reveal his secret would mean as much damage to her as it would to him. She no more wanted people to know he was her father than he did she was his child.

His guys had found them in a state of dishevelment, Aurora's clothes torn, the room in disarray. Conclusions had been drawn—but Reuben never had been one to read the gossip rags.

Of course, he had regrets. Rebecca Stuttgart, dead—but no questions asked because, although the sonofabitch had so nearly brought him down that night, Enrique Marquez was the perfect scapegoat. Reuben had mourned with the rest of them, said what a tragedy it was, what a great woman and wife she'd been, and decided that Marquez would probably have killed her anyway if he hadn't got there first.

But then there was the boy. Then there was Ralph...

He was the cost Reuben had paid in full. Ralph was the only child he could ever publicly claim to be his: his inheritor, his successor, his future, and the reason he had agreed to put up with his irksome housekeeper for so many years.

Reuben had been forbidden to ever contact the child again. The knowledge broke something in him that he realised must be a heart. Margaret Jensen had enough ammunition to sink him for good, and the problem with knocking up a nonentity was that, when the shit hit, she had nothing to lose. He, on the other hand, did. Reuben van der Meyde had dozens of children all across Hollywood, all across the globe, but none who would ever know they were his.

He put his eye to the scope and adjusted the lens.

The irony wasn't lost.

It was the longest two minutes of Stevie Speller's life. She attempted distraction. She made the bed, brushed her teeth, checked her phone, opened the window...

Outside, on the street, a mother chided her child. Normal people. Ordinary lives.

She and Xander had been in New York for six months. For both of them, Reuben van der Meyde's party had marked a point of no return. They had moved into a six-storey redbrick in Greenwich Village and were pursuing a quieter life. Hollywood was over.

Xander found it easier to escape the limelight. He was currently at work on his debut novel. He said it was fiction but Stevie suspected it was autobiographical, at least in part. It wasn't hard to recognise the two school friends, but the boys' story he was, as yet, holding close to his chest. Xander would share the ghosts of his past when he was ready. They both would.

For Stevie, it had been harder. Marty King couldn't understand why she was opting out: her presence on Cacatra that fateful night meant she was more bankable now than ever. Though she tried never to think of it, it came back to her in her dreams. How she had so nearly ripped the ground from under Hollywood, the mother of all scandals right there on her lips. She couldn't decide if she was grateful to JB Moreau for having stepped in when he did, saving her from exposing the truth. She believed he had done so to protect the island, rather than through any loyalty to Xander. Her husband, however, believed different.

Some days Stevie missed acting, but not enough. Instead, she decided to go back to university and pursue a degree in Psychology, a subject she had always wanted to explore. In time, her journey through LA would become a peculiar sort of detour, one from which she'd learned more about human desires and frailties than she could from any book.

Her phone beeped with a message. Bibi Reiner.

She opened it, unable to stop herself smiling.

News? x

Stevie took a deep breath. She padded back into the bathroom, picked up the little white stick and looked. And looked again.

Aurora Nash spent the best part of a year travelling through Europe. After her showdown with Tom, she'd had no choice. LA could never be the same again.

She had started in Asia and the Antipodes, letting her hair grow, wearing no make-up and shapeless, practical clothes and giving up caring what she looked like. She sat on beaches with strangers and shared last cigarettes and found she could be normal if she wanted and that people treated you how your behaviour demanded to be treated, famous or not. In Europe she went through Italy, into Spain and France, through England and then, at last, up to Scandinavia.

Once, in London, walking down Embankment early one morning, she had thought she passed van der Meyde's son and Margaret Jensen. The half-brother she could never know.

Then again, he was one of who knew how many. It would send her crazy if she let it.

Perhaps she could have taken a leaf from Margaret's book and forced Reuben into a confession. It had been tempting. But then she'd remembered the people whose lives she would demolish and how it wasn't her right to do so. All those kids in blissful ignorance. Let them live it. She wouldn't wish her own discovery on anyone.

Weeks ago, in a bar outside Helsinki, she had heard one

of Tom and Sherilyn's records. This time, the tears hadn't come. She didn't need to cry any more.

Returning to her hostel, Aurora had taken a pen and paper and started to write him a letter. It had taken days, countless drafts, before she was happy. Everything she'd wanted to say but had never felt able: all on the line, a clean slate.

Aurora's world had been obliterated. But it was what she saved from the wreckage that mattered.

She consulted the scrap of paper to make sure, a stalling tactic as much as anything because she knew this was the place. The house was as she'd pictured. It was a wooden building outside Rovaniemi, brown and white, the roof hidden under a drift and a bank of ferns behind. The porch was in need of repair. A plastic swing, discarded, was half buried in the snow. The car out front was scratched, its front tyre flat. Clearly the money this woman had been promised had never made it out of Reuben van der Meyde's bank account.

Aurora hitched the strap of her rucksack and pushed open the gate. Her hands and feet were freezing, the snow a foot deep.

A new dawn, a new horizon. Life was starting over.

She went to the porch and put her hand out to knock.

Before she could, a shadow came to the door, as if it had been waiting. The catch went. A fair-haired woman answered, eyes so blue, and when they saw Aurora they filled with tears.

They needed no words.

The woman held her arms out and Aurora walked straight into them.

Jacqueline Spark exited her office on North Harper Avenue and hailed a cab to the airport. The thought of visiting Cacatra after everything that had happened wasn't top on her list of priorities, but if that was where Lori wanted to get married then that was where it was happening.

Since the van der Meyde debacle, Jacqueline and Lori had become, rightly or wrongly, LA's dream team. Jacqueline had been promoted at One Touch but had soon outgrown her role, electing to break out on her own and embark on a new business. With it, Spark PR was born. Lori Garcia was her first client: world-famous supermodel, muse, mother—and a woman for whom men were prepared to kill. It was a potent combination.

At LAX, Jacqueline bought herself a latte. She was against this, but knew she could not change Lori's mind. Though Omar Garcia would always be credited to the late Maximo, she could understand Lori's desire to unite her family. Jacqueline's job was to make sure her client knew what she was doing. Failing that, to pick up the pieces.

She sipped hot coffee and waited for her flight to be announced.

For the first time in his life, Lance Chlomsky had a girlfriend.

Since the van der Meyde party he'd been hot property, made hotter by his involvement with the police in the early stages of the Maximo Diaz investigation. As the guy who'd found him, Lance had acquired the sort of heroic-slash-dangerous status that proved irresistible to women. With offers now in the pipeline for an autobiography, a charity single and even a walk-on part in one of his best-loved sitcoms, he was riding on air. Not bad for the boy who up until six months ago had resigned himself to never getting to first base with a girl, let alone finding one who was content to give him head all day long.

'You're so hot,' crooned Darnelle, looping her arms around his scrawny rib cage.

Lance scrutinised his pimply face in the mirror. He squeezed one of the whiteheads on his chin and watched with satisfaction as it yielded fudgy matter.

Oh yeah, this was what it was about. When he'd met Juan/Enrique on their training week he never would have dreamed that scary-looking sonofabitch would be responsible for changing his life. But change his life, he had—and most definitely for the better.

Lance ignored the niggling feeling that said he hadn't been entirely honest with the cops. That Marquez hadn't been the only one down in the galley that unforgettable night while the tray he'd taken out had been prepared. That JB Moreau had been down there, too. That it had been JB who spoke to him, and JB who told him what to do.

Forget it, it wasn't important.

He was made.

Lori Garcia kissed her father's cheek at the flower-strewn altar. Tony took his seat, Omar on his lap, and the gathering fell quiet in preparation for the vows to be said.

Waves pounded the shores of Cacatra, her and JB's paradise.

This was where it began again: the start of the rest of their lives. JB had been unable to let it go, the closest place to home he had. He was king of this island, and Lori, at his side, its queen.

Their happy ever after.

Lori joined her betrothed. His silver eyes glinted like jewels in a dark place.

JB pulled her close. 'Do you?' he murmured.

She smiled at him, never so sure of anything. 'I do.'

* * * * *

If you enjoyed your trip to

TEMPTATION ISLAND

then join

Victoria Fox

on some other mini-adventures in her

Short Tales of Temptation

Rivals
Pride
Ambition

Available in eBook
Visit www.victoriafoxwrites.co.uk

Read on for a sneak peek of
Rivals

RIVALS

'It's *unbearably* bloody hot. Can someone get me a drink before I burst into flames?'

Emily Windermere fanned herself with small, porcelain hands, gazing whimsically upon her beauty in the make-up girl's mirror. Even when she was roasting beneath layers of net and taffeta, trussed up in a bodice and choked by a necklace of ribbons, her wide-eyed reflection—those pools of hazel bordered by delicate lashes, that thicket of copper framing a flawless, cream-skinned complexion—remained as serenely lovely as an English garden on the first day of spring.

It was the English summer that was the problem.

'Ugh! Wasps!' Irritably Emily batted her arms, causing the make-up girl's brush to stab her in the eye. 'My God, is it too much to hope I'm not blind by the end of this?'

'Here you go, Ms Windermere.' A nervous runner was proffering a glass of cloudy lemonade, one of the on-set requisites stipulated by her management.

'That'll explain why I'm getting mauled by insects,' she complained, accepting it all the same. 'Can't we take care of this inside my trailer?'

'I need the light, I'm afraid,' said the make-up girl through gritted teeth.

It was Friday morning, a fortnight into filming, and, contrary to the studio's concerns that a London June wouldn't produce *enough* light, they now had rather too much of it. The city was enduring a heatwave that showed no signs of abating, golden sun blazing across Hampstead Heath from an unbroken swimming-pool sky. Cast were sweating through Victorian petticoats and frock coats, while crew chased to allay the disgruntled company, struggling under clipboards and sound equipment and taking occasional refuge for a cigarette in the shelter of a crisp white parasol.

'They're ready for you,' prompted the runner, anxiously smiling as Emily rose with majesty from her seat, mustering her lacy skirts and, with a dainty finger, removing the spot of perspiration that had gathered in her philtrum.

She thought of Christopher Fenwick awaiting her in his breeches.

'And I'm ready for them,' she breathed.

© Victoria Fox 2012

Don't miss what happens next in

Rivals

Emily Windermere, darling of British film, has a starring role in the summer's hottest period drama—but it's her scandalous affair off-screen that's set to raise temperatures. Meanwhile Julia Chambers has been cast as the dowdy maid yet again; she's lived her whole life in Emily's shadow and when her rival moves to take the one thing Julia holds dear, she decides it's payback time.

"A juicy tale of glamour, corruption and ambition." – Jo Rees

POWER

Marriage to Hollywood heartthrob Cole Steel secured Lana Falcon a glittering place on the red carpet. But running from a wicked past she has trapped herself in a gilded cage— the price of freedom... her soul?

REVENGE

Kate di Laurentis' career is fading as quickly as her looks... What could be worse than discovering her husband's latest mistress is Hollywood's hottest starlet? Her only option—the most shocking revenge!

LUST

Chloe French's innocent beauty has captured a million hearts, but no one's warned her of the dangerous, dark temptation of rockstar Nate—will lust destroy her?

GREED

Las Vegas king Robert St Louis's fairytale wedding to Sin City's richest heiress is tabloid gold... But scandal circles like a vulture—dirty secrets are about to be exposed!

BETRAYAL

From the deepest desires come the deadliest deeds...and these four couples are about to pay for their sins...

Sexy. Sensational... Sinfully good. If you love Jackie Collins, then you'll devour Victoria Fox!

www.mirabooks.co.uk